HE STARED OUT ONCE MORE
TOWARD THE SEA

He imagined a newborn city congealing suddenly out of the mists: shining towers, great domed palaces, golden mosaics. That would be no great effort for them. They could just summon it forth whole out of time. And why not? They had Timbuctoo. They had Alexandria. They could have anything they like. Suddenly he felt frightened.

"You're so quiet all of a sudden, Charles," said Gioia, "tell me what you're looking for out there."

"Byzantium."

Gioia frowned. "Byzantium doesn't exist."

Charles looked at her. "How could we *not* do Byzantium, Gioia? We certainly will do Byzantium. I know we will. It's only a matter of time. And we have all the time in the world."

A shadow crossed her face. "Do we? Do we?"

—from Robert Silverberg's
Nebula Award-winning short story
"Sailing to Byzantium"

D0057428

Look for all these Tor books edited by Terry Carr

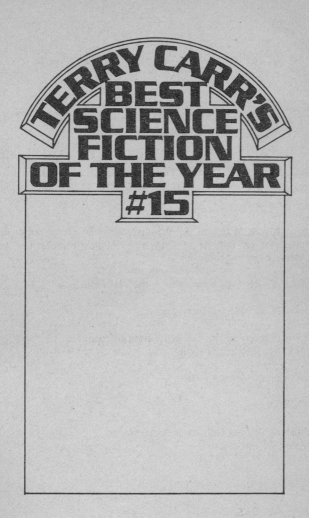

TERRY CARR'S BEST SCIENCE FICTION OF THE YEAR #15

TOR

A TOM DOHERTY ASSOCIATES BOOK

TERRY CARR'S BEST SCIENCE FICTION OF THE YEAR #15

Copyright © 1986 by Terry Carr

First printing: August 1986

A TOR Book

Published by Tom Doherty Associates, Inc.
49 West 24 Street
New York, N.Y. 10010

Cover art by Ron Walotsky

ISBN: 0-812-53267-8
CAN. ED.: 0-812-53268-6

Printed in the United States

0 9 8 7 6 5 4 3 2 1

ACKNOWLEDGMENTS

"Sailing to Byzantium" by Robert Silverberg. Copyright © 1985 by Agberg Ltd. From *Isaac Asimov's Science Fiction Magazine*, February 1985, by permission of the author.

"Flying Saucer Rock & Roll" by Howard Waldrop. Copyright © 1984 by Omni Publications International Ltd. From *Omni*, January 1985, by permission of the author.

"Bluff" by Harry Turtledove. Copyright © 1985 by Davis Publications, Inc. From *Analog*, February 1985, by permission of the author. Originally published as by "Eric G. Iverson."

"A Spanish Lesson" by Lucius Shepard. Copyright © 1985 by Mercury Press, Inc. From *Fantasy and Science Fiction*, December 1985, by permission of the author.

"Snow" by John Crowley. Copyright © 1985 by Omni Publications International Ltd. From *Omni*, November 1985, by permission of the author and his agents, Kirby McCauley Ltd.

"Shanidar" by David Zindell. Copyright © 1985 by David Zindell. From *Writers of the Future*, by permission of the author.

"All My Darling Daughters" by Connie Willis. Copyright © 1985 by Connie Willis. From *Fire Watch*, by permission of the author.

"Of Space/Time and the River" by Gregory Benford. Copyright © 1985 by Abbenford Associates. Originally published by Cheap Street Press. Reprinted by permission of the author.

"A Gift from the GrayLanders" by Michael Bishop. Copyright © 1985 by Davis Publications, Inc. From *Isaac Asimov's Science Fiction Magazine*, September 1985, by permission of the author.

"Praxis" by Karen Joy Fowler. Copyright © 1985 by Davis Publications, Inc. From *Isaac Asimov's Science Fiction Magazine*, March 1985, by permission of the author.

"The People on the Precipice" by Ian Watson. Copyright © 1985 by Ian Watson. From *Interzone*, Autumn 1985, by permission of the author.

"The Only Neat Thing to Do" by James Tiptree, Jr. Copyright © 1985 by James Tiptree, Jr. From *Fantasy and Science Fiction*, October 1985, by permission of the author and her agent, Virginia Kidd.

CONTENTS

INTRODUCTION

Among critics and long-time readers of science fiction, the first thing they complain about in this genre (and the fantasy genre) is the incredible proliferation in recent years of series novels. Their names are legion: the Darkover series, the Riverworld series, the Dune series, the Sime/Gen series, the Dragonriders series, etc., etc. It seems that every time a writer produces an sf or fantasy novel that proves to be popular, it follows as the night the day that there will be a sequel next year and then a third book to form a trilogy; usually there will come even more books carrying the series on potentially forever.

The rap against such open-ended series is made on grounds of normal literary practice: a novel should be complete in itself; its world and characters should be fashioned strictly to make and illustrate whatever points about the human condition the author had in mind, and the feeling is that no second, third, fifth, or eighth novels should be necessary for this purpose. Writers of classic novels such as Tolstoy, Dickens, Flaubert, and Steinbeck felt no need to write sequels or series to follow even their most popular novels; therefore if sf and fantasy writers indulge in such things, they must be catering to the wishes of their readers, who after all are mostly adolescents and don't understand or care about the purities that characterize novel writing in its highest forms.

For the most part, I believe these criticisms are correct. In the long history of sf and fantasy, sequels and series have been very much the exception rather than the rule with major writers. Did H. G. Wells ever write a sequel to any of his classic science fiction novels? Did Robert A. Heinlein, or Philip K. Dick, or Ursula K. Le Guin? No, of course they didn't; they were and are writers who understood the criteria of classic novel writing, and cleaved to them.

The one area of "classic" writing in which sequels and series have been common is juvenile fiction, as you probably can remember from the books you read as a child. Remember the animal books of Thornton W. Burgess, and those about Freddy the Pig, etc.; recall that the Oz novels of L. Frank Baum were continued after his death by Ruth Plumly Thompson and others; and there was the Narnia series by C. S. Lewis, plus many others. For a somewhat older readership, we had the Mars, Venus, and Pellucidar series by Edgar Rice Burroughs (not to mention the even longer Tarzan series).

These books, along with the many series about characters such as Frank Reade, Jr., Tom Swift, and Nancy Drew, seem to have established series novels as the province of juvenile readers. The suspicion is that very young readers have enough trouble getting used to imagining characters and worlds, even fairly commonplace ones, without being burdened with new sets of characters and settings in every book they read, so that series novels are necessary to keep them coming back to read more. And the "purities" of literature are seen as being above their heads anyway. Therefore it's rather easy for those who grumble about series novels in science fiction and fantasy to dismiss them as essentially juvenile fiction.

And probably this is for the most part a correct assessment. But in my opinion it's not necessarily correct for all such series, because science fiction and fantasy form a genre of writing that appeals to older readers as much as to younger ones: the genre has attributes that can provide enjoyment for people of most any age. Science fiction is, after all, built not only on the traditional literary criteria but also on the sheer fascination of imagination, of seeing grand or startling views of our future, and this additional dimension is precisely what makes sf different from other literature.

The strange, delightful, powerful evocations of other worlds that we get in science fiction are often as important as the characters we meet there . . . and the themes in sf stories are sometimes so large that a single novel truly cannot present them fully. So there are cases in which sequels and series are completely appropriate, and the current flourishing market for trilogies and series can be seen not merely as one that encourages writers to keep going over the same old ground in novel after novel, but also as a situation that challenges truly ambitious writers to imagine future worlds and future histories that will best be told about at great length. The publishing trend is one that can bring out the very best, the most thoughtful and imaginative, in science fiction.

In fact, we've already begun to see the fruits of these possibilities. I'll mention only one such trilogy, a set of three novels that are written on a truly grand scale that would have been impossible in earlier decades of sf publishing. Consider Brian W. Aldiss's Helliconia series: the work of an accomplished artist writing seriously about a world that requires more wordage than any single novel could hold today. Aldiss's trilogy, along with a few others, demonstrates that sequels and series novels aren't limited to the life-stories of space tyrants or adventurers looking forever for some lost planet. There are greater possibilities available to us now, and we'll be seeing more and more literary results in the years to come.

Naturally you won't find such grand visions in a book of short stories, novelettes, and novellas; but the truth is that most every grand vision begins with a smaller one. The number of superb novels that have begun as shorter stories that were expanded as the authors thought more about them is a long one (*Flowers for Algernon* by Daniel Keyes, for instance), so it's just possible that you'll find in this selection of the most thought-provoking science fiction stories of 1985 a story or two, or three, that will later provide the basis for a marvelous novel or even an irresistible series of novels.

Not that that's necessary in order for you to enjoy the many fine stories here. Short stories and such have their own criteria and delights—and those pleasures can be as great as any you can find in the longest novel series ever written. A fine short story is, in fact, a great epic compressed to its essentials. So here's a book of epics; just add imagination, and enjoy.

—Terry Carr

SAILING TO BYZANTIUM

Robert Silverberg

Imagine the people of Earth in the far future have brought you to their world—a marvelous time when everyone is on permanent vacation in the six fabulous cities of this bright new world. But your lover, who seems to be an outcast of some sort, abruptly leaves you, and as you search the world for her you gradually begin to see the darker side of this far tomorrow.

Robert Silverberg's most recent novel is Tom o' Bedlam.

At dawn he arose and stepped out onto the patio for his first look at Alexandria, the one city he had not yet seen. That year the five cities were Chang-an, Asgard, New Chicago, Timbuctoo, Alexandria: the usual mix of eras, cultures, realities. He and Gioia, making the long flight from Asgard in the distant north the night before, had arrived late, well after sundown, and had gone straight to bed. Now, by the gentle apricot-hued morning light, the fierce spires and battlements of Asgard seemed merely something he had dreamed.

The rumor was that Asgard's moment was finished, anyway. In a little while, he had heard, they were going to tear it down and replace it, elsewhere, with Mohenjo-daro. Though there were never more than five cities, they changed constantly. He could remember a time when they had had Rome of the Caesars instead of Chang-an, and Rio de Janeiro rather than Alexandria. These people saw no point in keeping anything very long.

It was not easy for him to adjust to the sultry intensity of Alexandria after the frozen splendors of Asgard. The wind, coming off the water, was brisk and torrid both at once. Soft turquoise wavelets lapped at the jetties. Strong presences assailed his senses: the hot heavy sky, the stinging scent of the red lowland sand borne on the breeze, the sullen swampy aroma of the nearby sea. Everything trembled and glimmered in the early light. Their hotel was beautifully situated, high on the northern slope of the huge artificial mound known as the Paneium that was sacred to the goat-footed god. From here they had a total view of the city: the wide noble boulevards, the soaring obelisks and monuments, the palace of Hadrian just below the hill, the stately and awesome Library, the temple of Poseidon, the teeming marketplace, the royal lodge that Mark Antony had built after his defeat at Actium. And of course the Lighthouse, the wondrous many-windowed Lighthouse, the seventh wonder of the world, that immense pile of marble and limestone and reddish-purple Aswan granite rising in majesty at the end of its mile-long causeway. Black smoke from the beacon-fire at its summit curled lazily into the sky. The city was awakening. Some temporaries in short white kilts appeared and began to trim the dense dark hedges that bordered the great public buildings. A few citizens wearing loose robes of vaguely Grecian style were strolling in the streets.

There were ghosts and chimeras and phantasies everywhere about. Two slim elegant centaurs, a male and a female, grazed on the hillside. A burly thick-thighed swordsman appeared on the porch of the temple of Poseidon holding a Gorgon's severed head; he waved it in a wide arc, grinning broadly. In the street below the hotel gate three small pink sphinxes, no bigger than housecats, stretched and yawned and began to prowl the curbside. A larger one, lion-sized, watched warily from an alleyway: their mother, surely. Even at this distance he could hear her loud purring.

Shading his eyes, he peered far out past the Lighthouse and across the water. He hoped to see the dim shores of Crete or Cyprus to the north, or perhaps the great dark curve of Anatolia. *Carry me toward that great Byzantium*, he thought. *Where all is ancient, singing at the oars*. But he beheld only the endless empty sea, sun-bright and blinding though the morning was just beginning. Nothing was ever where he expected it to be. The continents did not seem to be in their proper places any longer. Gioia, taking him aloft long ago in her little flitterflitter, had shown him that. The tip of South America was canted far out into the Pacific; Africa was weirdly foreshortened; a broad tongue of ocean separated Europe and Asia. Australia did not appear to exist at all. Perhaps they had dug it up and used it for other things. There was no trace of the world he once had known. This was the fiftieth century. "The fiftieth century after *what*?" he had asked several times, but no one seemed to know, or else they did not care to say.

"Is Alexandria very beautiful?" Gioia called from within.

"Come out and see."

Naked and sleepy-looking, she padded out onto the white-tiled patio and nestled up beside him. She fit neatly under his arm. "Oh, yes, yes!" she said softly. "So very beautiful, isn't it? Look, there, the palaces, the Library, the Lighthouse! Where will we go first? The Lighthouse, I think. Yes? And then the marketplace—I want to see the Egyptian magicians—and the stadium, the races—will they be having races today, do you think? Oh, Charles, I want to see everything!"

"Everything? All on the first day?"

"All on the first day, yes," she said. "Everything."

"But we have plenty of time, Gioia."

"Do we?"

He smiled and drew her tight against his side.

"Time enough," he said gently.

He loved her for her impatience, for her bright bubbling eagerness. Gioia was not much like the rest in that regard, though she seemed identical in all other ways. She was short, supple, slender, dark-eyed, olive-skinned, narrow-hipped, with wide shoulders and flat muscles. They were all like that, each one indistinguishable from the rest, like a horde of millions of brothers and sisters—a world of small, lithe, childlike Mediterraneans, built for juggling, for bull-dancing, for sweet white wine at midday and rough red wine at night. They had the same slim bodies, the same broad mouths, the same great glossy eyes. He had never seen anyone who appeared to be younger than twelve or older than twenty. Gioia was somehow a little different, although he did not quite know how; but he knew that it was for that imperceptible but significant difference that he loved her. And probably that was why she loved him also.

He let his gaze drift from west to east, from the Gate of the Moon down broad Canopus Street and out to the harbor, and off to the tomb of Cleopatra at the tip of long slender Cape Lochias. Everything was here and all of it perfect, the obelisks, the statues and marble colonnades, the courtyards and shrines and groves, great Alexander himself in his coffin of crystal and gold: a splendid gleaming pagan city. But there were oddities—an unmistakable mosque near the public gardens, and what seemed to be a Christian church not far from the Library. And those ships in the harbor, with all those red sails and bristling masts—surely they were medieval, and late medieval at that. He had seen such anachronisms in other places before. Doubtless these people found them amusing. Life was a game for them. They played at it unceasingly. Rome, Alexandria, Timbuctoo—why not? Create an Asgard of translucent bridges and shimmering ice-girt palaces, then grow weary of it and take it away? Replace it with Mohenjodaro? Why not? It seemed to him a great pity to destroy those lofty Nordic feasting-halls for the sake of building a squat, brutal, sun-baked city of brown brick; but these people did not look at things the way he did. Their cities were only temporary. Someone in Asgard had said that Timbuctoo would be the next to go, with Byzantium rising in its place. Well, why not? Why not? They could have anything they liked. This was the fiftieth century, after all. The only rule was that there could be no more than five cities at once. "Limits," Gioia had informed him solemnly when they first began to travel together, "are very important." But she did not know why, or did not care to say.

He stared out once more toward the sea.

He imagined a newborn city congealing suddenly out of mists, far across the water: shining towers, great domed palaces, golden mosaics. That would be no great effort for them. They could just summon it forth whole out of time, the Emperor on his throne and the Emperor's drunken soldiery roistering in the streets, the brazen clangor of the cathedral gong rolling through the Grand Bazaar, dolphins leaping beyond the shoreside pavilions. Why not? They had Timbuctoo. They had Alexandria. Do you crave Constantinople? Then behold Constantinople! Or Avalon, or Lyonesse, or Atlantic. They could have anything they liked. It is pure Schopenhauer here: the world as will and imagination. Yes! These slender dark-eyed people journeying tirelessly from miracle to miracle. Why not Byzantium next? Yes! Why not? *That is no country for old men*, he thought. *The young in one another's arms, the birds in the trees*—yes! Yes! Anything they liked. They even had him. Suddenly he felt frightened. Questions he had not asked for a long time burst through into his consciousness. *Who am I? Why am I here? Who is this woman beside me?*

"You're so quiet all of a sudden, Charles," said Gioia, who could not abide silence for very long. "Will you talk to me? I want you to talk to me. Tell me what you're looking for out there."

He shrugged. "Nothing."

"Nothing?"

"Nothing in particular."

"I could see you seeing something."

"Byzantium," he said. "I was imagining that I could look straight across the water to Byzantium. I was trying to get a glimpse of the walls of Constantinople."

"Oh, but you wouldn't be able to see as far as that from here. Not really."

"I know."

"And anyway Byzantium doesn't exist."

"Not yet. But it will. Its time comes later on."

"Does it?" she said. "Do you know that for a fact?"

"On good authority. I heard it in Asgard," he told her. "But even if I hadn't, Byzantium would be inevitable, don't you think? Its time would have to come. How could we not do Byzantium, Gioia? We certainly will do Byzantium, sooner or later. I know we will. It's only a matter of time. And we have all the time in the world."

A shadow crossed her face. "Do we? Do we?"

He knew very little about himself, but he knew that he

was not one of them. That he knew. He knew that his name was Charles Phillips and that before he had come to live among these people he had lived in the year 1984, when there had been such things as computers and television sets and baseball and jet planes, and the world was full of cities, not merely five but thousands of them, New York and London and Johannesburg and Paris and Liverpool and Bangkok and San Francisco and Buenos Aires and a multitude of others, all at the same time. There had been four and a half billion people in the world then; now he doubted that there were as many as four and a half million. Nearly everything had changed beyond comprehension. The moon still seemed the same, and the sun; but at night he searched in vain for familiar constellations. He had no idea how they had brought him from then to now, or why. It did no good to ask. No one had any answers for him; no one so much as appeared to understand what it was that he was trying to learn. After a time he had stopped asking; after a time he had almost entirely ceased wanting to know.

He and Gioia were climbing the Lighthouse. She scampered ahead, in a hurry as always, and he came along behind her in his more stolid fashion. Scores of other tourists, mostly in groups of two or three, were making their way up the wide flagstone ramps, laughing, calling to one another. Some of them, seeing him, stopped a moment, stared, pointed. He was used to that. He was so much taller than any of them; he was plainly not one of them. When they pointed at him he smiled. Sometimes he nodded a little acknowledgment.

He could not find much of interest in the lowest level, a massive square structure two hundred feet high built of huge marble blocks: within its cool musty arcades were hundreds of small dark rooms, the offices of the Lighthouses's keepers and mechanics, the barracks of the garrison, the stables for the three hundred donkeys that carried the fuel to the lantern far above. None of that appeared inviting to him. He forged onward without halting until he emerged on the balcony that led to the next level. Here the Lighthouse grew narrower and became octagonal: its face, granite now and handsomely fluted, rose in a stunning sweep above him.

Gioia was waiting for him there. "This is for you," she said, holding out a nugget of meat on a wooden skewer. "Roast lamb. Absolutely delicious. I had one while I was waiting for you." She gave him a cup of some cool green sherbet also, and darted off to buy a pomegranate. Dozens of temporaries were roaming the balcony, selling refreshments of all kinds.

He nibbled at the meat. It was charred outside, nicely pink and moist within. While he ate, one of the temporaries came up to him and peered blandly into his face. It was a stocky swarthy male wearing nothing but a strip of red and yellow cloth about its waist. "I sell meat," it said. "Very fine roast lamb, only five drachmas."

Phillips indicated the piece he was eating. "I already have some," he said.

"It is excellent meat, very tender. It has been soaked for three days in the juices of—"

"Please," Phillips said. "I don't want to buy any meat. Do you mind moving along?"

The temporaries had confused and baffled him at first, and there was still much about them that was unclear to him. They were not machines—they looked like creatures of flesh and blood—but they did not seem to be human beings, either, and no one treated them as if they were. He supposed they were artificial constructs, products of a technology so consummate that it was invisible. Some appeared to be more intelligent than others, but all of them behaved as if they had no more autonomy than characters in a play, which was essentially what they were. There were untold numbers of them in each of the five cities, playing all manner of roles: shepherds and swineherds, street-sweepers, merchants, boatmen, vendors of grilled meats and cool drinks, hagglers in the marketplace, schoolchildren, charioteers, policemen, grooms, gladiators, monks, artisans, whores and cutpurses, sailors—whatever was needed to sustain the illusion of a thriving, populous urban center. The dark-eyed people, Gioia's people, never performed work. They were not enough of them to keep a city's functions going, and in any case they were strictly tourists, wandering with the wind, moving from city to city as the whim took them, Chang-an to New Chicago,

New Chicago to Timbuctoo, Timbuctoo to Asgard, Asgard to Alexandria, onward, ever onward.

The temporary would not leave him alone. Phillips walked away and it followed him, cornering him against the balcony wall. When Gioia returned a few minutes later, lips prettily stained with pomegranate juice, the temporary was still hovering about him, trying with lunatic persistence to sell him a skewer of lamb. It stood much too close to him, almost nose to nose, great sad cowlike eyes peering intently into his as it extolled with mournful mooing urgency the quality of its wares. It seemed to him that he had had trouble like this with temporaries on one or two earlier occasions. Gioia touched the creature's elbow lightly and said, in a short sharp tone Phillips had never heard her use before, "He isn't interested. Get away from him." It went at once. To Phillips she said, "You have to be firm with them."

"I was trying. It wouldn't listen to me."

"You ordered it to go away, and it refused?"

"I asked it to go away. Politely. Too politely, maybe."

"Even so," she said. "It should have obeyed a human, regardless."

"Maybe it didn't think I was human," Phillips suggested. "Because of the way I look. My height, the color of my eyes. It might have thought I was some kind of temporary myself."

"No," Gioia said, frowning. "A temporary won't solicit another temporary. But it won't ever disobey a citizen, either. There's a very clear boundary. There isn't ever any confusion. I can't understand why it went on bothering you." He was surprised at how troubled she seemed: far more so, he thought, than the incident warranted. A stupid device, perhaps miscalibrated in some way, overenthusiastically pushing its wares—what of it? What of it? Gioia, after a moment, appeared to come to the same conclusion. Shrugging, she said, "It's defective, I suppose. Probably such things are more common than we suspect, don't you think?" There was something forced about her tone that bothered him. She smiled and handed him her pomegranate. "Here. Have a bite, Charles. It's wonderfully sweet. They used to be extinct, you know. Shall we go on upward?"

*   *   *

The octagonal midsection of the Lighthouse must have
been several hundred feet in height, a grim claustrophobic
tube almost entirely filled by the two broad spiraling ramps
that wound around the huge building's central well. The
ascent was slow: a donkey team was a little way ahead of
them on the ramp, plodding along laden with bundles of
kindling for the lantern. But at last, just as Phillips was
growing winded and dizzy, he and Gioia came out onto the
second balcony, the one marking the transition between
the octagonal section and the Lighthouse's uppermost sto-
rey, which was cylindrical and very slender.

She leaned far out over the balustrade. "Oh, Charles,
look at the view! Look at it!"

It was amazing. From one side they could see the entire
city, and swampy Lake Mareotis and the dusty Egyptian
plain beyond it, and from the other they peered far out into
the gray and choppy Mediterranean. He gestured toward
the innumerable reefs and shallows that infested the waters
leading to the harbor entrance. "No wonder they needed a
lighthouse here," he said. "Without some kind of gigantic
landmark they'd never have found their way in from the
open sea."

A blast of sound, a ferocious snort, erupted just above
him. He looked up, startled. Immense statues of trumpet-
wielding Tritons jutted from the corners of the Lighthouse
at this level; that great blurting sound had come from the
nearest of them. A signal, he thought. A warning to the
ships negotiating that troubled passage. The sound was
produced by some kind of steam-powered mechanism, he
realized, operated by teams of sweating temporaries clustered about bonfires at the base of each Triton.

Once again he found himself swept by admiration for
the clever way these people carried out their reproductions
of antiquity. Or *were* they reproductions, he wondered? He
still did not understand how they brought their cities into
being. For all he knew, this place was the authentic Alexandria itself, pulled forward out of its proper time just as
he himself had been. Perhaps this was the true and original
Lighthouse, and not a copy. He had no idea which was the
case, nor which would be the greater miracle.

"How do we get to the top?" Gioia asked.

"Over there, I think. That doorway."

The spiraling donkey-ramps ended here. The loads of lantern fuel went higher via a dumb-waiter in the central shaft. Visitors continued by way of a cramped staircase, so narrow at its upper end that it was impossible to turn around while climbing. Gioia, tireless, sprinted ahead. He clung to the rail and labored up and up, keeping count of the tiny window-slits to ease the boredom of the ascent. The count was nearing a hundred when finally he stumbled into the vestibule of the beacon chamber. A dozen or so visitors were crowded into it. Gioia was at the far side, by the wall that was open to the sea.

It seemed to him he could feel the building swaying in the winds, up here. How high were they? Five hundred feet, six hundred, seven? The beacon chamber was tall and narrow, divided by a catwalk into upper and lower sections. Down below, relays of temporaries carried wood from the dumb-waiter and tossed it on the blazing fire. He felt its intense heat from where he stood, at the rim of the platform on which the giant mirror of polished metal was hung. Tongues of flame leaped upward and danced before the mirror, which hurled its dazzling beam far out to sea. Smoke rose through a vent. At the very top was a colossal statue of Poseidon, austere, ferocious, looming above the lantern.

Gioia sidled along the catwalk until she was at his side. "The guide was talking before you came," she said, pointing. "Do you see that place over there, under the mirror? Someone standing there and looking into the mirror gets a view of ships at sea that can't be seen from here by the naked eye. The mirror magnifies things."

"Do you believe that?"

She nodded toward the guide. "It said so. And it also told us that if you look in a certain way, you can see right across the water into the city of Constantinople."

She is like a child, he thought. They all are. He said, "You told me yourself this very morning that it isn't possible to see that far. Besides, Constantinople doesn't exist right now."

"It will," she replied. "*You* said that to me, this very morning. And when it does, it'll be reflected in the Lighthouse mirror. That's the truth. I'm absolutely certain of it.'' She swung about abruptly toward the entrance of the beacon chamber. "Oh, look, Charles! Here comes Nissandra and Aramayne! And there's Hawk! There's Stengard!" Gioia laughed and waved and called out names. "Oh, everyone's here! *Everyone!*''

They came jostling into the room, so many newcomers that some of those who had been there were forced to scramble down the steps on the far side. Gioia moved among them, hugging, kissing. Phillips could scarcely tell one from another—it was hard for him even to tell which were the men and which the women, dressed as they all were in the same sort of loose robes—but he recognized some of the names. These were her special friends, her set, with whom she had journeyed from city to city on an endless round of gaiety in the old days before he had come into her life. He had met a few of them before, in Asgard, in Rio, in Rome. The beacon-chamber guide, a squat wide-shouldered old temporary wearing a laurel wreath on its bald head, reappeared and began its potted speech, but no one listened to it; they were all too busy greeting one another, embracing, giggling. Some of them edged their way over to Phillips and reached up, standing on tiptoes, to touch their fingertips to his cheek in that odd hello of theirs. "Charles," they said gravely, making two syllables out of the name, as these people often did. "So good to see you again. Such a pleasure. You and Gioia—such a handsome couple. So well suited to each other.''

Was that so? He supposed it was.

The chamber hummed with chatter. The guide could not be heard at all. Stengard and Nissandra had visited New Chicago for the water-dancing—Aramayne bore tales of a feast in Chang-an that had gone on for *days*—Hawk and Hekna had been to Timbuctoo to see the arrival of the salt caravan, and were going back there soon—a final party soon to celebrate the end of Asgard that absolutely should not be missed—the plans for the new city, Mohenjo-daro—we have reservations for the opening, we wouldn't pass it up for anything—and, yes, they were definitely going to do Constantinople after that, the planners were already deep into their Byzantium research—so good to see you, you look so beautiful all the time—have you been to the Library yet? The zoo? To the temple of Serapis?—

To Phillips they said, "What do you think of our Alexandria, Charles? Of course you must have known it well in your day. Does it look the way you remember it?" They were always asking things like that. They did not seem to comprehend that the Alexandria of the Lighthouse and the Library was long lost and legendary by his time. To them, he suspected, all the places they had brought back into existence were more or less contemporary. Rome of the Caesars, Alexandria of the Ptolemies, Venice of the Doges, Chang-an of the T'angs, Asgard of the Aesir, none any less real than the next nor any less unreal, each one simply a facet of the distant past, the fantastic immemorial past, a plum plucked from that dark backward and abysm of time. They had no contexts for separating one era from another. To them all the past was one borderless timeless realm. Why then should he not have seen the Lighthouse before, he who had leaped into this era from the New York of 1984? He had never been able to explain it to them. Julius Caesar and Hannibal, Helen of Troy and Charlemagne, Rome of the gladiators and New York of the Yankees and Mets, Gilgamesh and Tristan and Othello and Robin Hood and George Washington and Queen Victoria—to them, all equally real and unreal, none of them any more than bright figures moving about on a painted canvas. The past, the past, the elusive and fluid past—to them it was a single place of infinite accessibility and infinite connectivity. Of course they would think he had seen the Lighthouse before. He knew better than to try again to explain things. "No," he said simply. "This is my first time in Alexandria."

They stayed there all winter long, and possibly some of the spring. Alexandria was not a place where one was sharply aware of the change of seasons, nor did the passage of time itself make itself very evident when one was living one's entire life as a tourist.

During the day there was always something new to see. The zoological garden, for instance: a wondrous park, miraculously green and lush in this hot dry climate, where astounding animals roamed in enclosures so generous that they did not seem like enclosures at all. Here were camels, rhinoceroses, gazelles, ostriches, lions, wild asses; and here too, casually adjacent to those familiar African beasts, were hippogriffs, unicorns, basilisks, and fire-snorting dragons with rainbow scales. Had the original zoo of Alexandria had dragons and unicorns? Phillips doubted it. But this one did; evidently it was no harder for the backstage craftsmen to manufacture mythic beasts than it was for them to turn out camels and gazelles. To Gioia and her friends all of them were equally mythical, anyway. They were just as awed by the rhinoceros as by the hippogriff. One was no more strange—nor any less—than the other. So far as Phillips had been able to discover, none of the mammals or birds of his era had survived into this one except for a few cats and dogs, though many had been reconstructed.

And then the Library! All those lost treasures, reclaimed from the jaws of time! Stupendous columned marble walls, airy high-vaulted reading-rooms, dark coiling stacks stretching away to infinity. The ivory handles of seven hundred thousand papyrus scrolls bristling on the shelves. Scholars and librarians gliding quietly about, smiling faint scholarly smiles but plainly preoccupied with serious matters of the mind. They were all temporaries, Phillips realized. Mere props, part of the illusion. But were the scrolls illusions too? "Here we have the complete dramas of Sophocles," said the guide with a blithe wave of its hand, indicating shelf upon shelf of texts. Only seven of his hundred twenty-three plays had survived the successive burnings of the library in ancient times by Romans, Christians, Arabs: were the lost ones here, the *Triptolemus*, the *Nausicaa*, the *Jason*, and all the rest? And would he find here too, miraculously restored to being, the other vanished treasures of ancient literature—the memoirs of Odysseus, Cato's history of Rome, Thucydides' life of Pericles, the missing volumes of Livy? But when he asked if he might explore the stacks, the guide smiled apologetically and said that all the librarians were busy just now. Another time, perhaps? Perhaps, said the guide. It made no difference, Phillips decided. Even if these people somehow had brought back those lost masterpieces of antiquity, how would he read them? He knew no Greek.

The life of the city buzzed and throbbed about him. It was a dazzlingly beautiful place: the vast bay thick with

sails, the great avenues running rigidly east–west, north–
south, the sunlight rebounding almost audibly from the
bright walls of the palaces of kings and gods. They have
done this very well, Phillips thought: very well indeed. In
the marketplace hard-eyed traders squabbled in half a dozen
mysterious languages over the price of ebony, Arabian
incense, jade, panther-skins. Gioia bought a dram of pale
musky Egyptian perfume in a delicate tapering glass flask.
Magicians and jugglers and scribes called out stridently to
passersby, begging for a few moments of attention and a
handful of coins for their labor. Strapping slaves, black
and tawny and some that might have been Chinese, were
put up for auction, made to flex their muscles, to bare their
teeth, to bare their breasts and thighs to prospective buyers.
In the gymnasium naked athletes hurled javelins and dis-
cuses, and wrestled with terrifying zeal. Gioia's friend
Stengard came rushing up with a gift for her, a golden
necklace that would not have embarrassed Cleopatra. An
hour later she had lost it, or perhaps had given it away
while Phillips was looking elsewhere. She bought another,
even finer, the next day. Anyone could have all the money
he wanted, simply by asking: it was as easy to come by as
air, for these people.

Being here was much like going to the movies, Phillips
told himself. A different show every day: not much plot,
but the special effects were magnificent and the detail-
work could hardly have been surpassed. A megamovie, a
vast entertainment that went on all the time and was being
played out by the whole population of Earth. And it was
all so effortless, so spontaneous: just as when he had gone
to a movie he had never troubled to think about the myriad
technicians behind the scenes, the cameramen and the
costume designers and the set-builders and the electricians
and the model-makers and the boom operators, so too here
he chose not to question the means by which Alexandria
had been set before him. It felt real. It *was* real. When he
drank the strong red wine it gave him a pleasant buzz. If
he leaped from the beacon chamber of the Lighthouse he
suspected he would die, though perhaps he would not stay
dead for long: doubtless they had some way of restoring
him as often as was necessary. Death did not seem to be a
factor in these people's lives.

By day they saw sights. By night he and Gioia went to parties, in their hotel, in seaside villas, in the palaces of the high nobility. The usual people were there all the time, Hawk and Hekna, Aramayne, Stengard and Shelimir, Nissandra, Asoka, Afonso, Protay. At the parties there were five or ten temporaries for every citizen, some as mere servants, others as entertainers or even surrogate guests, mingling freely and a little daringly. But everyone knew, all the time, who was a citizen and who just a temporary. Phillips began to think his own status lay somewhere between. Certainly they treated him with a courtesy that no one ever would give a temporary, and yet there was a condescension to their manner that told him not simply that he was not one of them but that he was someone or something of an altogether different order of existence. That he was Gioia's lover gave him some standing in their eyes, but not a great deal: obviously he was always going to be an outsider, a primitive, ancient and quaint. For that matter he noticed that Gioia herself, though unquestionably a member of the set, seemed to be regarded as something of an outsider, like a tradesman's great-granddaughter in a gathering of Plantagenets. She did not always find out about the best parties in time to attend; her friends did not always reciprocate her effusive greetings with the same degree of warmth; sometimes he noticed her straining to hear some bit of gossip that was not quite being shared with her. Was it because she had taken him for her lover? Or was it the other way around: that she had chosen to be his lover precisely because she was *not* a full member of their caste?

Being a primitive gave him, at least, something to talk about at their parties. "Tell us about war," they said. "Tell us about elections. About money. About disease." They wanted to know everything, though they did not seem to pay close attention: their eyes were quick to glaze. Still, they asked. He described traffic jams to them, and politics, and deodorants, and vitamin pills. He told them about cigarettes, newspapers, subways, telephone directories, credit cards, and basketball.

"Which was your city?" they asked. New York, he told them. "And when was it? The seventh century, did you say?" The twentieth, he told them. They exchanged glances and nodded. "We will have to do it," they said. "The World Trade Center, the Empire State Building, the Citicorp Center, the Cathedral of St. John the Divine: how fascinating! Yankee Stadium. The Verrazzano Bridge. We will do it all. But first must come Mohenjo-daro. And then, I think, Constantinople. Did your city have many people?" Seven million, he said. Just in the five boroughs alone. They nodded, smiling amiably, unfazed by the number.

Seven million, seventy million—it was all the same to them, he sensed. They would just bring forth the temporaries in whatever quantity was required. He wondered how well they would carry the job off. He was no real judge of Alexandrias and Asgards, after all. Here they could have unicorns and hippogriffs in the zoo, and live sphinxes prowling in the gutters, and it did not trouble him. Their fanciful Alexandria was as good as history's, or better. But how sad, how disillusioning it would be, if the New York that they conjured up had Greenwich Village uptown and Times Square in the Bronx, and the New Yorkers, gentle and polite, spoke with the honeyed accents of Savannah or New Orleans. Well, that was nothing he needed to brood about just now. Very likely they were only being courteous when they spoke of doing his New York. They had all the vastness of the past to choose from: Nineveh, Memphis of the Pharaohs, the London of Victoria or Shakespeare or Richard the Third, Florence of the Medici, the Paris of Abelard and Heloise or the Paris of Louis XIV, Moctezuma's Tenochtitlan and Atahuallpa's Cuzco; Damascus, St. Petersburg, Babylon, Troy. And then there were all the cities like New Chicago, out of time that was time yet unborn to him but ancient history to them. In such richness, such an infinity of choices, even mighty New York might have to wait a long while for its turn. Would he still be among them by the time they got around to it? By then, perhaps, they might have become bored with him and returned him to his own proper era. Or possibly he would simply have grown old and died. Even here, he supposed, he would eventually die, though no one else ever seemed to. He did not know. He realized that in fact he did not know anything.

The north wind blew all day long. Vast flocks of ibises

appeared over the city, fleeing the heat of the interior, and screeched across the sky with their black necks and scrawny legs extended. The sacred birds, descending by the thousands, scuttered about in every crossroad, pouncing on spiders and beetles, on mice, on the debris of the meatshops and the bakeries. They were beautiful but annoyingly ubiquitous, and they splashed their dung over the marble buildings; each morning squadrons of temporaries carefully washed it off. Gioia said little to him now. She seemed cool, withdrawn, depressed; and there was something almost intangible about her, as though she were gradually becoming transparent. He felt it would be an intrusion upon her privacy to ask her what was wrong. Perhaps it was only restlessness. She became religious, and presented costly offerings at the temples of Serapis, Isis, Poseidon, Pan. She went to the necropolis west of the city to lay wreaths on the tombs in the catacombs. In a single day she climbed the Lighthouse three times without any sign of fatigue. One afternoon he returned from a visit to the Library and found her naked on the patio; she had anointed herself all over with some aromatic green salve. Abruptly she said, "I think it's time to leave Alexandria, don't you?"

She wanted to go to Mohenjo-daro, but Mohenjo-daro was not yet ready for visitors. Instead they flew eastward to Chang-an, which they had not seen in years. It was Phillips' suggestion: he hoped that the cosmopolitan gaudiness of the old T'ang capital would lift her mood.

They were to be guests of the Emperor this time: an unusual privilege, which ordinarily had to be applied for far in advance, but Phillips had told some of Gioia's highly placed friends that she was unhappy, and they had quickly arranged everything. Three endlessly bowing functionaries in flowing yellow robes and purple sashes met them at the Gate of Brilliant Virtue in the city's south wall and conducted them to their pavilion, close by the imperial palace and the Forbidden Garden. It was a light, airy place, thin walls of plastered brick braced by graceful columns of some dark, aromatic wood. Fountains played on the roof of green and yellow tiles, creating an unending cool rainfall of recirculating water. The balustrades were of carved marble, the door-fittings were of gold.

There was a suite of private rooms for him, and another for her, though they would share the handsome damask-draped bedroom at the heart of the pavilion. As soon as they arrived Gioia announced that she must go to her rooms to bathe and dress. "There will be a formal reception for us at the palace tonight," she said. "They say the imperial receptions are splendid beyond anything you could imagine. I want to be at my best." The Emperor and all his ministers, she told him, would receive them in the Hall of the Supreme Ultimate; there would be a banquet for a thousand people; Persian dancers would perform, and the celebrated jugglers of Chung-nan. Afterward everyone would be conducted into the fantastic landscape of the Forbidden Garden to view the dragon-races and the fireworks.

He went to his own rooms. Two delicate little maid-servants undressed him and bathed him with fragrant sponges. The pavilion came equipped with eleven temporaries who were to be their servants: soft-voiced unobtrusive cat-like Chinese, done with perfect verisimilitude, straight black hair, glowing skin, epicanthic folds. Phillips often wondered what happened to a city's temporaries when the city's time was over. Were the towering Norse heroes of Asgard being recycled at this moment into wiry dark-skinned Dravidians for Mohenjo-daro? When Timbuctoo's day was done, would its brightly robed black warriors be converted into supple Byzantines to stock the arcades of Constantinople? Or did they simply discard the old temporaries like so many excess props, stash them in warehouses somewhere, and turn out the appropriate quantities of the new model? He did not know; and once when he had asked Gioia about it she had grown uncomfortable and vague. She did not like him to probe for information, and he suspected it was because she had very little to give. These people did not seem to question the workings of their own world; his curiosities were very twentieth-century of him, he was frequently told, in that gently patronizing way of theirs. As his two little maids patted him with their sponges he thought of asking them where they had served before Chang-an. Rio? Rome? Haroun al-Raschid's Baghdad? But these fragile girls, he knew, would only giggle and retreat if he tried to question them. Interrogating temporaries was not only improper, but pointless: it was like interrogating one's luggage.

When he was bathed and robed in rich red silks he wandered the pavilion for a little while, admiring the tinkling pendants of green jade dangling on the portico, the lustrous auburn pillars, the rainbow hues of the intricately interwoven girders and brackets that supported the roof. Then, wearying of his solitude, he approached the bamboo curtain at the entrance to Gioia's suite. A porter and one of the maids stood just within. They indicated that he should not enter; but he scowled at them and they melted from him like snowflakes. A trail of incense led him through the pavilion to Gioia's innermost dressing-room. There he halted, just outside the door.

Gioia sat naked with her back to him at an ornate dressing-table of some rare flame-colored wood inlaid with bands of orange and green porcelain. She was studying herself intently in a mirror of polished bronze held by one of her maids: picking through her scalp with her fingernails, as a woman might do who was searching out her gray hairs.

But that seemed strange. Gray hair, on Gioia? On a citizen? A temporary might display some appearance of aging, perhaps, but surely not a citizen. Citizens remained forever young. Gioia looked like a girl. Her face was smooth and unlined, her flesh was firm, her hair was dark: that was true of all of them, every citizen he had ever seen. And yet there was no mistaking what Gioia was doing. She found a hair, frowned, drew it taut, nodded, plucked it. Another. Another. She pressed the tip of her finger to her cheek as if testing it for resilience. She tugged at the skin below her eyes, pulling it downward. Such familiar little gestures of vanity; but so odd here, he thought, in this world of the perpetually young. Gioia, worried about growing old? Had he simply failed to notice the signs of age on her? Or was it that she worked hard behind his back at concealing them? Perhaps that was it. Was he wrong about the citizens, then? Did they age even as the people of less blessed eras had always done, but simply have better ways of hiding it? How old was she, anyway? Thirty? Sixty? Three hundred?

Gioia appeared satisfied now. She waved the mirror away; she rose; she beckoned for her banquet robes. Phillips, still standing unnoticed by the door, studied her with admiration: the small round buttocks, almost but not quite boyish, the elegant line of her spine, the surprising breadth of her shoulders. No, he thought, she is not aging at all. Her body is still like a girl's. She looks as young as on the day they first had met, however long ago that was—he could not say; it was hard to keep track of time here; but he was sure some years had passed since they had come together. Those gray hairs, those wrinkles and sags for which she had searched just now with such desperate intensity, must all be imaginary, mere artifacts of vanity. Even in this remote future epoch, then, vanity was not extinct. He wondered why she was so concerned with the fear of aging. An affectation? Did all these timeless people take some perverse pleasure in fretting over the possibility that they might be growing old? Or was it some private fear of Gioia's, another symptom of the mysterious depression that had come over her in Alexandria?

Not wanting her to think that he had been spying on her, when all he had really intended was to pay her a visit, he slipped silently away to dress for the evening. She came to him an hour later, gorgeously robed, swaddled from chin to ankles in a brocade of brilliant colors shot through with threads of gold, face painted, hair drawn up tightly and fastened with ivory combs: very much the lady of the court. His servants had made him splendid also, a lustrous black surplice embroidered with golden dragons over a sweeping floor-length gown of shining white silk, a necklace and pendant of red coral, a five-cornered gray felt hat that rose in tower upon tower like a ziggurat. Gioia, grinning, touched her fingertips to his cheek. "You look marvelous!" she told him. "Like a grand mandarin!"

"And you like an empress," he said. "Of some distant land: Persia, India. Here to pay a ceremonial visit on the Son of Heaven." An excess of love suffused his spirit, and, catching her lightly by the wrist, he drew her toward him, as close as he could manage it considering how elaborate their costumes were. But as he bent forward and downward, meaning to brush his lips lightly and affectionately against the tip of her nose, he perceived an unexpected strangeness, an anomaly: the coating of white paint that was her makeup seemed oddly to magnify rather than mask the contours of her skin, highlighting and revealing details he had never observed before. He saw a pattern of fine lines radiating from the corners of her eyes, and the unmistakable beginning of a quirk-mark in her cheek just to the left of her mouth, and perhaps the faint indentation of frown-lines in her flawless forehead. A shiver traveled along the nape of his neck. So it was not affectation, then, that had had her studying her mirror so fiercely. Age was in truth beginning to stake its claim on her, despite all that he had come to believe about these people's agelessness. But a moment later he was not so sure. Gioia turned and slid gently half a step back from him—she must have found his stare disturbing—and the lines he had thought he had seen were gone. He searched for them and saw only girlish smoothness once again. A trick of the light? A figment of an overwrought imagination? He was baffled.

"Come," she said. "We mustn't keep the Emperor waiting."

Five mustachioed warriors in armor of white quilting and seven musicians playing cymbals and pipes escorted them to the Hall of the Supreme Ultimate. There they found the full court arrayed: princes and ministers, high officials, yellow-robed monks, a swarm of imperial concubines. In a place of honor to the right of the royal thrones, which rose like gilded scaffolds high above all else, was a little group of stern-faced men in foreign costumes, the ambassadors of Rome and Byzantium, of Arabia and Syria, of Korea, Japan, Tibet, Turkestan. Incense smouldered in enameled braziers. A poet sang a delicate twanging melody, accompanying himself on a small harp. Then the Emperor and Empress entered: two tiny aged people, like waxen images, moving with infinite slowness, taking steps no greater than a child's. There was the sound of trumpets as they ascended their thrones. When the little Emperor was seated—he looked like a doll up there, ancient, faded, shrunken, yet still somehow a figure of extraordinary power—he stretched forth both his hands, and enormous gongs began to sound. It was a scene of astonishing splendor, grand and overpowering.

These are all temporaries, Phillips realized suddenly. He

saw only a handful of citizens—eight, ten, possibly as many as a dozen—scattered here and there about the vast room. He knew them by their eyes, dark, liquid, knowing. They were watching not only the imperial spectacle but also Gioia and him; and Gioia, smiling secretly, nodding almost imperceptibly to them, was acknowledging their presence and their interest. But those few were the only ones in here who were autonomous living beings. All the rest—the entire splendid court, the great mandarins and paladins, the officials, the giggling concubines, the haughty and resplendent ambassadors, the aged Emperor and Empress themselves, were simply part of the scenery. Had the world ever seen entertainment on so grand a scale before? All this pomp, all this pageantry, conjured up each night for the amusement of a dozen or so viewers?

At the banquet the little group of citizens sat together at a table apart, a round onyx slab draped with translucent green silk. There turned out to be seventeen of them in all, including Gioia; Gioia appeared to know all of them, though none, so far as he could tell, was a member of her set that he had met before. She did not attempt introductions. Nor was conversation at all possible during the meal: there was a constant astounding roaring din in the room. Three orchestras played at once and there were troupes of strolling musicians also, and a steady stream of monks and their attendants marched back and forth between the tables loudly chanting sutras and waving censers to the deafening accompaniment of drums and gongs. The Emperor did not descend from his throne to join the banquet; he seemed to be asleep, though now and then he waved his hand in time to the music. Gigantic half-naked brown slaves with broad cheekbones and mouths like gaping pockets brought forth the food, peacock tongues and breast of phoenix heaped on mounds of glowing saffron-colored rice, served on frail alabaster plates. For chopsticks they were given slender rods of dark jade. The wine, served in glistening crystal beakers, was thick and sweet, with an aftertaste of raisins, and no beaker was allowed to remain empty for more than a moment.

Phillips felt himself growing dizzy: when the Persian dancers emerged he could not tell whether there were five of them or fifty, and as they performed their intricate whirling routines it seemed to him that their slender muslin-veiled forms were blurring and merging one into another. He felt frightened by their proficiency, and wanted to look away, but he could not. The Chung-nan jugglers that followed them were equally skillful, equally alarming, filling the air with scythes, flaming torches, live animals, rare porcelain vases, pink jade hatchets, silver bells, gilded cups, wagon-wheels, bronze vessels, and never missing a catch. The citizens applauded politely but did not seem impressed. After the jugglers, the dancers returned, performing this time on stilts; the waiters brought platters of steaming meat of a pale lavender color, unfamiliar in taste and texture: filet of camel, perhaps, or haunch of hippopotamus, or possibly some choice chop from a young dragon. There was more wine. Feebly Phillips tried to wave it away, but the servitors were implacable. This was a drier sort, greenish-gold, austere, sharp on the tongue. With it came a silver dish, chilled to a polar coldness, that held shaved ice flavored with some potent smoky-flavored brandy. The jugglers were doing a second turn, he noticed. He thought he was going to be ill. He looked helplessly toward Gioia, who seemed sober but fiercely animated, almost manic, her eyes blazing like rubies. She touched his cheek fondly.

A cool draft blew through the hall: they had opened one entire wall, revealing the garden, the night, the stars. Just outside was a colossal wheel of oiled paper stretched on wooden struts. They must have erected it in the past hour: it stood a hundred fifty feet high or even more, and on it hung lanterns by the thousands, glimmering like giant fireflies. The guests began to leave the hall. Phillips let himself be swept along into the garden, where under a yellow moon strange crook-armed trees with dense black needles loomed ominously. Gioia slipped her arm through his. They went down to a lake of bubbling crimson fluid and watched scarlet flamingo-like birds ten feet tall fastidiously spearing angry-eyed turquoise eels. They stood in awe before a fat-bellied Buddha of gleaming blue tilework, seventy feet high. A horse with a golden mane came prancing by, striking showers of brilliant red sparks wherever its hooves touched the ground. In a grove of lemon trees that seemed to have the power to wave their slender limbs about, Phillips came upon the Emperor, standing by himself and rocking gently back and forth. The old man seized Phillips by the hand and pressed something into his palm, closing his fingers tight about it; when he opened his fist a few moments later he found his palm full of gray irregular pearls. Gioia took them from him and cast them into the air, and they burst like exploding firecrackers, giving off splashes of colored light. A little later, Phillips realized that he was no longer wearing his surplice or his white silken undergown. Gioia was naked too, and she drew him gently down into a carpet of moist blue moss, where they made love until dawn, fiercely at first, then slowly, languidly, dreamily. At sunrise he looked at her tenderly and saw that something was wrong.

"Gioia?" he said doubtfully.

She smiled. "Ah, no. Gioia is with Fenimon tonight. I am Belilala."

"With—Fenimon?"

"They are old friends. She had not seen him in years."

"Ah. I see. And you are—?"

"Belilala," she said again, touching her fingertips to his cheek.

It was not unusual, Belilala said. It happened all the time; the only unusual thing was that it had not happened to him before now. Couples formed, traveled together for a while, drifted apart, eventually reunited. It did not mean that Gioia had left him forever. It meant only that just now she chose to be with Fenimon. Gioia would return. In the meanwhile he would not be alone. "You and I met in New Chicago," Belilala told him. "And then we saw each other again in Timbuctoo. Have you forgotten? Oh, yes, I see that you have forgotten!" She laughed prettily; she did not seem at all offended.

She looked enough like Gioia to be her sister. But, then, all the citizens looked more or less alike to him. And apart from their physical resemblance, so he quickly came to realize, Belilala and Gioia were not really very similar. There was a calmness, a deep reservoir of serenity, in Belilala that Gioia, eager and volatile and ever impatient, did not seem to have. Strolling the swarming streets of Chang-an with Belilala, he did not perceive in her any of

Gioia's restless feverish need always to know what lay beyond, and beyond, and beyond even that. When they toured the Hsing-ch'ing Palace, Belilala did not after five minutes begin—as Gioia surely would have done—to seek directions to the Fountain of Hsuan-tsung or the Wild Goose Pagoda. Curiosity did not consume Belilala as it did Gioia. Plainly she believed that there would always be enough time for her to see everything she cared to see. There were some days when Belilala chose not to go out at all, but was content merely to remain at their pavilion playing a solitary game with flat porcelain counters, or viewing the flowers of the garden.

He found, oddly, that he enjoyed the respite from Gioia's intense world-swallowing appetites; and yet he longed for her to return. Belilala—beautiful, gentle, tranquil, patient—was too perfect for him. She seemed unreal in her gleaming impeccability, much like one of those Sung celadon vases that appear too flawless to have been thrown and glazed by human hands. There was something a little soulless about her: an immaculate finish outside, emptiness within. Belilala might almost have been a temporary, he thought, though he knew she was not. He could explore the pavilions and palaces of Chang-an with her, he could make graceful conversation with her while they dined, he could certainly enjoy coupling with her; but he could not love her or even contemplate the possibility. It was hard to imagine Belilala worriedly studying herself in a mirror for wrinkles and gray hairs. Belilala would never be any older than she was at this moment; nor could Belilala ever have been any younger. Perfection does not move along an axis of time. But the perfection of Belilala's glossy surface made her inner being impenetrable to him. Gioia was more vulnerable, more obviously flawed—her restlessness, her moodiness, her vanity, her fears—and therefore she was more accessible to his own highly imperfect twentieth-century sensibility.

Occasionally he saw Gioia as he roamed the city, or thought he did. He had a glimpse of her among the miracle-vendors in the Persian Bazaar, and outside the Zoroastrian temple, and again by the goldfish pond in the Serpentine Park. But he was never quite sure that the woman he saw was really Gioia, and he never could get close enough to her to be certain: she had a way of vanishing as he approached, like some mysterious Lorelei luring him onward and onward in a hopeless chase. After a while he came to realize that he was not going to find her until she was ready to be found.

He lost track of time. Weeks, months, years? He had no idea. In this city of exotic luxury, mystery, and magic all was in constant flux and transition and the days had a fitful, unstable quality. Buildings and even whole streets were torn down of an afternoon and re-erected, within days, far away. Grand new pagodas sprouted like toadstools in the night. Citizens came in from Asgard, Alexandria, Timbuctoo, New Chicago, stayed for a time, disappeared, returned. There was a constant round of court receptions, banquets, theatrical events, each one much like the one before. The festivals in honor of past emperors and empresses might have given some form to the year, but they seemed to occur in a random way, the ceremony marking the death of T'ai Tsung coming around twice the same year, so it seemed to him, once in a season of snow and again in high summer, and the one honoring the ascension of the Empress Wu being held twice in a single season. Perhaps he had misunderstood something. But he knew it was no use asking anyone.

One day Belilala said unexpectedly, "Shall we go to Mohenjo-daro?"

"I didn't know it was ready for visitors," he replied.

"Oh, yes. For quite some time now."

He hesitated. This had caught him unprepared. Cautiously he said, "Gioia and I were going to go there together, you know."

Belilala smiled amiably, as though the topic under discussion were nothing more than a choice of that evening's restaurant.

"Were you?" she asked.

"It was all arranged while we were still in Alexandria. To go with you instead—I don't know what to tell you, Belilala." Phillips sensed that he was growing terribly flustered. "You know that I'd like to go. With you. But on the other hand I can't help feeling that I shouldn't go there until I'm back with Gioia again. If I ever am." How foolish this sounds, he thought. How clumsy, how adolescent. He found that he was having trouble looking straight at her. Uneasily he said, with a kind of desperation in his voice, "I did promise her—there was a commitment, you understand—a firm agreement that we would go to Mohenjo-daro together—"

"Oh, but Gioia's already there!" said Belilala in the most casual way.

He gaped as though she had punched him.

"What?"

"She was one of the first to go, after it opened. Months and months ago. You didn't know?" she asked, sounding surprised, but not very. "You really didn't know?"

That astonished him. He felt bewildered, betrayed, furious. His cheeks grew hot, his mouth gaped. He shook his head again and again, trying to clear it of confusion. It was a moment before he could speak. "Already there?" he said at last. "Without waiting for me? After we had talked about going there together—after we had agreed—"

Belilala laughed. "But how could she resist seeing the newest city? You know how impatient Gioia is!"

"Yes. Yes."

He was stunned. He could barely think.

"Just like all short-timers," Belilala said. "She rushes here, she rushes there. She must have it all, now, now, right away, at once, instantly. You ought never expect her to wait for you for anything for very long: the fit seizes her, and off she goes. Surely you must know that about her by now."

"A short-timer?" He had not heard that term before.

"Yes. You knew that. You must have known that." Belilala flashed her sweetest smile. She showed no sign of comprehending his distress. With a brisk wave of her hand she said, "Well, then, shall we go, you and I? To Mohenjo-daro?"

"Of course," Phillips said bleakly.

"When would you like to leave?"

"Tonight," he said. He paused a moment. "What's a short-timer, Belilala?"

Color came to her cheeks. "Isn't it obvious?" she asked.

*   *   *

Had there ever been a more hideous place on the face of the earth than the city of Mohenjo-daro? Phillips found it difficult to imagine one. Nor could he understand why, out of all the cities that had ever been, these people had chosen to restore this one to existence. More than ever they seemed alien to him, unfathomable, incomprehensible.

From the terrace atop the many-towered citadel he peered down into grim claustrophobic Mohenjo-daro and shivered. The stark, bleak city looked like nothing so much as some prehistoric prison colony. In the manner of an uneasy tortoise it huddled, squat and compact, against the gray monotonous Indus River plain: miles of dark burnt-brick walls enclosing miles of terrifying orderly streets, laid out in an awesome, monstrous gridiron pattern of maniacal rigidity. The houses themselves were dismal and forbidding too, clusters of brick cells gathered about small airless courtyards. There were no windows, only small doors that opened not onto the main boulevards but onto the tiny mysterious lanes that ran between the buildings. Who had designed this horrifying metropolis? What harsh, sour souls they must have had, these frightening and frightened folk, creating for themselves in the lush fertile plains of India such a Supreme Soviet of a city!

"How lovely it is," Belilala murmured. "How fascinating!"

He stared at her in amazement.

"Fascinating? Yes," he said. "I suppose so. The same way that the smile of a cobra is fascinating."

"What's a cobra?"

"Poisonous predatory serpent," Phillips told her. "Probably extinct. Or formerly extinct, more likely. It wouldn't surprise me if you people had re-created a few and turned them loose in Mohenjo to make things livelier."

"You sound angry, Charles."

"Do I? That's not how I feel."

"How do you feel, then?"

"I don't know," he said after a long moment's pause. He shrugged. "Lost, I suppose. Very far from home."

"Poor Charles."

"Standing here in this ghastly barracks of a city, listening to you tell me how beautiful it is, I've never felt more alone in my life."

"You miss Gioia very much, don't you?"

He gave her another startled look.

"Gioia has nothing to do with it. She's probably been having ecstasies over the loveliness of Mohenjo just like you. Just like all of you. I suppose I'm the only one who can't find the beauty, the charm. I'm the only one who looks out there and sees only horror, and then wonders why nobody else sees it, why in fact people would set up a place like this for *entertainment,* for *pleasure*—"

Her eyes were gleaming. "Oh, you are angry! You really are!"

"Does that fascinate you too?" he snapped. "A demonstration of genuine primitive emotion? A typical quaint twentieth-century outburst?" He paced the rampart in short quick anguished steps. "Ah. Ah. I think I understand it now, Belilala. Of course: I'm part of your circus, the star of the sideshow. I'm the first experiment in setting up the next stage of it, in fact." Her eyes were wide. The sudden harshness and violence in his voice seemed to be alarming and exciting her at the same time. That angered him even more. Fiercely he went on, "Bringing whole cities back out of time was fun for a while, but it lacks a certain authenticity, eh? For some reason you couldn't bring the inhabitants too; you couldn't just grab a few million prehistorics out of Egypt or Greece or India and dump them down in this era, I suppose because you might have too much trouble controlling them, or because you'd have the problem of disposing of them once you were bored with them. So you had to settle for creating temporaries to populate your ancient cities. But now you've got me. I'm something more real than a temporary, and that's a terrific novelty for you, and novelty is the thing you people crave more than anything else: maybe the *only* thing you crave. And here I am, complicated, unpredictable, edgy, capable of anger, fear, sadness, love, and all those other formerly extinct things. Why settle for picturesque architecture when you can observe picturesque emotion, too? What fun I must be for all of you! And if you decide that I was really interesting, maybe you'll ship me back where I came from and check out a few other ancient types—a Roman gladiator, maybe, or a Renaissance pope, or even a Neanderthal or two—"

"Charles," she said tenderly. "Oh, Charles, Charles, Charles, how lonely you must be, how lost, how troubled! Will you ever forgive me? Will you ever forgive us all?"

Once more he was astounded by her. She sounded entirely sincere, altogether sympathetic. Was she? Was she, really? He was not sure he had ever had a sign of genuine caring from any of them before, not even Gioia. Nor could he bring himself to trust Belilala now. He was afraid of her, afraid of all of them, of their brittleness, their slyness, their elegance. He wished he could go to her and have her take him in her arms; but he felt too much the shaggy prehistoric just now to be able to risk asking that comfort of her.

He turned away and began to walk around the rim of the citadel's massive wall.

"Charles?"

"Let me alone for a little while," he said.

He walked on. His forehead throbbed and there was a pounding in his chest. All stress systems going full blast, he thought: secret glands dumping gallons of inflammatory substances into his bloodstream. The heat, the inner confusion, the repellent look of this place—

Try to understand, he thought. Relax. Look about you. Try to enjoy your holiday in Mohenjo-daro.

He leaned warily outward, over the edge of the wall. He had never seen a wall like this; it must be forty feet thick at the base, he guessed, perhaps even more, and every brick perfectly shaped, meticulously set. Beyond the great rampart, marshes ran almost to the edge of the city, although close by the wall the swamps had been dammed and drained for agriculture. He saw lithe brown farmers down there, busy with their wheat and barley and peas. Cattle and buffaloes grazed a little farther out. The air was heavy, dank, humid. All was still. From somewhere close at hand came the sound of a droning, whining stringed instrument and a steady insistent chanting.

Gradually a sort of peace pervaded him. His anger subsided. He felt himself beginning to grow calm again. He looked back at the city, the rigid interlocking streets, the maze of inner lanes, the millions of courses of precise brickwork.

It is a miracle, he told himself, that this city is here in

this place and at this time. And it is a miracle that I am here to see it.

Caught for a moment by the magic within the bleakness, he thought he began to understand Belilala's awe and delight, and he wished now that he had not spoken to her so sharply. The city was alive. Whether it was the actual Mohenjo-daro of thousands upon thousands of years ago, ripped from the past by some wondrous hook, or simply a cunning reproduction, did not matter at all. Real or not, this was the true Mohenjo-daro. It had been dead and now, for the moment, it was alive again. These people, these *citizens*, might be trivial, but reconstructing Mohenjo-daro was no trivial achievement. And that the city that had been reconstructed was oppressive and sinister-looking was unimportant. No one was compelled to live in Mohenjo-daro any more. Its time had come and gone, long ago; those little dark-skinned peasants and craftsmen and merchants down there were mere temporaries, mere inanimate things, conjured up like zombies to enhance the illusion. They did not need his pity. Nor did he need to pity himself. He knew that he should be grateful for the chance to behold these things. Some day, when this dream had ended and his hosts had returned him to the world of subways and computers and income tax and television networks, he would think of Mohenjo-daro as he had once beheld it, lofty walls of tightly woven dark brick under a heavy sky, and he would remember only its beauty.

Glancing back, he searched for Belilala and could not for a moment find her. Then he caught sight of her carefully descending a narrow staircase that angled down the inner face of the citadel wall.

"Belilala!" he called.

She paused and looked his way, shading her eyes from the sun with her hand. "Are you all right?"

"Where are you going?"

"To the baths," she said. "Do you want to come?"

He nodded. "Yes. Wait for me, will you? I'll be right there." He began to run toward her along the top of the wall.

The baths were attached to the citadel: a great open tank the size of a large swimming pool, lined with bricks set on edge in gypsum mortar and waterproofed with asphalt, and eight smaller tanks just north of it in a kind of covered arcade. He supposed that in ancient times the whole complex had had some ritual purpose, the large tank used by common folk and the small chambers set aside for the private ablutions of priests or nobles. Now the baths were maintained, it seemed, entirely for the pleasure of visiting citizens. As Phillips came up the passageway that led to the main bath he saw fifteen or twenty of them lolling in the water or padding languidly about, while temporaries of the dark-skinned Mohenjo-daro type served them drinks and pungent little morsels of spiced meat as though this were some sort of luxury resort. Which was, he realized, exactly what it was. The temporaries wore white cotton loincloths; the citizens were naked. In his former life he had encountered that sort of casual public nudity a few times on visits to California and the south of France, and it had made him mildly uneasy. But he was growing accustomed to it here.

The changing-rooms were tiny brick cubicles connected by rows of closely placed steps to the courtyard that surrounded the central tank. They entered one and Belilala swiftly slipped out of the loose cotton robe that she had worn since their arrival that morning. With arms folded she stood leaning against the wall, waiting for him. After a moment he dropped his own robe and followed her outside. He felt a little giddy, sauntering around naked in the open like this.

On the way to the main bathing area they passed the private baths. None of them seemed to be occupied. They were elegantly constructed chambers, with finely jointed brick floors and carefully designed runnels to drain excess water into the passageway that led to the primary drain. Phillips was struck with admiration for the cleverness of the prehistoric engineers. He peered into this chamber and that to see how the conduits and ventilating ducts were arranged, and when he came to the last room in the sequence he was surprised and embarrassed to discover that it was in use. A brawny grinning man, big-muscled, deep-chested, with exuberantly flowing shoulder-length red hair and a flamboyant, sharply tapering beard, was thrashing about merrily with two women in the small tank. Phillips had a quick glimpse of a lively tangle of arms, legs, breasts, buttocks.

"Sorry," he muttered. His cheeks reddened. Quickly he ducked out, blurting apologies as he went. "Didn't realize the room was occupied—no wish to intrude—"

Belilala had proceeded on down the passageway. Phillips hurried after her. From behind him came peals of cheerful raucous booming laughter and high-pitched giggling and the sound of splashing water. Probably they had not even noticed him.

He paused a moment, puzzled, playing back in his mind that one startling glimpse. Something was not right. Those women, he was fairly sure, were citizens: little slender elfin dark-haired girlish creatures, the standard model. But the man? That great curling sweep of red hair? Not a citizen. Citizens did not affect shoulder-length hair. And *red*? Nor had he ever seen a citizen so burly, so powerfully muscular. Or one with a beard. But he could hardly be a temporary, either. Phillips could conceive no reason why there would be so Anglo-Saxon-looking a temporary at Mohenjo-daro; and it was unthinkable for a temporary to be frolicking like that with citizens, anyway.

"Charles?"

He looked up ahead. Belilala stood at the end of the passageway, outlined in a nimbus of brilliant sunlight. "Charles?" she said again. "Did you lose your way?"

"I'm right here behind you," he said. "I'm coming."

"Who did you meet in there?"

"A man with a beard."

"With a what?"

"A beard," he said. "Red hair growing on his face. I wonder who he is."

"Nobody I know," said Belilala. "The only one I know with hair on his face is you. And yours is black, and you shave it off every day." She laughed. "Come along, now! I see some friends by the pool!"

He caught up with her and they went hand in hand out into the courtyard. Immediately a waiter glided up to them, an obsequious little temporary with a tray of drinks. Phillips waved it away and headed for the pool. He felt terribly exposed: he imagined that the citizens disporting themselves here were staring intently at him, studying his hairy primitive body as though he were some mythical creature, a Minotaur, a werewolf, summoned up for their amusement. Belilala drifted off to talk to someone and he slipped into the water, grateful for the concealment it offered. It was deep, warm, comforting. With swift powerful strokes he breast-stroked from one end to the other.

A citizen perched elegantly on the pool's rim smiled at him. "Ah, so you've come at last, Charles!" Char-less. Two syllables. Someone from Gioia's set: Stengard, Hawk, Aramayne? He could not remember which one. They were all so much alike.

Phillips returned the man's smile in a half-hearted, tentative way. He searched for something to say and finally asked, "Have you been here long?"

"Weeks. Perhaps months. What a splendid achievement this city is, eh, Charles? Such utter unity of mood—such a total statement of a uniquely single-minded esthetic—"

"Yes. Single-minded is the word," Phillips said drily.

"Gioia's word, actually. Gioia's phrase. I was merely quoting."

Gioia. He felt as if he had been stabbed.

"You've spoken to Gioia lately?" he said.

"Actually, no. It was Hekna who saw her. You do remember Hekna, eh?" He nodded toward two naked women standing on the brick platform that bordered the pool, chatting, delicately nibbling morsels of meat. They could have been twins. "There is Hekna, with your Belilala." Hekna, yes. So this must be Hawk, Phillips thought, unless there has been some recent shift of couples. "How sweet she is, your Belilala," Hawk said. "Gioia chose very wisely when she picked her for you."

Another stab: a much deeper one. "Is that how it was?" he said. "Gioia *picked* Belilala for me?"

"Why, of course!" Hawk seemed surprised. It went without saying, evidently. "What did you think? That Gioia would merely go off and leave you to fend for yourself?"

"Hardly. Not Gioia."

"She's very tender, very gentle, isn't she?"

"You mean Belilala? Yes, very," said Phillips carefully. "A dear woman, a wonderful woman. But of course I hope to get together with Gioia again soon." He paused.

"They say she's been in Mohenjo-daro almost since it opened."

"She was here, yes."

"Was?"

"Oh, you know Gioia," Hawk said lightly. "She's moved along by now, naturally."

Phillips leaned forward. "Naturally," he said. Tension thickened his voice. "Where has she gone this time?"

"Timbuctoo, I think. Or New Chicago. I forget which one it was. She was telling us that she hoped to be in Timbuctoo for the closing-down party. But then Fenimon had some pressing reason for going to New Chicago. I can't remember what they decided to do." Hawk gestured sadly. "Either way, a pity that she left Mohenjo before the new visitor came. She had such a rewarding time with you, after all: I'm sure she'd have found much to learn from him also."

The unfamiliar term twanged an alarm deep in Phillips' consciousness. *"Visitor?"* he said, angling his head sharply toward Hawk. "What visitor do you mean?"

"You haven't met him yet? Oh, of course, you've only just arrived."

Phillips moistened his lips. "I think I may have seen him. Long red hair? Beard like this?"

"That's the one! Willoughby, he's called. He's—what?— a Viking, a pirate, something like that. Tremendous vigor and force. Remarkable person. We should have many more visitors, I think. They're far superior to temporaries, everyone agrees. Talking with a temporary is a little like talking to one's self, wouldn't you say? They give you no significant illumination. But a visitor—someone like this Willoughby—or like you, Charles—a visitor can be truly enlightening, a visitor can transform one's view of reality—"

"Excuse me," Phillips said. A throbbing began behind his forehead. "Perhaps we can continue this conversation later, yes?" He put the flats of his hands against the hot brick of the platform and hoisted himself swiftly from the pool. "At dinner, maybe—or afterward—yes? All right?" He set off at a quick half-trot back toward the passageway that led to the private baths.

As he entered the roofed part of the structure his throat

grew dry, his breath suddenly came short. He padded quickly up the hall and peered into the little bath-chamber. The bearded man was still there, sitting up in the tank, breast-high above the water, with one arm around each of the women. His eyes gleamed with fiery intensity in the dimness. He was grinning in marvelous self-satisfaction; he seemed to brim with intensity, confidence, gusto.

Let him be what I think he is, Phillips prayed. I have been alone among these people long enough.

"May I come in?" he asked.

"Aye, fellow!" cried the man in the tub thunderously. "By my troth, come ye in, and bring your lass as well! God's teeth, I wot there's room aplenty for more folk in this tub than we!"

At that great uproarious outcry Phillips felt a powerful surge of joy. What a joyous rowdy voice! How rich, how lusty, how totally uncitizenlike!

And those oddly archaic words! *God's teeth? By my troth?* What sort of talk was that? What else but the good pure sonorous Elizabethan diction! Certainly it had something of the roll and fervor of Shakespeare about it. And spoken with—an Irish brogue, was it? No, not quite: it was English, but English spoken in no manner Phillips had ever heard.

Citizens did not speak that way. But a *visitor* might.

So it was true. Relief flooded Phillips' soul. Not alone, then! Another relict of a former age—another wanderer—a companion in chaos, a brother in adversity—a fellow voyager, tossed even farther than he had been by the tempests of time—

The bearded man grinned heartily and beckoned to Phillips with a toss of his head. "Well, join us, join us, man! 'Tis good to see an English face again, amidst all these Moors and rogue Portugals! But what have ye done with thy lass? One can never have enough wenches, d'ye not agree?"

The force and vigor of him were extraordinary: almost too much so. He roared, he bellowed, he boomed. He was so very much what he ought to be that he seemed more a character out of some old pirate movie than anything else, so blustering, so real, that he seemed unreal. A stage-

Elizabethan, larger than life, a boisterous young Falstaff without the belly.

Hoarsely, Phillips said, "Who are you?"

"Why, Ned Willoughby's son Francis am I, of Plymouth. Late of the service of Her Most Protestant Majesty, but most foully abducted by the powers of darkness and cast away among these blackamoor Hindus, or whatever they be. And thyself?"

"Charles Phillips." After a moment's uncertainty he added, "I'm from New York."

"*New* York? What place is that? In faith, man, I know it not!"

"A city in America."

"A city in America, forsooth! What a fine fancy that is! In America, you say, and not on the Moon, or perchance underneath the sea?" To the women Willoughby said, "D'ye hear him? He comes from a city in America! With the face of an Englishman, though not the manner of one, and not quite the proper sort of speech. A city in America! A *city*. God's blood, what will I hear next?"

Phillips trembled. Awe was beginning to take hold of him. This man had walked the streets of Shakespeare's London, perhaps. He had clinked canisters with Marlowe or Essex or Walter Raleigh; he had watched the ships of the Armada wallowing in the Channel. It strained Phillips' spirit to think of it. This strange dream in which he found himself was compounding its strangeness now. He felt like a weary swimmer assailed by heavy surf, winded, dazed. The hot close atmosphere of the baths was driving him toward vertigo. There could be no doubt of it any longer. He was not the only primitive—the only *visitor*—who was wandering loose in this fiftieth century. They were conducting other experiments as well. He gripped the sides of the door to steady himself and said, "When you speak of Her Most Protestant Majesty, it's Elizabeth the First you mean, is that not so?"

"Elizabeth, aye! As to the First, that is true enough, but why trouble to name her thus? There is but one. First and Last, I do trow, and God save her, there is no other!"

Phillips studied the other man warily. He knew that he must proceed with care. A misstep at this point and he would forfeit any chance that Willoughby would take him seriously. How much metaphysical bewilderment, after all, could this man absorb? What did he know, what had anyone of his time known, of past and present and future and the notion that one might somehow move from one to the other as readily as one would go from Surrey to Kent? That was a twentieth-century idea, late nineteenth at best, a fantastical speculation that very likely no one had even considered before Wells had sent his time traveler off to stare at the reddened sun of the earth's last twilight. Willoughby's world was a world of Protestants and Catholics, of kings and queens, of tiny sailing vessels, of swords at the hip and ox-carts on the road: that world seemed to Phillips far more alien and distant than was this world of citizens and temporaries. The risk that Willoughby would not begin to understand him was great.

But this man and he were natural allies against a world they had never made. Phillips chose to take the risk.

"Elizabeth the First is the queen you serve," he said. "There will be another of her name in England, in due time. Has already been, in fact."

Willoughby shook his head like a puzzled lion. "Another Elizabeth, d'ye say?"

"A second one, and not much like the first. Long after your Virgin Queen, this one. She will reign in what you think of as the days to come. That I know without doubt."

The Englishman peered at him and frowned. "You see the future? Are you a soothsayer, then? A necromancer, mayhap? Or one of the very demons that brought me to this place?"

"Not at all," Phillips said gently. "Only a lost soul, like yourself." He stepped into the little room and crouched by the side of the tank. The two citizen-women were staring at him in bland fascination. He ignored them. To Willoughby he said, "Do you have any idea where you are?"

The Englishman had guessed, rightly enough, that he was in India: "I do believe these little brown Moorish folk are of the Hindu sort," he said. But that was as far as his comprehension of what had befallen him could go.

It had not occurred to him that he was no longer living in the sixteenth century. And of course he did not begin to suspect that this strange and somber brick city in which he found himself was a wanderer out of an era even more remote than his own. Was there any way, Phillips wondered, of explaining that to him?

He had been here only three days. He thought it was devils that had carried him off. "While I slept did they come for me," he said. "Mephistophilis Sathanas and his henchmen seized me—God alone can say why—and swept me in a moment out to this torrid realm from England, where I had reposed among friends and family. For I was between one voyage and the next, you must understand, awaiting Drake and his ship—you know Drake, the glorious Francis? God's blood, there's a mariner for ye! We were to go to the Main again, he and I, but instead here I be in this other place—" Willoughby leaned close and said, "I ask you, soothsayer, how can it be, that a man go to sleep in Plymouth and wake up in India? It is passing strange, is it not?"

"That it is," Phillips said.

"But he that is in the dance must needs dance on, though he do but hop, eh? So do I believe." He gestured toward the two citizen-women. "And therefore to console myself in this pagan land I have found me some sport among these little Portugal women—"

"Portugal?" said Phillips.

"Why, what else can they be, but Portugals? Is it not the Portugals who control all these coasts of India? See, the people are of two sorts here, the blackamoors and the others, the fair-skinned ones, the lords and masters who lie here in these baths. If they be not Hindus, and I think they are not, then Portugals is what they must be." He laughed and pulled the women against himself and rubbed his hands over their breasts as though they were fruits on a vine. "Is that not what you are, you little naked shameless Papist wenches? A pair of Portugals, eh?"

They giggled, but did not answer.

"No," Phillips said. "This is India, but not the India you think you know. And these women are not Portuguese."

"Not Portuguese?" Willoughby said, baffled.

"No more so than you. I'm quite certain of that."

Willoughby stroked his beard. "I do admit I found them very odd, for Portugals. I have heard not a syllable of their

Portugee speech on their lips. And it is strange also that they run naked as Adam and Eve in these baths, and allow me free plunder of their women, which is not the way of Portugals at home, God wot. But I thought me, this is India, they choose to live in another fashion here—''

"No," Phillips said. "I tell you, these are not Portuguese, nor any other people of Europe who are known to you."

"Prithee, who are they, then?"

Do it delicately, now, Phillips warned himself. *Delicately*.

He said, "It is not far wrong to think of them as spirits of some kind—demons, even. Or sorcerers who have magicked us out of our proper places in the world." He paused, groping for some means to share with Willoughby, in a way that Willoughby might grasp, this mystery that had enfolded them. He drew a deep breath. "They've taken us not only across the sea," he said, "but across the years as well. We have both been hauled, you and I, far into the days that are to come."

Willoughby gave him a look of blank bewilderment.

"Days that are to come? Times yet unborn, d'ye mean? Why, I comprehend none of that!"

"Try to understand. We're both castaways in the same boat, man! But there's no way we can help each other if I can't make you see—"

Shaking his head, Willoughby muttered, "In faith, good friend, I find your words the merest folly. Today is today, and tomorrow is tomorrow, and how can a man step from one to t'other until tomorrow be turned into today?"

"I have no idea," said Phillips. Struggle was apparent on Willoughby's face; but plainly he could perceive no more than the haziest outline of what Phillips was driving at, if that much. "But this I know," he went on, "that your world and all that was in it is dead and gone. And so is mine, though I was born four hundred years after you, in the time of the second Elizabeth."

Willoughby snorted scornfully. "Four hundred—"

"You must believe me!"

"Nay! Nay!"

"It's the truth. Your time is only history to me. And mine and yours are history to *them*—ancient history. They call us visitors, but what we are is captives." Phillips felt himself quivering in the intensity of his effort. He was aware how insane this must sound to Willoughby. It was beginning to sound insane to him. "They've stolen us out of our proper times—seizing us like gypsies in the night—"

"Fie, man! You rave with lunacy!"

Phillips shook his head. He reached out and seized Willoughby tightly by the wrist. "I beg you, listen to me!" The citizen-women were watching closely, whispering to one another behind their hands, laughing. "Ask then!" Phillips cried. "Make them tell you what century this is! The sixteenth, do you think? Ask them!"

"What century could it be, but the sixteenth of our Lord?"

"They will tell you it is the fiftieth."

Willoughby looked at him pityingly. "Man, man, what a sorry thing thou art! The fiftieth, indeed!" He laughed. "Fellow, listen to me, now. There is but one Elizabeth, safe upon her throne in Westminster. This is India. The year is Anno 1591. Come, let us you and I steal a ship from these Portugals, and make our way back to England, and peradventure you may get from there to your America—"

"There is no England."

"Ah, can you say that and not be mad?"

"The cities and nations we knew are gone. These people live like magicians, Francis." There was no use holding anything back now, Phillips thought leadenly. He knew that he had lost. "They conjure up places of long ago, and build them here and there to suit their fancy, and when they are bored with them they destroy them, and start anew. There is no England. Europe is empty, featureless, void. Do you know what cities there are? There are only five in all the world. There is Alexandria of Egypt. There is Timbuctoo in Africa. There is New Chicago in America. There is a great city in China—in Cathay, I suppose you would say. And there is this place, which they call Mohenjo-daro, and which is far more ancient than Greece, than Rome, than Babylon."

Quietly Willoughby said, "Nay. This is mere absurdity. You say we are in some far tomorrow, and then you tell me we are dwelling in some city of long ago."

"A conjuration, only," Phillips said in desperation. "A likeness of that city. Which these folk have fashioned somehow for their own amusement. Just as we are here, you and I: to amuse them. Only to amuse them.''

''You are completely mad.''

''Come with me, then. Talk with the citizens by the great pool. Ask them what year this is; ask them about England; ask them how you come to be here.'' Once again Phillips grasped Willoughby's wrist. ''We should be allies. If we work together, perhaps we can discover some way to get ourselves out of this place, and—''

''Let me be, fellow.''

''Please—''

''Let me be!'' roared Willoughby, and pulled his arm free. His eyes were stark with rage. Rising in the tank, he looked about furiously as though searching for a weapon. The citizen-women shrank back away from him, though at the same time they seemed captivated by the big man's fierce outburst. ''Go to, get you to Bedlam! Let me be, madman! Let me be!''

Dismally Phillips roamed the dusty unpaved streets of Mohenjo-daro alone for hours. His failure with Willoughby had left him bleak-spirited and somber: he had hoped to stand back to back with the Elizabethan against the citizens, but he saw now that that was not to be. He had bungled things; or, more likely, it had been impossible ever to bring Willoughby to see the truth of their predicament.

In the stifling heat he went at random through the confusing congested lanes of flat-roofed, windowless houses and blank, featureless walls until he emerged into a broad marketplace. The life of the city swirled madly around him: the pseudo-life, rather, the intricate interactions of the thousands of temporaries who were nothing more than wind-up dolls set in motion to provide the illusion that pre-Vedic India was still a going concern. Here vendors sold beautiful little carved stone seals portraying tigers and monkeys and strange humped cattle, and women bargained vociferously with craftsmen for ornaments of ivory, gold, copper, and bronze. Weary-looking women squatted behind immense mounds of newly made pottery, pinkish-red with black designs. No one paid any attention to him. He was the outsider here, neither citizen nor temporary. They belonged.

He went on, passing the huge granaries where workmen ceaselessly unloaded carts of wheat and others pounded grain on great circular brick platforms. He drifted into a public restaurant thronging with joyless silent people standing elbow to elbow at small brick counters, and was given a flat round piece of bread, a sort of tortilla or chapatti, in which was stuffed some spiced mincemeat that stung his lips like fire. Then he moved onward, down a wide, shallow, timbered staircase into the lower part of the city, where the peasantry lived in cell-like rooms packed together as though in hives.

It was an oppressive city, but not a squalid one. The intensity of the concern with sanitation amazed him: wells and fountains and public privies everywhere, and brick drains running from each building, leading to covered cesspools. There was none of the open sewage and pestilent gutters that he knew still could be found in the India of his own time. He wondered whether ancient Mohenjo-daro had in truth been so fastidious. Perhaps the citizens had redesigned the city to suit their own ideals of cleanliness. No: most likely what he saw was authentic, he decided, a function of the same obsessive discipline that had given the city its rigidity of form. If Mohenjo-daro had been a verminous filthy hole, the citizens probably would have re-created it in just that way, and loved it for its fascinating, reeking filth.

Not that he had ever noticed an excessive concern with authenticity on the part of the citizens; and Mohenjo-daro, like all the other restored cities he had visited, was full of the usual casual anachronisms. Phillips saw images of Shiva and Krishna here and there on the walls of buildings he took to be temples, and the benign face of the mother-goddess Kali loomed in the plazas. Surely those deities had arisen in India long after the collapse of the Mohenjo-daro civilization. Were the citizens indifferent to such matters of chronology? Or did they take a certain naughty pleasure in mixing the eras—a mosque and a church in Greek Alexandria, Hindu gods in prehistoric Mohenjo-daro? Perhaps their records of the past had become contaminated with errors over the thousands of years. He would not have been surprised to see banners bearing portraits of Gandhi and Nehru being carried in procession through the streets. And there were phantasms and chimeras at large here again too, as if the citizens were untroubled by the boundary between history and myth: little fat elephant-headed Ganeshas blithely plunging their trunks into water-fountains, a six-armed three-headed woman sunning herself on a brick terrace. Why not? Surely that was the motto of these people: *Why not, why not, why not?* They could do as they pleased, and they did. Yet Gioia had said to him, long ago, "Limits are very important." In what, Phillips wondered, did they limit themselves, other than the number of their cities? Was there a quota, perhaps, on the number of "visitors" they allowed themselves to kidnap from the past? Until today he had thought he was the only one; now he knew there was at least one other; possibly there were more elsewhere, a step or two ahead or behind him, making the circuit with the citizens who traveled endlessly from New Chicago to Chang-an to Alexandria. We should join forces, he thought, and compel them to send us back to our rightful eras. *Compel?* How? File a class-action suit, maybe? Demonstrate in the streets? Sadly he thought of his failure to make common cause with Willoughby. We are natural allies, he thought. Together perhaps we might have won some compassion from these people. But to Willoughby it must be literally unthinkable that Good Queen Bess and her subjects were sealed away on the far side of a barrier hundreds of centuries thick. He would prefer to believe that England was just a few months' voyage away around the Cape of Good Hope, and that all he need do was commandeer a ship and set sail for home. Poor Willoughby: probably he would never see his home again.

The thought came to Phillips suddenly:

Neither will you.

And then, after it:

If you could go home, would you really want to?

One of the first things he had realized here was that he knew almost nothing substantial about his former existence. His mind was well stocked with details on life in twentieth-century New York, to be sure; but of himself he could say not much more than that he was Charles Phillips and had come from 1984. Profession? Age? Parents' names? Did he have a wife? Children? A cat, a dog, hobbies? No data: none. Possibly the citizens had stripped such things from him when they brought him here, to spare him from the pain of separation. They might be capable of that kindness. Knowing so little of what he had lost, could he truly say that he yearned for it? Willoughby seemed to remember much more of his former life, and longed for it all the more. He was spared that. Why not stay here, and go on and on from city to city, sightseeing all of time past as the citizens conjured it back into being? Why not? Why not? The chances were that he had no choice about it, anyway.

He made his way back up toward the citadel and to the baths once more. He felt a little like a ghost, haunting a city of ghosts.

Belilala seemed unaware that he had been gone for most of the day. She sat by herself on the terrace of the baths, placidly sipping some thick milky beverage that had been sprinkled with a dark spice. He shook his head when she offered him some.

"Do you remember I mentioned that I saw a man with red hair and a beard this morning?" Phillips said. "He's a visitor. Hawk told me that."

"Is he?" Belilala asked.

"From a time about four hundred years before mine. I talked with him. He thinks he was brought here by demons." Phillips gave her a searching look. "I'm a visitor too, isn't that so?"

"Of course, love."

"And how was *I* brought here? By demons also?"

Belilala smiled indifferently. "You'd have to ask someone else. Hawk, perhaps. I haven't looked into these things very deeply."

"I see. Are there many visitors here, do you know?"

A languid shrug. "Not many, no, not really. I've only heard of three or four besides you. There may be others by now, I suppose." She rested her hand lightly on his. "Are you having a good time in Mohenjo, Charles?"

He let her question pass as though he had not heard it.

"I asked Hawk about Gioia," he said.

"Oh?"

"He told me that she's no longer here, that she's gone on to Timbuctoo or New Chicago, he wasn't sure which."

"That's quite likely. As everybody knows, Gioia rarely stays in the same place very long."

Phillips nodded. "You said the other day that Gioia is a short-timer. That means she's going to grow old and die, doesn't it?"

"I thought you understood that, Charles."

"Whereas you will not age? Nor Hawk, nor Stengard, nor any of the rest of your set?"

"We will live as long as we wish," she said. "But we will not age, no."

"What makes a person a short-timer?"

"They're born that way, I think. Some missing gene, some extra gene—I don't actually know. It's extremely uncommon. Nothing can be done to help them. It's very slow, the aging. But it can't be halted."

Phillips nodded. "That must be very disagreeable," he said. "To find yourself one of the few people growing old in a world where everyone stays young. No wonder Gioia is so impatient. No wonder she runs around from place to place. No wonder she attached herself so quickly to the barbaric hairy visitor from the twentieth century, who comes from a time when *everybody* was a short-timer. She and I have something in common, wouldn't you say?"

"In a manner of speaking, yes."

"We understand aging. We understand death. Tell me: is Gioia likely to die very soon, Belilala?"

"Soon? Soon?" She gave him a wide-eyed child-like stare. "What is soon? How can I say? What you think of as soon and what I think of as soon are not the same things, Charles." Then her manner changed: she seemed to be hearing what he was saying for the first time. Softly she said, "No, no, Charles. I don't think she will die very soon."

"When she left me in Chang-an, was it because she had become bored with me?"

Belilala shook her head. "She was simply restless. It had nothing to do with you. She was never bored with you."

"Then I'm going to go looking for her. Wherever she may be, Timbuctoo, New Chicago, I'll find her. Gioia and I belong together."

"Perhaps you do," said Belilala. "Yes. Yes, I think

you really do." She sounded altogether unperturbed, unrejected, unbereft. "By all means, Charles. Go to her. Follow her. Find her. Wherever she may be."

They had already begun dismantling Timbuctoo when Phillips got there. While he was still high overhead, his flitterflitter hovering above the dusty tawny plain where the River Niger met the sands of the Sahara, a surge of keen excitement rose in him as he looked down at the square gray flat-roofed mud brick buildings of the great desert capital. But when he landed he found gleaming metal-skinned robots swarming everywhere, a horde of them scuttling about like giant shining insects, pulling the place apart.

He had not known about the robots before. So that was how all these miracles were carried out, Phillips realized: an army of obliging machines. He imagined them bustling up out of the earth whenever their services were needed, emerging from some sterile subterranean storehouse to put together Venice or Thebes or Knossos or Houston or whatever place was required, down to the finest detail, and then at some later time returning to undo everything that they had fashioned. He watched them now, diligently pulling down the adobe walls, demolishing the heavy metal-studded gates, bulldozing the amazing labyrinth of alleyways and thoroughfares, sweeping away the market. On his last visit to Timbuctoo that market had been crowded with a horde of veiled Tuaregs and swaggering Moors, black Sudanese, shrewd-faced Syrian traders, all of them busily dickering for camels, horses, donkeys, slabs of salt, huge green melons, silver bracelets, splendid vellum Korans. They were all gone now, that picturesque crowd of swarthy temporaries. Nor were there any citizens to be seen. The dust of destruction choked the air. One of the robots came up to Phillips and said in a dry crackling insect-voice, "You ought not to be here. This city is closed."

He stared at the flashing, buzzing band of scanners and sensors across the creature's glittering tapered snout. "I'm trying to find someone, a citizen who may have been here recently. Her name is—"

"This city is closed," the robot repeated inexorably.

They would not let him stay as much as an hour. There

is no food here, the robot said, no water, no shelter. This is not a place any longer. You may not stay. You may not stay. You may not stay.

This is not a place any longer.

Perhaps he could find her in New Chicago, then. He took to the air again, soaring northward and westward over the vast emptiness. The land below him curved away into the hazy horizon, bare, sterile. What had they done with the vestiges of the world that had gone before? Had they turned their gleaming metal beetles loose to clean everything away? Were there no ruins of genuine antiquity anywhere? No scrap of Rome, no shard of Jerusalem, no stump of Fifth Avenue? It was all so barren down there: an empty stage, waiting for its next set to be built. He flew on a great arc across the jutting hump of Africa and on into what he supposed was southern Europe: the little vehicle did all the work, leaving him to doze or stare as he wished. Now and again he saw another flitterflitter pass by, far away, a dark distant winged teardrop outlined against the hard clarity of the sky. He wished there was some way of making radio contact with them, but he had no idea how to go about it. Not that he had anything he wanted to say; he wanted only to hear a human voice. He was utterly isolated. He might just as well have been the last living man on Earth. He closed his eyes and thought of Gioia.

"Like this?" Phillips asked. In an ivory-paneled oval room sixty stories above the softly glowing streets of New Chicago he touched a small cool plastic canister to his upper lip and pressed the stud at its base. He heard a foaming sound; and then blue vapor rose to his nostrils.

"Yes," Cantilena said. "That's right."

He detected a faint aroma of cinnamon, cloves, and something that might almost have been broiled lobster. Then a spasm of dizziness hit him and visions rushed through his head: Gothic cathedrals, the Pyramids, Central Park under fresh snow, the harsh brick warrens of Mohenjo-daro, and fifty thousand other places all at once, a wild roller-coaster ride through space and time. It seemed to go on for centuries. But finally his head cleared and he looked about, blinking, realizing that the whole thing had taken only a moment. Cantilena still stood at his elbow. The other citizens in the room—fifteen, twenty of them—had scarcely moved. The strange little man with the celadon skin over by the far wall continued to stare at him.

"Well?" Cantilena asked. "What did you think?"

"Incredible."

"And very authentic. It's an actual New Chicagoan drug. The exact formula. Would you like another?"

"Not just yet," Phillips said uneasily. He swayed and had to struggle for his balance. Sniffing that stuff might not have been such a wise idea, he thought.

He had been in New Chicago a week, or perhaps it was two, and he was still suffering from the peculiar disorientation that that city always aroused in him. This was the fourth time that he had come here, and it had been the same every time. New Chicago was the only one of the reconstructed cities of this world that in its original incarnation had existed *after* his own era. To him it was an outpost of the incomprehensible future; to the citizens it was a quaint simulacrum of the archaeological past. That paradox left him aswirl with impossible confusions and tensions.

What had happened to *old* Chicago was of course impossible for him to discover. Vanished without a trace, that was clear: no Water Tower, no Marina City, no Hancock Center, no Tribune building, not a fragment, not an atom. But it was hopeless to ask any of the million-plus inhabitants of New Chicago about their city's predecessor. They were only temporaries; they knew no more than they had to know, and all that they had to know was how to go through the motions of whatever it was that they did by way of creating the illusion that this was a real city. They had no need of knowing ancient history.

Nor was he likely to find out anything from a citizen, of course. Citizens did not seem to bother much about scholarly matters. Phillips had no reason to think that the world was anything other than an amusement park to them. Somewhere, certainly, there had to be those who specialized in the serious study of the lost civilizations of the past—for how, otherwise, would these uncanny reconstructed cities be brought into being? "The planners," he had once heard Nissandra or Aramayne say, "are already deep into their Byzantium research.'' But who were the planners? He had no idea. For all he knew, they were the robots. Perhaps the robots were the real masters of this whole era, who created the cities not primarily for the sake of amusing the citizens but in their own diligent attempt to comprehend the life of the world that had passed away. A wild speculation, yes; but not without some plausibility, he thought.

He felt oppressed by the party gaiety all about him. ''I need some air,'' he said to Cantilena, and headed toward the window. It was the merest crescent, but a breeze came through. He looked out at the strange city below.

New Chicago had nothing in common with the old one but its name. They had built it, at least, along the western shore of a large inland lake that might even be Lake Michigan, although when he had flown over it had seemed broader and less elongated than the lake he remembered. The city itself was a lacy fantasy of slender pastel-hued buildings rising at odd angles and linked by a webwork of gently undulating aerial bridges. The streets were long parentheses that touched the lake at their northern and southern ends and arched gracefully westward in the middle. Between each of the great boulevards ran a track for public transportation—sleek aquamarine bubble-vehicles gliding on soundless wheels—and flanking each of the tracks were lush strips of park. It was beautiful, astonishingly so, but insubstantial. The whole thing seemed to have been contrived from sunbeams and silk.

A soft voice beside him said, ''Are you becoming ill?''

Phillips glanced around. The celadon man stood beside him: a compact, precise person, vaguely Oriental in appearance. His skin was of a curious gray-green hue like no skin Phillips had ever seen, and it was extraodinarily smooth in texture, as though he were made of fine porcelain.

He shook his head. ''Just a little queasy,'' he said. ''This city always scrambles me.''

''I suppose it can be disconcerting,'' the little man replied. His tone was furry and veiled, the inflection strange. There was something feline about him. He seemed sinewy, unyielding, almost menacing. ''Visitor, are you?''

Phillips studied him a moment. ''Yes,'' he said.

''So am I, of course.''

"Are you?"

"Indeed." The little man smiled. "What's your locus? Twentieth century? Twenty-first at the latest, I'd say."

"I'm from 1984. 1984 A.D."

Another smile, a self-satisfied one. "Not a bad guess, then." A brisk tilt of the head. "Y'ang-Yeovil."

"Pardon me?" Phillips said.

"Y'ang-Yeovil. It is my name. Formerly Colonel Y'ang-Yeovil of the Third Septentriad."

"Is that on some other planet?" asked Phillips, feeling a bit dazed.

"Oh, no, not at all," Y'ang-Yeovil said pleasantly. "This very world, I assure you. I am quite of human origin. Citizen of the Republic of Upper Han, native of the city of Port Ssu. And you—forgive me—your name—?"

"I'm sorry. Phillips. Charles Phillips. From New York City, once upon a time."

"Ah, New York!" Y'ang-Yeovil's face lit with a glimmer of recognition that quickly faded. "New York—New York—it was very famous, that I know—"

This is very strange, Phillips thought. He felt greater compassion for poor bewildered Francis Willoughby now. This man comes from a time so far beyond my own that he barely knows of New York—he must be a contemporary of the real New Chicago, in fact; I wonder whether he finds this version authentic—and yet to the citizens this Y'ang-Yeovil too is just a primitive, a curio out of antiquity—

"New York was the largest city of the United States of America," Phillips said.

"Of course. Yes. Very famous."

"But virtually forgotten by the time the Republic of Upper Han came into existence, I gather."

Y'ang-Yeovil said, looking uncomfortable, "There were disturbances between your time and mine. But by no means should you take from my words the impression that your city was—"

Sudden laughter resounded across the room. Five or six newcomers had arrived at the party. Phillips stared, gasped, gaped. Surely that was Stengard—and Aramayne beside him—and that other woman, half-hidden behind them—

"If you'll pardon me a moment—" Phillips said, turning abruptly away from Y'ang-Yeovil. "Please excuse me. Someone just coming in—a person I've been trying to find ever since—"

He hurried toward her.

"Gioia?" he called. "Gioia, it's me! Wait! Wait!"

Stengard was in the way. Aramayne, turning to take a handful of the little vapor-sniffers from Cantilena, blocked him also. Phillips pushed through them as though they were not there. Gioia, halfway out the door, halted and looked toward him like a frightened deer.

"Don't go," he said. He took her hand in his.

He was startled by her appearance. How long had it been since their strange parting on that night of mysteries in Chang-an? A year? A year and a half? So he believed. Or had he lost all track of time? Were his perceptions of the passing of the months in this world that unreliable? She seemed at least ten or fifteen years older. Maybe she really was; maybe the years had been passing for him here as in a dream, and he had never known it. She looked strained, faded, worn. Out of a thinner and strangely altered face her eyes blazed at him almost defiantly, as though saying, *See? See how ugly I have become?*

He said, "I've been hunting for you for—I don't know how long it's been, Gioia. In Mohenjo, in Timbuctoo, now here. I want to be with you again."

"It isn't possible."

"Belilala explained everything to me in Mohenjo. I know that you're a short-timer—I know what that means, Gioia. But what of it? So you're beginning to age a little. So what? So you'll only have three or four hundred years, instead of forever. Don't you think I know what it means to be a short-timer? I'm just a simple ancient man of the twentieth century, remember? Sixty, seventy, eighty years is all we would get. You and I suffer from the same malady, Gioia. That's what drew you to me in the first place. I'm certain of that. That's why we belong with each other now. However much time we have, we can spend the rest of it together, don't you see?"

"You're the one who doesn't see, Charles," she said softly.

"Maybe. Maybe I still don't understand a damned thing

about this place. Except that you and I—that I love you—that I think you love me—''

"I love you, yes. But you don't understand. It's precisely because I love you that you and I—you and I can't—''

With a despairing sigh she slid her hand free of his grasp. He reached for her again, but she shook him off and backed up quickly into the corridor.

"Gioia?''

"Please,'' she said. "No. I would never have come here if I knew you were here. Don't come after me. Please. Please.''

She turned and fled.

He stood looking after her for a long moment. Cantilena and Aramayne appeared, and smiled at him as if nothing at all had happened. Cantilena offered him a vial of some sparkling amber fluid. He refused with a brusque gesture. Where do I go now? he wondered. What do I do? He wandered back into the party.

Y'ang-Yeovil glided to his side. "You are in great distress,'' the little man murmured.

Phillips glared. "Let me be.''

"Perhaps I could be of some help.''

"There's no help possible,'' said Phillips. He swung about and plucked one of the vials from a tray and gulped its contents. It made him feel as if there two of him, standing on either side of Y'ang-Yeovil. He gulped another. Now there were four of him. "I'm in love with a citizen,'' he blurted. It seemed to him that he was speaking in chorus.

"Love. Ah. And does she love you?''

"So I thought. So I think. But she's a short-timer. Do you know what that means? She's not immortal like the others. She ages. She's beginning to look old. And so she's been running away from me. She doesn't want me to see her changing. She thinks it'll disgust me, I suppose. I tried to remind her just now that I'm not immortal either, that she and I could grow old together, but she—''

"Oh, no,'' Y'ang-Yeovil said quietly. "Why do you think you will age? Have you grown any older in all the time you have been here?''

Phillips was nonplussed. "Of course I have. I—I—''

"Have you?" Y'ang-Yeovil smiled. "Here. Look at your-self." He did something intricate with his fingers and a shimmering zone of mirror-like light appeared between them. Phillips stared at his reflection. A youthful face stared back at him. It was true, then. He had simply not thought about it. How many years had he spent in this world? The time had simply slipped by: a great deal of time, though he could not calculate how much. They did not seem to keep close count of it here, nor had he. But it must have been many years, he thought. All that endless travel up and down the globe—so many cities had come and gone—Rio, Rome, Asgard, those were the first three that came to mind—and there were others; he could hardly re-member every one. Years. His face had not changed at all. Time had worked its harshness on Gioia, yes, but not on him.

"I don't understand," he said. "Why am I not aging?"

"Because you are not real," said Y'ang-Yeovil. "Are you unaware of that?"

Phillips blinked. "Not—real?"

"Did you think you were lifted bodily out of your own time?" the little man asked. "Ah, no, no, there is no way for them to do such a thing. We are not actual time travelers: not you, not I, not any of the visitors. I thought you were aware of that. But perhaps your era is too early for a proper understanding of these things. We are very cleverly done, my friend. We are ingenious constructs, marvelously stuffed with the thoughts and attitudes and events of our own times. We are their finest achievement, you know: far more complex even than one of these cities. We are a step beyond the temporaries—more than a step, a great deal more. They do only what they are instructed to do, and their range is very narrow. They are nothing but machines, really. Whereas we are autonomous. We move about by our own will; we think, we talk, we even, so it seems, fall in love. But we will not age. How could we age? We are not real. We are mere artificial webworks of mental responses. We are mere illusions, done so well that we deceive even our-selves. You did not know that? Indeed, you did not know?"

He was airborne, touching destination buttons at ran-dom. Somehow he found himself heading back toward

Timbuctoo. *This city is closed. This is not a place any longer.* It did not matter to him. Why should anything matter?

Fury and a choking sense of despair rose within him. I am software, Phillips thought. I am nothing but software. *Not real. Very cleverly done. An ingenious construct. A mere illusion.*

No trace of Timbuctoo was visible from the air. He landed anyway. The gray sandy earth was smooth, unturned, as though there had never been anything there. A few robots were still about, handling whatever final chores were required in the shutting-down of a city. Two of them scuttled up to him. Huge bland gleaming silver-skinned insects, not friendly.

"There is no city here," they said. "This is not a permissible place."

"Permissible by whom?"

"There is no reason for you to be here."

"There's no reason for me to be anywhere," Phillips said. The robots stirred, made uneasy humming sounds and ominous clicks, waved their antennae about. They seem troubled, he thought. They seem to dislike my attitude. Perhaps I run some risk of being taken off to the home for unruly software for debugging. "I'm leaving now," he told them. "Thank you. Thank you very much." He backed away from them and climbed into his flitterflitter. He touched more destination buttons.

We move about by our own will. We think, we talk, we even fall in love.

He landed in Chang-an. This time there was no reception committee waiting for him at the Gate of Brilliant Virtue. The city seemed larger and more resplendent: new pagodas, new palaces. It felt like winter: a chilly cutting wind was blowing. The sky was cloudless and dazzlingly bright. At the steps of the Silver Terrace he encountered Francis Willoughby, a great hulking figure in magnificent brocaded robes, with two dainty little temporaries, pretty as jade statuettes, engulfed in his arms. "Miracles and wonders! The silly lunatic fellow is here too!" Willoughby roared. "Look, look, we are come to far Cathay, you and I!"

We are nowhere, Phillips thought. *We are mere illusions, done so well that we deceive even ourselves.*

To Willoughby he said, "You look like an emperor in those robes, Francis."

"Aye, like Prester John!" Willoughby cried. "Like Tamburlaine himself! Aye, am I not majestic?" He slapped Phillips gaily on the shoulder, a rough playful poke that spun him halfway about, coughing and wheezing. "We flew in the air, as the eagles do, as the demons do, as the angels do! Soared like angels! Like angels!" He came close, looming over Phillips. "I would have gone to England, but the wench Belilala said there was an enchantment on me that would keep me from England just now; and so we voyaged to Cathay. Tell me this, fellow, will you go witness for me when we see England again? Swear that all that has befallen us did in truth befall? For I fear they will say I am as mad as Marco Polo, when I tell them of flying to Cathay."

"One madman backing another?" Phillips asked. "What can I tell you? You still think you'll reach England, do you?" Rage rose to the surface in him, bubbling hot. "Ah, Francis, Francis, do you know your Shakespeare? Did you go to the plays? We aren't real. *We aren't real.* We are such stuff as dreams are made on, the two of us. That's all we are. O brave new world! What England? Where? There's no England. There's no Francis Willoughby. There's no Charles Phillips. What we are is—"

"Let him be, Charles," a cool voice cut in.

He turned. Belilala, in the robes of an empress, was coming down the steps of the Silver Terrace.

"I know the truth," he said bitterly. "Y'ang-Yeovil told me. The visitor from the twenty-fifth century. I saw him in New Chicago."

"Did you see Gioia there too?" Belilala asked.

"Briefly. She looks much older."

"Yes. I know. She was here recently."

"And has gone on, I suppose?"

"To Mohenjo again, yes. Go after her, Charles. Leave poor Francis alone. I told her to wait for you. I told her that she needs you, and you need her."

"Very kind of you. But what good is it, Belilala? I don't even exist. And she's going to die."

"You exist. How can you doubt that you exist? You feel, don't you? You suffer. You love. You love Gioia: is that not so? And you are loved by Gioia. Would Gioia love what is not real?''

"You think she loves me?''

"I know she does. Go to her, Charles. Go. I told her to wait for you in Mohenjo.''

Phillips nodded numbly. What was there to lose?

"Go to her,'' said Belilala again. "Now.''

"Yes,'' Phillips said. "I'll go now.'' He turned to Willoughby. "If ever we meet in London, friend, I'll testify for you. Fear nothing. All will be well, Francis.''

He left them and set his course for Mohenjo-daro, half expecting to find the robots already tearing it down. Mohenjo-daro was still there, no lovelier than before. He went to the baths, thinking he might find Gioia there. She was not; but he came upon Nissandra, Stengard, Fenimon. "She has gone to Alexandria,'' Fenimon told him. "She wants to see it one last time, before they close it.''

"They're almost ready to open Constantinople,'' Stengard explained. "The capital of Byzantium, you know, the great city by the Golden Horn. They'll take Alexandria away, you understand, when Byzantium opens. They say it's going to be marvelous. We'll see you there for the opening, naturally?''

"Naturally,'' Phillips said.

He flew to Alexandria. He felt lost and weary. All this is hopeless folly, he told himself. I am nothing but a puppet jerking about on its strings. But somewhere above the shining breast of the Arabian sea the deeper implications of something that Belilala had said to him started to sink in, and he felt his bitterness, his rage, his despair, all suddenly beginning to leave him. *You exist. How can you doubt that you exist? Would Gioia love what is not real?* Of course. Of course. Y'ang-Yeovil had been wrong: visitors were something more than mere illusions. Indeed Y'ang-Yeovil had voiced the truth of their condition without understanding what he was really saying: *We think, we talk, we fall in love.* Yes. That was the heart of the situation. The visitors might be artificial, but they were not unreal. Belilala had been trying to tell him that just the other night. *You suffer. You love. You love Gioia. Would Gioia love what is not real?* Surely he was real, or at any rate real enough. What he was was something strange, something that would probably have been all but incomprehensible to the twentieth-century people whom he had been designed to simulate. But that did not mean that he was unreal. Did one have to be of woman born to be real? No. No. No. His kind of reality was a sufficient reality. He had no need to be ashamed of it. And, understanding that, he understood that Gioia did not need to grow old and die. There was a way by which she could be saved, if only she would embrace it. If only she would.

When he landed in Alexandria he went immediately to the hotel on the slopes of the Paneium where they had stayed on their first visit, so very long ago; and there she was, sitting quietly on a patio with a view of the harbor and the Lighthouse. There was something calm and resigned about the way she sat. She had given up. She did not even have the strength to flee from him any longer.

"Gioia," he said gently.

She looked older than she had in New Chicago. Her face was drawn and sallow and her eyes seemed sunken; and she was not even bothering these days to deal with the white strands that stood out in stark contrast against the darkness of her hair. He sat down beside her and put his hand over hers, and looked out toward the obelisks, the palaces, the temples, the Lighthouse. At length he said, "I know what I really am, now."

"Do you, Charles?" She sounded very far away.

"In my era we called it software. All I am is a set of commands, responses, cross-references, operating some sort of artificial body. It's infinitely better software than we could have imagined. But we were only just beginning to learn how, after all. They pumped me full of twentieth-century reflexes. The right moods, the right appetites, the right irrationalities, the right sort of combativeness. Somebody knows a lot about what it was like to be a twentieth-century man. They did a good job with Willoughby, too, all that Elizabethan rhetoric and swagger. And I suppose they got Y'ang-Yeovil right. *He* seems to think so: who better to judge? The twenty-fifth century, the Republic of Upper Han, people with gray-green skin, half Chinese and half Martian for all I know. *Somebody* knows. Somebody here is very good at programming, Gioia."

She was not looking at him.

"I feel frightened, Charles," she said in that same distant way.

"Of me? Of the things I'm saying?"

"No, not of you. Don't you see what has happened to me?"

"I see you. There are changes."

"I lived a long time wondering when the changes would begin. I thought maybe they wouldn't, not really. Who wants to believe they'll get old? But it started when we were in Alexandria that first time. In Chang-an it got much worse. And now—now—"

He said abruptly, "Stengard tells me they'll be opening Constantinople very soon."

"So?"

"Don't you want to be there when it opens?"

"I'm becoming old and ugly, Charles."

"We'll go to Constantinople together. We'll leave tomorrow, eh? What do you say? We'll charter a boat. It's a quick little hop, right across the Mediterranean. Sailing to Byzantium! There was a poem, you know, in my time. Not forgotten, I guess, because they've programmed it into me. All these thousands of years, and someone still remembers old Yeats. *The young in one another's arms, birds in the trees.* Come with me to Byzantium, Gioia."

She shrugged. "Looking like this? Getting more hideous every hour? While *they* stay young forever? While *you*—" She faltered; her voice cracked; she fell silent.

"Finish the sentence, Gioia."

"Please. Let me alone."

"You were going to say, 'While *you* stay young forever too, Charles,' isn't that it? You knew all along that I was never going to change. I didn't know that, but you did."

"Yes. I knew. I pretended that it wasn't true—that as I aged, you'd age too. It was very foolish of me. In Chang-an, when I first began to see the real signs of it—that was when I realized I couldn't stay with you any longer. Because I'd look at you, always young, always remaining the same age, and I'd look at myself, and—" She gestured, palms upward. "So I gave you to Belilala and ran away."

"All so unnecessary, Gioia."

"I didn't think it was."

"But you don't have to grow old. Not if you don't want to!"

"Don't be cruel, Charles," she said tonelessly. "There's no way of escaping what I have."

"But there is," he said.

"You know nothing about these things."

"Not very much, no," he said. "But I see how it can be done. Maybe it's a primitive simple-minded twentieth-century sort of solution, but I think it ought to work. I've been playing with the idea ever since I left Mohenjo. Tell me this, Gioia: Why can't you go to them, to the programmers, to the artificers, the planners, whoever they are, the ones who create the cities and the temporaries and the visitors. And have yourself made into something like me!"

She looked up, startled. "What are you saying?"

"They can cobble up a twentieth-century man out of nothing more than fragmentary records and make him plausible, can't they? Or an Elizabethan, or anyone else of any era at all, and he's authentic, he's convincing. So why couldn't they do an even better job with you? Produce a Gioia so real that even Gioia can't tell the difference? But a Gioia that will never age—a Gioia-construct, a Gioia-program, a visitor-Gioia! Why not? Tell me why not, Gioia."

She was trembling. "I've never heard of doing any such thing!"

"But don't you think it's possible?"

"How would I know?"

"Of course it's possible. If they can create visitors, they can take a citizen and duplicate her in such a way that—"

"It's never been done. I'm sure of it. I can't imagine any citizen agreeing to any such thing. To give up the body—to let yourself be turned into—into—"

She shook her head, but it seemed to be a gesture of astonishment as much as of negation.

He said, "Sure. To give up the body. Your natural body, your aging, shrinking, deteriorating short-timer body. What's so awful about that?"

She was very pale. "This is craziness, Charles. I don't want to talk about it any more."

"It doesn't sound crazy to me."

"You can't possibly understand."

"Can't I? I can certainly understand being afraid to die. I don't have a lot of trouble understanding what it's like to be one of the few aging people in a world where nobody grows old. What I can't understand is why you aren't even willing to consider the possibility that—"

"No," she said. "I tell you, it's crazy. They'd laugh at me."

"Who?"

"All of my friends. Hawk, Stengard, Aramayne—" Once again she would not look at him. "They can be very cruel, without even realizing it. They despise anything that seems ungraceful to them, anything sweaty and desperate and cowardly. Citizens don't do sweaty things, Charles. And that's how this will seem. Assuming it can be done at all. They'll be terribly patronizing. Oh, they'll be sweet to me, yes, dear Gioia, how wonderful for you, Gioia, but when I turn my back they'll laugh. They'll say the most wicked things about me. I couldn't bear that."

"They can afford to laugh," Phillips said. "It's easy to be brave and cool about dying when you know you're going to live forever. How very fine for them; but why should you be the only one to grow old and die? And they won't laugh, anyway. They're not as cruel as you think. Shallow, maybe, but not cruel. They'll be glad that you've found a way to save yourself. At the very least, they won't have to feel guilty about you any longer, and that's bound to please them. You can—"

"Stop it," she said.

She rose, walked to the railing of the patio, stared out toward the sea. He came up behind her. Red sails in the harbor, sunlight glittering along the sides of the Lighthouse, the palaces of the Ptolemies stark white against the sky. Lightly he rested his hand on her shoulder. She twitched as if to pull away from him, but remained where she was.

"Then I have another idea," he said quietly. "If you won't go to the planners, *I* will. Reprogram me, I'll say. Fix things so that I start to age at the same rate you do. I'll be more authentic, anyway, if I'm suposed to be playing the part of a twentieth-century man. Over the years I'll very gradually get some lines in my face, my hair will turn gray, I'll walk a little more slowly—we'll grow old to-

gether, Gioia. To hell with your lovely immortal friends.
We'll have each other. We won't need them.''

She swung around. Her eyes were wide with horror.

"Are you serious, Charles?''

"Of course.''

"No,'' she murmured. "No. Everything you've said to
me today is monstrous nonsense. Don't you realize that?''

He reached for her hand and enclosed her fingertips in
his. "All I'm trying to do is find some way for you and
me to—''

"Don't say any more,'' she said. "Please.'' Quickly, as
though drawing back from a suddenly flaring flame, she
tugged her fingers free of his and put her hand behind her.
Though his face was just inches from hers he felt an
immense chasm opening between them. They stared at one
another for a moment; then she moved deftly to his left,
darted around him, and ran from the patio.

Stunned, he watched her go, down the long marble
corridor and out of sight. It was folly to give pursuit, he
thought. She was lost to him: that was clear, that was
beyond any question. She was terrified of him. Why cause
her even more anguish? But somehow he found himself
running through the halls of the hotel, along the winding
garden path, into the cool green groves of the Paneium. He
thought he saw her on the portico of Hadrian's palace, but
when he got there the echoing stone halls were empty. To
a temporary that was sweeping the steps he said, "Did you
see a woman come this way?'' A blank sullen stare was
his only answer.

Phillips cursed and turned away.

"Gioia?'' he called. "Wait! Come back!''

Was that her, going into the Library? He rushed past the
startled mumbling librarians and sped through the stacks,
peering beyond the mounds of double-handled scrolls into
the shadowy corridors. "Gioia? *Gioia!*'' It was a desecration,
bellowing like that in this quiet place. He scarcely cared.

Emerging by a side door, he loped down to the harbor.
The Lighthouse! Terror enfolded him. She might already be
a hundred steps up that ramp, heading for the parapet from
which she meant to fling herself into the sea. Scattering
citizens and temporaries as if they were straws, he ran
within. Up he went, never pausing for breath, though his

synthetic lungs were screaming for respite, his ingeniously designed heart was desperately pounding. On the first balcony he imagined he caught a glimpse of her, but he circled it without finding her. Onward, upward. He went to the top, to the beacon chamber itself: no Gioia. Had she jumped? Had she gone down one ramp while he was ascending the other? He clung to the rim and looked out, down, searching the base of the Lighthouse, the rocks offshore, the causeway. No Gioia. I will find her somewhere, he thought. I will keep going until I find her. He went running down the ramp, calling her name. He reached ground level and sprinted back toward the center of town. Where next? The temple of Poseidon? The tomb of Cleopatra?

He paused in the middle of Canopus Street, groggy and dazed.

"Charles?" she said.

"Where are you?"

"Right here. Beside you." She seemed to materialize from the air. Her face was unflushed, her robe bore no trace of perspiration. Had he been chasing a phantom through the city? She came to him and took his hand, and said softly, tenderly, "Were you really serious, about having them make you age?"

"If there's no other way, yes."

"The other way is so frightening, Charles."

"Is it?"

"You can't understand how much."

"More frightening than growing old? Than dying?"

"I don't know," she said. "I suppose not. The only thing I'm sure of is that I don't want you to get old, Charles."

"But I won't have to. Will I?" He stared at her.

"No," she said. "You won't have to. Neither of us will."

Phillips smiled. "We should get away from here," he said after a while. "Let's go across to Byzantium, yes, Gioia? We'll show up in Constantinople for the opening. Your friends will be there. We'll tell them what you've decided to do. They'll know how to arrange it. Someone will."

"It sounds so strange," said Gioia. "To turn myself into—into a visitor? A visitor in my own world?"

"That's what you've always been, though."

"I suppose. In a way. But at least I've been *real* up to now."

"Whereas I'm not?"

"Are you, Charles?"

"Yes. Just as real as you. I was angry at first, when I found out the truth about myself. But I came to accept it. Somewhere between Mohenjo and here, I came to see that it was all right to be what I am: that I perceive things, I form ideas, I draw conclusions. I am very well designed, Gioia. I can't tell the difference between being what I am and being completely alive, and to me that's being real enough. I think, I feel, I experience joy and pain. I'm as real as I need to be. And you will be too. You'll never stop being Gioia, you know. It's only your body that you'll cast away, the body that played such a terrible joke on you anyway." He brushed her cheek with his hand. "It was all said for us before, long ago:

"Once out of nature I shall never take
My bodily form from any natural thing,
But such a form as Grecian goldsmiths make
of hammered gold and gold enamelling
To keep a drowsy Emperor awake—"

"Is that the same poem?" she asked.

"The same poem, yes. The ancient poem that isn't quite forgotten yet."

"Finish it, Charles."

—*"Or set upon a golden bough to sing*
To lords and ladies of Byzantium
Of what is past, or passing, or to come."

"How beautiful. What does it mean?"

"That it isn't necessary to be mortal. That we can allow ourselves to be gathered into the artifice of eternity, that we can be transformed, that we can move on beyond the flesh. Yeats didn't mean it in quite the way I do—he wouldn't have begun to comprehend what we're talking about, not a word of it—and yet, and yet—the underlying truth is the same. Live, Gioia! With me!'' He turned to her and saw color coming into her pallid cheeks. ''It does make sense, what I'm suggesting, doesn't it? You'll attempt it, won't you? Whoever makes the visitors can be induced to remake you. Right? What do you think: can they, Gioia?''

She nodded in a barely perceptible way. ''I think so,'' she said faintly. ''It's very strange. But I think it ought to be possible. Why not, Charles? Why not?''

''Yes,'' he said. ''Why not?''

In the morning they hired a vessel in the harbor, a low sleek pirogue with a blood-red sail, skippered by a rascally-looking temporary whose smile was irresistible. Phillips shaded his eyes and peered northward across the sea. He thought he could almost make out the shape of the great city sprawling on its seven hills, Constantine's New Rome beside the Golden Horn, the mighty dome of Hagia Sophia, the somber walls of the citadel, the palaces and churches, the Hippodrome, Christ in glory rising above all else in brilliant mosaic streaming with light.

''Byzantium,'' Phillips said. ''Take us there the shortest and quickest way.''

''It is my pleasure,'' said the boatman with unexpected grace.

Gioia smiled. He had not seen her looking so vibrantly alive since the night of the imperial feast in Chang-an. He reached for her hand—her slender fingers were quivering lightly—and helped her into the boat.

FLYING SAUCER ROCK & ROLL

Howard Waldrop

Science fiction stories aren't always set in the future. Sometimes sf writers have to take us back to the past in order to catch up on things such as UFO visitations, as in this detailed and evocative tale set in the early 1960s.

Howard Waldrop won a Nebula Award for his novelette "The Ugly Chickens." His first solo novel was Them Bones.

They could have been contenders.

Talk about Danny and the Juniors, talk about the Spaniels, the Contours, Sonny Till and the Orioles. They made it to the big time: records, tours, sock hops at $500 a night. Fame and glory.

But you never heard of the Kool-Tones, because they achieved their apotheosis and their apocalypse on the same night, and then they broke up. Some still talk about that night, but so much happened, the Kool-Tones get lost in the shuffle. And who's going to believe a bunch of kids, anyway? The cops didn't, and their parents didn't. It was only two years after the President had been shot in Dallas, and people were still scared. This, then, is the Kool-Tones' story:

Leroy was smoking a cigar through a hole he'd cut in a pair of thick, red wax lips. Slim and Zoot were tooting away on Wowee whistles. It was a week after Halloween, and their pockets were still full of trick-or-treat candy they'd muscled off little kids in the projects. Ray, slim and nervous, was hanging back. "We shouldn't be here, you know? I mean, this ain't the Hellbenders' territory, you know? I don't know whose it is, but, like, Vinnie and the guys don't come this far." He looked around.

Zoot, who was white and had the beginnings of a mustache, took the yellow wax-candy kazoo from his mouth. He bit off and chewed up the big C pipe. "I mean, if you're scared, Ray, you can go back home, you know?"

"Nah!" said Leroy. "We need Ray for the middle parts." Leroy was twelve years old and about four feet tall. He was finishing his fourth cigar of the day. He looked like a small Stymie Beard from the old Our Gang comedies.

He still wore the cut-down coat he'd taken with him when he'd escaped from his foster home.

He was staying with his sister and her boyfriend. In each of his coat pockets he had a bottle: one Coke and one bourbon.

"We'll be all right," said Cornelius, who was big as a house and almost eighteen. He was shaped like a big ebony golf tee, narrow legs and waist blooming out to an A-bomb mushroom of arms and chest. He was a yard wide at the shoulders. He looked like he was always wearing football pads.

"That's right," said Leroy, taking out the wax lips and wedging the cigar back into the hole in them. "I mean, the kid who found this place didn't say anything about it being somebody's *spot*, man."

"What's that?" asked Ray.

They looked up. A small spot of light moved slowly across the sky. It was barely visible, along with a few stars, in the lights from the city.

"Maybe it's one of them UFOs you're always talking about, Leroy," said Zoot.

"Flying saucer, my left ball," said Cornelius. "That's Telstar. You ought to read the papers."

"Like your mama makes you?" asked Slim.

"Aww . . ." said Cornelius.

They walked on through the alleys and the dark streets. They all walked like a man.

"This place is Oz," said Leroy.

"Hey!" yelled Ray, and his voice filled the area, echoed back and forth in the darkness, rose in volume, died away.

"Wow."

They were on what had been the loading dock of an old freight and storage company. It must have been closed sometime during the Korean War or maybe in the unimaginable eons before World War II. The building took up most of the block, but the loading area on the back was sunken and surrounded by the stone wall they had climbed. If you stood with your back against the one good loading door, the place was a natural amphitheater.

Leroy chugged some Coke, then poured bourbon into the half-empty bottle. They all took a drink, except Cornelius, whose mother was a Foursquare Baptist and could smell liquor on his breath three blocks away.

Cornelius drank only when he was away from home two or three days.

"Okay, Kool-Tones," said Leroy. "Let's hit some notes."

They stood in front of the door. Leroy to the fore, the others behind him in a semicircle: Cornelius, Ray, Slim, and Zoot.

"One, two, three," said Leroy quietly, his face toward the bright city beyond the surrounding buildings.

He had seen all the movies with Frankie Lymon and the Teenagers in them and knew the moves backwards. He jumped in the air and came down, and Cornelius hit it: "*Bah-doo, bah-doo, ba-doo—uhh.*"

It was a bass from the bottom of the ocean, from the Marianas Trench, a voice from Death Valley on a wet night, so far below sea level you could feel the absence of light in your mind. And then Zoot and Ray came in: "*Ooh-oooh, ooh-oooh,*" with Leroy humming under, and then Slim stepped out and began the lead tenor part of "Sincerely," by the Crows. And they went through that one perfectly, flawlessly, the dark night and the dock walls throwing their voices out to the whole breathing city.

"Wow," said Ray, when they finished, but Leroy held up his hand, and Zoot leaned forward and took a deep breath and sang: "*Dee-dee-woo-oo, dee-eee—wooo-oo, dee-uhmm-doo-way.*"

And Ray and Slim chanted: "A-weem-wayyy, a-weem-wayyy."

And then Leroy, who had a falsetto that could take hair off an opossum, hit the high notes from "The Lion Sleeps Tonight," and it was even better than the first song, and not even the Tokens on their number-two hit had ever sounded greater.

Then they started clapping their hands, and at every clap the city seemed to jump with expectation, joining in their dance, and they went through a shaky-legged Skyliners-type routine and into: "*Hey-ahh-stuh-huh, hey-ahh-stuh-uhh,*" of Maurice Williams and the Zodiacs' "Stay," and when Leroy soared his "*Hoh-wahh-yuh?*" over Zoot's singing, they all thought they would die.

And without pause, Ray and Slim started: "*Shoo-be-doop, shoo-doop-do-be-doop, shoo-doopbe-do-be-doop,*" and Cornelius was going, "*Ah-rem-em, ah-rem-em, ah-rem-emm bah.*"

And they went through the Five Satins' "(I Remember) In the Still of the Night."

"Hey, wait," said Ray, as Slim "*woo-uh-wooo-uh-woo-ooo-ah-woo-ah*"-ed to a finish, "I thought I saw a guy out there."

"You're imagining things," said Zoot. But they all stared out into the dark anyway.

There didn't seem to be anything there.

"Hey, look," said Cornelius. "Why don't we try putting the bass part of 'Stormy Weather' with the high part of 'Crying in the Chapel'? I tried it the other night, but I can't—"

"Shit, man!" said Slim. "That ain't the way it is on the records. You gotta do it like on the records."

"Records are going to hell, anyway. I mean, you got Motown and some of that, but the rest of it's like the Beatles and Animals and Rolling Stones and Wayne shitty Fontana and the Mindbenders and . . ."

Leroy took the cigar from his mouth. "Fuck the Beatles," he said. He put the cigar back in his mouth.

"Yeah, you're right, I agree. But even the other music's not the—"

"Aren't you kids up past your bedtime?" asked a loud voice from the darkness.

They jerked erect. For a minute, they hoped it was only the cops.

Matches flared in the darkness, held up close to faces. The faces had all their eyes closed so they wouldn't be blinded and unable to see in case the Kool-Tones made a break for it. Blobs of face and light floated in the night, five, ten, fifteen, more.

Part of a jacket was illuminated. It was the color reserved for the kings of Tyre.

"Oh, shit!" said Slim. "Trouble. Looks like the Purple Monsters."

The Kool-Tones drew into a knot.

The matches went out and they were in a breathing darkness.

"You guys know this turf is reserved for friends of the local protective, athletic, and social club, viz., us?" asked the same voice. Chains clanked in the black night.

"We were just leaving," said Cornelius.

The noisy chains rattled closer.

You could hear knuckles being slapped into fists out there.

Slim hoped someone would hurry up and hit him so he could scream.

"Who are you guys with?" asked the voice, and a flashlight shone in their eyes, blinding them.

"Aww, they're just little kids," said another voice.

"Who you callin' little, turd?" asked Leroy, shouldering his way between Zoot and Cornelius's legs.

A *wooooooo*! went up from the dark, and the chains rattled again.

"For God's sake, shut up, Leroy!" said Ray.

"Who you people think you are, anyway?" asked another, meaner voice out there.

"We're the Kool-Tones," said Leroy. "We can sing it slow, and we can sing it low, and we can sing it loud, and we can make it go!"

"I hope you like that cigar, kid," said the mean voice, "because after we piss on it, you're going to have to eat it."

"Okay, okay, look," said Cornelius. "We didn't know it was your turf. We come from over in the projects and . . ."

"Hey, man, Hellbenders, Hellbenders!" The chains sounded like tambourines now.

"Naw, naw. We ain't Hellbenders. We ain't nobody but the Kool-Tones. We just heard about this place. We didn't know it was yours," said Cornelius.

"We only let Bobby and the Bombers sing here," said a voice.

"Bobby and the Bombers can't sing their way out of the men's room," said Leroy. Slim clamped Leroy's mouth, burning his hand on the cigar.

"You're gonna regret that," said the mean voice, which stepped into the flashlight beam, "because I'm Bobby, and four more of these guys out here are the Bombers."

"We didn't know you guys were part of the Purple Monsters!" said Zoot.

"There's lots of stuff you don't know," said Bobby. "And when we're through, there's not much you're gonna *remember*."

"I only know the Del Vikings are breaking up," said Zoot. He didn't know why he said it. Anything was better than waiting for the knuckle sandwiches.

Bobby's face changed. "No shit?" Then his face set in hard lines again. "Where'd a punk like you hear something like that?"

"My cousin," said Zoot. "He was in the Air Force with two of them. He writes to 'em. They're tight. One of them said the act was breaking up because nobody was listening to their stuff anymore."

"Well, that's rough," said Bobby. "It's tough out there on the road."

"Yeah," said Zoot. "It really is."

Some of the tension was gone, but certain delicate ethical questions remained to be settled.

"I'm Lucius," said a voice. "Warlord of the Purple Monsters." The flashlight came on him. He was huge. He was like Cornelius, only he was big all the way to the ground. His feet looked like blunt I beams sticking out of the bottom of his jeans. His purple satin jacket was a bright fluorescent blot on the night. "I hate to break up this chitchat"—he glared at Bobby—"but the fact is you people are on Purple Monster territory, and some tribute needs to be exacted."

Ray was digging in his pockets for nickels and dimes.

"Not money. Something that will remind you not to do this again."

"Tell you what," said Leroy. He had worked himself away from Slim. "You think Bobby and the Bombers can sing?"

"Easy!" said Lucius to Bobby, who had started forward with the Bombers. "Yeah, kid. They're the best damn group in the city."

"Well, *I* think we can outsing 'em," said Leroy, and smiled around his dead cigar.

"Oh, jeez," said Zoot. "They got a record, and they've—"

"I *said*, we can outsing Bobby and the Bombers, anytime, any place," said Leroy.

"And what if you can't?" asked Lucius.

"You guys like piss a lot, don't you?" There was a general movement toward the Kool-Tones. Lucius held up his hand. "Well," said Leroy, "how about all the members of the losing group drink a quart apiece?"

Hands of the Kool-Tones reached out to still Leroy. He danced away.

"I like that," said Lucius. "I really like that. That all right, Bobby?"

"I'm going to start saving it up now."

"Who's gonna judge?" asked one of the Bombers.

"The same as always," said Leroy. "The public. Invite 'em in."

"Who do we meet with to work this out?" asked Lucius.

"Vinnie of the Hellbenders. He'll work out the terms."

Slim was beginning to see he might not be killed that night. He looked on Leroy with something like worship.

"How we know you guys are gonna show up?" asked Bobby.

"I swear on Sam Cooke's grave," said Leroy.

"Let 'em pass," said Bobby.

They crossed out of the freight yard and headed back for the projects.

"Shit, man!"

"Now you've done it!"

"I'm heading for Florida."

"What the hell, Leroy, are you crazy?"

Leroy was smiling. "We can take them, easy," he said, holding up his hand flat.

He began to sing "Chain Gang." The other Kool-Tones joined in, but their hearts weren't in it. Already there was a bad taste in the back of their throats.

Vinnie was mad.

The black outline of a mudpuppy on his white silk jacket seemed to swell as he hunched his shoulders toward Leroy.

"What the shit you mean, dragging the Hellbenders into this without asking us first? That just ain't done, Leroy."

"Who else could take the Purple Monsters in case they wasn't gentlemen?" asked Leroy.

Vinnie grinned. "You're gonna die before you're fifteen, kid."

"That's my hope."

"Creep. Okay, we'll take care of it."

"One thing," said Leroy. "No instruments. They gotta get us a mike and some amps, and no more than a quarter of the people can be from Monster territory. And it's gotta be at the freight dock."

"That's one thing?" asked Vinnie.

"A few. But that place is great, man. We can't lose there."

Vinnie smiled, and it was a prison-guard smile, a Nazi smile. "If you lose, kid, after the Monsters get through with you, the Hellbenders are gonna have a little party."

He pointed over his shoulder to where something resembling testacles floated in alcohol in a mason jar on a shelf. "We're putting five empty jars up there tomorrow. That's what happens to people who get the Hellbenders involved without asking and then don't come through when the pressure's on. You know what I mean?"

Leroy smiled. He left smiling. The smile was still frozen to his face as he walked down the street.

This whole thing was getting too grim.

Leroy lay on his cot listening to his sister and her boyfriend porking in the next room.

It was late at night. His mind was still working. Sounds beyond those in the bedroom came to him. Somebody staggered down the project hallway, bumping from one wall to another. Probably one man Jones. Chances are he wouldn't make it to his room all the way at the end of the corridor. His daughter or one of her kids would probably find him asleep in the hall in a pool of barf.

Leroy turned over on the rattly cot, flipped on his seven-transistor radio, and jammed it up to his ear. Faintly came the sounds of another Beatles song.

He thumbed the tuner, and the four creeps blurred into four or five other Englishmen singing some other stupid song about coming to places he would never see.

He went through the stations until he stopped on the third note of the Monotones' "Book of Love." He sang along in his mind.

Then the deejay came on, and everything turned sour again. "Another golden oldie, 'Book of Love,' by the Monotones. Now here's the WBKD pick of the week, the fabulous Beatles with 'I've Just Seen a Face,' " Leroy pushed the stations around the dial, then started back.

Weekdays were shit. On weekends you could hear good old stuff, but mostly the stations all played Top 40, and that was English invasion stuff, or if you were lucky, some Motown. It was Monday night. He gave up and turned to an all-night blues station, where the music usually meant something. But this was like, you know, the sharecropper hour or something, and all they were playing was whiny cotton-choppin' work blues from some damn Alabama singer who had died in 1932, for God's sake.

Disgusted, Leroy turned off the radio.

His sister and her boyfriend had quit for a while, so it was quieter in the place. Leroy lit a cigarette and thought of getting out of here as soon as he could.

I mean, Bobby and the Bombers had a record, a real big-hole forty-five on WhamJam. It wasn't selling worth shit from all Leroy heard, but that didn't matter. It was a record, and it was real, it wasn't just singing under some street lamp. Slim said they'd played it once on WABC, on the *Hit-or-Flop* show, and it was a flop, but people heard it. Rumor was the Bombers had gotten sixty-five dollars and a contract for the session. They'd had a couple of gigs at dances and such, when the regular band took a break. They sure as hell couldn't be making any money, or they wouldn't be singing against the Kool-Tones for free kicks.

But they had a record out, and they were working.

If only the Kool-Tones got work, got a record, went on tour. Leroy was just twelve, but he knew how hard they were working on their music. They'd practice on street corners, on the stoop, just walking, getting the notes down right—the moves, the facial expressions of all the groups they'd seen in movies and on Slim's mother's TV.

There were so many places to be out there. There was a real world with people in it who weren't punching somebody for berries, or stealing the welfare and stuff. Just someplace open, someplace away from everything else.

He flipped on the flashlight beside his cot, pulled it under the covers with him, and opened his favorite book. It was Edward J. Ruppelt's *Report on Unidentified Flying Objects*. His big brother John William, whom he had never seen, sent it to him from his Army post in California as soon as he found Leroy had run away and was living with his sister. John William also sent his sister part of his allotment every month.

Leroy had read the book again and again. He knew it by heart already. He couldn't get a library card under his own name because the state might trace him that way. (They'd already been around asking his sister about him. She lied. But she too had run away from a foster home as soon as she was old enough, so they hadn't believed her and would be back.) So he'd had to boost all his books. Sometimes it took days, and newsstand people got mighty suspicious when you were black and hung around for a long time, waiting for the chance to kipe stuff. Usually they gave you the hairy eyeball until you went away.

He owned twelve books on UFOs now, but the Ruppelt was still his favorite. Once he'd gotten a book by some guy named Truman or something, who wrote poetry inspired by the people from Venus. It was a little sad, too, the things people believed sometimes. So Leroy hadn't read any more books by people who claimed they'd been inside the flying saucers or met the Neptunians or such. He read only the ones that gave histories of the sightings and asked questions, like why was the Air Force covering up? Those books never told you what was in the UFOs, and that was good because you could imagine it for yourself.

He wondered if any of the Del Vikings had seen flying saucers when they were in the Air Force with Zoot's cousin. Probably not, or Zoot would have told him about it. Leroy always tried to get the rest of the Kool-Tones interested in UFOs, but they all said they had their own problems, like girls and cigarette money. They'd go with him to see *Invasion of the Saucermen* or *Earth Vs. the Flying Saucers* at the movies, or watch *The Thing* on Slim's mother's TV on the *Creature Feature*, but that was about it.

Leroy's favorite flying-saucer sighting was the Mantell case, in which a P-51 fighter plane, which was called the Mustang, chased a UFO over Kentucky and then crashed after it went off the Air Force radar. Some say Captain Mantell died of asphyxiation because he went to 20,000 feet and didn't have on an oxygen mask, but other books said he saw "something metallic and of tremendous size" and was going after it. Ruppelt thought it was a Skyhook balloon, but he couldn't be sure. Others said it was a real UFO and that Mantell had been shot down with Z-rays.

It had made Leroy's skin crawl when he had first read it.

But his mind went back to the Del Vikings. What had caused them to break up? What was it really like out there on the road? Was music getting so bad that good groups couldn't make a living at it anymore?

Leroy turned off the flashlight and put the book away. He put out the cigarette, lit a cigar, went to the window, and looked up the airshaft. He leaned way back against the cool window and could barely see one star overhead. Just one star.

He scratched himself and lay back down on the bed.

For the first time, he was afraid about the contest tomorrow night.

We got to be good, he said to himself. *We got to be good*.

In the other room, the bed started squeaking again.

The Hellbenders arrived early to check out the turf. They'd been there ten minutes when the Purple Monsters showed up. There was handshaking all around, talk a little while, then they moved off into two separate groups. A few civilians came by to make sure this was the place they'd heard about.

"Park your cars out of sight, if you got 'em," said Lucius. "We don't want the cops to think anything's going on here."

Vinnie strut-walked over to Lucius.

"This crowd's gonna be bigger than I thought. I can tell."

"People come to see somebody drink some piss. You know, give the public what it wants. . . ." Lucius smiled.

"I guess so. I got this weird feelin', though. Like, you know, if your mother tells you she dreamed about her aunt, like right before she died and all?"

"I know what feelin' you mean, but I ain't got it," said Lucius.

"Who you got doing the electrics?"

"Guy named Sparks. He was the one lit up Choton Field."

At Choton Field the year before, two gangs wanted to fight under the lights. So they went to a high-school football stadium. Somebody got all the lights and the P.A. on without going into the control booth.

Cops drove by less than fifty feet away, thinking there was a practice scrimmage going on, while down on the field guys were turning one another into bloody strings. Somebody was on the P.A. giving a play-by-play. From the outside it sounded cool. From the inside, it looked like a pizza with all the topping ripped off it.

"Oh," said Vinnie. "Good man."

He used to work for Con Ed, and he still had his I.D. card. Who was going to mess with Consolidated Edison? He drove an old, gray pickup with a smudge on the side that had once been a power-company emblem. The truck was filled to the brim with cables, wires, boots, wrenches, tape, torches, work lights, and rope.

"Light man's here!" said somebody.

Lucius shook hands with him and told him what they wanted. He nodded.

The crowd was getting larger, groups and clots of people drifting in, though the music wasn't supposed to start for another hour. Word traveled fast.

Sparks attached a transformer and breakers to a huge, thick cable.

Then he got out his climbing spikes and went up a pole like a monkey, the heavy *chunk-chunk* drifting down to the crowd every time he flexed his knees. His tool belt slapped against his sides.

He had one of the guys in the Purple Monsters throw him up the end of the inch-thick electrical cable.

The sun had just gone down, and Sparks was a silhouette against the purpling sky that poked between the buildings.

A few stars were showing in the eastern sky. Lights were on all through the autumn buildings. Thanksgiving was in a few weeks, then Christmas.

The shopping season was already in full swing, and the streets would be bathed in neon, in holiday colors. The city stood up like big, black fingers all around them.

Sparks did something to the breakdown box on the pole.

There was an immense blue scream of light that stopped everybody's heart.

New York City went dark.

"Fucking *wow*!"

A raggedy-assed cheer of wonder ran through the crowd.

There were crashes, and car horns began to honk all over town.

"Uh, Lucius," Sparks yelled down the pole after a few minutes. "Have the guys go steal me about thirty automobile batteries."

The Purple Monsters ran off in twenty different directions.

"Ahhhyyyhhyyh," said Vinnie, spitting a toothpick out of his mouth. "The Monsters get to have all the fun."

It was 5:27 P.M. on November 9, 1965. At the Ossining changing station a guy named Jim was talking to a guy named Jack.

Then the trouble phone rang. Jim checked all his dials before he picked it up.

He listened, then hung up.

"There's an outage all down the line. They're going to switch the two hundred K's over to the Buffalo net and reroute them back through here. Check all the load levels. Everything's out from Schenectady to Jersey City."

When everything looked ready, Jack signaled to Jim.

Jim called headquarters, and they watched the needles jump on the dials.

Everything went black.

Almost everything.

Jack hit all the switches for backup relays, and nothing happened.

Almost nothing.

Jim hit the emergency battery work lights. They flicked and went out.

"What the hell?" asked Jack.

He looked out the window.

Something large and bright moved across a nearby reservoir and toward the changing station.

"Holy Mother of Christ!" he said.

Jim and Jack went outside.

The large bright thing moved along the lines toward the station. The power cables bulged toward the bottom of the thing, whipping up and down, making the stanchions sway. The station and the reservoir were bathed in a blue glow as the thing went over. Then it took off quickly toward Manhattan, down the straining lines, leaving them in complete darkness.

Jim and Jack went back into the plant and ate their lunches.

Not even the phone worked anymore.

It was really black by the time Sparks got his gear set up. Everybody in the crowd was talking about the darkness of the city and the sky. You could see all over the place, everywhere you looked.

There was very little noise from the city around the loading area.

Somebody had a radio on. There were a few Jersey and Pennsy stations on. One of them went off while they listened.

In the darkness, Sparks worked by the lights of his old truck. What he had in front of him resembled something from an alchemy or magnetism treatise written early in the eighteenth century. Twenty or so car batteries were hooked up in series with jumper cables. He'd tied those in with amps, mikes, transformers, a light board, and lights on the dock area.

"Stand clear!" he yelled. He bent down with the last set of cables and stuck an alligator clamp on a battery spot.

There was a screeching blue jag of light and a frying noise. The lights flickered and came on, and the amps whined louder and louder.

The crowd, numbering around five hundred, gave out with prolonged huzzahs and applause.

"Test test test," said Lucius. Everybody held their hands over their ears.

"Turn that fucker down," said Vinnie. Sparks did. Then he waved to the crowd, got into his old truck, turned the lights off, and drove into the night.

"Ladies and gentlemen, the Purple Monsters . . ." said Lucius, to wild applause, and Vinnie leaned into the mike, "and the Hellbenders," more applause, then back to Lucius, "would like to welcome you to the first annual piss-off—I mean, sing-off—between our own Bobby and the Bombers," cheers, "and the challengers," said Vinnie, "the Kool-Tones!" More applause.

"They'll do two sets, folks," said Lucius, "taking turns. And at the end, the unlucky group, gauged by *your* lack of applause, will win a prize!"

The crowd went wild.

The lights dimmed out. "And now," came Vinnie's voice from the still blackness of the loading dock, "for your listening pleasure, Bobby and the Bombers!"

"Yayyyyyyyyyy!"

The lights, virtually the only lights in the city except for those that were being run by emergency generators, came up, and there they were.

Imagine frosted, polished elegance being thrust on the unwilling shoulders of a sixteen-year-old.

They had on blue jackets, matching pants, ruffled shirts, black ties, cuff links, tie tacks, shoes like obsidian mortar trowels. They were all black boys, and from the first note, you knew they were born to sing:

"*Bah bah*," sang Letus the bassman, "*doo-doo duh-duh doo-ahh, duh-doo-dee-doot*," sang the two tenors, Lennie and Conk, and then Bobby and Fred began trading verses of the Drifters' "There Goes My Baby," while the tenors wailed and Letus carried the whole with his bass.

Then the lights went down and came up again as Lucius said, "Ladies and gentlemen, the Kool-Tones!"

It was magic of a grubby kind.

The Kool-Tones shuffled on, arms pumping in best Frankie Lymon and the Teenagers fashion, and they ran in place as the hand-clapping got louder and louder and they leaned into the mikes.

They were dressed in waiters' red cloth jackets the Hellbenders had stolen from a laundry service for them that morning. They wore narrow black ties, except Leroy who had on a big, thick, red bow tie he'd copped from his sister's boyfriend.

Then Cornelius leaned over his mike and: *"Doook doook doook doookov,"* and Ray and Zoot joined with *"dook dook dook dookov,"* into Gene Chandler's "Duke of Earl," with Leroy smiling and doing all of Chandler's hand moves. Slim chugged away the *"iiiiiiiiyiyiyiyiiiii's"* in the background in runs that made the crowd's blood cold, and the lights went down. Then the Bombers were back, and in contrast to the up-tempo ending of "Duke of Earl" they started with a sweet tenor a cappella line and then: *"wooradad-da-dut, woo-radad-da-dat,"* of Shep and the Limelites' "Daddy's Home."

The Kool-Tones jumped back into the light. This time Cornelius started it off with *"Bomp-a-pa-bomp, bomp-pa-pa-bomp, dang-a-dang-dang, ding-a-dong-ding,"* and into the Marcels' "Blue Moon," not just a hit but a mere monster back in 1961. And they ran through the song, Slim taking the lead, and the crowd began to yell like mad halfway through. And Leroy—smiling, singing, rocking back and forth, doing James Brown tantrum-steps in front of the mike—knew, could feel, that they had them, that no matter what, they were going to win. And he ended with his whining part and Cornelius went *"Bomp-ba-ba-bomp-ba-bom,"* and paused and then deeper, *"booo mooo."*

The lights came up and Bobby and the Bombers hit the stage. At first Leroy, sweating, didn't realize what they were doing, because the Bombers, for the first few seconds, made this churning rinky-tink sound with the high voices. The bass, Letus, did this grindy sound with his throat. Then the Bombers did the only thing that could save them, a white boy's song, Bobby launching into Del Shannon's "Runaway," with both feet hitting the stage at once. Leroy thought he could taste that urine already.

The other Kool-Tones were transfixed by what was about to happen.

"They can't do that, man," said Leroy.

"They're gonna cop out."

"That's impossible. Nobody can do it."

But when the Bombers got to the break, this guy Fred stepped out to the mike and went: *"Eee-de-ee-dee-eedle-eee-eee, eee-deee-eedle-deeee, eedle-dee-eedle-dee-dee-dee, eewheetle-eeedle-dee-deedle-dee-eeeeee,"* in a spitting falsetto, half mechanical, half Martian cattle call—the organ break of "Runaway," done with the human voice.

The crowd was on its feet screaming, and the rest of the song was lost in stamping and cheers. When the Kool-Tones jumped out for the last song of the first set, there were some boos and yells for the Bombers to come back, but then Zoot started talking about his girl putting him down because he couldn't shake 'em down, but how now *he* was back to let her know. . . . They all jumped in the air and came down on the first line of "Do You Love Me?" by the Contours, and they gained some of the crowd back. But they finished a little wimpy, and then the lights went down and an absolutely black night descended. The stars were shining over New York City for the first time since World War II, and Vinnie said, "Ten minutes, folks!" and guys went over to piss against the walls or add to the consolation-prize bottles.

It was like halftime in the locker room with the score Green Bay 146, You 0.

"A cheap trick," said Zoot. "We don't *do* shit like that."

Leroy sighed. "We're gonna have to," he said. He drank from a Coke bottle one of the Purple Monsters had given him. "We're gonna have to do something."

"We're gonna have to drink pee-pee, and then Vinnie's gonna de-nut us, is what's gonna happen."

"No, he's not," said Cornelius.

"Oh, yeah?" asked Zoot. "Then what's that in the bottle in the clubhouse?"

"Pig's balls," said Cornelius. "They got 'em from a slaughterhouse."

"How do you know?"

"I just know," said Cornelius, tiredly. "Now let's just get this over with so we can go vomit all night."

"I don't want to hear any talk like that," said Leroy. "We're gonna go through with this and give it our best, just like we planned, and if that ain't good enough, well, it just ain't good enough."

"No matter what we do, ain't gonna be good enough."

"Come on, Ray, *man*!"

"I'll do my best, but my heart ain't in it."

They lay against the loading dock. They heard laughter from the place where Bobby and the Bombers rested.

"Shit, it's dark!" said Slim.

"It ain't just us, just the city," said Zoot. "It's the whole goddamn U.S."

"It's just the whole East Coast," said Ray. "I heard on the radio. Part of Canada, too."

"What is it?"

"Nobody knows."

"Hey, Leroy," said Cornelius. "Maybe it's those Martians you're always talking about."

Leroy felt a chill up his spine.

"Nah," said Slim. "It was that guy Sparks. He shorted out the whole East Coast up that pole there."

"Do you really believe that?" asked Zoot.

"I don't know what I believe anymore."

"I believe," said Lucius, coming out of nowhere with an evil grin on his face, "that it's *show time*."

They came to the stage running, and the lights came up, and Cornelius leaned on his voice and: "*Rabbalabbalabba ging gong, rabbalabbalabba ging gong*," and the others went "*wooooooooooo*" in the Edsels' "Rama Lama Ding Dong." They finished and the Bombers jumped into the lights and went into: "*Domm dom domm dom doobedoo, dom domm dom dobedoodbeedomm, wah-wahwahwahhh*," of the Del Vikings' "Come Go With Me."

The Kool-Tones came back with: "*Ahhhhhhhhaahh-woooowoooo, ow-ow-ow-ow-owh-woo*," of "Since I Don't Have You," by the Skyliners, with Slim singing in a clear, straight voice, better than he had ever sung that song before, and everybody else joined in, Leroy's voice fading into Slim's for the falsetto *weeeeooooow*'s so you couldn't tell where one ended and the other began.

Then Bobby and the Bombers were back, with Bobby telling you the first two lines and: *"Detooodwop, detooodwop, detooodwop,"* of the Flamingos' "I Only Have Eyes for You," calm, cool, collected, assured of victory, still running on the impetus of their first set's showstopper.

Then the Kool-Tones came back and Cornelius rared back and asked: *"Ahwunno wunno hooo? Be-do-be-hooo?"* Pause.

They slammed down into "Book of Love," by the Monotones, but even Cornelius was flagging, sweating now in the cool air, his lungs were husks. He saw one of the Bombers nod to another, smugly, and that made him mad. He came down on the last verse like there was no one else on the stage with him, and his bass roared so loud it seemed there wasn't a single person in the dark United States who didn't wonder who wrote that book.

And they were off, and Bobby and the Bombers were on now, and a low hum began to fill the air. Somebody checked the amp; it was okay. So the Bombers jumped into the air, and when they came down they were into the Cleftones' "Heart and Soul," and they *sang* that song, and while they were singing, the background humming got louder and louder.

Leroy leaned to the other Kool-Tones and whispered something. They shook their heads. He pointed to the Hellbenders and the Purple Monsters all around them. He asked a question they didn't want to hear. They nodded grudging approval, and then they were on again, for the last time.

"Dep dooomop dooomop doomop, doo ooo, oowah oowah ooowah ooowah," sang Leroy, and they all asked "Why Do Fools Fall in Love?" Leroy sang like he was Frankie Lymon—not just some kid from the projects who wanted to be him—and the Kool-Tones *were* the Teenagers, and they began to pull and heave that song like it was a dead whale. And soon they had it in the water, and then it was swimming a little, then it was moving, and then the sonofabitch started spouting water, and that was the place

where Leroy went into the falsetto "*wyyyyyyyyyyyyyyyyy-yyyyyy,*" and instead of chopping it where it should have been, he kept on. The Kool-Tones went *ooom wahooomwah* softly behind him, and still he held to that note, and the crowd began to applaud, and they began to yell, and Leroy held it longer, and they started stamping and screaming, and he held it until he knew he was going to cough up both his lungs, and he held it after that, and the Kool-Tones were coming up to meet him, and Leroy gave a tantrum-step, and his eyes were bugging, and he felt his lungs tear out by the roots and come unglued, and he held the last syllable, and the crowd wet itself and—

The lights went out and the amp went dead. Part of the crowd had a subliminal glimpse of something large, blue, and cool looming over the freight yard, bathing the top of the building in a soft glow.

In the dead air the voices of the Kool-Tones dropped in pitch as if they were pulled upward at a thousand miles an hour, and then they rose in pitch as if they had somehow come back at that same thousand miles an hour.

The blue thing was a looming blur and then was gone.

The lights came back on. The Kool-Tones stood there blinking: Cornelius, Ray, Slim, and Zoot. The space in front of the center mike was empty.

The crowd had an orgasm.

The Bombers were being violently ill over next to the building.

"God, that was *great!*" said Vinnie. "Just great!"

All four of the Kool-Tones were shaking their heads.

They should be tired, but this looked worse than that, thought Vinnie. They should be ecstatic. They looked like they didn't know they had won.

"Where's Leroy?" asked Cornelius.

"How the hell should I know?" Vinnie said, sounding annoyed.

"I remembered him smiling, like," said Zoot.

"And the blue thing. What about it?"

"What blue thing?" asked Lucius.

"I dunno. Something was blue."

"All I saw was the lights go off and that kid ran away," said Lucius.

"Which way?"

"Well, I didn't exactly see him, but he must have run some way. Don't know how he got by us. Probably thought you were going to lose and took it on the lam. I don't see how you'd worry when you can make your voices do that stuff."

"Up," said Zoot, suddenly.

"What?"

"We went up, and we came down. Leroy didn't come down with us."

"Of course not. He was still holding the same note. I thought the little twerp's balls were gonna fly out his mouth."

"No. We . . ." Slim moved his hands up, around, gave up. "I don't know what happened, do you?"

Ray, Zoot, and Cornelius all looked like they had thirty-two lane bowling alleys inside their heads and all the pin machines were down.

"Aw, shit," said Vinnie. "You won. Go get some sleep. You guys were really bitchin'."

The Kool-Tones stood there uncertainly for a minute.

"He was, like, smiling, you know?" said Zoot.

"He was always smiling," said Vinnie. "Crazy little kid."

The Kool-Tones left.

The sky overhead was black and spattered with stars. It looked to Vinnie as if it were deep and wide enough to hold anything. He shuddered.

"Hey!" he yelled. "Somebody bring me a beer!"

He caught himself humming. One of the Hellbenders brought him a beer.

BLUFF

Harry Turtledove

A recent theory in historical anthropology provides the basis for this fascinating story about a Terran expedition to a planet whose more or less humanoid inhabitants are at the Bronze Age level of civilization . . . and each of them is in direct voice contact with his or her god. Which makes for puzzlement and misunderstanding on both sides. . . .

Harry Turtledove has written many excellent stories under the penname "Eric G. Iverson," but beginning last year he changed his byline to his real name.

The pictures from the survey satellites came out of the fax machine one after the other, *chunk, chunk, chunk*. Ramon Castillo happened to be close by. He took them from the tray, more out of a sense of duty than in the expectation of finding anything interesting. The previous photo runs of the still-unnamed planet below had proven singularly dull.

There hadn't been a good shot of this river-valley system before, though. As he studied the print, his heavy eyebrows lifted like raven's wings. He felt a flush of excitement beneath his coppery skin, and damned himself for a fool. "Wishful thinking," he muttered aloud. Just the same, he slipped the print into the magnifying viewer.

His whoop brought people running from all over the

William Howells. Helga Stein was first into the fax compartment: a stocky blonde in her late twenties, her normally serious expression now replaced by surprise. "*Mein Gott*, was that you, Ramon?" she exclaimed; Castillo was usually very quiet.

Most of the time he found her intensely annoying; he was a cultural anthropologist and she a psychologist, and their different approaches to problems that touched them both led to frequent arguments. Now, though, he stepped away from the viewer and invited her forward with a courtly sweep of his arm. "You'll see for yourself," he said grandly. He spoke Latin with a facility that left everyone else aboard the *Howells* jealous.

"What am I looking for?" she asked, fiddling with the focus. By then the other members of the survey team were crowding in: physical anthropologist Sybil Hussie and her husband George Davies, who was a biologist (they were married just before upship, and George had endured in good spirits all the stale jokes about practicing what he studied); Xing Mei-lin the linguist; and Manolis Zakythinos, whose specialty was geology.

Even Stan Jeffries stuck his head in to see what the fuss was about. "Found the mountain of solid platinum, did you?" the navigator chuckled, seeing Helga peering into the viewer.

She looked up, puzzlement on her face. "What is that in Latin?" she asked; the ship's English-speakers consistently forgot to use the international scholarly tongue. Grumbling, Jeffries repeated himself.

"Ah," she said, distracted enough to be polite instead of freezing him for his heavyhanded wit. "Interpreting such photos is not my area of epxertise, you must understand; I leave that to Sybil or Manolis or Ramon who saw this first. But along the banks of this river there are I think cities set in the midst of a network of canals."

Yells like Castillo's ripped from the entire scientific crew. They all scrambled toward the viewer at the same time. "Ouch!" Sybil Hussie said as an elbow caught her in the ribs. "Have a care, there. This is no bloody rugby scrum—and try doing that into Latin, if anybody has a mind to."

At last, grudgingly, they formed a line. "You see?" Castillo said as they examined the print in turn. He was still voluble in his excitement. "Walled towns with major works of architecture at their centers; outlying hamlets; irrigation works that cover the whole flood-plain. Judging by the rest of the planet, I would guess that this is its very first civilization, equivalent to Sumer or Egypt back on Earth."

They had known for several days that the world was inhabited, but nothing at a level higher than tiny farming villages had shown up on any earlier pictures—certainly no culture worth contacting. Now, though—

"A chance to really see how a hydraulic civilization functions, instead of guessing from a random selection of 5,000-year-old finds," Ramon said dreamily.

Mei-lin spoke with down-to-earth practicality. "A chance for a new dissertation." Her Latin was not as fluent as his, but had a precision Caesar might have admired.

"Publications," Helga and George Davies said in the same breath. Everyone laughed.

"Maybe enough art objects to make us all rich," Jeffries put in.

Manolis Zakythinos made a small, disgusted noise. All the same, the navigator's words hung in the air. It had happened before, to other incoming survey teams. There was always a premium on new forms of beauty.

Zakythinos slipped out. Thinking he was still annoyed, Ramon started to go after him, but the geologist quickly returned with a bottle of ouzo. "To the crows with the vile excuse for vodka the food unit turns out," he cried, his deep-set brown eyes flashing. "This calls for a true celebration."

"Call the captain," someone said as, amid cheers, they repaired to the galley. Most of them stopped at their cabins for something special; Sybil was carrying a squat green bottle of Tanqueray that she put between bourbon and scotch. Odd, Ramon thought, how her husband favored the American drink while Jeffries, who was from the States, preferred scotch.

Castillo's own contribution came from the hills outside his native Bogota. He set the joints, rolled with almost compulsive neatness, beside the liquor. Being moderate by nature, he still had most of the kilo he had brought, and had given away a good deal of what was gone.

Given a choice, he would sooner have drunk beer, but space restrictions aboard the *Howells* made taking it impossible. He sighed and fixed himself a gin and tonic.

He was, inevitably and with inevitable fruitlessness, arguing with Helga about what the aliens below would be like when the buzz of conversation around them quieted for a moment. Blinking, Ramon looked up. Captain Katerina Tolmasova stood in the galley doorway.

Always, Ramon thought, she had that way of drawing attention to herself. Part of it lay in her staying in uniform long after the rest of them had relaxed into jeans or coveralls. But she would have worn her authority like a cloak over any clothes, or none.

In any clothes or none, also, she would have drawn male glances. Not even George Davies was immune, in spite of being a contented newlywed. She was tall, slim, dark: not at all the typical Russian. But her nationality showed in her broad, high cheekbones and in her eyes—enormous blue pools in which a man would gladly drown himself.

It still amazed Ramon, and sometimes frightened him a little, that they shared a bed.

She came over to him, smiling. "I am to understand that we have you to thank for this, ah, occasion?" Her voice made a slow music of Latin. It was the only language they had in common; he wondered how many times in the past thousand years it had been used for love-making.

Now he shrugged. "It could have been anyone. Whoever saw the pictures first would have recognized what was on them."

"I am glad you did, even so. Making contact is ever so much more interesting than weeks in the endless sameness of hyperdrive, though the instructors at the Astrograd Starship Academy would frown to hear me say so." She paused to sip vodka over ice—not the rough ship's brew, but Stolichnaya from her private hoard, which went down like a warm whisper—then went on, "Also I am glad we have here beings without a high technology. I shall worry less, of nights." The weapons of the *Howells,* of course, were under her control, along with everything else having to do with the safety of the ship.

"I hope," he said, touching her hand, "that I can help keep you from worrying."

"It is a shame romantic speeches have so little to do with life," she said. She sounded a little sad. Seeing the hurt spring into his eyes, she added quickly, "Not that they are not welcome even so. My quarters would be lonely without you tonight, the more so as afterwards we will be busy, first I guiding the ship down and then you with this new species. We shall not have much time together then; best enjoy while we may."

Pitkhanas, steward-king of the river-god Tabal for the town of Kussara, awoke with the words of the god ringing in his ears: "See to the dredging of the canals today, lest they be filled with silt!"

King though he was, he scrambled from his bed, throwing aside the light, silky coverlet; disobeying the divine voice was unimaginable. He hardly had a backward glance to spare for the superb form of his favorite wife Azzias.

She muttered a drowsy complaint at being disturbed. "I am sorry," he told her. "Tabal has ordered me to see to the dredging of the canals today, lest they be filled with silt."

"Ah," she said, and went back to sleep.

Slaves hurried forward to dress Pitkhanas, draping him in the gold-shot crimson robe of state, setting the conical crown on his head, and slipping his feet into sandals with silver buckles. As he was being clothed, he breakfasted on a small loaf, a leg of boiled fowl from the night before that would not stay fresh much longer, and a pot of fermented fruit juice.

Tabal spoke to him again as he was eating, echoing the previous command. He felt the beginnings of a headache, as always happened when he did not at once do what the god demanded. He hastily finished his food, wiped his mouth on the sleeve of his robe, and hurried out of the royal bedchamber. Servants scrambled to open doors before him.

The last portal swung wide; he strode out of the palace into the central square of Kussara. The morning breeze from the Til-Barsip river was refreshing, drying the sweat that prickled on him under the long robe.

Close by the palace entrance stood the tomb of his father Zidantas, whose skull topped the monument. Several commoners were laying offerings at the front of the tomb: fruits, bread, cheese. In the short skirts of thin stuff that were their sole garments, they were more comfortable than he. When they saw him, they went down on their knees, touching their heads to the ground.

"Praise to your father, my lord king," one of them quavered, his voice muffled. "He has told me where I misplaced a fine alabaster bowl."

"Good for you, then," Pitkhanas said. Dead no less than alive, his father always had a harsh way of speaking to him.

As now: "I thought you were going to see to the dredging of the canals today," Zidantas snapped.

"So I am," Pitkhanas said mildly, trying to avoid Zidantas's wrath.

"Then do it," his father growled. The old man had been dead for three years or so. At times his voice and manner were beginning to remind the king of Labarnas, his own grandfather and Zidantas's father. Labarnas rarely spoke from the tomb any more, save to old men and women who remembered him well. Zidantas's presence, though, was as real and pervasive in Kussara as that of Pitkhanas.

Surrounded by his attendants, the king hurried through the town's narrow, winding streets, stepping around or over piles of stinking garbage. The mud-brick housefronts were monotonous, but the two-story buildings provided welcome shade. Despite the breeze, the day was already hot.

Pitkhanas heard people chattering in the courtyards behind the tall blank walls of their homes. A woman's angry screech came from the roof where she and her husband had been sleeping: "Get up, you sot! Are you too sozzled to listen to the gods and work?"

The gods she spoke of were paltry, nattering things, fit for the lower classes: gods of the hearth, of the various crafts, of wayfaring. Pitkhanas had never heard them and did not know all their names; let the priests keep them straight. The great gods of the heavens and earth dealt with him directly, not through such intermediaries.

Kussara's eastern gate was sacred to Ninatta and Kulitta, the god and goddess of the two moons. Their statues stood in a niche above the arch, the stone images fairly bursting with youth. Below them, carts rumbled in and out, their ungreased axles squealing. Sentries paced the wall over the gate. The sun glinted off their bronze spearpoints.

The gate-captain, a scar-seamed veteran named Tushratta, bowed low before Pitkhanas. "How can this one serve you, my lord?"

"Tabal has reminded me that the canals need dredging," the king replied. "Tell some of your soldiers to gather peasants from the fields—three hundred over all will do—and set them to work at it."

"I hear you and obey as I hear and obey the gods," Tushratta said. He touched the alabaster eye-idol that he wore on his belt next to his dagger. They were common all through the Eighteen Cities, as channels to make the voices of the gods easier to understand.

Tushratta bawled the names of several warriors; some came down from the wall, others out of the barracks by the gate. "The canals need dredging," he told them. "Gather peasants from the field—three hundred over all will do—and set them to work at it."

The men dipped their heads, then fanned out into the green fields to do as they had been ordered. The peasants working at their plots knew instinctively what the soldiers were about, and tried to disappear. The warriors routed them out one by one. Soon they gathered the required number, most with hoes or digging-sticks already in their hands.

Pitkhanas gave them their commands, watched them troop off toward the canals in groups of ten or so. They splashed about, deepening the channels so the precious water could flow more freely. The king started to go back to the palace to tend to other business, then wondered whether he should stay awhile to encourage the canal-dredgers.

He paused, irresolute, glanced up at the images of the gods for guidance. Kulitta spoke to him: "Best you remain. Seeing the king as well as hearing his words reminds the worker of his purpose.''

''Thank you, mistress, for showing me the proper course,'' Pitkhanas murmured. He went out to the canals to let the peasants see him at close range. His retinue followed, a slave holding a parasol above his head to shield him from the strong sun.

''His majesty is gracious,'' Tushratta remarked to one of the king's attendants, a plump little man named Radus-piyama, who was priest to the sky-god Tarhund.

The priest clucked reproachfully. ''Did you not hear him answer the goddess? Of course he follows her will.''

Kulitta's advice had been good; the work went more swiftly than it would have without Pitkhanas's presence. Now and then a man or two would pause to stretch or have a moment's horseplay, splashing muddy water at each other, but they soon returned to their tasks. ''The canals need dredging,'' one reminded himself in stern tones very like the king's.

Because the goddess had told Pitkhanas to stay and oversee the peasants, he was close by when the sky ship descended. The first of it he knew was a low mutter in the air, like distant thunder—but the day was bright and cloudless. Then Radus-piyama cried out and pointed upward. Pitkhanas's gaze followed the priest's finger.

For a moment he did not see what Radus-piyama had spied, but then his eye caught the silver glint of light. It reminded him of the evening star seen at earliest twilight—but only for an instant, for it moved through the heavens like a stooping bird of prey, growing brighter and (he rubbed his eyes) larger. The noise in the sky became a deep roar that smote the ears. Pitkhanas clapped his hands over them. The sound still came through.

''Ninatta, Kulitta, Tarhund lord of the heavens, tell me the meaning of this portent,'' Pitkhanas exclaimed. The gods were silent, as if they did not know. The king waited, more afraid than he had ever been in his life.

If he knew fear, raw panic filled his subjects. The peasants toiling in the canals were screaming and shrieking. Some scrambled onto dry land and fled, while others took deep breaths and ducked under the water to hide from the monstrous heavenly apparition.

Even a few members of Pitkhanas's retinue broke and ran. The soldiers Tushratta had gathered were on the edge of running too, but the gate-captain's angry bellow stopped them: "Hold fast, you cowards! Where are your guts? Stand and protect your king." The command brought most of them back to their places, though a couple kept pelting back toward Kussara.

"Is it a bird, my lord?" Radus-piyama shouted through the thunder. The priest of Tarhund was still at Pitkhanas's side, still pointing to the thing in the sky. It had come close enough to show a pair of stubby wings, though those did not flap.

"Say rather a ship," Tushratta told him. Campaigning had, of necessity, made him a keen observer. "Look there: you can see a row of holes along either side, like the oarports of a big rivership."

"Where are the oars, then?" Radus-piyama asked. Tushratta shrugged, having no more idea than the tubby priest.

"Who would sail a ship through the sky?" Pitkhanas whispered. "The gods?" But they had not spoken to him, nor, as he could see from the fear of the men around him, to anyone else.

The ship, if that was what it was, crushed half a plot of grain beneath it when it touched ground about a hundred paces from the king and his retinue. A gust of warm air blew in their faces. The thunder gradually died. Several of Pitkhanas's attendants—and several of the soldiers—moaned and hid their eyes with their arms, certain their end had come. Had it not been beneath his royal dignity, the king would have done the same.

Tushratta, though, was staring with interest at the marks painted along the sides of the ship below the holes that looked like oarports. "I wonder if that is writing," he said.

"It doesn't look like writing," Radus-piyama protested. All the Eighteen Cities of the Til-Barsip valley used the same script; most of its symbols still bore a strong resemblance to the objects they represented, though rebus-puns and specific grammatical determinants became more subtle and complex generation by generation.

The gate-captain said stubbornly, "There are more ways

to write than ours, sir. I've fought against the hill-barbarians, and seen their villages. They use some of our signs for their language, but they have signs of their own, too, ones we don't have in the valley."

"Foreigners," Radus-piyama snorted. "I despise foreigners."

"So do I, but I have had to deal with them," Tushratta said. Foreigners were dangerous. They worshiped gods different from those of the Eighteen Cities, gods who spoke to them in their own unintelligible tongues. And if they spoke with angry voices, war was sure to follow.

A door swung open in the side of the ship. Pitkhanas felt his hearts pounding in his chest; excitement began to replace fear. Perhaps they were all inside the sky ship, having come to Kussara for some reason of their own. What an honor! Almost everyone heard the gods scores of times each day, but they were rarely seen.

A ramp slid down from the open doorway. The king saw a stir of motion behind it . . . and his hopes of meeting the gods face-to-face were dashed, for the people emerging from the sky ship were the most foreign foreigners he had ever seen.

He wondered if they *were* people. The tallest of them was half a head shorter than the Kussaran average. Instead of blue-gray or green-gray skins, theirs were of earthy shades, rather like dried mud bricks. One was darker than that, and another almost golden. Some had black hair like the folk of the Eighteen Cities and all the other peoples they knew, but the heads of others were topped with brownish-yellow or even orange-red locks. One had hair on his face!

Their gear was as unfamiliar as their persons. They wore trousers of some heavy blue fabric, something like those of the hillmen but tight, not baggy. Despite the heat, they were all in tunics, dyed with colors Pitkhanas had never seen on cloth. They held a variety of curious implements.

"Some of those will be warriors," Tushratta said as the royal party drew nearer.

"How can you tell that?" the king asked. To him the square black box one of them was lifting to his face—no, *her* face; by the breasts it was a woman, though what was a woman doing in the company of voyagers?—was as alien as the long, thin contraptions of wood and metal borne by the hairy-faced stranger and a couple of others.

"The way they carry them, my lord," the gate-captain answered, pointing to the trio with the long things. "And the way they watch us—they have something of the soldier to them."

Once it was pointed out to him, Pitkhanas could also see what Tushratta had noticed. He would never have spotted it for himself, though. "How can you observe so clearly, with the voices of the gods mute?" he said. That awful silence inside his head left him bewildered.

Tushratta shrugged. "I have seen soldiers among us and among the barbarians in the hills, my lord. My eyes tell me how these men are like them. Were the gods speaking, they would say the same, surely."

The golden-skinned stranger, the smallest of them all, descended from the ramp of the sky ship and slowly approached Pitkhanas and his followers. He held his hands out before him. The gesture was plainly peaceful, but not fully reassuring to the king; the foreigners, he saw, had only one thumb on each hand.

A moment later, the breath hissed from his nostrils in anger. "They insult me—it is a woman they send as herald!" This foreigner was so slimly made that only up close did the difference become apparent.

Hearing Pitkhanas's exclamation, one of the soldiers stepped forward to seize the offender. But before he could lay hands on her, she touched a button on her belt and shot into the air, hovering overhead at five times the height of a man.

The soldier, the attendants, the king gaped in astonishment. The sky ship was entirely outside their experience, too alien for them to gauge the power it represented. This, though—"Do not try to injure them again, or they will destroy us all!" Zidantas shouted to Pitkhanas.

"Of course, sire," the king gasped, putting his palms to his temples in relief that his dead father's voice had returned to him. "Do not try to injure them again, or they will destroy us all!" he called to his men, adding, "Abase yourselves, so they can see your repentance."

Heedless of their robes and skirts, his followers went to their knees in the soft mud of the field. Pitkhanas himself bowed from the waist, holding his eyes to the ground.

One of the strangers on the ramp of the sky ship called out something. His voice sounded like any other man's, but the words were meaningless to the king.

A soft touch on his shoulder made him look up. The foreign woman was standing before him, her feet touching the ground once more. She gestured that he should straighten himself: When he had, she bowed in return, as deeply as he had. She pointed to his men and motioned for them to rise too.

"Stand up," he told them.

As they were doing so, the woman went to her knees in the mud herself, careless of her rich, strange clothing. She got up quickly, echoing Pitkhanas's command with a questioning note in her voice.

He corrected her, using the singular verb-form this time instead of the plural. She understood at once, pointing to one man and repeating the singular and then at several and using the plural. He smiled, dipped his head, and spread his arms wide to show that she was right.

It began there.

"May I speak with you, my lord?" Radus-piyama asked.

"Yes," Pitkhanas said, a little wearily. He could feel in his belly what was about to come from the priest. Radus-piyama had been saying the same thing for many days now.

Nor did he surprise the king; with more passion than one would have expected to find in his small, round frame, he burst out, "My lord, I ask you again to expel the dirt-colored foreigners from Kussara. Tarhund has spoken to me once more, urging me to set this task upon you, lest they corrupt Kussara and all the Eighteen Cities."

"The god has given me no such command," Pitkhanas replied, as he had all the previous times Radus-piyama had asked him to get rid of the strangers. "If I hear it from his lips, be sure I shall obey. But until then these people from the far land called Terra are welcome here. They bring many fine gifts and things to trade." His hand went to his belt. The knife that hung there was a present from the Terrajin; it was made from a gray metal that was stronger than the best bronze and held a better edge.

"Come with me to the temple, then," Radus-piyama

said. "Perhaps in his own home you will know the god's will more clearly."

Pitkhanas hesitated. Tarhund spoke to him: "Go with my priest to my house in Kussara. If I have further commands for you, you should best hear them there."

"The god bids me go with you to his house in Kussara," the king told Radus-piyama. "If he has further commands for me, I should best hear them there."

Radus-piyama showed his teeth in a delighted grin. "Splendid, my lord! Surely Tarhund will show you the proper course. I had begun to fear that you no longer heard the gods at all, that you had become as deaf to them as the Terrajin are."

Pitkhanas made an angry noise in the back of his throat. "Not agreeing with you, priest, does not leave one accursed. Tushratta, for instance, prospers, yet he is most intimate with the Terrajin of anyone in Kussara."

Radus-piyama had begun to cringe in the face of the king's temper, but at mention of the officer he recovered and gave a contemptuous sneer. "Choose someone else as an example, my lord, not Tushratta. The gods have gradually been forgetting him for years. Why, he told me once that without his eye-idol he rarely hears them. Aye, he is a fit one to associate with the foreigners. He even has to cast the bones to learn what course he should take."

"Well, so do we all, now and then," the king reproved. "They show us the will of the gods."

"Oh, no doubt, my lord," Radus-piyama said. "But no one I know of has to use the bones as often as Tushratta. If the gods spoke to him more, he would have fewer occasions to call on such less certain ways of learning what they wanted of him."

"He is a good soldier," Pitkhanas said stiffly. Radus-piyama, seeing that he could not sway the king on this question, bowed his head in acquiescence. "To the temple, then," Pitkhanas said.

As usual near midday, the central square of Kussara was jammed with people. Potters and smiths traded their wares for grain or beer. Rug-makers displayed their colorful products in the hope of attracting customers wealthy enough to afford them. "Clear, fresh river-water!" a hawker called. "No need to drink it muddy from the canal!" He had two large clay jugs slung over his shoulder on a carrying-pole. Harlots swayed boldly through the crowd. Slaves followed them with their eyes or dozed in whatever shade they could find. More gathered at a small shrine, offering a handful of meal or fruit to its god in exchange for advice.

Pitkhanas also saw a couple of Terrajin in the square. The foreigners still drew stares from peasants new in town and attracted small groups of curious children wherever they went, but most of Kussara had grown used to them in the past year-quarter. Their odd clothes and coloring, the metal boxes they carried that clicked or hummed, were accepted peculiarities now, like the feather-decked turbans of the men from the city of Hurma or the habit the people of the town of Yuzat had of spitting after every sentence.

The Terraj called Kastiyo was haggling with a carpenter over the price of a stool as the king and Radus-piyama came by. "I know wood is valuable because you have to trade to get it," the Terraj was saying, "but surely this silver ring is a good payment." Kastiyo fumbled for words and spoke slowly, but he made himself understood; after tiny Jingmaylin, he probably had the best grasp of Kussara's language.

The carpenter weighed the ring in his hand. "Is it enough?"

"Who—ah, whom—do you ask?" the Terraj said.

"Why, my god, of course: Kadashman, patron of wood-workers. He says the bargain is fair." The carpenter lifted the stool, gave it to Kastiyo, and held out his hand for the ring.

The foreigner passed it to him, but persisted, "How is it you know what the god says?"

"I hear him, naturally, just as I hear you; but you will go away and he is always with me." The carpenter looked as confused as the Terraj. Then he brightened. "Perhaps you do not know Kadashman because you are not a wood-worker and he has no cause to speak to you. But surely your own gods talk to you in much the same way."

"I have never heard a god," Kastiyo said soberly. "None of my people has. That is why we is—*are*—so interested in learning more about those of Kussara."

The carpenter's jaw dropped at Kastiyo's admission. "You see?" Radus-piyama said to Pitkhanas. "Out of their own mouths comes proof of their accursedness."

"They have gods, or a god," the king answered. "I have asked them that."

Radus-piyama laughed. "How could there be only one god? And even if there were, would he not speak to his people?"

To that Pitkhanas had no reply. He and the priest walked in silence to the temple of Tarhund, the Great House, as it was called: after the shrine of Tabal, the tallest and most splendid building in Kussara. The temples towered over the palace of the steward-king, who was merely the gods' servant. The huge rectangular tower of mud-brick rose in ever smaller stages to Tarhund's chamber at the very top.

Together, Pitkhanas and Radus-piyama climbed the temple's 316 steps—one for each day of the year. Under-priests bowed to their chief and to the king, who could see the surprise on their faces at his unscheduled visit.

"Is the god properly robed?" Radus-piyama called when they were nearly at the top.

The door to Tarhund's chambers swung open. A priest whose skin was gray with age emerged, his walk a slow hobble helped by a stick. "That he is, sir," he replied, "and pronounces himself greatly pleased with his new vestments, too."

"Excellent, Millawanda," Radus-piyama said. "Then he will give our king good advice about the Terrajin."

Millawanda's eyesight was beginning to fail, and he had not noticed Pitkhanas standing beside Radus-piyama. The king waved for him not to bother when he started a shaky bow. "Thank you, my lord. Yes, Tarhund has mentioned the foreigners to me. He says—"

"I will hear for myself what he says, thank you," Pitkhanas said. He stepped toward the god's chambers. When Radus-piyama started to follow him, he waved him back; he was still annoyed that the priest had feared Tarhund was not speaking to him any more.

Tarhund stood in his niche, an awesome figure, taller than a man. Torchlight played off the gold leaf that covered his face, hands, and feet, and off the gold and silver threads running through the thick, rich cloth of his new ankle-length robe. In his left hand he held the solid-gold globe of the sun, in his right black stormclouds.

The king suddenly saw with horror that he had forgotten to bring any offering when the god summoned him. He groveled on his belly before Tarhund as the lowliest of his slaves would have before him. Stripping off his sandals with their silver buckles, he set them on the table in front of the god next to the gifts of food, beer, and incense from the priests. "Accept these from this worm, your servant," he implored.

Tarhund's enormous eyes of polished jet gripped and held him. The god's words echoed in Pitkhanas's ears: "You may speak."

"Thank you, my master." Still on the floor, the king poured out everything that had happened since the coming of the Terrajin. "Are they stronger than you, lord, and your brother and sister gods? When we first met them, their powers and strangeness silenced your voices, and we despaired. You returned as we grew to know them, but now you speak in one way to your priests and in another to me. What shall I do? Shall I destroy the Terrajin, or order them to leave? Or shall I let them go on as they would, seeing that they have done no harm yet? Say on; let me know your will."

The god took so long answering that Pitkhanas trembled and felt his limbs grow weak with fear. If the strangers *were* mightier than the gods— But at last Tarhund replied, though his voice seemed faint and far away, almost a divine mumble: "Let them go on as they would. Seeing that they have done no harm yet, they will keep on behaving well."

Pitkhanas knocked his forehead against mud brick. "I hear and obey, my master." He dared another question: "My lord, how is it that the Terrajin hear no gods of their own?"

Tarhund spoke again, but only in a gabble from which the king could understand nothing. Tears filled his eyes. He asked, "Is it as Radus-piyama says, that they are accursed?"

"No." This time the god's answer came quick, clear, and sharp. "Accursed men would work evil. They do not. Tell Radus-piyama to judge them by their deeds."

"Aye, my master." Sensing that the divine audience was over, Pitkhanas rose and left Tarhund's chamber.

Radus-piyama and Millawanda were waiting expectantly outside. The king said, "The god has declared to me that the Terrajin are not accursed. Accursed men would work evil. They do not, and they will keep on behaving well. Judge them by their deeds. This is Tarhund's command to me, and mine to you. Hear it always."

The priests blinked in surprise. But their obedience to the king was as ingrained as their service to Tarhund. "I hear you and obey as I hear and obey the god," Radus-piyama acknowledged, Millawanda following him a moment later.

Satisfied, Pitkhanas started down the long stairway of Tarhund's Great House. Had he conveyed his orders in writing, the priests might somehow have found a way to bend them to their own desires. Now, though, his wishes and Tarhund's would both be ringing in their ears. They would give him no more trouble over the Terrajin.

The tape of Ramon Castillo dickering with the Kussaran woodworker ended. The video screen went dark. Helga Stein lifted her headphones, rubbed her ears. "Another one," she sighed.

"What was that?" Castillo was still wearing his 'phones, which muffled her words. "Sorry." He took them off quickly.

"It's nothing," Helga said wearily. She turned to Mei-lin, who had been going over the tape with them. "Did I understand that correctly—the native calling on a deity named Kadashman at the decision-point?"

"Oh yes," the linguist answered at once. To Ramon she added, "You do very well with the language. He had no trouble following you at all."

"Thanks," he said; Mei-lin was not one to give praise lightly. But he had to object, " 'Calling on' isn't quite what happened. He asked a question, got an answer, and acted on it. Look for yourselves."

When he reached to rewind the tape, Helga stopped him. "Don't bother; all of us have seen the like dozens of times already. The local's eyes get far away for a few seconds, or however long it takes, then he comes out of it and does whatever he does. But what does it *mean*?"

" 'Eyes get far away,' " Ramon said. "That's not a

bad way to put it, I suppose, but to me it just looks as though the natives are listening."

"To what?" Helga flared, her face going pink. "And if you say 'a god,' I'll brain you with this table."

"It's bolted to the floor," he pointed out.

"Ach!" She snarled a guttural oath that was emphatically not Latin, stormed out of the workroom.

"You should not tease her so, Ramon," Mei-lin said quietly. Trouble rested on her usually calm features.

"I didn't mean to," the cultural anthropologist replied, still taken aback at Helga's outburst. "I simply have a very literal mind. I was going to suggest that if she had to hit me, the stool I bought would serve better."

Mei-lin smiled a dutiful smile. "At least you and Sybil have your stools and other artifacts you can put your hands on to study. All Helga and I can do is examine patterns, and none of the patterns here makes any sense that I can find."

"You shouldn't expect an alien species to think as we do."

"Spare me the tautology," the linguist snapped; her small sarcasm shocked Castillo much more than Helga's losing her temper. "For that matter, I sometimes wonder if these Kussarans think at all."

Ramon was shocked again, for she plainly meant it. "What about this, then?" he said, holding up the stool. It was a fine piece of craftsmanship, the legs beautifully fitted to the seat, the dyed-leather seatcover secured by bronze tacks to the wood below. "What about their walls and temples and houses, their cloth, their fields and canals, their writing, their language?"

"What about their language?" she retorted. "As I said, you've learned it quite well. You tell me how to say 'to think' in Kussaran."

"Why, it's—" Castillo began, and then stopped, his mouth hanging open. *"No sé,"* he admitted, startled back into Spanish, a slip he rarely made.

"I don't know either, or how to say 'to wonder' or 'to doubt' or 'to believe' or any other word that relates to cognition. And any Kussaran who says, 'I feel it in my bones' suffers from arthritis. Your 'literal mind' would make you a wildeyed dreamer among these people, Ramon. How can they live without reflecting on life? Is it any wonder that Helga and I feel we're eating soup with a fork?''

"No-o," he said slowly. Then he laughed. "Maybe their precious gods do their thinking for them." The laugh was not one of amusement. The problem of the gods vexed him as much as it did Helga. Where she fretted over failing to understand the locals' psychological makeup, he had the feeling he was seeing their cultural patterns only through fog—superficial shapes were clear, but whatever was behind them was hidden in the mist.

Mei-lin failed to find his suggestion even sardonically amusing. "There are no gods. If there were, our instruments would have detected them."

"Telepathy," Ramon probed, hoping to get a rise out of her.

She did not take the bait. All she said was, "Assuming it exists (which I don't), telepathy from whom? The bugs we've scattered around show that the king, the ministers, the priests talk to their gods as often as the peasants do—oftener, if anything. There are no secret rulers, Ramon."

"I know." His shoulders sagged a little. "In fact, the Kussarans who hold the fewest one-sided conversations are some of the soldiers and merchants—and everyone else looks down on them on account of it."

"Still, if they were all as interested in us as Tushratta, our job would be ten times easier."

"True enough." The gate-captain spent as much of his time at the *Howells* as his duties allowed. "I wouldn't be surprised if he's around so much because we have no gods at all and give him someone to feel superior to."

"You're getting as cynical as Stan Jeffries," she said, which canceled his pleasure at her earlier compliment. Feeling his face grow hot, he rose and took a hasty leave.

As he passed the galley, he thought there was some god working, and probably a malignant one, for Jeffries himself called, "Hey, Ramon, come sit in for a while. Reiko's engine-watch just started, and we're short-handed."

The inevitable poker game had begun when the *Howells* was still in parking orbit around Terra. Castillo rarely played. Not only were the regulars some of his least favorite people on the ship, they also won money from him with great regularity.

He was about to decline again when he saw Tushratta was one of the players. The Kussarans gambled among themselves with dice, and the soldier was evidently picking up a new game. He looked rather uncomfortable in a Terran chair: it was too small for him and did not quite suit his proportions.

"What does he use to buy chips?" Ramon asked, sitting down across from the native.

João Gomes, one of the engine-room technicians, said a little too quickly, "Oh, we give them to him. He just plays for fun."

Castillo raised an eyebrow. The technician flushed. Jeffries said, "Why fight it, João? He can always ask Tushratta himself. All right, Ramon, he buys it with native goods: pots and bracelets and such. When he wins, we pay off with our own trinkets: a pair of scissors, a pocketknife, a flashlight." He stared defiantly at the anthropologist. "Want to make something of it?"

That sort of dealing was technically against regulations, but Ramon said, "I suppose not, provided I get photos of all the Kussaran artifacts you've gotten from him."

"Naturally," Jeffries agreed. Faces fell all around the table. Castillo hid a smile. Of course the poker players had been planning to hide the small trinkets and sell them for their own profit when they got home. It happened on every expedition that found intelligent natives, one way or another. The anthropologist was also certain he would not see everything.

Tushratta pointed at the deck of cards. "Deal," he said in heavily accented but understandable Latin.

To keep things simple for the beginner, they stuck with five-card stud and one joker. "A good skill game, anyway," Jeffries said. "You can tell where you stand. You play something like seven stud, low in the hole wild, and you don't know whether to shit or go blind."

Ramon lost a little, won a little, lost a little more. He might have done better if he hadn't been paying as much attention to Tushratta as to the cards—or, he told himself with characteristic honesty, he might not. As was to be expected among more experienced players, the native lost, but not too badly. His worst flaw, Castillo thought, was a tendency not to test bluffs: a problem the anthropologist had himself.

When Tushratta ran low on chips, he dug in his pouch and produced a cylinder seal, a beautifully carved piece of alabaster about the size of his little finger designed to be rolled on a mud tablet to show that he had written it. The stake Gomes gave him for it seemed honest.

A couple of hands later, the Kussaran and Jeffries got into an expensive one. Ramon was dealing, but folded after his third card. Everyone else dropped out on the next one, with varied mutters of disgust.

"Last card," the anthropologist said. He tossed them out.

Someone gave a low whistle. Jeffries, grinning, had four diamonds up. A couple of chairs away, Tushratta was sitting behind two pairs: treys and nines.

"Your bet, Tushratta," Ramon said. The Kussaran did, heavily.

"Ah, now we separate the sheep from the goats," Jeffries said, and raised. But the navigator's grin slipped when Tushratta raised back. "Oh, you bastard," he said in English. He shoved in more chips. "Call."

Looking smug, Tushratta showed his hole card: a third nine. "Ouch," Jeffries said. "No wonder you bumped it up, with a full house." Castillo was not sure how much of that Tushratta understood, but the Kussaran knew he had won. He raked in the pot with both hands, started stacking the chips in neat piles of five in front of him.

Jeffries managed a sour grin. "Not that you needed the boat," he said to Tushratta. He turned over his own fifth card. It was a club.

Laughter erupted around the table. "That'll teach you, Stan," Gomes said. "Serves you right."

Tushratta knocked several piles of chips onto the floor. He made no move to pick them up; he was staring at Jeffries's hole card as though he did not believe his eyes. "You had nothing," he said.

The navigator had learned enough Kussaran to follow him. "A pair of sixes, actually."

Tushratta waved that away, as of no importance. He spoke slowly, sounding, Ramon thought, uncertain where his words were leading him: "You saw my two pairs showing. You could not beat them, but you kept betting. Why did you do that?"

"It was a bluff that didn't work," Jeffries answered. The key word came out in Latin. He turned to Castillo for help. "Explain it to him, Ramon; you're smoother with the lingo than I am."

"I'll try," the anthropologist said; he did not know the word for "bluff" either. Circumlocution, then: "You saw Jeffries's four diamonds. He wanted to make you drop by acting as though he had a flush. He did not know you had three nines. If you only had the two pairs that were up, you would lose against a flush, and so you might not bet against it. That was what he wanted—that is what bluff is."

"But he did not have a flush," Tushratta protested, almost in a wail.

"But he seemed to, did he not? Tell me, if you had only had the two pair, what would you have done when he raised?"

Tushratta pressed the heels of his hands against his eyes. He was silent for almost a full minute. At last he said, very low, "I would have folded."

Then he did retrieve the chips he had spilled, carefully restacked them. "I have had enough poker for today. What will you give me for these? There are many more here than I had yesterday."

They settled on a hand-held mirror, three butane lighters, and a hatchet. Ramon suspected the latter would be used on skulls, not timber. For the moment, though, Tushratta was anything but warlike. Still in the brown study that had gripped him since he won the hand from Jeffries, he took up his loot and left, talking to himself.

Castillo did not think he was communing with his mysterious gods; it sounded more like an internal argument. "But he didn't . . . But he seemed to . . . But he didn't . . . Bluff . . ."

"What's all that about?" Jeffries asked.

When the anthropologist translated, Gomes chuckled. "There you go, Stan, corrupting the natives." The navigator threw a chip at him.

*   *   *

"I laughed with the rest of them," Castillo said as he recounted the poker game in his cabin that night, "but looking back, I'm not sure João wasn't absolutely right. Katerina, I'd swear the idea of deceit had never crossed Tushratta's mind."

Frowning, the captain sat up in bed, her hair spilling softly over her bare shoulders. Her specialty was far removed from Ramon's, but she brought an incisive, highly logical mind to bear on any problem she faced. "Perhaps he was merely taken aback by a facet of the game that he had not thought of before."

"It went deeper than that," the anthropologist insisted. "He had to have the whole notion of bluffing defined for him, and it hit him hard. And as for thinking, Mei-lin has me wondering if the Kussarans really do."

"Really do what? Think? Don't be absurd, Ramon; of course they do. How could they have built this civilization of theirs without thinking?"

Castillo smiled. "Exactly what I said this afternoon." He repeated Mei-lin's argument for Katerina, finished, "As far as I can see, she has a point. Concepts can't exist in a culture without words to express them."

"Just so," the captain agreed. "As Marx said, it is not the consciousness of men that determines their existence, but rather their social existence determines their consciousness."

You and your Marx, Castillo thought fondly. He did not say that aloud, any more than he would have challenged Manolis Zakythinos's Orthodox Christianity. What he did say was, "Here's Kussara in front of us as evidence to the contrary."

"Only because we do not understand it," Katerina said firmly, her secular faith unshakable.

Still, Ramon could not deny the truth in her words, and admitted as much. "Their gods, for instance. We may not be able to see or hear them, but they're real as mud brick to the Kussarans."

"All primitive peoples talk to their gods," Katerina said.

"But not all of them have gods who answer back," the anthropologist replied, "and the locals certainly listen to theirs. In fact, they—"

His voice trailed away as his mind began working furiously. Suddenly he leaned over and kissed Katerina with a fervor that had nothing to do with lovemaking. He sprang out of bed, hurrying over to the computer terminal at his desk. Katerina exclaimed in surprise and a little indignation. He paid no attention, which was a measure of his excitement.

It took him a while to find the database he needed; it was not one he used often. When at last he did, he could hardly keep his fingers from trembling as he punched in his search commands. He felt like shouting when the readout began flowing across the screen.

Instead, he whispered, "I know, I know."

"You're crazy," Helga Stein said flatly when Ramon finished his presentation at a hastily called meeting the next morning. It was, he thought with a giddiness brought on by lack of sleep, a hell of a thing for a psychologist to say, but then Latin was a blunt language. And glances round the table showed that most of their colleagues agreed with her. Only Mei-lin seemed to be withholding judgment.

"Argue with the evidence, not with me," he said. "As far as I can see, it all points toward the conclusion I've outlined: the Kussarans are not conscious beings."

"Oh, piffle, Ramon," Sybil Hussie said. "My old cat Bill back in Manchester is a conscious being."

Castillo wished he was someplace else; he was too shy to enjoy putting forth a strange idea to a hostile audience. But he was also too stubborn to fold up in the face of mockery. "No, Sybil," he said, "your old Bill, that mangy creature—I've met him, you know—isn't conscious, he's simply aware."

"Well, what is the difference?" Manolis Zakythinos asked.

"Or, better, how do you define consciousness?" George Davies put in.

"With Helga over there waiting to pounce on me, I won't even try. Let her do it."

The psychologist blinked when Ramon tossed the ball to her, rather like a prosecution witness unexpectedly summoned by the defense. Her answer came slowly: "Consciousness is an action, not an essence. It manipulates meanings in a metaphorical space in a way analogous to manipulating real objects in real space. In 'meanings' I include the mental image a conscious being holds of itself. Consciousness operates on whatever the conscious being is thinking about, choosing relevant elements and building patterns from them as experience has taught it. I must agree with Ramon, Sybil: your cat is not a conscious being. It is aware, but it is not aware of itself being aware. If you want a short definition, that is what consciousness is.''

Davies was already sputtering protests. ''It's bloody incomplete, is what it is. What about thinking? What about learning?''

Reluctantly, Helga said, ''One does not have to be conscious to think.'' That turned a storm of protest against her that dwarfed anything Ramon had faced. She waited for it to end. ''I will show you, then. Give me the next number in this sequence: one, four, seven, ten—''

''Thirteen.'' The response came instantly, from three or four people at once.

''How did you know that?'' she asked them. ''Were you aware of yourselves reasoning that you had to add three to the last number and then carrying out the addition? Or did you simply recognize the pattern and see what the next element *had* to be? From the speed with which you answered, I'd guess the latter—and where is the conscious thought there?''

Abrupt silence fell round the conference table. It was, Ramon thought, an introspective sort of silence; the very stuff of consciousness.

George Davies broke it. ''You picked too simple an example, Helga. Give us something more complicated.''

''What about typing, then, or playing a synthesizer? In both of them, the only way to perform well is to suppress your consciousness. The moment you start thinking about what you are doing, instead of doing it, you will go wrong.''

That—thoughtful—silence descended once more. When Helga spoke again, she looked first toward Castillo, grudging respect in her eyes. ''You've convinced me of the possibility, at least, Ramon, or rather made me convince myself.''

"I like it," Mei-lin said with sudden decision. "It fits. The total lack of mental imagery in the Kussaran language has been obvious to me for weeks. If the Kussarans are not conscious, they have no need for it."

"How do they get along without consciousness?" Davies challenged. "How can they function?"

"You do yourself, all the time," Ramon said. Before the biologist could object, he went on, "Think of a time when you were walking somewhere deep in a conversation with someone. Haven't you ever looked up and said, "Oh, we're here," with no memory of having crossed a street or two or gone by a park? Your consciousness was busy elsewhere, and the rest of your intelligence coped for you. Take away the part that was talking with your friend and you have what the Kussarans are like all the time. They get along just fine on pattern recognition and habit."

"And what happens when those aren't enough?" Davies asked, stabbing out a triumphant finger. "What happens when a Kussaran turns his old familiar corner and the smithy's caught fire and the whole street is burning? What then?"

Castillo licked his lips. He wished the question had not come so soon, or so bluntly. No help for it now, though. He took a deep breath and answered, "Then his gods tell him what to do."

He had not known so few people could make so much noise. For a moment he actually wondered if the attack was going to be physical; George Davies and his wife bounced halfway out of their chairs as they showered him with abuse. So did Helga, who shouted, "I was right the first time, Ramon—you *are* crazy." Even Mei-lin was shaking her head.

"Shouldn't you hear me out before you lock me up?" Castillo said tightly, almost shaking with anger.

"Why listen to more drivel?" Sybil Hussie said with a toss of her head.

"No, he is right," Zakythinos said. "Let him back up his claim, if he can. If he can convince such an, ah, skeptical audience, he deserves to be taken seriously."

"Thank you, Manolis." Ramon had himself under tight control again; railing back at them would not help. "Let me start out by saying that what I'm proposing isn't new;

the idea was first put forward by Jaynes over a hundred and fifty years ago, back in the 1970's, for ancient Terran civilizations.''

Helga rolled her eyes. "*Ach*, that period. Gods from outer space, is it?''

"Nothing like that," Castillo said, adding with some relish, "Jaynes was a psychologist, as a matter of fact.''

"And what sort of gods, if I may make so bold as to ask, would a psychologist have?'' Sybil said in a tone calculated to put Helga's teeth on edge as well as Ramon's.

The cultural anthropologist, though, had his answer ready: "Auditory and sometimes visual hallucinations, generated by the right side of the brain—the part that deals with patterns and broad perceptions rather than logic and speech. They would not be recognized as hallucinations, you understand; they would be perceived as divine voices. And, operating with the stored-up experience of a person's life, they would find the behavior pattern that fit any new or unexpected situation, and tell him what to do. No conscious thought would be involved at all.''

"It is drivel—'' Sybil began, but her husband was shaking his head.

"I wonder,'' he said slowly. "Kussaran life is organized neurologically on the same general pattern as Terran; dissection of native corpses and work with domestic animals clearly shows that. There are differences, of course—brain functions, for instance, seem to be arranged fore-and-aft, rather than axially as with us.''

"That's your province, of course,'' Ramon said. If George was arguing on those terms, he had to be considering the idea.

"These 'divine voices,' '' Helga said. "They would be related to the voices schizophrenics hear?''

"Very closely,'' Castillo agreed. "But they would be normal and universal, not something to be resisted and feared by the vestiges of the conscious mind-pattern. And the threshold for producing them could be much lower than it is in schizophrenics—anything unusual or unfamiliar would touch them off. So could the sight of an idol; that may be why Kussara is so littered with them.''

Davies sat straighter in his chair, a mannerism he had when he was coming up with an objection he thought telling. "What possible evolutionary advantage could there be to a way of life based on hallucination?"

"Social control," Ramon answered. "Remember, these aren't conscious beings we're talking about. They cannot visualize a connected series of activities, as we do. The only way for one of them weeding a field, say, to keep at his job all day long without someone standing over him, would be to keep hearing the voice of a chief or king saying over and over, 'Pull them out!' "

"Hmm," was all the biologist said.

"And since the king is part of the system too," Helga mused, "he would hear the voices of whatever high gods his culture had. They would be the only ones with enough authority to direct him."

"Perhaps of his ancestors also," Ramon said. "Remember that shrine by Pitkhanas's palace—it's a monument to his father, the last king of the city. There are offerings there, as to the gods."

"So there are." The psychologist paused, her eyes going big and round. "*Lieber Gott!* For such beings, belief in an afterlife would come naturally, and with reason. If a woman still heard, for instance, her mother's voice after her mother had died, would her mother not still be alive for her, in a very real sense of the word?"

"I hadn't even thought of that," Ramon whispered.

George Davies remained unconvinced. "If this style of perception is so wonderful, why aren't we all still blissfully unconscious?"

Castillo gave credit where it was due. "A remark of Katerina's put me on this track. Work it through. As a society gets increasingly complex, more and more layers of gods get added, to take care of all social levels. Look at Kussara now, with a separate deity for the carpenters and one for every other trade. Eventually, the system breaks down under its own weight.

"Writing helps, too. Writing makes a more complicated society possible, but it also weakens the authority of hallucinations. It's easier to evade a command when it's on a tablet in front of you that can be thrown away than when the king's voice sounds in your ear.

"And finally, the structure is geared to stability. It would have to come apart during war and crisis. What good are the commands of your gods if you're dealing with someone from a different culture, with a different language and strange gods of his own? Their orders would be as likely to get you killed as to save you.

"And in noticing how oddly the foreigners acted, you might account for it through something different inside them. And once you conceived of strangers with interior selves, you might suppose you had one too; the beginning of consciousness itself, maybe."

"There is evidence for that," Mei-lin broke in excitedly. "Remember, Ramon, how you remarked that the Kussarans who talked least with their gods were warriors and traders? They are exactly the ones with the greatest contact with foreigners—they may be on the very edge of becoming conscious beings."

All the anthropologist could do was nod. He felt dazed; the others were running with his hypothesis now in ways he had not imagined. And that, he thought, was as it should be. The concept was too big for any one man to claim it all.

Still sounding sour, George said, "I suppose we can work up experiments to test all this, if it's there." That was fitting too. If the idea had merit, it would come through inquiry unscathed or, better, refined and improved. If not, it did not deserve to survive.

Ramon could hardly wait to find out.

Holding his hands to his ears against the thunder, Pitkhanas watched the sky ship shrink as it rose into the heavens. It was the size of his fist at arm's length . . . the size of a night-flitterer . . . a point of silver light . . . gone.

The king saw how the great weight of the ship had pressed the ground where it had rested down half a forearm's depth. The grain that had been under it, of course, was long dead; the fields around the spot were rank and untended.

The fertility-goddess Yarris addressed Pitkhanas reproachfully. "That is good cropland. Set peasants to restoring its former lushness."

"It shall be done, mistress," he murmured, and relayed the command to his ministers.

His dead father spoke up. "Have warriors out to guard

the peasants, to keep the men of Maruwas down the river from raiding as they did when you were a boy. See you to it.''

Pitkhanas turned to Tushratta. ''Zidantas warns me to have warriors out to guard the peasants, to keep the men of Maruwas down the river from raiding as they did when I was a boy. See you to it.''

Tushratta bowed. ''I hear you and obey as I hear and obey the gods.'' The king walked off, never doubting his order would be obeyed.

In fact Tushratta did not hear the gods at all any more. Their voices had been slowly fading in his ears since his campaigns against the hillmen, but he knew to the day when they had vanished for good. ''*Bluff*,'' he said under his breath. He used the Terraj word; there was nothing like it in Kussaran.

He missed the gods terribly. He had even beseeched them to return—and how strange a thing was that, for the gods should always be present! Without their counsel, he felt naked and empty in the world.

But he went on. Indeed, he prospered. Perhaps the gods still listened to him, even if they would not speak. In the half-year since they left him, he had risen from gate-captain to warmaster of Kussara—the previous holder of that office having suddenly died. With himself he had brought certain other officers—young men who looked to him for guidance—and the detachments that obeyed them.

He would, he decided, follow Pitkhanas's command after all—but in his own fashion. As leader of the soldiers in the fields he would pick, hmm, Kushukh, who was not loyal to him . . . but who did head the palace guards.

How to get Kushukh to leave his post? ''*Bluff*,'' Tushratta muttered again. He still used the concept haltingly, like a man trying to speak a foreign language he did not know well. Standing as it were to one side of himself, seeing himself saying or doing one thing but intending another, took an effort that made sweat spring out on his forehead.

He would say . . . would say . . . His fist clenched as the answer came. He would tell Kushukh that Pitkhanas had said no one else could do the job as well. That should suffice.

And then, leading his own picked men, Tushratta would

go to the palace and . . . He looked ahead again, to
Pitkhanas's corpse being dragged away; to himself wearing
the royal robes and enjoying the royal treasures; to lying
with Azzias, surely the most magnificent creature the gods
ever made. Standing outside himself for those images was
easy. He had looked at them many, many times already.

After he had become king, Kushukh would prove no
problem; locked in the old ways, he would hear and obey
Tushratta just as he heard and obeyed the gods, just as he
had heard and obeyed Pitkhanas. Tushratta was less certain
of his own backers. He had not explained to them what a
bluff was, as Kastiyo had for him. But he had repeatedly
used the thing-that-seemed-this-but-was-that; he could not
have risen half so quickly otherwise. They were quick
lads. They might well see what it meant on their own.

If so—if he could never be sure that what one of them
told him, what one of them did, was not a *bluff*—how was
he to rule? They would not follow his orders merely
because it was he who gave them. Must he live all his days
in fear? That made him look ahead in a way he did not
like, to see himself cowering on the throne he had won.

But why did he have to be the one cowering? If one of
his backers tried to move against him and failed (and he
would not be such easy meat as Pitkhanas, for he would
always be watchful), why not treat that one so harshly that
the rest were made afraid? No matter then whether or not
they had his commands always ringing in their heads.
They would obey anyhow, out of terror.

Would that be enough?

Tushratta could hardly wait to find out.

A SPANISH LESSON

Lucius Shepard

Here's a mystery-filled novelette about a young man living on Spain's Costa del Sol who becomes involved with people who are . . . not of this world. Just what their world is becomes gradually clear as the story approaches its memorable climax.

Lucius Shepard burst onto the science fiction/fantasy scene a few years ago with a large number of beautifully written, strangely imagined stories including his first novel, Green Eyes. *In 1985 he easily won the John W. Campbell Award as the best new writer in the genre.*

That winter of '64 when I was seventeen and prone to obey the impulses of my heart as if they were illuminations produced by years of contemplative study, I dropped out of college and sailed to Europe, landing in Belfast, hitchhiking across Britain, down through France and Spain, and winding up on the Costa del Sol—to be specific, in a village near Malaga by the name of Pedregalejo—where one night I was to learn something of importance. What had attracted me to the village was not its quaintness, its vista of the placid Mediterranean and neat white stucco houses and little bandy-legged fishermen mending nets; rather, it was the fact that the houses along the shore were occupied by a group of expatriates, mostly Americans, who posed for me a bohemian ideal.

The youngest of them was seven years older than I, the

eldest three times my age, and among them they had amassed a wealth of experience that caused me envy and made me want to become like them: bearded, be-earringed, and travel-wise. There was, for example, Leonard Somstaad, a Swedish poet with the poetic malady of a weak heart and a fondness for *marjoun* (hashish candy); there was Art Shapiro, a wanderer who had for ten years migrated between Pedregalejo and Istanbul; there was Don Washington, a black ex-GI and blues singer, whose Danish girlfriend—much to the delight of the locals—was given to nude sunbathing; there was Robert Braehme, a New York actor who, in the best theatrical tradition, attempted halfheartedly to kill several of the others, suffered a nervous breakdown, and had to be returned to the States under restraint.

And then there was Richard Shockley, a tanned, hooknosed man in his late twenties, who was the celebrity of the group. A part-time smuggler (mainly of marijuana) and a writer of some accomplishment. His first novel, *The Celebrant*, had created a minor critical stir. Being a fledgling writer myself, it was he whom I most envied. In appearance and manner he suited my notion of what a writer should be. For a while he took an interest in me, teaching me smuggling tricks and lecturing on the moral imperatives of art; but shortly thereafter he became preoccupied with his own affairs and our relationship deteriorated.

In retrospect I can see that these people were unremarkable; but at the time they seemed impossibly wise, and in order to align myself with them, I rented a small beach house, bought a supply of notebooks, and began to fill them with page after page of attempted poetry.

Though I had insinuated myself into the group, I was not immediately accepted. My adolescence showed plainly against the backdrop of their experience. I had no store of anecdotes, no expertise with flute or guitar, and my conversation was lacking in hip savoir faire. In their eyes I was a kid, a baby, a clever puppy who had learned how to beg, and I was often the object of ridicule. Three factors saved me from worse ridicule: my size (six foot three, one-ninety), my erratic temper, and my ability to consume enormous quantities of drugs. This last was my great trick, my means of gaining respect. I would perform feats of ingestion that would leave Don Washington, a consummate doper, shaking his head in awe. Pills, powders, herbs—I was indiscriminate, and I initiated several dangerous dependencies in hopes of achieving equal status.

Six weeks after moving to the beach, I raised myself a notch in the general esteem by acquiring a girlfriend, a fey California blonde named Anne Fisher. It amuses me to recall the event that led Anne to my bed, because it smacked of the worst of cinema verité, an existential moment opening onto a bittersweet romance. We were walking on the beach, a rainy day, sea and sky blending in a slate fog toward Africa, both of us stoned near to the point of catatonia, when we happened upon a drowned kitten. Had I been unaccompanied, I might have inspected the corpse for bugs and passed on; but as it was, being under Anne's scrutiny, I babbled some nonsense about "this inconstant image of the world," half of which I was parroting from a Eugenio Montale poem, and proceeded to give the kitten decent burial beneath a flat rock.

After completing this nasty chore, I stood and discovered Anne staring at me wetly, her maidenly nature overborne by my unexpected sensitivity. No words were needed. We were alone on the beach, with Nina Simone's bluesy whisper issuing from a window of one of the houses, gray waves slopping at our feet. As if pressed together by the vast emptiness around us, we kissed. Anne clawed my back and ground herself against me: you might have thought she had been thirsting for me all her nineteen years, but I came to understand that desperation was born of philosophical bias and not sexual compulsion. She was deep into sadness as a motif for passion, and she liked thinking of us as two worthless strangers united by a sudden perception of life's pathetic fragility. Fits of weeping and malaise alternating with furious bouts of lovemaking were her idea of romantic counterpoint.

By the time she left me some months later, I had grown thoroughly sick of her; but she had—I believed—served her purpose in establishing me as a full-fledged expatriate.

Wrong. I soon found that I was still the kid, the baby, and I realized that I would remain so until someone of even lesser status moved to the beach, thereby nudging me closer to the mainstream. This didn't seem likely, and in truth I no longer cared. I had lost respect for the group: had I not, at seventeen, become as hiply expatriated as they, and wouldn't I, when I reached their age, be off to brighter horizons? Then as is often the case with reality, presenting us with what we desire at the moment desire begins to flag, two suitably substandard people rented the house next to mine.

Their names were Tom and Alise, and they were identical twins a couple of years older than I, hailing from—if you were to believe their story—Canada. Yet they had no knowledge of things Canadian, and their accent was definitely northern European. Not an auspicious entrée into a society as picky as Pedregalejo's. Everyone was put off by them, especially Richard Shockley, who saw them as a threat. "Those kind of people make trouble for everybody else," he said to me once. "They're just too damn weird." (It has always astounded me that those who pride themselves on eccentricity are so quick to deride this quality in strangers.) Others as well testified to the twins' weirdness: they were secretive, hostile; they had been seen making strange passes in the air on the beach, and that led some to believe they were religious nuts; they set lanterns in their windows at night and left them burning until dawn.

Their most disturbing aspect, however, was their appearance. Both were scarcely five feet tall, emaciated, pale, with black hair and squinty dark eyes and an elfin cleverness of feature that Shockley described as "prettily ugly, like Munchkins." He suggested that this look might be a product of inbreeding, and I thought he might be right: the twins had the sort of dulled presence that one associates with the retarded or the severely tranquilized. The fishermen treated them as if they were the devil's spawn, crossing themselves and spitting at the sight of them, and the expatriates were concerned that the fishermen's enmity would focus the attention of the Guardia Civil upon the beach.

The Guardia—with their comic-opera uniforms, their machine guns, their funny patent leather hats that from a distance looked like Mickey Mouse ears—were a legitimate menace. They had a long-standing reputation for murder and corruption, and were particularly fond of harassing foreigners. Therefore I was not surprised when a committee led by Shockley asked me to keep an eye on my new neighbors, the idea being that we should close ranks against them, even to the point of reporting any illegalities.

Despite knowing that refusal would consolidate my status as a young nothing, I told Shockley and his pals to screw off. I'm not able to take pride in this—had they been friendlier to me in the past, I might have gone along with the scheme; but as it was, I was happy to reject them. And further, in the spirit of revenge, I went next door to warn Tom and Alise.

My knock roused a stirring inside the house, whispers, and at last the door was cracked and an eye peeped forth. "Yes?" said Alise.

"Uh," I said, taken aback by this suspicious response. "My name's Lucius: From next door. I've got something to tell you about the people around here." Silence. "They're afraid of you," I went on. "They're nervous, because they've got dope and stuff, and they think you're going to bring the cops down on them."

Alise glanced behind her, more whispers, and then she said, "Why would we do that?"

"It's not that you'd do it on purpose," I said. "It's just that you're . . . different. You're attracting a lot of attention, and everyone's afraid that the cops will investigate you and then decide to bust the whole beach."

"Oh." Another conference, and finally she said, "Would you please come in?"

The door swung open, creaking like a coffin lid centuries closed, and I crossed the threshold. Tom was behind the door, and after shutting it, Alise ranged herself beside him. Her chest was so flat, their features so alike, it was only the length of her hair that allowed me to tell them apart. She gestured at a table-and-chairs set in the far corner, and, feeling a prickle of nervousness, I took a seat there. The room was similar to the living room of my house: white-washed walls, unadorned and flaking; cheap production-line furniture (the signal difference being that they had two beds instead of one); a gas stove in a niche to the left of the door. Mounted just above the light switch was a plastic crucifix; a frayed cord ran up behind the cross to the fixture on the ceiling, giving the impression that Christ had some role to play in the transmission of the current.

They had kept the place scrupulously neat; the one sign of occupancy was a pile of notebooks and a sketch-pad lying on the table. The pad was open to what appeared to be a rendering of complex circuitry. Before I could get a better look at it, Tom picked up the pad and tossed it onto the stove. Then they sat across from me, hands in their laps, as meek and quiet as two white mice. It was dark in the room, knife-edges of golden sunlight slanting through gaps in the shutter boards, and the twins' eyes were like dirty smudges on their pale skins.

"I don't know what more to tell you," I said. "And I don't have any idea what you should do. But I'd watch myself." They did not exchange glances or in any way visibly communicate, yet there was a peculiar tension to their silence, and I had the notion that they were again conferring: this increased my nervousness.

"We realize we're different," said Tom at length; his voice had the exact pitch and timbre of Alise's, soft and faintly burred. "We don't want to cause harm, but there's something we have to do here. It's dangerous, but we have to do it. We can't leave until it's done."

"We think you're a good boy," chimed in Alise, rankling me with this characterization. "We wonder if you would help us?"

I was perplexed. "What can I do?"

"The problem is one of appearances," said Tom. "We can't change the way we look, but perhaps we can change the way others perceive us. If we were to become more a part of the community, we might not be so noticeable."

"They won't have anything to do with you," I told him. "They're too. . . ."

"We have an idea," Alise cut in.

"Yes," said Tom. "We thought if there was the appearance of a romantic involvement between you and Alise, people might take us for granted. We hoped you would be agreeable to having Alise move in with you."

"Now wait!" I said, startled. "I don't mind helping you, but I. . . ."

"It would only be for appearances' sake," said Alise, deadpan. "There'd be no need for physical contact, and I would try not to be an imposition. I could clean for you and do the shopping."

Perhaps it was something in Alise's voice or a subtle shift in attitude, but for whatever reason, it was then that I sensed their desperation. They were very, very afraid . . . of what, I had no inkling. But fear was palpable, a thready pulse in the air. It was a symptom of my youth that I did not associate their fear with any potential threat to myself; I was merely made the more curious. "What sort of danger are you in?" I asked.

Once again there was that peculiar nervy silence, at the end of which Tom said, "We ask that you treat this as a confidence."

"Sure," I said casually. "Who am I gonna tell?"

The story Tom told was plausible; in fact, considering my own history—a repressive, intellectual father who considered me a major disappointment, who had characterized my dropping out as "the irresponsible actions of a glandular case"—it seemed programmed to enlist my sympathy. He said that they were not Canadian but German, and had been raised by a dictatorial stepfather after their mother's death. They had been beaten, locked in closets, and fed so poorly that their growth had been affected. Several months before, after almost twenty years of virtual confinement, they had managed to escape, and since then they had kept one step ahead of detectives hired by the stepfather. Now, penniless, they were trying to sell some antiquities that they had stolen from their home; and once they succeeded in this, they planned to travel east, perhaps to India, where they would be beyond detection. But they were afraid that they would be caught while waiting for the sale to go through; they had had too little practice with the world to be able to pass as ordinary citizens.

"Well," I said when he had finished. "If you want to move in"—I nodded at Alise—"I guess it's all right. I'll do what I can to help you. But first thing you should do is quit leaving lanterns in your window all night. That's what really weirds the fishermen out. They think you're doing some kind of magic or something." I glanced back and forth between them. "What are you doing?"

"It's just a habit," said Alise. "Our stepfather made us sleep with the lights on."

"You'd better stop it," I said firmly; I suddenly saw myself playing Anne Sullivan to their Helen Keller, paving their way to a full and happy life, and this noble self-image caused me to wax enthusiastic. "Don't worry," I told them. "Before I'm through, you people are going to pass for genu-*wine* All-American freaks. I guarantee it!"

If I had expected thanks, I would have been disappointed. Alise stood, saying that she'd be right back, she was going to pack her things, and Tom stared at me with an expression that—had I not been so pleased with myself—I might have recognized for pained distaste.

The beach at Pedregalejo inscribed a grayish white crescent for about a hundred yards along the Mediterranean, bounded on the west by a rocky point and on the east by a condominium under construction, among the first of many that were gradually to obliterate the beauty of the coast. Beyond the beachfront houses occupied by the expatriates were several dusty streets lined with similar houses, and beyond them rose a cliff of ocher rock surmounted by a number of villas, one of which had been rented by an English actor who was in the area shooting a bullfighting movie: I had been earning my living of late as an extra on the film, receiving the equivalent of five dollars a day and lunch (also an equivalent value, consisting of a greasy sandwich and soda pop).

My house was at the extreme eastern end of the beach and differed from the rest in that it had a stucco porch that extended into the water. Inside, as mentioned, it was almost identical to the twins' house; but despite this likeness, when Alise entered, clutching an airline bag to her chest, she acted as if she had walked into an alien spacecraft. At first, ignoring my invitation to sit, she stood stiffly in the corner, flinching every time I passed; then, keeping as close to the walls as a cat exploring new territory, she inspected my possessions, peeking into my backpack, touching the strings of my guitar, studying the crude watercolors with which I had covered up flaking spots in the whitewash. Finally she sat at the table, knees pressed tightly together, and stared at her hands. I tried to draw her into a conversation but received mumbles in reply, and eventually, near sunset, I took a notebook and a bagful of dope, and went out onto the porch to write.

When I was even younger than I was in 1964, a boy, I'd

assumed that all seas were wild storm-tossed enormities, rife with monsters and mysteries; and so at first sight, the relatively tame waters of the Mediterranean had proved a disappointment. However as time had passed, I'd come to appreciate the Mediterranean's subtle shifts in mood. On that particular afternoon the sea near to shore lay in a rippled sheet stained reddish orange by the dying light; farther out, a golden haze obscured the horizon and made the skeletal riggings of the returning fishing boats seem like the crawling of huge insects in a cloud of pollen. It was the kind of antique weather from which you might expect the glowing figure of Agamemnon, say, or of some martial Roman soul to emerge with ghostly news concerning the sack of Troy or Masada.

I smoked several pipefuls of dope—it was Moroccan kef, a fine grade of marijuana salted with flecks of white opium—and was busy recording the moment in overwrought poetry, when Alise came up beside me and, again reminding me of a white mouse, sniffed the air. "What's that?" she asked, pointing at the pipe. I explained and offered a toke. "Oh, no," she said, but continued peering at the dope and after a second added, "My stepfather used to give us drugs. Pills that made us sleepy."

"This might do the same thing," I said airily, and went back to my scribbling.

"Well," she said a short while later. "Perhaps I'll try a little."

I doubt that she had ever smoked before. She coughed and hacked, and her eyes grew red-veined and weepy, but she denied that the kef was having any effect. Gradually, though, she lapsed into silence and sat staring at the water; then, perhaps five minutes after finishing her last pipe, she ran into the house and returned with a sketchpad. "This is wonderful," she said. "Wonderful! Usually it's so hard to see." And began sketching with a charcoal pencil.

I giggled, taking perverse delight in having gotten her high, and asked, "What's wonderful?" She merely shook her head, intent on her work. I would have pursued the question, but at that moment I noticed a group of expatriates strolling toward us along the beach. "Here's your chance to act normal," I said, too stoned to recognize the cruelty of my words.

She glanced up. "What do you mean?"

I nodded in the direction of the proto-hippies. They appeared to be as ripped as we were: one of the women was doing a clumsy, skipping dance along the tidal margin, and the others were staggering, laughing, shouting encouragement. Silhouetted against the violent colors of sunset with their floppy hats and jerky movements, they had the look of shadow actors in a medieval mystery play. "Kiss me," I suggested to Alise. "Or act affectionate. Reports of your normalcy will be all over the beach before dark."

Alise's eyes widened, but she set down her pad. She hesitated briefly then edged her chair closer; she leaned forward, hesitated again, waiting until the group had come within good viewing range, and pressed her lips to mine.

Though I was not in the least attracted to Alise, kissing her was a powerful sexual experience. It was a chaste kiss. Her lips trembled but did not part, and it lasted only a matter of seconds; yet for its duration, as if her mouth had been coated with some psychochemical, my senses sharpened to embrace the moment in microscopic detail. Kissing had always struck me as a blurred pleasure, a smashing together of pulpy flesh accompanied by a flurry of groping. But with Alise I could feel the exact conformation of our lips, the minuscule changes in pressure as they settled into place, the rough material of her blouse grazing my arm, the erratic measures of her breath (which was surprisingly sweet). The delicacy of the act aroused me as no other kiss had before, and when I drew back I half-expected her to have been transformed into a beautiful princess. Not so. She was as ever small and pale. Prettily ugly.

Stunned, I turned toward the beach. The expatriates were gawping at us, and their astonishment reoriented me. I gave them a cheery wave, put my arm around Alise and, inclining my head to hers in a pretense of young love, I led her into the house.

That night I went to sleep while she was off visiting Tom. I tried to station myself on the extreme edge of the bed, leaving her enough room to be comfortable; but by the time she returned, I had rolled onto the center of the mattress, and when she slipped in beside me, turning on her side, her thin buttocks cupped spoon-style by my groin, I came drowsily awake and realized that my erection was butting between her legs. Once again physical contact with her caused a sharpening of my senses, and due to the intimacy of the contact, my desire, too, was sharpened. I could no more have stopped myself than I could have stopped breathing. Gently, as gently as though she were the truest of trueloves—and, indeed, I felt that sort of tenderness toward her—I began moving against her, thrusting more and more forcefully until I had eased partway inside. All this time she had made no sound, no comment, but now she cocked her leg back over my hip, wriggled closer and let me penetrate her fully.

It had been a month since Anne had left, and I was undeniably horny; but not even this could explain the fervor of my performance that night. I lost track of how many times we made love. And yet we never exchanged endearments, never spoke or in any way acknowledged one another as lovers. Though Alise's breath quickened, her face remained set in that characteristic deadpan, and I wasn't sure if she was deriving pleasure from the act or simply providing a service, paying rent. It didn't matter. I was having enough fun for both of us. The last thing I recall is that she had mounted me, female superior, her skin glowing ghost-pale in the dawn light, single-scoop breasts barely jiggling; her charcoal eyes were fixed on the wall, as if she saw there an important destination toward which she was galloping me post-haste.

My romance with Alise—this, and the fact that she and Tom had taken to smoking vast amounts of kef and wandering the beach glassy-eyed, thus emulating the behavior of the other expatriates—had more or less the desired effect upon everyone . . . everyone except Richard Shockley. He accosted me on my way to work one morning and told me in no uncertain terms that if I knew what was good for me, I should break all ties with the twins. I had about three inches and thirty pounds on him, and—for reasons I will shortly explain—I was in an irascible mood: I gave him a push and asked him to keep out of my business or suffer the consequences.

"You stupid punk!" he said, but backed away.

"Punk?" I laughed—laughter has always been for me a

spark to fuel rage—and followed him. "Come on, Rich. You can work up a better insult than that. A verbal guy like you. Come on! Give me a reason to get really crazy."

We were standing in one of the dusty streets back of the beach, not far from a bakery, a little shop with dozens of loaves of bread laid neatly in the window, and that moment a member of the Guardia Civil poked his head out the door. He was munching a sweet roll, watching us with casual interest: a short, swarthy man, wearing an olive green uniform with fancy epaulets, an automatic rifle slung over his shoulder, and sporting one of those goofy patent leather hats. Shockley blanched at the sight, wheeled around and walked away. I was about to walk away myself, but the guardsman beckoned. With a sinking feeling in the pit of my stomach. I went over to him.

"*Cobarde*," he said, gesturing at Shockley.

My Spanish was poor, but I knew that word: *coward*. "Yeah," I said. "In *inglés*, *cobarde* means chickenshit."

"Cheek-sheet," he said; then, more forcefully: "Cheek-sheet!"

He asked me to teach him some more English; he wanted to know all the curse words. His name was Francisco, he had fierce bad breath, and he seemed genuinely friendly. But I knew damn well that he was most likely trying to recruit me as an informant. He talked about his family in Seville, his girlfriend, how beautiful it was in Spain. I smiled, kept repeating, "*Sí, sí*," and was very relieved when he had to go off on his rounds.

Despite Shockley's attitude, the rest of the expatriates began to accept the twins, lumping us together as weirdos of the most perverted sort, yet explicable in our weirdness. From Don Washington I learned that Tom, Alise, and I were thought to be involved in a ménage à trois, and when I attempted to deny this, he said it was no big thing. He did ask, however, what I saw in Alise. I gave some high school reply about it all being the same in the dark, but in truth I had no answer to his question. Since Alise had moved in, my life had assumed a distinct pattern. Each morning I would hurry off to Malaga to work on the movie set; each night I would return home and enter into brainless rut with Alise. I found this confusing. Separated from Alise, I felt only mild pity for her, yet her proximity would drive me into a lustful frenzy. I lost interest in writing, in Spain, in everything except Alise's undernourished body. I slept hardly at all, my temper worsened, and I began to wonder if she were a witch and had ensorcelled me. Often I would come home to discover her and Tom sitting stoned on my porch, the floor littered with sketches of those circuitlike designs (actually they less resembled circuits than a kind of mechanistic vegetation). I asked once what they were. "A game," replied Alise, and distracted me with a caress.

Two weeks after she moved in, I shouted at the assistant director of the movie (he had been instructing me on how to throw a wineskin with the proper degree of adulation as the English actor-matador paraded in triumph around the bullring) and was fired. After being hustled off the set. I vowed to get rid of Alise, whom I blamed for all my troubles. But when I arrived home, she was nowhere to be seen. I stumped over to Tom's house and pounded on the door. It swung open, and I peeked inside. Empty. Half a dozen notebooks were scattered on the floor. Curiosity overrode my anger. I stepped in and picked up a notebook.

The front cover was decorated with a hand-drawn swastika, and while it is not uncommon to find swastikas on notebook covers—they make for entertaining doodling—the sight of this one gave me a chill. I leafed through the pages, noticing that though the entries were in English, there were occasional words and phrases in German, these having question marks beside them, then I went back and read the first entry.

> *The Führer had been dead three days, and still no one had ventured into the office where he had been exposed to the poisoned blooms, although a servant had crawled along the ledge to the window and returned with the news that the corpse was stiffened in its leather tunic, its cheeks bristling with a dead man's growth and strings of desiccated blood were hanging from its chin. But as we well remembered his habit of reviving the dead for a final bout of torture, we were afraid that he might have set an igniter in his cells to ensure rebirth, and so we*

*waited while the wine in his goblet turned to vinegar
and then to a murky gas that hid him from our view.
Nothing had changed. The garden of hydrophobic
roses fertilized with his blood continued to lash and
slather, and the hieroglyphs of his shadow selves
could be seen patrolling the streets.*

The entry went on in like fashion for several pages,
depicting a magical-seeming Third Reich ruled by a dead
or moribund Hitler, policed by shadow men known collec-
tively as the Disciples, and populated by a terrified citi-
zenry. All the entries were similar in character, but in the
margins were brief notations, most having to do with
either Tom's or Alise's physical state, and one passage in
particular caught my eye:

*Alise's control of her endocrine system continues
to outpace mine. Could this simply be a product of
male and female differences? It seems likely, since
we have all else in common.*

Endocrine? Didn't that have something to do with glands
and secretions? and if so, couldn't this be a clue to Alise's
seductive powers? I wished that old Mrs. Adkins (General
Science, fifth period) had been more persevering with me.
I picked up another notebook. No swastika on the cover,
but on the foreleaf was written: "Tom and Alise, 'born'
March 1944." The entire notebook contained a single
entry, apparently autobiographical, and after checking out
the window to see if the twins were in sight, I sat down to
read it.

Five pages later I had become convinced that Tom was
either seriously crazy or that he and Alise were the subjects of an insane Nazi experiment . . . or both. The word
clone was not then in my vocabulary, but this was exactly
what Tom claimed that he and Alise were. They, he said,
along with eighteen others, had been grown from a single
cell (donor unknown), part of an attempt to speed up
development of a true Master Race. A successful attempt,
according to him, for not only were the twenty possessed
of supernormal physical and mental abilities, but they were
stronger and more handsome than the run of humanities:

this seemed to me wish fulfillment pure and simple, and other elements of the story—for example, the continuation of an exotic Third Reich past 1945—seemed delusion. But upon reading further, learning that they had been sequestered in a cave for almost twenty years, being educated by scientific personnel, I realized that Tom and Alise could have been told these things and have assumed their truth. One could easily make a case for some portion of the Reich having survived the war.

I was about to put down the notebook when I noticed several loose sheets of paper stuck in the rear; I pulled them out and unfolded them. The first appeared to be a map of part of a city, with a large central square labeled "Citadel," and the rest were covered in a neat script that—after reading a paragraph or two—I deduced to be Alise's.

Tom says that since I'm the only one ever to leave the caves (before we all finally left them, that is) I should set down my experiences. He seems to think that having even a horrid past is preferable to having none, and insists that we should document it as well as we can. For myself, I would like to forget the past, but I'll write down what I remember to satisfy his compulsiveness.

When we were first experimenting with the tunnel, we knew nothing more about it than that it was a metaphysical construct of some sort. Our control of it was poor and we had no idea how far it reached or through what medium penetrated. Nor had we explored it to any great extent. It was terrifying. The only constant was that it was always dark, with fuzzy, different-colored lights shining at what seemed tremendous distances away. Often you would feel disembodied, and sometimes your body was painfully real, subject to odd twinges and shocks. Sometimes it was hard to move—like walking through black glue, and other times it was as if the darkness were a frictionless substance that squeezed you along faster than you wanted to go. Horrible afterimages materialized and vanished on all sides—monsters, animals, things to which I couldn't put a name. We

*were almost as frightened of the tunnel as we were
of our masters. Almost.*

*One night after the guards had taken some of the
girls into their quarters, we opened the tunnel and
three of us entered it. I was in the lead when our
control slipped and the tunnel began to constrict. I
started to turn back, and the next I knew I was
standing under the sky, surrounded by windowless
buildings. Warehouses, I think. The street was deserted, and I had no idea where I was. In a panic, I
ran down the street and soon I heard the sounds of
traffic. I turned a corner and stopped short. A broad
avenue lined with gray buildings—all decorated with
carved eagles—led away from where I stood and
terminated in front of an enormous building of black
stone. I recognized it at once from pictures we had
been shown—Hitler's Citadel.*

*Though I was still very afraid, perhaps even more
so, I realized that I had learned two things of importance. First, that no matter through what otherworldly medium it stretched, the tunnel also negotiated
a worldly distance. Second, I understood that the
portrait painted of the world by our masters was more
or less accurate. We had never been sure of this,
despite having been visited by Disciples and other of
Hitler's creatures, their purpose being to frighten us
into compliance.*

*I only stood a few minutes in that place, yet I'll
never be able to forget it. No description could
convey its air of menace, its oppressiveness. The
avenue was thronged with people, all—like our
guards—shorter and less attractive than I and my
siblings, all standing stock-still, silent, and gazing at
the Citadel. A procession of electric cars was passing through their midst, blowing horns, apparently to
celebrate a triumph, because no one was obstructing
their path. Several Disciples were prowling the fringes
of the crowd, and overhead a huge winged shape
was flying. It was no aircraft; its wings beat, and it
swooped and soared like a live thing. Yet it must
have been forty or fifty feet long. I couldn't make out
what it was; it kept close to the sun, and therefore*

*was always partly in silhouette. (I should mention
that although the sun was at meridian, the sky was a
deep blue such as I have come to associate with the
late afternoon skies of this world, and the sun itself
was tinged with red, its globe well defined—I think it
may have been farther along the path to dwarfism
than the sun of this world.) All these elements
contributed to the menace of the scene, but the
dominant force was the Citadel. Unlike the other
buildings, no carvings adorned it. No screaming
eagles, no symbols of terror and war. It was a
construct of simple curves and straight lines; but
that simplicity implied an animal sleekness, commu-
nicated a sense of great power under restraint, and I
had the feeling that at any moment the building
might come alive and devour everyone within its reach.
It seemed to give its darkness to the air.*

*I approached a man standing nearby and asked
what was going on. He looked at me askance, then
checked around to see if anyone was watching us.
"Haven't you heard?" he said.*

"I've been away," I told him.

*This, I could see, struck him as peculiar, but he
accepted the fact and said, "They thought he was
coming back to life, but it was a false alarm. Now
they're offering sacrifices."*

*The procession of cars had reached the steps of the
Citadel, and from them emerged a number of people
with their hands bound behind their backs, and a lesser
number of very large men, who began shoving them up
the steps toward the main doors. Those doors swung
open, and from the depths of the Citadel issued a
kind of growling music overlaid with fanfares of trumpets. A reddish glow—feeble at first, then brightening
to a blaze—shone from within. The light and the music
set my heart racing. I backed away, and as I did, I
thought I saw a face forming in the midst of that red
glow. Hitler's face, I believe. But I didn't wait to vali-
date this. I ran, ran as hard as I could back to the
street behind the warehouses, and there, to my relief, I
discovered that the tunnel had once again been opened.*

*   *   *

I leaned back, trying to compare what I had read with my knowledge of the twins. Those instances of silent communication. Telepathy? Alise's endocrinal control. Their habit of turning lamps on to burn away the night—could this be some residual behavior left over from cave life? Tom had mentioned that the lights had never been completely extinguished, merely dimmed. Was this all an elaborate fantasy he had concocted to obscure their pitiful reality? I was certain this was the case with Alise's testimony. Whatever, I found that I was no longer angry at them, that they had been elevated in my thoughts from nuisance to mystery. Looking back, I can see that my new attitude was every bit as discriminatory as my previous one. I felt for them an adolescent avidity such as I might have exhibited toward a strange pet. They were neat, weird, with the freakish appeal of Venus's-flytraps and sea monkeys. Nobody else had one like them, and having them to myself made me feel superior. I would discover what sort of tricks they could perform, take notes on their peculiarities, and then, eventually growing bored, I'd move along to a more consuming interest. Though I was intelligent enough to understand that this attitude was—in its indulgence and lack of concern for others—typically ugly-American, I saw no harm in adopting it. Why, they might even benefit from my attention.

At that moment I heard voices outside. I skimmed the notebook toward the others on the floor and affected nonchalance. The door opened; they entered and froze upon seeing me. "Hi," I said. "Door was open, so I waited for you here. What have you been up to?"

Tom's eyes flicked to the notebooks, and Alise said, "We've been walking."

"Yeah?" I said this with great good cheer, as if pleased that they had been taking exercise. "Too bad I didn't get back earlier. I could have gone with you."

"Why *are* you back?" asked Tom, gathering the notebooks.

I didn't want to let on about the loss of my job, thinking that the subterfuge would give me a means of keeping track of them. "Some screwup on the set," I told him. "They had to put off filming. What say we go into town?"

From that point on, no question I asked them was

casual; I was always testing, probing, trying to ferret out some of their truth.

"Oh, I don't know," said Tom. "I thought I'd have a swim."

I took a mental note: Why do subjects exhibit avoidance of town? For an instant I had an unpleasant vision of myself, a teenage monster gloating over his two gifted white mice, but this was overborne by my delight in the puzzle they presented. "Yeah," I said breezily. "A swim would be nice."

That night making love with Alise was a whole new experience. I wasn't merely screwing; I was exploring the unknown, penetrating mystery. Watching her pale, passionless face, I imagined the brain behind it to be a strange, glowing jewel, with facets instead of convolutions. *National Enquirer* headlines flashed through my head. Nazi Mutants Alive in Spain. American Teen Uncovers Hitler's Secret Plot. Of course there would be no such publicity. Even if Tom's story were true—and I was far from certain that it was—I had no intention of betraying them. I wasn't that big a jerk.

For the next month I maintained the illusion that I was still employed by the film company, and left home each morning at dawn; but rather than catching the bus into Malaga, I would hide between the houses, and as soon as Tom and Alise went off on one of their walks (they always walked west along the beach, vanishing behind a rocky point), I would sneak into Tom's house and continue investigating the notebooks. The more I read, the more firmly I believed the story. There was a flatness to the narrative tone that reminded me of a man I had heard speaking about the concentration camps, dully recounting atrocities, staring into space, as if the things he said were putting him into a trance. For example:

> . . . *It was on July 2nd that they came for Urduja and Klaus. For the past few months, they had been making us sleep together in a room lit by harsh fluorescents. There were no mattresses, no pillows, and they took our clothes so we could not use them as covering. It was like day under those trays of*

white light, and we lay curled around each other for warmth. They gassed us before they entered, but we had long since learned how to neutralize the gas, and so we were all awake, linked, pretending to be asleep. Three of them came into the room, and three more stood at the door with guns. At first it seemed that this would be just another instance of rape. The three men violated Urduja one after the other. She kept up her pretense of unconsciousness, but she felt everything. We tried to comfort her, sending out our love and encouragement. But I could sense her hysteria, her pain. They were rough with her, and when they had finished, her thighs were bloody. She was very brave and gave no cry; she was determined not to give us away. Finally they picked her and Klaus up and carried them off. An hour later we felt them die. It was horrible, as if part of my mind had short-circuited, a corner of it left forever dim.

We were angry and confused. Why would they kill what they had worked so hard to create? Some of us, Uwe and Peter foremost among them, wanted to give up the tunnel and revenge ourselves as best we could; but the rest of us managed to calm things down. Was it revenge we wanted, we asked, or was it freedom? If freedom was to be our choice, then the tunnel was our best hope. Would I—I wonder—have lobbied so hard for the tunnel if I had known that only Alise and I would survive it?

The story ended shortly before the escape attempt was to be made; the remainder of the notebooks contained further depictions of that fantastic Third Reich—genetically created giants who served as executioners, fountains of blood in the squares of Berlin, dogs that spoke with human voices and spied for the government—and also marginalia concerning the twins' abilities, among them being the control of certain forms of energy: these particular powers had apparently been used to create the tunnel. All this fanciful detail unsettled me, as did several elements of the story. Tom had stated that the usual avenues of escape had been closed to the twenty clones, but what was a tunnel if not a usual avenue of escape? Once he had mentioned that the tunnel was "unstable." What did that mean? And he seemed to imply that the escape had not yet been effected.

By the time I had digested the notebooks, I had begun to notice the regular pattern of the twins' walks; they would disappear around the point that bounded the western end of the beach, and then a half hour later, they would return, looking worn-out. Perhaps, I thought, they were doing something there that would shed light on my confusion, and so one morning I decided to follow them.

The point was a spine of blackish rock shaped like a lizard's tail that extended about fifty feet out into the water. Tom and Alise would always wade around it. I, however, scrambled up the side and lay flat like a sniper atop it. From my vantage I overlooked a narrow stretch of gravelly shingle, a little trough scooped out between the point and low, brown hills that rolled away inland. Tom and Alise were sitting ten or twelve feet below, passing a kef pipe, coughing, exhaling billows of smoke.

That puzzled me. Why would they come here just to get high? I scrunched into a more comfortable position. It was a bright, breezy day; the sea was heaving with a light chop, but the waves slopping onto the shingle were ripples. A few fishing boats were herding a freighter along the horizon. I turned my attention back to the twins. They were standing, making peculiar gestures that reminded me of T'ai Chi, though these were more labored.

Then I noticed that the air above the tidal margin had become distorted as with a heat haze . . . yet it was not hot in the least. I stared at the patch of distorted air—it was growing larger and larger—and I began to see odd translucent shapes eddying within it: they were similar to the shapes that the twins were always sketching. There was a funny pressure in my ears; a drop of sweat slid down the hollow of my throat, leaving a cold track.

Suddenly the twins broke off gesturing and leaned against each other; the patch of distorted air misted away. The twins were breathing heavily, obviously exhausted. They sat down a couple of feet from the water's edge, and after a long silence Tom said, "We should try again to be certain."

"Why don't we finish it now?" said Alise. "I'm so tired of this place."

"It's too dangerous in the daylight." Tom shied a pebble out over the water. "If they're waiting at the other end, we might have to run. We'll need the darkness for cover."

"What about tonight?"

"I'd rather wait until tomorrow night. There's supposed to be a storm front coming, and nobody will be outside."

Alise sighed.

"What's wrong?" Tom asked. "Is it Lucius?"

I listened with even more intent.

"No," she said. "I just want it to be over."

Tom nodded and gazed out to sea. The freighter looked to have moved a couple of inches eastward; gulls were flying under the sun, becoming invisible as they passed across its glaring face, and then swooping away like bits of winged matter blown from its core. Tom picked up the kef pipe. "Let's try it again," he said.

At that instant someone shouted, "Hey!" Richard Shockley came striding down out of the hills behind the shingle. Tom and Alise got to their feet. "I can't believe you people are so fucking uncool," said Shockley, walking up to them; his face was dark with anger, and the breeze was lashing his hair, as if it, too, were enraged. "What the hell are you trying to do? Get everyone busted?"

"We're not doing anything," said Alise.

"Naw!" sneered Shockley. "You're just breaking the law in plain view. Plain fucking view!" His fists clenched, and I thought for a moment he was going to hit them. They were so much smaller than he that they looked like children facing an irate parent.

"You won't have to be concerned with us much longer," said Tom. "We're leaving soon."

"Good," said Shockley. "That's real good. But lemme tell you something, man. I catch you smoking out here again, and you might be leaving quicker than you think."

"What do you mean?" asked Alise.

"Don't you worry about what I fucking mean," said Shockley. "You just watch your behavior. We had a good scene going here until you people showed up, and I'll be damned if I'm going to let you blow it." He snatched the pipe from Tom's hand and slung it out to sea. He shook his finger in Tom's face. "I swear, man! One more fuckup, and I'll be on you like white on rice!'' Then he stalked off around the point.

As soon as he was out of sight, without a word exchanged between them, Tom and Alsie waded into the water and began groping beneath the surface, searching for the pipe. To my amazement, because the shallows were murky and full of floating litter, they found it almost instantly.

I was angry at Shockley, both for his treatment of the twins and for his invasion of what I considered my private preserve, and I headed toward his house to tell him to lay off. When I entered I was greeted by a skinny, sandy-haired guy—Skipper by name—who was sprawled on pillows in the front room; from the refuse of candy wrappers, crumpled cigarette packs, and empty pop bottles surrounding him, I judged him to have been in this position for quite some time. He was so opiated that he spoke in mumbles and he could scarcely open his eyes, but from him I learned the reason for Shockley's outburst. ''You don't wanna see him now, man,'' said Skipper, and flicked out his tongue to retrieve a runner of drool that had leaked from the corner of his mouth. ''Dude's on a rampage, y'know?''

''Yeah,'' I said. ''I know.''

''Fucker's paranoid,'' said Skipper. ''Be paranoid myself if I was holding a key of smack.''

''Heroin?''

''King H,'' said Skipper with immense satisfaction, as if pronouncing the name of his favorite restaurant, remembering past culinary treats. ''He's gonna run it up to Copenhagen soon as— ''

''Shut the hell up!'' It was Shockley, standing in the front door. ''Get out,'' he said to me.

''Be a pleasure.'' I strolled over to him. ''The twins are leaving tomorrow night. Stay off their case.''

He squared his shoulders, trying to be taller. ''Or what?''

''Gee, Rich,'' I said. ''I'd hate to see anything get in the way of your mission to Denmark.''

Though in most areas of experience I was a neophyte compared to Shockley, he was just a beginner compared to me as regarded fighting. I could tell a punch was coming from the slight widening of his eyes, the tensing of his shoulders. It was a silly, schoolgirlish punch. I stepped inside it, forced him against the wall, and jammed my forearm under his chin. "Listen, Rich," I said mildly. "Nobody wants trouble with the Guardia, right?" My hold prevented him from speaking, but he nodded. Spit bubbled between his teeth. "Then there's no problem. You leave the twins alone, and I'll forget about the dope. O.K.?" Again he nodded. I let him go, and he slumped to the floor, holding his throat. "See how easy things go when you just sit down and talk about them?" I said, and grinned. He glared at me. I gave him a cheerful wink and walked off along the beach.

I see now that I credited Shockley with too much wisdom; I assumed that he was an expert smuggler and would maintain a professional calm. I underestimated his paranoia and gave no thought to his reasons for dealing with a substance as volatile as heroin: they must have involved a measure of desperation, because he was not a man prone to taking whimsical risks. But I wasn't thinking about the consequences of my actions. After what I had seen earlier beyond the point, I believed that I had figured out what Tom and Alise were up to. It seemed implausible, yet equally inescapable. And if I was right, this was my chance to witness something extraordinary. I wanted nothing to interfere.

Gray clouds blew in the next morning from the east, and a steady downpour hung a silver beaded curtain from the eaves of my porch. I spent the day pretending to write and watching Alise out of the corner of my eye. She went about her routines, washing the dishes, straightening up, sketching—the sketching was done with a bit more intensity than usual. Finally, late that afternoon having concluded that she was not going to tell me she was leaving, I sat down beside her at the table and initiated a conversation. "You ever read science fiction?" I asked.

"No," she said, and continued sketching.

"Interesting stuff. Lots of weird ideas. Time travel, aliens. . . ." I jiggled the table, causing her to look up, and fixed her with a stare. "Alternate worlds."

She tensed but said nothing.

"I've read your notebooks," I told her.

"Tom thought you might have." She closed the sketchpad.

"And I saw you trying to open the tunnel yesterday. I know that you're leaving."

She fingered the edge of the pad. I couldn't tell if she was nervous or merely thinking.

I kept after her. "What I can't figure out is *why* you're leaving. No matter who's chasing you, this world can't be as bad as the one described in the notebooks. At least we don't have anything like the Disciples."

"You've got it wrong," she said after a silence. "The Disciples are of my world."

I had more or less deduced what she was admitting to, but I hadn't really been prepared to accept that it was true, and for a moment I retrenched, believing again that she was crazy, that she had tricked me into swallowing her craziness as fact. She must have seen this in my face or read my thoughts, because she said then, "It's the truth."

"I don't understand," I said. "Why are you going back?"

"We're not; we're going to collapse the tunnel, and to do that we have to activate it. It took all of us to manage it before; Tom and I wouldn't have been able to see the configurations clearly enough if it hadn't been for your drugs. We owe you a great deal." A worry line creased her brow. "You mustn't spy on us tonight. It could be dangerous."

"Because someone might be waiting," I said. "The Disciples?"

She nodded. "We think one followed us into the tunnel and was trapped. It apparently can't control the fields involved in the tunnel, but if it's nearby when we activate the opening. . . ." She shrugged.

"What'll you do if it is?"

"Lead it away from the beach," she said.

She seemed assured in this, and I let the topic drop. "What are they, anyway?" I asked.

"Hitler once gave a speech in which he told us they were magical reproductions of his soul. Who knows? They're horrid enough for that to be true."

"If you collapse the tunnel, then you'll be safe from pursuit. Right?"

"Yes."

"Then why leave Pedregalejo?"

"We don't fit in," she said, and let the words hang in the air a few seconds. "Look at me. Can you believe that in my world I'm considered beautiful?"

An awkward silence ensued. Then she smiled. I'd never seen her smile before. I can't say it made her beautiful—her skin looked dead pale in the dreary light, her features asexual—but in the smile I could detect the passive confidence with which beauty encounters the world. It was the first time I had perceived her as a person and not as a hobby, a project.

"But that's not the point," she went on. "There's somewhere we want to go."

"Where?"

She reached into her airline bag, which was beside the chair, and pulled out a dog-eared copy of *The Tibetan Book of the Dead*. "To find the people who understand this."

I scoffed. "You believe that crap?"

"What would you know?" she snapped. "It's chaos inside the tunnel. It's. . . ." She waved her hand in disgust, as if it weren't worth explaining anything to such an idiot.

"Tell me about it," I said. Her anger had eroded some of my skepticism.

"If you've read the notebooks, you've seen my best attempt at telling about it. Ordinary referents don't often apply inside the tunnel. But it appears to pass by places described in this book. You catch glimpses of lights, and you're drawn to them. You seem to have an innate understanding that the lights are the entrances to worlds, and you sense that they're fearsome. But you're afraid that if you don't stop at one of them, you'll be killed. The others let themselves be drawn. Tom and I kept going. This light, this world, felt less fearsome than the rest." She gave a doleful laugh. "Now I'm not so sure."

"In one of the notebooks," I said, "Tom wrote that the others didn't survive."

"He doesn't really know," she said. "Perhaps he wrote that to make himself feel better about having wound up here. That would be like him."

We continued talking until dark. It was the longest time I had spent in her company without making love, and yet—because of this abstinence—we were more lovers then than we had ever been before. I listened to her not with an eye toward collecting data, but with genuine interest, and though everything she told me about her world smacked of insanity, I believed her. There were, she said, rivers that sprang from enormous crystals, birds with teeth, bats as large as eagles, cave cities, wizards, winged men who inhabited the thin Andean air. It was a place of evil grandeur, and at its heart, its ruler, was the dead Hitler, his body uncorrupting, his death a matter of conjecture, his terrible rule maintained by a myriad of servants in hopes of his rebirth.

At the time, Alise's world seemed wholly alien to me, as distinct from our own as Jupiter or Venus. But now I wonder if—at least in the manner of its rule—it is not much the same: Are we not also governed by the dead, by the uncorrupting laws they have made, laws whose outmoded concepts enforce a logical tyranny upon a populace that no longer meets their standards of morality? And I wonder further if each alternate world (Alise told me they were infinite in number) is but a distillation of the one adjoining, and if somewhere at the heart of this complex lies a compacted essence of a world, a blazing point of pure principle that plays cosmic Hitler to its shadow selves.

The storm that blew in just after dark was like the Mediterranean an age-worn elemental. Distant thunder, a few strokes of lightning spreading glowing cracks down the sky, a blustery wind. Alise cautioned me again against following her, and told me she'd be back to say goodbye. I told her I'd wait, but as soon as she and Tom had left, I set out toward the point. I would no more have missed their performance than I would have turned down, say, a free ticket to see the Rolling Stones. A few drops of rain were falling, but a foggy moon was visible through high clouds inland. Shadows were moving in the lighted windows of the houses; shards of atonal jazz alternated with mournful gusts of wind.

Once Tom and Alise glanced back, and I dropped flat in the mucky sand, lying flat until they had waded around the point. By the time I reached the top of the rocks, the rain had stopped. Directly below me were two shadows and the glowing coal of the kef pipe. I was exhilarated. I wished my father were there so I could say to him, "All your crap about 'slow and steady wins the race,' all your rationalist bullshit, it doesn't mean anything in the face of this. There's mystery in the world, and if I'd stayed in school, I'd never have known it."

I was so caught up in thinking about my father's reactions that I lost track of Tom and Alise. When I looked down again, I found that they had taken a stand by the shore and were performing those odd, graceful gestures. Just beyond them, its lowest edge level with the water, was a patch of darkness blacker than night, roughly circular and approximately the size of a circus ring. Lightning was still striking down out to sea, but the moon had sailed clear of the clouds, staining silver the surrounding hilltops, bringing them close, and in that light I could see that the patch of darkness had depth . . . depth, and agitated motion. Staring into it was like staring into a fire while hallucinating, watching the flames adopt the forms of monsters, only in this case there were no flames but the vague impressions of monstrous faces melting up from the tunnel walls, showing a shinier black, then fading. I was at an angle to the tunnel, and while I could see inside it, I could also see that it had no exterior walls, that it was a hole hanging in midair, leading to an unearthly distance. Every muscle in my body was clenched, pressure was building in my ears, and I heard a static hiss overriding the grumble of thunder and the mash of the waves against the point.

My opinion of the twins had gone up another notch. Anyone who would enter that fuming nothingness was worthy of respect. They looked the image of courage: two pale children daring the darkness to swallow them. They kept on with their gestures until the depths of the tunnel began to pulse like a black gulping throat. The static hiss grew louder, oscillating in pitch, and the twins tipped their heads to the side, admiring their handiwork.

Then a shout in Spanish, a beam of light probing at the twins from the seaward reach of the point.

Seconds later Richard Shockley splashed through the shallows and onto shore; he was holding a flashlight, and the wind was whipping his hair. Behind him came a short dark-skinned man carrying an automatic rifle, wearing the hat and uniform of the Guardia Civil. As he drew near I recognized him to be Francisco, the guardsman who had tried to cozy up to me. He had a Band-Aid on his chin, which—despite his weapon and traditions—made him seem an innocent.

The two men's attention was fixed on the twins, and they didn't notice the tunnel, though they passed close to its edge. Francisco began to harangue the twins in Spanish, menacing them with his gun.

I crept nearer and heard the word *heroína*. Heroin. I managed to hear enough to realize what had happened. Shockley, either for the sake of vengeance or—more likely—panicked by what he considered a threat to his security, had planted heroin in Tom's house and informed on him, hoping perhaps to divert suspicion and ingratiate himself with the Guardia. Alise was denying the charges, but Francisco was shouting her down.

And then he caught sight of the tunnel. His mouth fell open and he backed against the rocks directly beneath me.

Shockley spotted it, too. He shined his flashlight into the tunnel, and the beam was sheared off where it entered the blackness, as if it had been bitten in half. For a moment they were frozen in a tableau. Only the moonlight seemed in motion, coursing along Francisco's patent leather hat.

What got into me then was not bravery or any analogue thereof, but a sudden violent impulse such as had often landed me in trouble. I jumped feet first onto Francisco's back. I heard a grunt as we hit the ground, a snapping noise, and the next I knew I was scrambling off him, reaching for his gun, which had flown a couple of yards away. I had no clue of how to operate the safety or even of where it was located. But Shockley wasn't aware of that. His eyes were popped, and he sidled along the rocks toward the water, his head twitching from side to side, searching for a way out.

Hefting the cold, slick weight of the gun gave me a sense of power—a feeling tinged with hilarity—and as I came to my feet, aiming at Shockley's chest, I let out a purposefully demented laugh. "Tell me, Rich," I said. "Do you believe in God?"

He held out a hand palm-up and said, "Don't," in a choked voice.

"Remember that garbage you used to feed me about the moral force of poetry?" I said. "How you figure that jibes with setting up these two?" I waved the rifle barrel at the twins; they were staring into the tunnel, unmindful of me and Shockley.

"You don't understand," said Shockley.

"Sure I do, Rich." I essayed another deranged-teenage-killer laugh. "You're not a nice guy."

In the moonlight his face looked glossy with sweat. "Wait a minute," he said. "I'll. . . ."

Then Alise screamed, and I never did learn what Shockley had in mind. I spun around and was so shocked that I nearly dropped the gun. The tunnel was still pulsing, its depths shrinking and expanding like the gullet of a black worm, and in front of it stood a . . . my first impulse is to say "a shadow," but that description would not do justice to the Disciple. To picture it you must imagine the mold of an androgynous human body constructed from a material of such translucency that you couldn't see it under any condition of light; then you must further imagine that the mold contains a black substance (negatively black) that shares the proper ties of both gas and fluid, which is slipping around inside, never filling the mold completely—at one moment presenting to you a knife-edge, the next a frontal silhouette, and at other times displaying all the other possible angles of attitude, shifting among them. Watching it made me dizzy. Tom and Alise cowered from it, and when it turned full face to me, I, too, cowered. Red, glowing pin-pricks appeared in the places where its eyes should have been, the pin-pricks swelled, developing into real eyes. The pupils were black planets eclipsing bloody suns.

I wanted to run, but those eyes held me. Insanity was like a heat in them. They radiated fury, loathing, hatred, and I wonder now if anything human, even some perverted fraction of mad Hitler's soul, could have achieved such an alien resolve. My blood felt as thick as syrup, my scrotum tightened. Then something splashed behind me, and though I couldn't look away from the eyes, I knew that Shockley had run. The Disciple moved after him. And how it moved!

It was as if it were turning sideways and vanishing, repeating the process over and over, and doing this so rapidly that it seemed to be strobing, winking in and out of existence, each wink transporting it several feet farther along. Shockley never had a chance. It was too dark out near the end of the point for me to tell what really happened, but I saw two shadows merge and heard a bubbling scream.

A moment later the Disciple came whirling back toward the shore.

Instinctively I clawed the trigger of Francisco's gun—the safety had not been on. Bullets stitched across the Disciple's torso, throwing up geysers of blackness that almost instantly were reabsorbed into his body, as if by force of gravity. Otherwise they had no effect. The Disciple stopped just beyond arm's reach, nailing me with its burning gaze, flickering with the rhythm of a shadow cast by a fire. Only its eyes were constant, harrowing me.

Somone shouted—I think it was Tom, but I'm not sure; I had shrunk so far within myself that every element of the scene except the glowing red eyes had a dim value. Abruptly the Disciple moved away. Tom was standing at the mouth of the tunnel. When the Disciple had come half the distance toward him, he took a step forward and—like a man walking into a black mirror—disappeared.

The Disciple sped into the tunnel after him. For a time I could see their shapes melting up and fading among the other, more monstrous shapes.

A couple of minutes after they had entered it, the tunnel collapsed. Accompanied by a keening hiss, the interior walls constricted utterly and flecks of ebony space flew up from the mouth. Night flowed in to take its place. Alise remained standing by the shore, staring at the spot where the tunnel had been. In a daze, I walked over and put an arm around her shoulder, wanting to comfort her. But she shook me off and went a few steps into the water, as if to say that she would rather drown than accept my consolation.

My thoughts were in chaos, and needing something to focus them, I knelt beside Francisco, who was still lying facedown. I turned him onto his back, and his head turned with a horrid, grating sound. Blood and sand crusted his mouth. He was dead, his neck broken. For a long while I sat there, noticing the particulars of death, absorbed by them: how the blood within him had begun to settle to one side, discoloring his cheek/how his eyes, though glazed, had maintained a bewildered look. The Band-Aid on his chin had come unstuck, revealing a shaving nick. I might have sat there forever, hypnotized by the sight; but then a bank of clouds overswept the moon, and the pitch-darkness shocked me, alerted me to the possible consequences of what I had done.

From that point on I was operating in a kind of luminous panic, inspired by fear to acts of survival. I dragged Francisco's body into the hills; I waded into the water and found Shockley's body floating in the shallows. Every inch of his skin was horribly charred, and as I hauled him to his resting place beside Francisco, black flakes came away on my fingers. After I had covered the bodies with brush, I led Alise—by then unresisting—back to the house, packed for us both, and hailed a taxi for the airport. There I had a moment of hysteria, realizing that she would not have a passport. But she did. A Canadian one, forged in Malaga. We boarded the midnight flight to Casablanca, and the next day—because I was still fearful of pursuit—we began hitchhiking east across the desert.

Our travels were arduous. I had only three hundred dollars, and Alise had none. Tom's story about their having valuables to sell had been more or less true, but in our haste we had left them behind. In Cairo, partly due to our lack of funds and partly to medical expenses incurred by Alise's illness (amoebic dysentery), I was forced to take a job. I worked for a perfume merchant in the Khan el-Khalili Bazaar, steering tourists to his shop, where they could buy rare essences and drugs and change money at the black market rates. In order to save enough to pay our passage east, I began to cheat my employer, servicing some of his clients myself—and when he found me out, I had to flee with Alise, who had not yet shaken her illness.

I felt responsible for her, guilty about my role in the proceedings. I'd come to terms with Francisco's death. Naturally I regretted it, and sometimes I would see that dark, surprised face in my dreams. But acts of violence did not trouble my heart then as they do now. I had grown up violent in a violent culture, and I was able to rationalize the death as an accident. And, too, it had been no saint I had killed.

I could not, however, rationalize my guilt concerning Alise, and this confounded me. Hadn't I tried to save her and Tom? I realized that my actions had essentially been an expression of adolescent fury, yet they had been somewhat on the twins' behalf. And no one could have stood against the Disciple. What more could I have done? Nothing, I told myself. But this answer failed to satisfy me.

In Afghanistan, Alise suffered a severe recurrence of her dysentery. This time I had sufficient funds (money earned by smuggling, thanks to Shockley's lessons) to avoid having to work, and we rented a house on the outskirts of Kabul. We lived there three months, until she had regained her health. I fed her yogurt, red meat, vegetables; I bought her books and a tape recorder and music to play on it; I brought people in whom I thought she might be interested to visit her.

I wish I could report that we grew to be friends, but she had withdrawn into herself and thus remained a mystery to me, something curious and inexplicable. She would lie in her room—a cubicle of white washed stone—with the sunlight slanting in across her bed, paling her further, transforming her into a piece of ivory sculpture, and would gaze out the window for hours, seeing, I believe, not the exotic traffic on the street—robed horsemen from the north, ox-drawn carts, and Chinese-made trucks—but some otherworldly vista. Often I wanted to ask her more about her world, about the tunnel and Tom and a hundred other things. But while I could not institute a new relationship with her, I did not care to reinstitute our previous one. And so my questions went unasked. And so certain threads of this narrative must be left untied, reflecting the messiness of reality as opposed to the neatness of fiction.

Though this story is true, I do not ask that you believe it. To my mind it is true enough, and if you have read it to the end, then you have sufficiently extended your belief. In any case, it is a verity that the truth becomes a lie when it is written down, and it is the art of writing to wring as much truth as possible from its own dishonest fabric. I have but a single truth to offer, one that came home to me on the last day I saw Alise, one that stands outside both the story and the act of writing it.

We had reached the object of our months-long journey, the gates of a Tibetan nunnery on a hill beneath Dhaulagiri in Nepal, a high blue day with a chill wind blowing. It was here that Alise planned to stay. Why? She never told me more than she had in our conversation shortly before she and Tom set out to collapse the tunnel. The gates—huge wooden barriers carved with the faces of gods—swung open, and the female lamas began to applaud, their way of frightening off demons who might try to enter. They formed a crowd of yellow robes and tanned, smiling faces that seemed to me another kind of barrier, a deceptively plain facade masking some rarefied contentment. Alise and I had said a perfunctory good-bye, but as she walked inside, I thought—I hoped—that she would turn back and give vent to emotion.

She did not. The gates swung shut, and she was gone into the only haven that might accept her as commonplace.

Gone, and I had never really known her.

I sat down outside the gates, alone for the first time in many months, with no urgent destination or commanding purpose, and took stock. High above, the snowy fang of Dhaulagiri rared against a cloudless sky; its sheer faces depended to gentler slopes seamed with the ice-blue tongues of glaciers, and those slopes eroded into barren brown hills such as the one upon which the nunnery was situated. That was half the world.

The other half, the half I faced, was steep green hills terraced into barley fields, and winding through them a river, looking as unfeatured as a shiny aluminum ribbon. Hawks were circling the middle distance, and somewhere, perhaps from the monastery that I knew to be off among the hills, a horn sounded a great bass note like a distant dragon signaling its hunger or its rage.

I sat at the center of these events and things, at the dividing line of these half-worlds that seemed to me less in opposition than equally empty, and I felt that emptiness pouring into me. I was so empty, I thought that if the wind were to strike me at the correct angle, I might chime like a bell . . . and perhaps it did, perhaps the clarity of the Himalayan weather and this sudden increment of emptiness acted to produce a tone, an illumination, for I saw myself then as Tom and Alise must have seen me. Brawling, loutish, indulgent. The two most notable facts of my life were negatives: I had killed a man, and I had encountered the unknown and let it elude me. I tried once again to think what more I could have done, and this time, rather than arriving at the usual conclusion, I started to understand what lesson I had been taught on the beach at Pedregalejo.

Some years ago a friend of mine, a writer and a teacher of writing, told me that my stories had a tendency to run on past the climax, and that I frequently ended them with a moral, a technique he considered outmoded. He was, in the main, correct. But it occurs to me that sometimes a moral—whether or not clearly stated by the prose—is what provides us with the real climax, the good weight that makes the story resonate beyond the measure of the page. So, in this instance, I will go contrary to my friend's advice and tell you what I learned, because it strikes me as being particularly applicable to the American consciousness, which is insulated from much painful reality, and further because it relates to a process of indifference that puts us all at risk.

When the tragedies of others become for us diversions, sad stories with which to enthrall our friends, interesting bits of data to toss out at cocktail parties, a means of presenting a pose of political concern, or whatever . . . when this happens we commit the gravest of sins, condemn ourselves to ignominy, and consign the world to a dangerous course. We begin to justify our casual overview of pain and suffering by portraying ourselves as do-gooders incapacitated by the inexorable forces of poverty, famine, and war. "What can I do?" we say. "I'm only one person, and these things are beyond my control. I care about the world's trouble, but there are no solutions."

Yet no matter how accurate this assessment, most of us are relying on it to be true, using it to mask our indulgence, our deep-seated lack of concern, our pathological self-involvement. In adopting this attitude we delimit the possibilities for action by letting events progress to a point at which, indeed, action becomes impossible, at which we can righteously say that nothing can be done. And so we are born, we breed, we are happy, we are sad, we deal with consequential problems of our own, we have cancer or a car crash, and in the end our actions prove insignificant. Some will tell you to feel guilt or remorse over the vast inaction of our society is utter foolishness; life, they insist, is patently unfair, and all anyone can do is to look out for his own interests. Perhaps they are right; perhaps we are so mired in our self-conceptions that we can change nothing. Perhaps this is the way of the world. But, for the sake of my soul and because I no longer wish to hide my sins behind a guise of mortal incapacity, I tell you it is not.

SNOW

John Crowley

When you lose your beloved wife to death, all you really have left are memories of her. But in the future, perhaps there will be the means to store recordings of everything she did—providing you can pay for the mechanism that makes this possible. And even if you can, you may find that there are problems in such memory recordings too.

John Crowley's novels include Engine Summer *and* Little, Big.

I don't think Georgie would ever have got one for herself: She was at once unsentimental and a little in awe of death. No, it was her first husband—an immensely rich and (from Georgie's description) a strangely weepy guy, who had got it for her. Or for himself, actually, of course. He was to be the beneficiary. Only he died himself shortly after it was installed. If *installed* is the right word. After he died, Georgie got rid of most of what she'd inherited from him, liquidated it. It was cash that she had liked best about that marriage anyway; but the Wasp couldn't really be got rid of. Georgie ignored it.

In fact the thing really was about the size of a wasp of the largest kind, and it had the same lazy and mindless fight. And of course it really was a bug, not of the insect kind but of the surveillance kind. And so its name fit all around: one of those bits of accidental poetry the world generates without thinking. O Death, where is thy sting?

166

Georgie ignored it, but it was hard to avoid; you had to be a little careful around it; it followed Georgie at a variable distance, depending on her motions and the numbers of other people around her, the level of light, and the tone of her voice. And there was always the danger you might shut it in a door or knock it down with a tennis racket.

It cost a fortune (if you count the access and the perpetual-care contract, all prepaid), and though it wasn't really fragile, it made you nervous.

It wasn't recording all the time. There had to be a certain amount of light, though not much. Darkness shut it off. And then sometimes it would get lost. Once when we hadn't seen it hovering around for a time, I opened a closet door, and it flew out, unchanged. It went off looking for her, humming softly. It must have been shut in there for days.

Eventually it ran out, or down. A lot could go wrong, I suppose, with circuits that small, controlling that many functions. It ended up spending a lot of time bumping gently against the bedroom ceiling, over and over, like a winter fly. Then one day the maids swept it out from under the bureau, a husk. By that time it had transmitted at least eight thousand hours (eight thousand was the minimum guarantee) of Georgie: of her days and hours, her comings in and her goings out, her speech and motion, her living self—all on file, taking up next to no room, at The Park. And then, when the time came, you could go there, to The Park, say on a Sunday afternoon; and in quiet landscaped surroundings (as The Park described it) you would find her personal resting chamber; and there, in privacy, through the miracle of modern information storage and retrieval systems, you could access her; her alive, her as she was in every way, never changing or growing any older, fresher (as The Park's brochure said) than in memory ever green.

I married Georgie for her money, the same reason she married her first, the one who took out The Park's contract for her. She married me, I think, for my looks; she always had a taste for looks in men. I wanted to write. I made a calculation that more women than men make, and decided that to be supported and paid for by a rich wife would give me freedom to do so, to "develop." The calculation worked out no better for me than it does for most women who make it. I carried a typewriter and a case of miscellaneous paper from Ibiza to Gstaad to Bial to London, and typed on beaches, and learned to ski. Georgie liked me in ski clothes.

Now that those looks are all but gone, I can look back on myself as a young hunk and see that I was in a way a rarity, a type that you run into often among women, far less among men, the beauty unaware of his beauty, aware that he affects women profoundly and more or less instantly but doesn't know why; thinks he is being listened to and understood, that his soul is being seen, when all that's being seen is long-lashed eyes and a strong, square, tanned wrist turning in a lovely gesture, stubbing out a cigarette. Confusing. By the time I figured out why I had for so long been indulged and cared for and listened to, why I was interesting, I wasn't as interesting as I had been. At about the same time I realized I wasn't a writer at all. Georgie's investment stopped looking as good to her, and my calculation had ceased to add up; only by that time I had come, pretty unexpectedly, to love Georgie a lot, and she just as unexpectedly had come to love and need me too, as much as she needed anybody. We never really parted, even though when she died I hadn't seen her for years. Phone calls, at dawn or four A.M. because she never, for all her travel, really grasped that the world turns and cocktail hour travels around with it. She was a crazy, wasteful, happy woman, without a trace of malice or permanence or ambition in her—easily pleased and easily bored and strangely serene despite the hectic pace she kept up. She cherished things and lost them and forgot them: things, days, people. She had fun, though, and I had fun with her; that was her talent and her destiny, not always an easy one. Once, hung over in a New York hotel, watching a sudden snowfall out the immense window, she said to me, "Charlie, I'm going to die of fun."

And she did. Snow-foiling in Austria, she was among the first to get one of those snow leopards, silent beasts as fast as speedboats. Alfredo called me in California to tell me, but with the distance and his accent and his eagerness to tell me *he* wasn't to blame, I never grasped the details.

I was still her husband, her closest relative, heir to the
little she still had, and beneficiary, too, of The Park's
access concept. Fortunately, The Park's services included
collecting her from the morgue in Gstaad and installing her
in her chamber at The Park's California unit. Beyond
signing papers and taking delivery when Georgie arrived
by freight airship at Van Nuys, there was nothing for me
to do. The Park's representative was solicitous and made
sure I understood how to go about accessing Georgie, but I
wasn't listening. I am only a child of my time, I suppose.
Everything about death, the fact of it, the fate of the
remains, and the situation of the living faced with it,
seems grotesque to me, embarrassing, useless. And everything done about it only makes it more grotesque, more
useless: Someone I loved is dead; let me therefore dress in
clown's clothes, talk backwards, and buy expensive machinery to make up for it. I went back to L.A.

A year or more later, the contents of some safe-deposit
boxes of Georgie's arrived from the lawyer's: some bonds
and such stuff and a small steel case, velvet lined, that
contained a key, a key deeply notched on both sides and
headed with smooth plastic, like the key to an expensive
car.

Why did I go to The Park that first time? Mostly because
I had forgotten about it: Getting that key in the mail was
like coming across a pile of old snapshots you hadn't cared
to look at when they were new but which after they have
aged come to contain the past, as they did not contain the
present. I was curious.

I understood very well that The Park and its access
concept were very probably only another cruel joke on the
rich, preserving the illusion that they can buy what can't
be bought, like the cryonics fad of thirty years ago. Once
in Ibiza, Georgie and I met a German couple who also had
a contract with The Park; their Wasp hovered over them
like a Paraclete and made them self-conscious in the
extreme—they seemed to be constantly rehearsing the eternal show being stored up for their descendants. Their
deaths had taken over their lives, as though they were
pharaohs. Did they, Georgie wondered, exclude the Wasp
from their bedroom? Or did its presence there stir them to

greater efforts, proofs of undying love and admirable vigor for the unborn to see?

No, death wasn't to be cheated that way, any more than by pyramids, by masses said in perpetuity. It wasn't Georgie saved from death that I would find. But there were eight thousand hours of her life with me, genuine hours, stored there more carefully than they could be in my porous memory; Georgie hadn't excluded the Wasp from her bedroom, our bedroom, and she who had never performed for anybody could not have conceived of performing for it. And there would be me, too, undoubtedly, caught unintentionally by the Wasp's attention: Out of those thousands of hours there would be hundreds of myself, and myself had just then begun to be problematic to me, something that had to be figured out, something about which evidence had to be gathered and weighed. I was thirty-eight years old.

That summer, then, I borrowed a Highway Access Permit (the old HAPpy cards of those days) from a county lawyer I knew and drove the coast highway up to where The Park was, at the end of a pretty beach road, all alone above the sea. It looked from the outside like the best, most peaceful kind of Italian country cemetery, a low stucco wall topped with urns, amid cypresses, an arched gate in the center. A small brass plaque on the gate: PLEASE USE YOUR KEY. The gate opened, not to a square of shaded tombstones but onto a ramped corridor going down: The cemetery wall was an illusion, the works were underground. Silence, or nameless Muzak-like silence; solitude— either the necessary technicians were discreetly hidden or none were needed. Certainly the access concept turned out to be simplicity itself, in operation anyway. Even I, who am an idiot about information technology, could tell that. The Wasp was genuine state-of-the-art stuff, but what we mourners got was as ordinary as home movies, as old letters tied up in ribbon.

A display screen near the entrance told me down which corridor to find Georgie, and my key let me into a small screening room where there was a moderate-size TV monitor, two comfortable chairs, and dark walls of chocolate-brown carpeting. The sweet-sad Muzak. Georgie herself was evidently somewhere in the vicinity, in the wall or under the floor, they weren't specific about the charnel-house aspect of the place. In the control panel before the TV were a keyhole for my key and two bars: ACCESS and RESET.

I sat, feeling foolish and a little afraid, too, made more uncomfortable by being so deliberately soothed by neutral furnishings and sober tools. I imagined, around me, down other corridors, in other chambers, others communed with their dead as I was about to do, that the dead were murmuring to them beneath the stream of Muzak; that they wept to see and hear, as I might, but I could hear nothing. I turned my key in its slot, and the screen lit up. The dim lights dimmed further, and the Muzak ceased. I pushed ACCESS, obviously the next step. No doubt all these procedures had been explained to me long ago at the dock when Georgie in her aluminum box was being off-loaded, and I hadn't listened. And on the screen she turned to look at me—only not at me, though I started and drew breath—at the Wasp that watched her. She was in mid-sentence, mid-gesture. Where? When? *Or put it on the same card with the others*, she said, turning away. Someone said something, Georgie answered, and stood up, the Wasp panning and moving erratically with her, like an amateur with a home-video camera. A white room, sunlight, wicker. Ibiza. Georgie wore a cotton blouse, open; from a table she picked up lotion, poured some on her hand, and rubbed it across her freckled breastbone. The meaningless conversation about putting something on a card went on, ceased. I watched the room, wondering what year, what season I had stumbled into. Georgie pulled off her shirt— her small round breasts tipped with large, childlike nipples, child's breasts she still had at forty, shook delicately. And she went out onto the balcony, the Wasp following, blinded by sun, adjusting. *If you want to do it that way*, someone said. The someone crossed the screen, a brown blur, naked. It was me. Georgie said: *Oh, look, hummingbirds*.

She watched them, rapt, and the Wasp crept close to her cropped blond head, rapt too, and I watched her watch. She turned away, rested her elbows on the balustrade. I couldn't remember this day. How should I? One of hundreds, of thousands. . . . She looked out to the bright sea, wearing her sleepwalking face, mouth partly open, and

absently stroked her breast with her oiled hand. An iridescent glitter among the flowers was the hummingbird.

Without really knowing what I did—I felt hungry, suddenly, hungry for pastness, for more—I touched the RESET
bar. The balcony in Ibiza vanished, the screen glowed
emptily. I touched ACCESS.

At first there was darkness, a murmur; then a dark back
moved away from before the Wasp's eye, and a dim scene
of people resolved itself. Jump. Other people, or the same
people, a party? Jump. Apparently the Wasp was turning
itself on and off according to the changes in light levels
here, wherever *here* was. Georgie in a dark dress having
her cigarette lit: brief flare of the lighter. She said, *Thanks.*
Jump. A foyer or hotel lounge. Paris? The Wasp jerkily
sought for her among people coming and going; it couldn't
make a movie, establishing shots, cutaways—it could only
doggedly follow Georgie, like a jealous husband, seeing
nothing else. This was frustrating. I pushed RESET. ACCESS.
Georgie brushed her teeth, somewhere, somewhen.

I understood, after one or two more of these terrible
leaps. Access was random. There was no way to dial up a
year, a day, a scene. The Park had supplied no program,
none; the eight thousand hours weren't filed at all; they
were a jumble, like a lunatic's memory, like a deck of
shuffled cards. I had supposed, without thinking about it,
that they would begin at the beginning and go on till they
reached the end. Why didn't they?

I also understood something else. If access was truly
random, if I truly had no control, then I had lost as good
as forever those scenes I had seen. Odds were on the order
of eight thousand to one (more? far more? probabilities are
opaque to me) that I would never light on them again by
pressing this bar. I felt a pang of loss for that afternoon in
Ibiza. It was doubly gone now. I sat before the empty
screen, afraid to touch ACCESS again, afraid of what I
would lose.

I shut down the machine (the light level in the room
rose, the Muzak poured softly back in) and went out into
the halls, back to the display screen in the entranceway.
The list of names slowly, greenly, rolled over like the list
of departing flights at an airport: Code numbers were
missing from beside many, indicating perhaps that they

weren't yet in residence, only awaited. In the *D*s, three names, and DIRECTOR—hidden among them as though he were only another of the dead. A chamber number. I went to find it and went in. The director looked more like a janitor or a night watchman, the semiretired type you often see caretaking little-visited places. He wore a brown smock like a monk's robe and was making coffee in a corner of his small office, out of which little business seemed to be done. He looked up startled, caught out, when I entered.

"Sorry," I said, "but I don't think I understand this system right."

"A problem?" he said. "Shouldn't be a problem." He looked at me a little wide-eyed and shy, hoping not to be called on for anything difficult. "Equipment's all working?"

"I don't know," I said. "It doesn't seem that it could be." I described what I thought I had learned about The Park's access concept. "That can't be right, can it?" I said. "That access is totally random . . ."

He was nodding, still wide-eyed, paying close attention.

"Is it?" I asked.

"Is it what?"

"Random."

"Oh, yes. Yes, sure. If everything's in working order."

I could think of nothing to say for a moment, watching him nod reassuringly. Then, "Why?" I asked. "I mean why is there no way at all to, to organize, to have some kind of organized access to the material?" I had begun to feel that sense of grotesque foolishness in the presence of death, as though I were haggling over Georgie's effects. "That seems stupid, if you'll pardon me."

"Oh no, oh no," he said. "You've read your literature? You've read all your literature?"

"Well, to tell the truth . . ."

"It's all just as described," the director said. "I can promise you that. If there's any problem at all. . . ."

"Do you mind," I said, "if I sit down?" I smiled. He seemed so afraid of me and my complaint, of me as mourner, possibly grief crazed and unable to grasp the simple limits of his responsibilities to me, that he needed soothing himself. "I'm sure everything's fine," I said. "I just don't think I understand. I'm kind of dumb about these things."

"Sure. Sure. Sure." He regretfully put away his coffee makings and sat behind his desk, lacing his fingers together like a consultant. "People get a lot of satisfaction out of the access here," he said, "a lot of comfort, if they take in the right spirit." He tried a smile. I wondered what qualifications he had had to show to get this job. "The random part. Now, it's all in the literature. There's the legal aspect—you're not a lawyer are you, no, no, sure, no offense. You see, the material here isn't *for* anything, except, well, except for communing. But suppose the stuff were programmed, searchable. Suppose there was a problem about taxes or inheritance or so on. There could be subpoenas, lawyers all over the place, destroying the memorial concept completely."

I really hadn't thought of that. Built-in randomness saved past lives from being searched in any systematic way. And no doubt saved The Park from being in the records business and at the wrong end of a lot of suits. "You'd have to watch the whole eight thousand hours," I said, "and even if you found what you were looking for there'd be no way to replay it. It would have gone by." It would slide into the random past even as you watched it, like that afternoon in Ibiza, that party in Paris. Lost. He smiled and nodded. I smiled and nodded.

"I'll tell you something," he said. "They didn't predict that. The randomness. It was a side effect, an affect of the storage process. Just luck." His grin turned down, his brows knitted seriously. "See, we're storing here at the molecular level. We have to go that small, for space problems. I mean your eight-thousand-hour guarantee. If we had gone tape or conventional, how much room would it take up? If the access concept caught on. A lot of room. So we went vapor trap and endless tracking. Size of my thumbnail. It's all in the literature." He looked at me strangely. I had a sudden intense sensation that I was being fooled, tricked, that the man before me in his smock was no expert, no technician; he was a charlatan, or maybe a madman impersonating a director and not belonging here at all. It raised the hair on my neck and passed. "So the randomness," he was saying. "It was an effect of going molecular. Brownian movement. All you do is lift the endless tracking for a microsecond and you get a rearrangement at the molecular level. We don't randomize. The molecules do it for us."

I remembered Brownian movement, just barely, from physics class. The random movement of molecules, the teacher said; it has a mathematical description. It's like the movement of dust motes you see swimming in a shaft of sunlight, like the swirl of snowflakes in a glass paperweight that shows a cottage being snowed on. "I see," I said. "I guess I see."

"Is there," he said, "any other problem?" He said it as though there might be some other problem and that he knew what it might be and that he hoped I didn't have it. "You understand the system, key lock, two bars, ACCESS, RESET. . . ."

"I understand," I said. "I understand now."

"Communing," he said, standing, relieved, sure I would be gone soon. "I understand. It takes a while to relax into the communing concept."

"Yes," I said. "It does."

I wouldn't learn what I had come to learn, whatever that was. The Wasp had not been good at storage after all, no, no better than my young soul had been. Days and weeks had been missed by its tiny eye. It hadn't seen well, and in what it had seen it had been no more able to distinguish the just-as-well-forgotten from the unforgettable than my own eye had been. No better and no worse—the same.

And yet, and yet—she stood up in Ibiza and dressed her breasts with lotion, and spoke to me: *Oh, look, humming-birds.* I had forgotten, and the Wasp had not; and I owned once again what I hadn't known I had lost, hadn't known was precious to me.

The sun was setting when I left The Park, the satin sea foaming softly, randomly around the rocks.

I had spent my life waiting for something, not knowing what, not even knowing I waited. Killing time. I was still waiting. But what I had been waiting for had already occurred and was past.

It was two years, nearly, since Georgie had died; two years until, for the first and last time, I wept for her—for her and for myself.

*　　*　　*

Of course I went back. After a lot of work and correctly placed dollars, I netted a HAPpy card of my own. I had time to spare, like a lot of people then, and often on empty afternoons (never on Sunday) I would get out onto the unpatched and weed-grown freeway and glide up the coast. The Park was always open. I relaxed into the communing concept.

Now, after some hundreds of hours spent there underground, now, when I have long ceased to go through those doors (I have lost my key, I think; anyway I don't know where to look for it), I know that the solitude I felt myself to be in was real. The watchers around me, the listeners I sensed in other chambers, were mostly my imagination. There was rarely anyone there.

These tombs were as neglected as any tombs anywhere usually are. Either the living did not care to attend much on the dead—when have they ever?—or the hopeful buyers of the contracts had come to discover the flaw in the access concept—as I discovered it, in the end.

ACCESS, and she takes dresses one by one from her closet, and holds them against her body, and studies the effect in a tall mirror, and puts them back again. She had a funny face, which she never made except when looking at herself in the mirror, a face made for no one but herself, that was actually quite unlike her. The mirror Georgie.

RESET.

ACCESS. By a bizarre coincidence here she is looking in another mirror. I think the Wasp could be confused by mirrors. She turns away, the Wasp adjusts; there is someone asleep, tangled in bedclothes on a big hotel bed, morning, a room-service cart. Oh, the Algonquin: myself. Winter. Snow is falling outside the tall window. She searches her handbag, takes out a small vial, swallows a pill with coffee, holding the cup by its body and not its handle. I stir, show a tousled head of hair. Conversation—unintelligible. Gray room, whitish snow light, color degraded. Would I now (I thought, watching us) reach out for her? Would I in the next hour take her, or she me, push aside the bedclothes, open her pale pajamas? She goes into the john, shuts the door. The Wasp watches stupidly, excluded, transmitting the door.

RESET, finally.

But what (I would wonder) if I had been patient, what if I had watched and waited?

Time, it turns out, takes an unconscionable time. The waste, the footless waste—it's no spectator sport. Whatever fun there is in sitting idly looking at nothing and tasting your own being for a whole afternoon, there is no fun in replaying it. The waiting is excruciating. How often, in five years, in eight thousand hours of daylight or lamplight, might we have coupled, how much time expended in lovemaking? A hundred hours, two hundred? Odds were not high of my coming on such a scene; darkness swallowed most of them, and the others were lost in the interstices of endless hours spent shopping, reading, on planes and in cars, asleep, apart. Hopeless.

ACCESS. She has turned on a bedside lamp. Alone. She hunts amid the Kleenex and magazines on the bedside table, finds a watch, looks at it dully, turns it right side up, looks again, and puts it down. Cold. She burrows in the blankets, yawning, staring, then puts out a hand for the phone but only rests her hand on it, thinking. Thinking at four A.M. She withdraws her hand, shivers a child's deep, sleepy shiver, and shuts off the light. A bad dream. In an instant it's morning, dawn; the Wasp slept, too. She sleeps soundly, unmoving, only the top of her blond head showing out of the quilt—and will no doubt sleep so for hours, watched over more attentively, more fixedly, than any peeping Tom could ever have watched over her.

RESET.

ACCESS.

"I can't hear as well as I did at first," I told the director. "And the definition is getting softer."

"Oh sure," the director said. "That's really in the literature. We have to explain that carefully. That this might be a problem."

"It isn't just my monitor?" I asked. "I thought it was probably only the monitor."

"No, no, not really, no," he said. He gave me coffee. We'd gotten to be friendly over the months. I think, as well as being afraid of me, he was glad I came around now and then; at least one of the living came here, one at least was using the services. "There's a *slight* degeneration that does occur."

"Everything seems to be getting gray."

His face had shifted into intense concern, no belittling this problem. "Mm-hm, mm-hm, see, at the molecular level where we're at, there *is* degeneration. It's just in the physics. It randomizes a little over time. So you lose—you don't lose a minute of what you've got, but you lose a little definition. A little color. But it levels off."

"It does?"

"We think it does. Sure it does, we promise it does. We *predict* that it will."

"But you don't know."

"Well, well you see we've only been in this business a short while. This concept is new. There were things we couldn't know." He still looked at me, but seemed at the same time to have forgotten me. Tired. He seemed to have grown colorless himself lately, old, losing definition. "You might start getting some snow," he said softly.

ACCESS RESET ACCESS.

A gray plaza of herringbone-laid stones, gray, clicking palms. She turns up the collar of her sweater, narrowing her eyes in a stern wind. Buys magazines at a kiosk: *Vogue, Harper's, La Mode. Cold*, she says to the kiosk girl. *Frio.* The young man I was takes her arm; they walk back along the beach, which is deserted and strung with cast seaweed, washed by a dirty sea. Winter in Ibiza. We talk, but the Wasp can't hear, the sea's sound confuses it; it seems bored by its duties and lags behind us.

RESET.

ACCESS. The Algonquin, terribly familiar morning, winter. She turns away from the snow window. I am in bed, and for a moment watching this I felt suspended between two mirrors, reflected endlessly. I had seen this before; I had lived it once and remembered it once, and remembered the memory, and here it was again, or could it be nothing but another morning, a similar morning. There were far more than one like this, in this place. But no; she turns from the window, she gets out her vial of pills, picks up the coffee cup by its body: I had seen this moment before, not months before, weeks before, here in this chamber. I had come upon the same scene twice.

What are the odds of it, I wondered, what are the odds of coming upon the same minutes again, these minutes.

I stir within the bedclothes.

I leaned forward to hear, this time, what I would say; it was something like *but fun anyway*, or something.

Fun, she says, laughing, harrowed, the degraded sound a ghost's twittering. *Charlie, someday I'm going to die of fun.*

She takes her pill. The Wasp follows her to the john, and is shut out.

Why am I here? I thought, and my heart was beating hard and slow. *What am I here for? What?*

RESET.

ACCESS.

Silvered icy streets, New York, Fifth Avenue. She is climbing, shouting from a cab's dark interior. *Just don't shout at me*, she shouts at someone; her mother I never met, a dragon. She is out and hurrying away down the sleety street with her bundles, the Wasp at her shoulder. I could reach out and touch her shoulder and make her turn and follow me out. Walking away, lost in the colorless press of traffic and people, impossible to discern within the softened snowy image.

Something was very wrong.

Georgie hated winter, she escaped it most of the time we were together, about the first of the year beginning to long for the sun that had gone elsewhere; Austria was all right for a few weeks, the toy villages and sugar snow and bright, sleek skiers were not really the winter she feared, though even in fire-warmed chalets it was hard to get her naked without gooseflesh and shudders from some draft only she could feel. We were chaste in winter. So Georgie escaped it: Antigua and Bali and two months in Ibiza when the almonds blossomed. It was continual false, flavorless spring all winter long.

How often could snow have fallen when the Wasp was watching her?

Not often; countable times, times I could count up

myself if I could remember as the Wasp could. Not often. Not always.

"There's a problem," I said to the director.

"It's peaked out, has it?" he said. "That definition problem?"

"Actually," I said, "it's gotten worse."

He was sitting behind his desk, arms spread wide across his chair's back, and a false, pinkish flush to his cheeks like undertaker's makeup. Drinking.

"Hasn't peaked out, huh?" he said.

"That's not the problem," I said. "The problem is the access. It's not random like you said."

"Molecular level," he said. "It's in the physics."

"You don't understand. It's not getting more random. It's getting less random. It's getting selective. It's freezing up."

"No, no, no," he said dreamily. "Access is random. Life isn't all summer and fun, you know. Into each life some rain must fall."

I sputtered, trying to explain. "But but . . ."

"You know," he said. "I've been thinking of getting out of access." He pulled open a drawer in the desk before him; it made an empty sound. He stared within it dully for a moment and shut it. "The Park's been good for me, but I'm just not used to this. Used to be you thought you could render a service, you know? Well, hell, you know, you've had fun, what do you care?"

He was mad. For an instant I heard the dead around me; I tasted on my tongue the stale air of underground.

"I remember," he said, tilting back in his chair and looking elsewhere, "many years ago, I got into access. Only we didn't call it that then. What I did was, I worked for a stock-footage house. It was going out of business, like they all did, like this place here is going to do, shouldn't say that, but you didn't hear it. Anyway, it was a big warehouse with steel shelves for miles, filled with film cans, film cans filled with old plastic film, you know? Film of every kind. And movie people, if they wanted old scenes of past time in their moves, would call up and ask for what they wanted, find me this, find me that. And we had everything, every kind of scene, but you know what the hardest thing to find was? Just ordinary scenes of daily

life. I mean people just doing things and living their
lives. You know what we *did* have? Speeches. People
giving speeches. Like presidents. You could have hours of
speeches, but not just people, whatchacallit, oh, washing
clothes, sitting in a park . . .''

"It might just be the reception," I said. "Somehow."

He looked at me for a long moment as though I had just
arrived. "Anyway," he said at last, turning away again,
"I was there awhile learning the ropes. And producers
called and said, 'Get me this, get me that.' And one
producer was making a film, some film of the past, and he
wanted old scenes, *old*, of people long ago, in the summer; having fun; eating ice cream; swimming in bathing
suits; riding in convertibles. Fifty years ago. Eighty years
ago.''

He opened his empty drawer again, found a toothpick,
and began to use it.

"So I accessed the earliest stuff. Speeches. More
speeches. But I found a scene here and there—people in
the street, fur coats, window-shopping, traffic. Old people, I mean they were young then, but people of the past;
they have these pinched kind of faces, you get to know
them. Sad, a little. On city streets, hurrying, holding their
hats. Cities were sort of black then, in film; black cars in
the streets, black derby hats. Stone. Well, it wasn't what
they wanted. I found summer for them, color summer, but
new. They wanted old. I kept looking back. I kept looking.
I did. The further back I went, the more I saw these
pinched faces, black cars, black streets of stone. Snow.
There isn't any summer there.''

With slow gravity he rose and found a brown bottle and
two coffee cups. He poured sloppily. "So it's not your
reception," he said. "Film takes longer, I guess, but it's
the physics. All in the physics. A word to the wise is
sufficient.''

The liquor was harsh, a cold distillate of past sunlight. I
wanted to go, get out, not look back. I would not stay
watching until there was only snow.

"So I'm getting out of access," the director said. "Let
the dead bury the dead, right? Let the dead bury the
dead.''

                    *   *   *

I didn't go back. I never went back, though the highways opened again and The Park isn't far from the town I've settled in. Settled; the right word. It restores your balance, in the end, even in a funny way your cheerfulness, when you come to know, without regrets, that the best thing that's going to happen in your life has already happened. And I still have some summer left to me.

I think there are two different kinds of memory, and only one kind gets worse as I get older: the kind where, by an effort of will, you can reconstruct your first car or your serial number or the name and figure of your high school physics teacher—a Mr. Holm, in a gray suit, a bearded guy, skinny, about thirty. The other kind doesn't worsen; if anything it grows more intense. The sleepwalking kind, the kind you stumble into as into rooms with secret doors and suddenly find yourself sitting not on your front porch but in a classroom. You can't at first think where or when, and a bearded, smiling man is turning in his hand a glass paperweight, inside which a little cottage stands in a swirl of snow.

There is no access to Georgie, except that now and then, unpredictably, when I'm sitting on the porch or pushing a grocery cart or standing at the sink, a memory of that kind will visit me, vivid and startling, like a hypnotist's snap of fingers.

Or like that funny experience you sometimes have, on the point of sleep, of hearing your name called softly and distinctly by someone who is not there.

SHANIDAR

David Zindell

In this legend from the far future, new writer David Zindell takes us to a strange world where life and death are very different from what we know, and quests can definitely be epic.

Zindell's first novel is forthcoming this year from Donald I. Fine Books, and those who've read his stories in Writers of the Future *and* Interzone *will be watching eagerly for it.*

He came into my cutting shop on a quiet night when the air was black and still, the only sound the far-off hissing and humming of the machines as they hovered over the city streets, melting and smoothing the ice for the following day. He was a pale young man with brown, lively eyes beneath the white hood of his parka, and he wore a beard so dense and black that you would have thought him born on Gehenna or Sheydveg and not, as he claimed, on Summerworld where the men are nearly hairless and their skin is as dark as coffee. With his heavy brows and large, muscular face he nearly had the look of the Alaloi which had been the fashion—you will presently understand why— some twenty years ago. As he stood there in the stone hallway knocking the slush from his skates, he explained that he had need of my services. "You are Rainer, the cutter?" he asked me in a low, conspiratorial voice. I told him that was what the people of the city called me. "I want you to use all your skills," he said. "I want to become an Alaloi."

I led him into my tearoom where he ejected the blades from his skates and flopped his dripping mittens on top of the marble table which I had imported from Urradeth at great cost. And though I didn't feel much like playing the host—my white tunic was spattered with blood and brains and I had matters to attend to—I offered him kvass or coffee and was surprised that he chose coffee.

"Kvass fogs the brain," he said, ignoring the frescoes on the stone walls around him and staring me in the eyes. "Drink makes men forget their purpose."

I sent for the domestic and I asked the young man, "And your purpose is to look like an Alaloi?"

He shook his head. "My purpose is to *become* an Alaloi. Completely."

I laughed and I said, "You know I can't do that; you know the law. I can change your flesh as you please but——"

"What about Goshevan?"

"Goshevan!" I shouted. "Why do the young men always come asking about Goshevan?" The domestic came and I embarrassed myself by shouting out an order for coffee and kvass. As it rolled away, I said, "There are more stories told about Goshevan than dead stars in the Vild. What do you know about Goshevan?"

"I know that he wanted what I want. He was a man with a dream who——"

"He was a dreamer! Do you want to know about Goshevan? I'll tell you the story that I tell all the young men who come to me seeking nightmares. Are you sitting comfortably? Then listen well. . . ."

The domestic brought our drink bubbling in two of those huge, insulated pots that they blow on Fostora. It clumsily poured the dark liquids into our delicate marble cups as I told the young man the story of Goshevan:

"There lived on Summerworld a young noble who took a greater interest in antiques and old books—some say he had been to Ksandaria and bribed the librarians into selling him part of the Kyoto collection of Old Earth—than he did in managing his estates. He was an erudite man who claimed that the proper study of man was man—not how to produce five tons more coffee per cubage. One day he tired of his life and said, 'My s-sons are weak-faced maggots who exist on the diseased flesh of this rotten civilization. They p-plot with my wives against me and laugh as my wives sleep with other men.' And so Goshevan sold his estates, freed his slaves, and told his family they would have to make their living by the sweat of their hands and the inspiration of their brains. He paid for a passage on a Darghinni long ship and made his way toward the Vild.

"Now everyone knows the Darghinni are tricksters and so is it any wonder they didn't warn him of the laughing pools on Darkmoon? Well, warn him they didn't, and Goshevan spent two seasons on that dim, lukewarm planet coughing at the lungmelt in his chest while the surgeons painstakingly cut the spirulli from his muscles and waited and watched and cut some more.

"When he was well, he found a Fravashi trader who was willing to take him to Yarkona; on Yarkona he shaved his head and wrapped his body in rags so that the harijan pilgrims he befriended there would allow him a corner on one of their sluggish prayer ships in which to float. And so, gray of hair and stinking of years of his own sweat and filth, he came to Neverness like any other seeker.

"Though it was late midwinter spring, and warm for that season, he was stunned by the cold and dazzled by the brightness of our city. And so he paid too much money for snow goggles and the finest of shagshay furs lined with silk belly. 'The streets are colored ice,' he said disbelievingly, for the only ice he had ever seen had been brought to him in exotic drinks by his slaves. And he marvelled at the purples and greens of the glissades and the laughing children who chased each other up and down the orange and yellow slidderies on ice skates. The silvery spires and towers were frozen with the ever present verglas of that season, scattering the white spring light so that the whole city gleamed and sparkled in a most disconcerting manner. 'There is beauty here,' he said. 'The false beauty of artifice and a civilization gone to rot.' And so, dressed in deep winter furs and wobbling on his newly bought skates, he struck out into the streets to preach to the people.

"In the great square outside the Hofgarten where the

people of the Unreal City, high and low, meet and take their refreshment, the scryers, eschatologists, and cantors as well as the harijan, splicers and whores, he said, 'I s-speak to that inside you which is less than m-man but also m-more.' And he raged because no one would listen to a short, overdressed farsider who stuttered and could barely stand on his skates. 'You p-pilots,' he said, 'you are the p-pride of the galaxy! You travel from Simoom to Urradeth and on to Jacaranda in less time than the Darghinni need to prepare the first of eighteen jumps from Summerworld to Darkroom. You penetrate the Vild, lost in your mathematics and dreamtime and tell yourself you have seen something of the ineffable and eternal. But you have forgotten how to take pleasure in a simple flower! You foreswear marriage and children and thus you are more and less than men!'

''When the pilots turned away from him to drink their kvass and eiswein, he told the historians and fabulists that they knew nothing of the true nature of man. And they, those haughty professionals of our city, snubbed him and went on talking about Gaiea and Old Earth as if he were invisible. So Goshevan spoke to the programmers and holists, the Fravashi aliens and Friends of God, the harijan, the wormrunners, the splicers, and at last, because he was filled with a great sadness and longing, he zipped up his furs and went deep into the Farsiders' Quarter where he might pay for the company of a friendly ear.

''Because he was lonely and had been without a woman for many years, he took his pleasure among the whores of the lesser glidderies, which at that time were stained crimson and were narrow and twisted like snakes. Because his soul was empty he smoked toalache and awoke one fine morning to find himself in bed with four courtesans from Jacaranda. They asked him if all dark little men were as potent as he and advised him that the joys of conjoining with the alien Friends of Man were such that no man who had known only women could comprehend them. Goshevan, horrified at what he had done and forgetting where he was, began swearing and shouting and ordered that the courtesans be sold as field slaves. He threw a bag of diamonds at them, clipped in the blades to his skates, and raced up and down the back glissades for two days before he came to his right mind.''

I paused here in my story to refill our cups. The young man was staring at me intently, watching my every move with those piercing brown eyes and, I felt, stripping my words bare for lies. The room was very quiet and cold; I could hear his slow, even breathing as he nodded his head and asked, ''And then?''

''And then Goshevan made a decision. You see, he had hoped to win people over to his dream, which was to go out into the wasteland and live as what he called 'natural man.' The Alaloi, of course, had been his model. When he found he could not emulate them, he decided to join them.''

''A noble vision,'' the young man said.

''It was insane!'' I half-shouted. ''Who were these Alaloi he so admired? Dreamers and madmen they were—and still are. They came to this world on the first wave of the swarming, when Old Earth was young and, some say, as radioactive as plutonium. Cavemen! They wanted to be cavemen! So they back-mutated their chromosomes, destroyed their ship, and went to live in the frozen forests. And now their great-grandchildren's great-great-grandchildren hunt mammoths for meat and die long before they've seen their hundredth winter.''

''But they die happy,'' the young man said.

''Who knows how they die?'' I said to him. ''Goshevan wanted to know. He sought me out because it was said that once as a journeyman I had pioneered the operation he wanted, cutting on my very own self to prove my worth as a flesh changer. 'Make me into an Alaloi,' he begged me, in this very room where we presently drink our coffee and kvass. And I told him, 'Go to any of the cetics in this quarter and they will cure you of your delusions.' And he said, 'I will p-pay you ten million talanns!' But his farsider money was worthless in the Unreal City and I told him so. 'Diamonds,' he said. 'I've two thousand carats of Yarkona bluestars.' 'For that price,' I said, 'I can add eight inches to your spine or make you into a beautiful woman. I can lighten your skin and make your hair as white as a Jacaranda courtesan's.' Then he looked at me cunningly and said, 'I'll trade information for your services: I know the fixed-points of Agathange.' I laughed at him and asked, 'How is it you know what the pilots of our city have been seeking for three thousand years?'

"Well, it happened that he *did* know. With the riches from the sale of his estates, he had bought the secret of the location of that fabled world from a renegade pilot he had met on Darkmoon. I consulted our city archives; the librarians were *very* excited. They sent a young pilot to verify my information, and I told Goshevan we might have to wait two or three hundred days before we would know.

"Ten thousand city disks his information was worth! The pilot who rediscovered Agathange was very good. Phased into his light ship, the *Infinite Sloop*, proving the theorems of probalistic topology—or whatever it is that our famous pilots do when they wish to fall through the space that isn't space—he rushed through the fallaways, fenestering from window to window with such precision and elegance that he returned from Agathange in forty days.

" 'You can be a rich man,' Goshevan said to me on a clear, sparkling day of false winter. 'Do as I ask and all the disks are yours.'

"I hesitated not for a moment. I took him into the changing room and I began to cut. It was a challenge, I lied to myself, a test of knowledge and skill—to a dedicated cutter, it wasn't disks that mattered. I enlarged the basal bone of his jaw and stimulated the alveolar bone to maximal growth so that his face could support the larger teeth I implanted. The angle of the face itself I broadened so that there would be more room for a chewing apparatus strong enough to crack marrowbones. And of course, since the face jutted out farther from the skull, I had to build up the brow ridge with synthetic bone to protect the eyes. And though this shaping took the better part of winter, it was only the beginning.

"As he writhed beneath my lasers and scalpels, all the while keeping his face as quiet and blank as a snowfield, I went to work on his body. To support his huge new muscles—which were grown by the Fravashi deep-space method—I built him new bones. I expanded the plates and spicules of the honeycombed interior and strengthened the shafts and tendon attachments, adding as much as three millimeters to the cortices of the longer bones such as his femur. I stippled his skin. I went beneath the dermis, excising most of his sweat glands to keep him from soaking his furs and freezing to death at the first hint of false winter. Because his dark skin would synthesize too little vitamin D to keep his bones calcified during the long twilight of deep winter, I inhibited his melanocytes—it is little known that all men, light or dark, have nearly the same number of melanocytes—I lightened his skin until he was as fair as a man from Thorskalle. The last thing I did for him, or so I thought at the time, was to grow out his fine, almost invisible body hair so that it covered him like brown fur from toe to eyebrow.

"I was very pleased with my handiwork and a little frightened because Goshevan had grown so strong—stronger, I think, than any Alaloi—that he could have torn my clavicle from my chest, had he so desired. But *he* was not pleased and he said, 'The most important thing there is, this thing you didn't do.' And I told him, 'I've made you so that no one among the Alaloi could tell you from his brother.' But he looked at me with his dark fanatic's eyes and asked me, 'And my s-sons, should my s-seed by some chance be compatible with the Alaloi women, who will there be to call my weak-jawed half-breed sons brother?' I had no answer for him other than a dispirited repeating of the law: 'A man may do with his flesh as he pleases,' I said, 'but his DNA belongs to his species.' And then he grabbed my forearm so tightly that I thought my muscles would split away from the bone and said, 'Strong men make their own laws.'

"Then, because I felt a moment of pity for this strange man who only wanted what all men want—which is a son after his own image and a few moments of peace—I broke the law of the civilized worlds. It was a challenge, do you understand? I irradiated his testes and bathed them with sonics, killing off the sperm. I couldn't, of course, engage the services of a master splicer because all my colleagues shunned such criminal activity. But I *was* a master cutter— some will tell you the best in the city—and what is gene-splicing but surgery on a molecular scale? So I went into his tubules and painstakingly sectioned out and mutated segments of his stem cells' DNA so that the newly produced germ cells would make for him sons after his new image.

"When I finished this most delicate of delicate surgeries, which took the better part of two years, Goshevan regarded himself in the mirror of my changing room and announced, 'Behold *Homo neandertalis*. Now I am less than a man but also more.'

" 'You look as savage as any savage,' I said. And then, thinking to scare him, I told him what was commonly believed about the Alaloi. 'They live in caves and have no language,' I said. 'They are bestially cruel to their children; they eat strangers, and perhaps each other.'

"Goshevan laughed as I said this and then he told me, 'On Old Earth during the holocaust century, a neanderthal burial site was discovered in a place called Shanidar near the Zagros mountains of Irak. The archeologists found the skeleton of a forty-year-old m-man who was missing his lower right arm. Shanidar I, they named him, and they determined he had lost his arm long before he died. In the burial site of another neanderthal, Shanidar IV, was the pollen of several kinds of flowers, mixed in with all the bone fragments, pebbles and dust. The question I have for you, Cutter, is: how savage could these people have been if they supported a cripple and honored their dead with bright colored wildflowers?' So I answered, 'The Alaloi are not the same.' And he said, 'We will see, we will see.'

"Here I freely admit I had underestimated him. I had supposed him to be a lunatic or at best, a self-deluder who hadn't a chance of getting ten miles away from our city. The covenant between the founder of Neverness and the Alaloi allows us this single island—large though it might be—and to our city fathers, this covenant is holy. Boats are useless because of the icebergs of the Sound, and the windjammers of would-be poachers and smugglers are shot from the air. Because I couldn't picture Goshevan walking out onto the Starnbergersee when it freezes over in deep winter, I asked him somewhat smugly how he intended to find his Alaloi.

" 'Dogs,' he said. 'I will attach dogs to a sled and let them pull me across the frozen sea.' And I asked, 'What

are dogs?' 'Dogs are carnivorous mammals from Old Earth,'
he said. 'They are like human slaves, only friendly and
eager to please.' And I said, 'Oh, you mean huzgies,'
which is what the Alaloi call their sled dogs. I laughed at
him then and watched the white skin beneath his hairy face
turn red as if slapped by a sudden cold wind. 'And how
will you smuggle such beasts into our city?' I asked him.

"So Goshevan parted the hair of his abdomen to show
me a thin band of hard white skin I had taken for an
appendectomy scar. 'Cut here,' he said, and after nerve-
blocking him, cut I did until I came to a strange-looking
organ adjoining the large intestine where his appendix
should have been. 'It's a false ovary,' he said. 'Clever are
the breeders of Darkmoon. Come. Cut again and see what
I've brought with me.' I removed the false organ, which
was red and slippery and made of one of those pungently
sweet-smelling bioplastics they synthesize on Darkmoon. I
made a quick incision and out spilled thousands of unfertil-
ized ova and a sac of sperm floating in krydda suspension
to keep them fresh and vital. He pointed at the milky
sperm sac and said, 'The seed of Darkmoon's finest Mutts.
I had originally hoped to train hundreds of sled teams.'

"How Goshevan brought the dogs to term and trained
them, I do not know because I didn't see him again for
two winters. I thought perhaps that he'd been caught and
banished or had his head split open and had his plasm
sucked out by some filthy slel necker.

"But as you will see, Goshevan was a resourceful man
and hard to kill. He came again to my shop on the deepest
of deep winter nights when the air was so black and cold
that even on the greatest of the glissades and slidderies,
The Run and The Way, nothing moved. In the hallway of
my shop he stood like a white bear, opening his shagshay
furs and removing the balaclava from his face with powerful, sweeping motions. I could see beneath his furs one of
those black and gold, heated kamelaikas that the racers
wear on festival days when they wish to keep warm and
still have their limbs free for stroking. 'This is my noble
savage?' I said to him as I fingered his wonderfully warm
undersuit. 'Even a f-fanatic such as I must make some
concessions to survival,' he said. And I asked him, 'What

will you do when the batteries die?' He gave me a look that was at once fearful and bursting with excitement, and he said, 'When the batteries die, I will either be dead or I will have found my home.'

"He said goodbye to me and went out onto the gliddery where his dogs were up on their hind legs, straining at their harnesses as they whined and barked and pushed their black noses into his parka. From my window, I could see him fumbling with the stiff leather straps and thumping the side of the lead dog with his huge mittens. He adjusted the load three times before he had it to his liking, taking pains that the sacks of dog meal were balanced and tightly lashed to the wooden frame. Then he was off, whistling in a curious manner as he glided around the corner of the cetic's shop and disappeared into the cold."

The tearoom felt cold as I said these words. I noticed that the young man was pursing his narrow lips tightly as he fiddled with his coffee. All at once, he let out his breath in a puff of steam that seemed to hang in the air. "But that isn't the end of your story, is it, Cutter? You haven't told the moral: how poor Goshevan died on the ice broken-hearted and disavowing his dream."

"Why is it you young people always want an ending? Does our universe come to an *end* or does it fold in upon itself? Are the Agathanians at the end of human evolution or do they represent a new species? And so on, and so on. Is there any end to the questions impatient young men ask?"

I took a quick gulp of the bitter kvass, burning my lips and throat so that I sat there dumbly sucking in the cold air like an old bellows. "No, you are right," I gasped out. "That is not the end of my story."

"Goshevan drove his dogs straight out onto the frozen Starnbergersee. Due west he went, running fast across the wind-packed snow for six hundred miles. He came to the first of the Thousand Islands and found mountains shrouded in evergreen forests where the thallows nested atop the steep granite cliffs filling the air for miles with their harsh cawings. But he found no Alaloi, and he urged his dogs carefully across the crevasses of the Fairleigh ice-shelf, back out onto the sea.

"Fifteen islands he crossed without finding a trace of a

human being. He had been gone sixty-two days when the crushing, deadly silent cold of deep winter began yielding to the terrible storms of midwinter spring. During a snow so heavy and wet that he had to stop every hundred yards to scrape the frozen slush from the steel runners of his sled, his lead dog, Yuri the Fierce, pulled them into a crevasse. Though he dug his boots into the sloppy snow and held on to the sled with all his strength, the pendulating weight of Yuri, Sasha and Ali as they swung back and forth over the lip of the ice was such that he felt himself being slowly dragged into the crevasse. It was only by the quick slashing of his hunting knife that he saved himself and the rest of his team. He cut the harness from which his strongest dogs dangled and watched helplessly as they tried to dig their black claws into the sides of the crevasse, all the while yelping pitifully as they fell to the ice below.

"Goshevan was stunned. Though the snow had stopped and he was within sight of the sixteenth and largest of the Thousand Islands, he realized he could go no farther without rest. He erected his tent and fed the dogs from the crumbly remnants of the last bag of food. There came a distant hissing that quickly grew into a roar as the storm returned, blasting across the Starnbergersee with such ferocity that he spent all that day and night tending the ice-screws of his tent so that he wouldn't be blown away. For nine days he lay there shivering inside his sleeping sack as the wind-whipped ice crystals did their work. By the tenth day, the batteries to his heated kamelaika were so low that he threw them in disgust against the shredded, useless walls of his tent. He dug a cave in the snow and pulled the last two of his starving dogs into the hole so that they might huddle close and keep each other warm. But Gasherbrum the Friendly, the smartest of his dogs, died on the eleventh day. And on the morning of the twelfth day, his beloved Kanika, whose paws were crusted with ice and blood, was as still as a deep winter night.

"When the storm broke on the fifteenth day, Goshevan was so crazy with thirst that he burned his frostbitten lips upon the metal cup in which he was melting snow. And though he was famished and weak as a snow worm, he could not bring himself to eat his dogs because he was both father and mother to them, and the thought of it made him so sick he would rather have died.

"From the leather and wood of his sled he fashioned a crude pair of snowshoes and set out across the drifts for a huge blue and white mountain he could see in the distance puncturing the sky. Kweitkel it was called, as he would later learn. Kweitkel, which meant 'white mountain' in the language of the Devaki, who were the tribe of Alaloi who found him dying in the thick forests of its eastern slope.

"His rescuers—five godlike men dressed in angelic white, or so it seemed to his fevered, delirious mind—brought him to a huge cave. Some days later he came awake to the wonderful smells of hot soup and roasting nuts. He heard soft voices speaking a strange, musical language that was a delight to his ear. Two children, a boy and a girl he thought, were sitting at the corners of the luxurious fur which covered him, peeking at him coyly through the spread-out fingers of their little hands and giggling.

"A man with great shoulders and a beard as black as a furfly came over to him. Between his blunt, scarred fingers he held a soup bowl made from yellowed bone and and scrimshawed with intricate figures of diving whales. As Goshevan gulped the soup, the man asked, 'Marek? Patwin? Olorun? Nodin? Mauli?' Goshevan, half-snow-blind and weak in the head as he was, forgot that I had made him so that no one among the Alaloi could tell him from his brothers. He thought he was being accused of being an alien so he shook his head furiously back and forth at the sound of each name. At last, when Lokni, which was the big man's name, had given up trying to discover the tribe to which he belonged, Goshevan pointed to his chest and said, 'I am man. I'm just a man.' 'Iaman,' Lokni repeated. 'Ni luria la Devaki.' And so it was that Lokni of the Devaki welcomed Goshevan of the Iaman tribe to his new home.

"Goshevan gained strength quickly, gorging upon a salty cheese curdled from shagshay milk and the baldo nuts the Devaki stored against the storms of midwinter spring. And though Katerina, who was Lokni's wife, offered him thick mammoth steaks running red with the life's blood beneath a charcoaled crust, he would eat no meat. He, who all his life had eaten only soft, decerebrated cultured meats, was horrified that such gentle people took their nourishment from the flesh of living animals. 'I don't think I can teach these savages the few right-actioned ways of civilized man,' he said to himself. 'Why should they listen to me, a total stranger?' And so for the first time since Summerworld he came to question the wisdom of what he had done.

"By the time Goshevan had put on fifty pounds of new muscle, the storms of midwinter spring had given way to the fine weather of false winter. There came cool sunny days; the occasional powdery snows were too light to cover the alpine fireweed and snow dahlia which blanketed the lower slopes of Kweitkel. The thallows were molting and the furflys laying eggs. For Tuwa, the mammoth, came calving time, and for the Devaki, it was time to slaughter mammoth.

"Goshevan was sick. Though he had quickly learned the language of the Devaki, and learned also to tolerate his body lice and filthy hair, he did not know how he could kill an animal. But when Lokni unsmilingly slapped a spear into his hand, he knew he would have to hunt with the eighteen other men, many of whom had come to wonder about his strange ways and questioned his manhood.

"At first the hunt went well. In one of the lovely valleys of Kweitkel's southern foothills, they spotted a mammoth herd gorging on arctic timothy and overripe, half-fermented snow apple. The great hairy beasts were carousing and drunkenly trampling through the acres of alpine fireweed which were everywhere aflame with bright reds and oranges and so beautiful that Goshevan wanted to cry. They drove the trumpeting mammoths down the valley and into a bog where three calves fell quickly beneath flint-tipped spears. But then Lokni mired himself near the edge of the bog, and Wemilo was trampled by an enraged cow. It fell to Goshevan to help Lokni. Though he reached out with his spear into the bog until his shoulder joint popped, he failed to close the distance. He heard voices and shouting and thunder and felt the ground moving beneath him. As he looked up to see the red-eyed cow almost upon him, he realized that the men were praying for his ghost, for it was known that no single man could stand against Tuwa's charge.

"Goshevan was terrified. He cast his spear at the mammoth's eye with such a desperate force that the point drove into the brain, and the great beast fell like a mountain. The Devaki were stunned. Never had they seen such a thing, and Haidar and Alani, who had doubted his bravery, said that he was more than a man. But Goshevan knew his feat was the result of blind luck and my surgery, and thus he came to despise himself because he had killed a magnificent being and was therefore less than a man.

"In the cave that night, the Devaki made a feast to mourn the passing of Tuwa's anima and to wish Wemilo's ghost enlightenment on the other side of day. Lokni sliced his own ear off his head with a sharp obsidian flake and laid the bloody flap of skin on Wemilo's cold forehead so that he might always hear the prayers of the tribe. Katerina bound her husband's wound with feather moss while the other women scattered snow dahlias over Wemilo's crushed body.

"Then Lokni turned to Goshevan and said, 'A man, to be a man, must have a woman, and you are too old to take a virgin bride.' He went over to Lara, who was sobbing over Wemilo's grave. 'Look at this poor woman. Long ago her father, Arani, deserted her to live with the hairless people of the Unreal City. She has no brothers. And now Wemilo dances with the stars. Look at this poor beautiful woman whose hair is still black and shiny and whose teeth are straight and white. Who will be a man to this woman?'

"Goshevan looked at Lara and though her eyes were full of tears, they were also hot and dark, full of beauty and life. He felt very excited and said, 'A man would be a fool not to desire this woman.' And then he thought to comfort her by saying, 'We'll be married and have many fine children to love.'

"A hush fell over the cave. The Devaki looked at each other as if they couldn't believe their ears. And Ushi wondered aloud, 'How can he not know that Lara has three daughters and one son?' 'Of course I know,' Goshevan said. 'It only means she is very fertile and will have no trouble bearing me sons.' Then Ushi let out a cry and began tearing at her hair. Katerina hid her eyes beneath her hand and Lokni asked, 'How can it be, Goshevan, that you do not know the Law?' And Goshevan, who was angry and confused, replied, 'How can I know your law when I'm from a faraway tribe?' Lokni looked at him and there was death in his eyes. 'The Law is the Law,' he said, 'and it is the same for every Alaloi. It can only be that the storm stole away your memory and froze part of your soul.' And then, because Lokni didn't want to kill the man who had saved his life and was about to marry his sister, he explained the Law.

" 'She may have but one more child. A woman may have five children: One child to give to the Serpent's Breath of deep winter, one child for the tusks of Tuwa, the mammoth. One child for the fever that comes in the night.' Lokni paused a moment as the Law passed from lip to lip, and all the tribe except Goshevan were chanting: 'A boy to become a man; a girl to become Devaki, Mother of the People.'

"Lokni cupped his hand around the back of Goshevan's neck and squeezed as he said, 'If we become too many, we will kill all the mammoth and have to hunt silk belly and shagshay for food. And when they are gone, we will have to cut holes in the ice of the sea so to spear the seals when they come up to breathe. When the seals are gone, we will be forced to murder Kikilia, the whale, who is wiser than we and as strong as God. When all the animals are gone, we will dig tangleroot and eat the larvae of furflys and break our teeth as we gnaw the lichen from the rocks. At last we will be so many, we will murder the forests to plant snow apple so that men will come to lust for land, and some men will come to have more land than others. And when there is no land left, the stronger men will get their sustenance from the labor of weaker men, who will have to sell their women and children so that they might have mash to eat. The strongest men will make war on each other so that they might have still more land. Thus we will become hunters of men and be doomed to hell in living and hell on the other side. And then, as it did on Earth in the time before the swarming, fire will rain from the sky, and the Devaki will be no more.' "

"And so Goshevan, who really wanted only one son, came to accept the Law of the Alaloi, for who knew bet-

ter than he the evils of owning slaves and lying with
whores?

"He married Lara at the end of false winter. In her long
black hair, she replaced the snow dahlias of her mourning
time with the fire flowers of the new bride and set to
sewing him the new shagshay parka he would need when
deep winter came. Each Devaki made them a wedding
gift. Eirene and Jael, the two giggling children who had
first greeted him so many months before, gave him a pair
of mittens and a carved tortrix horn for him to fill with the
potent beer that was brewed each winter from mashed
tangleroot. His finest gift, a work of breathtaking art and
symmetry, was the spear that Lokni gave him. It was long
and heavy and tipped with a blade of flint so sharp that it
cut through cured mammoth hide as easily as cheese."

I finished my drink, pausing a moment to catch my
breath. The sounds the young man's marble cup made
against the cold hard table seemed gritty and overloud. I
smelled cinnamon and honey; a minute later the domestic
served raisin bread spread with honey-cheese and brought
us fresh pots of coffee. Outside the tearoom, I could hear
the soft clack-clack of steel skates against the ice of the
gliddery. I wondered who would be so foolish, or desperate, to be out on such a night. The young man took my
hand in his, staring at me so intently that I had to look
away. "And Goshevan?" he asked. "He was happy with
the beautiful Lara? He was happy, wasn't he?"

"He was happy," I said, trying to slip my old hand
from the young man's grip. "He was so happy he came
to regard his body lice as his 'little pets' and didn't care
that he would have to pass the rest of his days without a
bath. His stuttering, which had embarrassed him all his life
and caused him great shame, came to a sudden end as he
found the liquid vowels and smooth consonants of the
Devaki language rolling easily off his tongue. He loved
Lara's children as his own and loved Lara as only a
desperate and romantic man can love a woman. Though
she had none of the exotic skills of the courtesans with
whom he had been so familiar, she loved him with such a
strength and passion that he came to divide his life into
two parts: the time before Lara, which was murky and dim

and full of confused memories, and the time after, which was full of light and joy and laughter. So it happened that when, the following midwinter spring, she pointed to her belly and smiled, he knew with a sureness that he had not spent his life in vain and was as happy as a man could be.

"The deep powder snows of winter were falling as Lara swelled like the ripened baldo nuts which the women picked and stored in great barrels staved with mammoth ribs and covered with mammoth hides. 'It will be a boy,' she said to him one night in early deep winter when the slopes of Kweitkel were silvery with the light of the moons. 'When I was carrying my girls I was sick every morning of the three seasons of growing. But with this one I wake up as hungry as Tuwa in midwinter spring.'

"When her time came, Katerina shooed Lokni and Goshevan, uncle and father, to the front of the cave where they waited while the women did their secret things. It was a night of such coldness that old Amalia said comes but twice every hundredyear. To the north, they could see green curtains of light hanging down from the black starry sky. 'The firefalls,' Lokni said. 'Sometimes they are faint and green as you see and other times as red as blood. The spirit of Wemilo and all our ancestors light the deep winter night to give us hope against the darkness.' And then he pointed at a bright triangle of stars twinkling brightly above the eastern horizon. 'Wakanda, Eanna, and Farfara,' he said. 'Men live there, I think. Shadow men without bodies. It is said they have no souls and take their nourishment from light.' And so they sat there for a long time shivering in their shagshay furs, talking of the things men talk about when they are full of strange longing and wonder at the mystery of life.

"There came a squalling from the cave. Goshevan clapped Lokni on the back and started laughing. But the cries of his newborn son were followed by a low wailing and then a whole chorus of women crying. He felt a horrible fear and leapt to his feet even as Lokni tried to hold him back.

"He ran to the warmest, deepest part of the cave where the men were not supposed to go. There, in the sick yellow light of the oil-stones, on a blood-soaked newl fur, he saw his son lying all wet and slippery and pink between Lara's bent legs. Katerina knelt over the struggling infant, holding a corner of the gray fur over his face. Goshevan knocked her away from his son so that she fell to the floor, winded and gasping for air. As Haidar and Palani grabbed his arms, Lokni came to him and with such a sadness that his voice broke and tears ran from his eyes, he said, 'It is the Law, my friend. Any born such as he must immediately make the journey to the other side.' Then Goshevan, who had been full of blind panic and rage, looked at his son. He saw that growing from the hips were two tiny red stumps, twitching pathetically where they should have been kicking. His son had no legs. And to Lokni, who had gathered up the baby in his arms, he said, 'The Devaki do not kill each other.' And Lokni said, 'A baby is not a Devaki until he is named.' Then Goshevan raged so that Einar and Pauli had to come hold him as well. 'I name him Shanidar,' he said. 'Shanidar, my son, whom I love more than life.' But Lokni shook his head because life is so hard the Devaki do not name their children until four winters have passed. With his forefinger, he made a star above the screaming baby's head and went out to bury him in the snow.

"Lokni, whose white parka was stained crimson with frozen blood, returned alone with his hands shielding his eyes as if to protect them from false winter's noonday sun. Goshevan broke free and picked up the mammoth spear which had been his wedding gift. He threw it at Lokni in desperation, too blind with pain and fear to see the point enter his stomach and emerge from his back. And he ran outside to find his son.

"An hour later he returned. And in his arms, frozen as hard as a mammoth leg, he held his quiet, motionless son. 'Lara,' he said. And like a drunkard, he stumbled towards his wife. But Lara, who had seen what had passed between her legs and what her husband had done, opened the great artery of her throat with her hide scraper before he could get too close. And when he cried out that he loved her and would die if she died, she told him that the essence of the Law is that life must be lived with honor and joy or not lived at all. So Lara died as he watched, and the best part of him died with her. Knowing that his life had come to an end, he unknotted the ties of his parka, exposing the black matted hair of his chest so that Einar and Alani and the others might more easily spear him. But Goshevan had learned nothing. Lokni, lying on his back with the blood running from a great hole in his abdomen, said, 'Go back to the City, foolish man. We will not kill you; we are not hunters of men.'

"They gave Goshevan a team of snarling dogs and a barrel of baldo nuts and sent him out onto the ice. And he, who should have died a hundred times, did not die because he was full of the madness which protects desperate men, and a new idea had come into his head. So he made his way back across the ice of the Starnbergersee. This time, he ate his dogs when they died and didn't care that his beard was crusted with their black, frozen blood. He came once again to Neverness as a seeker; he came to my cutting shop, wretched, starving, covered with filth and dead, frostbitten skin rotting on his face. He came to me and said, 'I seek life for my son.'

"He stood in this very room, above this table. From a leather bag full of snow and rimed with frost, he removed a twisted, pinkish lump of frozen meat and laid it on the table. 'This is my son,' he said. 'Use all your skills, Cutter, and return my son to me.'

"Goshevan told me his story, all the while cradling in his arms the leather bag to which he had returned his poor son's corpse. He was mad, so mad that I had to shout and repeat myself over and over before he would cease his ranting. 'There isn't a single cryologist in the city,' I told him, 'who can bring your son back to life.'

"But he never understood me. He went out onto the slidderies and glissades, telling his story to every cutter, splicer and cetic who would listen to him. Thus it came to be known throughout the city that I had tampered with his DNA and tampered badly. I was brought before the akashics and their accursed optical computers which laid bare my brain and recorded my actions and memories for all to see. 'If you ever again break the laws of our city,' the master akashic told me, 'you will be banished.' To ensure that I would obey the law, he ordered me to submit to their computer on the first day of each new year 'so long as you live.' Curiously, although I had scandalized most of the city, my 'Neanderthal Procedure' became immediately popular among the many farsiders who come to Neverness seeking to be other than what they are. For many years thereafter, the glidderies of our quarter were filled with squat hairy supermen who looked as if they could have been Goshevan's brother.

"And Goshevan, poor Goshevan—though he pleaded with and threatened every cryologist in the quarter—death is death, and no one could do more for him than give him a hot meal and a little toalache and send him on his way. The last I heard of him, he was trying to bribe his way to Agathange, where, he said, the men were no longer men and miracles were free to anyone who would surrender up his humanity. But everyone knows Agathanian resurrection is just a myth dreamed up by some fabulist drunk with the fire of toalache, no more real than the telepaths of The Golcanda. And so Goshevan disappeared into the back alleys of our Unreal City, no doubt freezing to death one dark winter's night. And there, my young friend, my story ends."

Painfully, I stood up to indicate that our conversation was over. But the young man kept to his chair, staring at me silently. His eyes grew so intense, so dark and disturbed, I thought that, perhaps, all men who desire the unobtainable must be touched with some degree of madness. I felt the acids of the kvass and coffee burning in my stomach as I said, "You must go now. You understand now, you understand why."

Suddenly, he slapped the table. The tearoom echoed with the loud rattle of teacups and the young man's trembling voice. "There the story does *not* end," he said. "This is the end, the true end of Goshevan's story that they tell in the silver mines of Summerworld."

I smiled at him then because the story of Goshevan is now a legend, and the endings to his story are as many as the Thousand Islands. Although I was certain to be bored by one of the fabulist myths in which Goshevan returns triumphantly to the Patwin or Basham or some other tribe of the Alaloi, one can never be *truly* certain. As I am a collector of such myths, I said, "Tell me your ending."

"Goshevan found Agathange," the young man said with

conviction. "You yourself said he was hard to kill, Cutter. He found Agathange where the men—I guess I really shouldn't call them men because they were many-sexed and looked more like seals than men—where the Agathanians brought Shanidar back to life. They fitted him with mechanical legs stronger than real legs. They made him fifty sets of replacement legs, in graduated lengths to accommodate his growth. They offered Goshevan the peace of Agathange's oceans, the wisdom and bliss of cortically implanted bio-chips. But Goshevan, he said he wasn't fit for an ice-world that was less than civilized and that he certainly wasn't worthy of a water world that was beyond civilization. He thanked his hosts and said, 'Shanidar will grow up to be a prince. I will bring him home to Summerworld where men such as we belong.'

"To Summerworld he came many years later as an old man with white hair and a stooped back. He called upon the favor of his old friends, asking for the loan of rich delta land so that he could reestablish his estates. But no one recognized him. They, those wily, arrogant lords swathed in their white summer silks, they saw only an old madman—who I guess must have looked more like a beast to them than a man—and a strange-looking boy with proscribed Agathanian legs. 'Goshevan,' said Leonid the Just, who had once helped Goshevan put down Summerworld's forty-eighth servile revolt, 'was as hairless as an elephant. He stuttered, too, if my poor memory serves me right.' And then—are you listening, Cutter?—then Leonid ordered them sold into the silver mines. Sondevan, the obese slavemaster, removed Shanidar's legs and strapped a cart to his abdomen so that he could wheel himself along the steel tracks that led into the ground. And though Goshevan was old, he was as strong as a water buffalo. They shoved a pick at him and set him hacking at a vein of sylvanite. 'Goshevan,' said the slavemaster, 'was my father's name. He was small and weak and let the Delta Lords buy his land for a tenth a talann per cubage. This ugly animal is not he.'

"The mines were cooler than the rice paddies, but they were hellishly hot compared with the frozen forests of Kweitkel. Goshevan—do you remember how you removed his sweat glands, Cutter?—Goshevan lasted two hours before he keeled over from heatstroke and fell into delirium. But before he died, he told his son the story of his birth and explained the Law of the Devaki. His last words before the slavemaster's silver mallet caved in his head were, 'Go back!'

"So I've come back," the young man said. The cutting shop was silent around us. As I stood there on the cold tile floor, I could hear the ragged hissing of my breath and taste the bittersweet tang of coffee coating my tongue and teeth. Suddenly, the young man rose to his feet so quickly that he bumped the table with his hip, sending one of my priceless teacups shattering against the floor. He opened his furs and dropped his trousers. There, badly fitted to his hips as if by some ignorant apprentice cutter, I could see the prosthetic legs—the kind they make badly on Fostora or Kainan—where they disappeared beneath reddened flaps of skin.

"I've come back to you, Grandfather," he said. "And you must do for me what you failed to do for Goshevan, who was my father."

And there my story really and truly ends. I do not know if the young man who came to me was the real Shanidar. I do not know if the story he told of Goshevan's death is really true. I prefer to believe his story, though it isn't stories that matter. What matters is precision and skill, the growing of new limbs for the legless and the altering, despite the law of civilization, the tampering with a young man's DNA when the need to tamper and heal is great. What matters is men who aren't afraid to change the shape and substance of their flesh so that they might seek out new beginnings.

When, on the first day of midwinter spring, I am brought before the master akashic and banished from my mysterious and beloved city, I will not seek out Agathange, tempting though the warmth of their oceans might be. I am too old to take on the body of a seal; I do not wish for the wisdom of cortically implanted biochips. To paraphrase the law: A man may do with his DNA as he pleases but his soul belongs to his people. It is to my people, the Devaki, that I must return. I have bitterly missed all these years the quiet white beauty of Kweitkel and besides, I must put flowers on my daughter Lara's grave. I, Arani, who once came to Neverness from the sixteenth and largest of the Thousand Islands like any other seeker, will take my grandson back across the frozen Starnbergersee. And for Goshevan, child of my lasers and microscopes, for my poor, brave, restless son-in-law I will pray as we pray for all who make the great journey: Goshevan, mi alasharia la shantih Devaki, may your spirit rest in peace on the other side of day.

ALL MY DARLING DAUGHTERS

Connie Willis

After only a few years writing science fiction, Connie Willis has already won awards and established herself as an accomplished and unpredictable writer. Certainly this novelette about a young woman in a boarding school in space holds many surprises—and some shocks. You won't easily forget it.

Connie Willis collaborated with Cynthia Felice on the novel Water Witch; *her first collection of stories is* Fire Watch, *where this story first appeared.*

> Barrett: I'll have her dog . . . Octavius.
> Octavius: Sir?
> Barrett: Her dog must be destroyed. At once.
> Octavius: I really d-don't see what the p-poor little
>   beast has d-done to . . .
> —*The Barretts of Wimpole Street*

The first thing my new roommate did was tell me her life story. Then she tossed up all over my bunk. Welcome to Hell. I know, I know. It was my own fucked fault that I was stuck with the stupid little scut in the first place. Daddy's darling had let her grades slip till she was back in the freshman dorm and she would stay there until the admin reported she was being a good little girl again. But he didn't have to put me in the charity ward, with all the little scholarship freshmen from the front colonies—fright-

ened virgies one and all. The richies had usually had their
share of jig-jig in boarding school, even if they were
mostly edge. And they were willing to learn.

Not this one. She wouldn't know a bone from a vaj, and
wouldn't know what went into which either. Ugly, too.
Her hair was chopped off in an old-fashioned bob I thought
nobody, not even front kids, wore anymore. Her name was
Zibet and she was from some godspit colony called
Marylebone Weep and her mother was dead and she had
three sisters and her father hadn't wanted her to come. She
told me all this in a rush of what she probably thought was
friendliness before she tossed her supper all over me and
my nice new slickspin sheets.

The sheets were the sum total of good things about the
vacation Daddy Dear had sent me on over summer break.
Being stranded in a forest of slimy slicksa trees and noble
natives was supposed to build my character and teach me
the hazards of bad grades. But the noble natives were good
at more than weaving their precious product with its near
frictionless surface. Jig-jig on slickspin is something entirely different, and I was close to being an expert on the
subject. I'd bet even Brown didn't know about this one.
I'd be more than glad to teach him.

"I'm so *sorry*," she kept saying in a kind of hiccup
while her face turned red and then white and then red
again like a fucked alert bell, and big tears seeped down
her face and dripped on the mess. "I guess I got a little
sick on the shuttle."

"I guess. Don't bawl, for jig's sake, it's no big deal.
Don't they have laundries in Mary Boning It?"

"Marylebone Weep. It's a natural spring."

"So are you, kid. So are you." I scooped up the wad,
with the muck inside. "No big deal. The dorm mother will
take care of it."

She was in no shape to take the sheets down herself, and
I figured Mumsy would take one look at those big fat tears
and assign me a new roommate. This one was not exactly
perfect. I could see right now I couldn't expect her to do
her homework and not bawl giant tears while Brown and I
jig-jigged on the new sheets. But she didn't have leprosy,
she didn't weigh eight hundred pounds, and she hadn't

gone for my vaj when I bent over to pick up the sheets. I could do a lot worse.

I could also be doing some better. Seeing Mumsy on my first day back was not my idea of a good start. But I trotted downstairs with the scutty wad and knocked on the dorm mother's door.

She is no dumb lady. You have to stand in a little box of an entryway waiting for her to answer your knock. The box works on the same principle as a rat cage, except that she's added her own little touch. Three big mirrors that probably cost her a year's salary to cart up from earth. Never mind—as a weapon, they were a real bargain. Because, Jesus Jiggin' Mary, you stand there and sweat and the mirrors tell you your skirt isn't straight and your hair looks scutty and that bead of sweat on your upper lip is going to give it away immediately that you are scared scutless. By the time she answers the door—five minutes if she's feeling kindly—you're either edge or you're not there. No dumb lady.

I was not on the defensive, and my skirts are never straight, so the mirrors didn't have any effect on me, but the five minutes took their toll. That box didn't have any ventilation and I was way too close to those sheets. But I had my speech all ready. No need to remind her who I was. The admin had probably filled her in but good. And I'd get nowhere telling her they were my sheets. Let her think they were the virgie's.

When she opened the door I gave her a brilliant smile and said, "My roommate's had a little problem. She's a new freshman, and I think she got a little excited coming up on the shuttle and—"

I expected her to launch into the "supplies are precious, everything must be recycled, cleanliness is next to godliness" speech you get for everything you do on this godspit campus. Instead she said, "What did you do to her?"

"What did I—look, she's the one who tossed up. What do you think I did, stuck my fingers down her throat?"

"Did you give her something? Sumurai? Float? Alcohol?"

"Jiggin' Jesus, she just got here. She walked in, she said she was from Mary's Prick or something, she tossed up."

"And?"

"And what? I may look depraved, but I don't think freshmen vomit at the sight of me."

From her expression, I figured Mumsy might. I stuck the smelly wad of sheets at her. "Look," I said, "I don't care what you do. It's not my problem. The kid needs clean sheets."

Her expression for the mucky mess was kinder than the one she had for me. "Recycling is not until Wednesday. She will have to sleep on her mattress until then."

Mary Masting, she could knit a sheet by Wednesday, especially with all the cotton flying around this fucked campus. I grabbed the sheets back.

"Jig you, scut," I said.

I got two months' dorm restricks and a date with the admin.

I went down to the third level and did the sheets myself. It cost a fortune. They want you to have an *awareness* of the harm you are doing the delicate environment by failing to abide, etc. Total scut. The environment's about as delicate as a senior's vaj. When Old Man Moulton bought this thirdhand Hell-Five, he had some edge dream of turning it into the college he went to as a boy. Whatever possessed him to even buy the old castoff is something nobody's ever figured out. There must have been a Lagrangian point on the top of his head.

The realtor must have talked hard and fast to make him think Hell could ever look like Ames, Iowa. At least there'd been some technical advances since it was first built or we'd all be *floating* around the godspit place. But he couldn't stop at simply gravitizing the place, fixing the plumbing, and hiring a few good teachers. Oh, no, he had to build a sandstone campus, put in a football field, and plant *trees!* This all cost a fortune, of course, which put it out of the reach of everybody but richies and trust kids, except for Moulton's charity scholarship cases. But you couldn't jig-jig in a plastic bag to fulfill your fatherly instincts back then, so Moulton had to build himself a college. And here we sit, stuck out in space with a bunch of fucked cottonwood trees that are trying to take over.

Jesus Bonin' Mary, cottonwoods! I mean, so what if we're a hundred years out of date. I can take the freshman beanies and the pep rallies. Dorm curfews didn't stop anybody a hundred years ago either. And face it, pleated skirts and cardigans make for easy access. But those godspit trees!

At first they tried the nature-dupe stuff. Freeze your vaj in winter, suffocate in summer, just like good old Iowa. The trees were at least bearable then. Everybody choked in cotton for a month, they baled the stuff up like Mississippi slaves and shipped it down to earth and that was it. But finally something was too expensive even for Daddy Moulton and we went on even-clime like all the other Hell-Fives. Nobody bothered to tell the trees, of course, so now they just spit and drop leaves whenever they feel like it, which is all the time. You can hardly make it to class without choking to death.

The trees do their dirty work down under, too, rooting happily away through the plumbing and the buried cables so that nothing works. Ever. I think the whole outer shell could blow away and nobody would ever know. The fucked root system would hold us together. And the admin wonders why we call it Hell. I'd like to upset their delicate balance once and for all.

I ran the sheets through on disinfect and put them in the spin. While I was sitting there, thinking evil thoughts about freshmen and figuring how to get off restricks, Arabel came wandering in.

"Tavvy, hi! When did you get back?" She is always too sweet for words. We played lezzies as freshmen, and sometimes I think she's sorry it's over. "There's a great party," she said.

"I'm on restricks," I said. Arabel's not the world's greatest authority on parties. I mean, herself and a plastic bone would be a great party. "Where is it?"

"My room. Brown's there," she said languidly. This was calculated to make me rush out of my pants and up the stairs, no doubt. I watched my sheets spin.

"So what are you doing down here?" I said.

"I came down for some float. Our machine's out. Why don't you come on over? Restricks never stopped you before."

"I've been to your parties, Arabel. Washing my sheets might be more exciting."

"You're right," she said, "it might." She fiddled with the machine. This was not like her at all.

"What's up?"

"Nothing's up." She sounded puzzled. "It's samurai-party time without the samurai. Not a bone in sight and no hope of any. That's why I came down here."

"Brown, too?" I asked. He was into a lot of edge stuff, but I couldn't quite imagine celibacy.

"Brown, too. They all just sit there."

"They're on something, then. Something new they brought back from vacation." I couldn't see what she was so upset about.

"No," she said. "They're not on anything. This is different. Come see. Please."

Well, maybe this was all a trick to get me to one of Arabel's scutty parties and maybe not. But I didn't want Mumsy to think she'd hurt my feelings by putting me on restricks. I threw the lock on the spin so nobody'd steal the sheets and went with her.

For once Arabel hadn't exaggerated. It was a godspit party, even by her low standards. You could tell that the minute you walked in. The girls looked unhappy, the boys looked uninterested. It couldn't be all bad, though. At least Brown was back. I walked over to where he was standing.

"Tavvy," he said, smiling, "how was your summer? Learn anything new from the natives?"

"More than my fucked father intended." I smiled back at him.

"I'm sure he had your best interests at heart," he said. I started to say something clever to that, then realized he wasn't kidding. Brown was just like I was. He had to be kidding. Only he wasn't. He wasn't smiling anymore either.

"He just wanted to protect you, for your own good."

Jiggin' Jesus, he had to be on something. "I don't need any protecting," I said. "As you well know."

"Yeah," he said, sounding disappointed. "Yeah." He moved away.

What in the scut was going on? Brown leaned against the wall, watching Sept and Arabel. She had her sweater off and was shimmying out of her skirt, which I have seen before, sometimes even helped with. What I had never seen before was the look of absolute desperation on her face. Something was very wrong. Sept stripped, and his bone was as big as Arabel could have wanted, but the look on her face didn't change. Sept shook his head almost disapprovingly at Brown and went down on Arabel.

"I haven't had any straight-up all summer," Brown said from behind me, his hand on my vaj. "Let's get out of here."

Gladly. "We can't go to my room," I said. "I've got a virgie for a roommate. How about yours?"

"No!" he said, and then more quietly, "I've got the same problem. New guy. Just off the shuttle. I want to break him in gently."

You're lying, Brown, I thought. And you're about to back out of this, too. "I know a place," I said, and practically raced him to the laundry room so he wouldn't have time to change his mind.

I spread one of the dried slickspin sheets on the floor and went down as fast as I could get out of my clothes. Brown was in no hurry, and the frictionless sheet seemed to relax him. He smoothed his hands the full length of my body. "Tavvy," he said, brushing his lips along the line from my hips to my neck, "your skin's so soft. I'd almost forgotten." He was talking to himself.

Forgotten what, for fucked's sake, he couldn't have been without any jig-jig all summer or he'd be showing it now, and he acted like he had all the time in the world.

"Almost forgotten . . . nothing like . . ."

Like what? I thought furiously. Just what have you got in that room? And what has it got that I haven't? I spread my legs and forced him down between them. He raised his head a little, frowning, then he started that long, slow, torturing passage down my skin again. Jiggin' Jesus, how long did he think I could wait?

"Come on," I whispered, trying to maneuver him with my hips. "Put it in, Brown. I want to jig-jig. Please."

He stood up in a motion so abrupt that my head smacked against the laundry-room floor. He pulled on his clothes, looking . . . what? Guilty? Angry?

I sat up. "What in the holy scut do you think you're doing?"

"You wouldn't understand. I just keep thinking about your father."

"My *father*? What in the scut are you talking about?"

"Look, I can't explain it. I just can't . . ." And left. Like that. With me ready to go off any minute and what do I get? A cracked head.

"I don't have a father, you scutty godfucker!" I shouted after him.

I yanked my clothes on and started pulling the other sheet out of the spin with a viciousness I would have liked to have spent on Brown. Arabel was back, watching from the laundry-room door. Her face still had that strained look.

"Did you see that last charming scene?" I asked her, snagging the sheet on the spin handle and ripping a hole in one corner.

"I didn't have to. I can imagine it went pretty much the way mine did." She leaned unhappily against the door. "I think they've all gone bent over the summer."

"Maybe." I wadded the sheets together into a ball. I didn't think that was it, though. Brown wouldn't have lied about a new boy in his room in that case. And he wouldn't have kept talking about my father in that edge way. I walked past Arabel. "Don't worry, Arabel, if we have to go lezzy again, you know you're my first choice."

She didn't even look particularly happy about that.

My idiot roommate was awake, sitting bolt upright on the bunk where I'd left her. The poor brainless thing had probably been sitting there the whole time I'd been gone. I made up the bunk, stripped off my clothes for the second time tonight, and crawled in. "You can turn out the light any time," I said.

She hopped over to the wall plate, swathed in a nightgown that dated as far back as Old Man Moulton's college days, or farther. "Did you get in trouble?" she asked, her eyes wide.

"Of course not. I wasn't the one who tossed up. If anybody's in trouble, it's you," I added maliciously.

She seemed to sag against the flat wallplate as if she were clinging to it for support. "My father—will they tell my father?" Her face was flashing red and white again.

And where would the vomit land this time? That would teach me to take out my frustrations on my roommate.

"Your father? Of course not. Nobody's in trouble. It was a couple of fucked sheets, that's all."

She didn't seem to hear me. "He said he'd come and get me if I got in trouble. He said he'd make me go home."

I sat up in the bunk. I'd never seen a freshman yet that wasn't dying to go home, at least not one like Zibet, with a whole loving family waiting for her instead of a trust and a couple of snotty lawyers. But Zibet here was scared scutless at the idea. Maybe the whole campus was going edge. "You didn't get in trouble," I repeated. "There's nothing to worry about."

She was still hanging onto that wallplate for dear life.

"Come on"—Mary Masting, she was probably having an attack of some kind, and I'd get blamed for that, too. "You're safe here. Your father doesn't even know about it."

She seemed to relax a little. "Thank you for not getting me in trouble," she said and crawled back into her own bunk. She didn't turn the light off.

Jiggin' Jesus, it wasn't worth it. I got out of bed and turned the fucked light off myself.

"You're a good person, you know that," she said softly into the darkness. Definitely edge. I settled down under the covers, planning to masty myself to sleep, since I couldn't get anything any other way, but very quietly. I didn't want any more hysterics.

A hearty voice suddenly exploded into the room. "To the young men of Moulton College, to all my strong sons, I say—"

"What's that?" Zibet whispered.

"First night in Hell," I said, and got out of bed for the thirtieth time.

"May all your noble endeavors be crowned with success," Old Man Moulton said.

I slapped my palm against the wallplate and then fumbled through my still-unpacked shuttle bag for a nail file. I stepped up on Zibet's bunk with it and started to unscrew the intercom.

"To the young women of Moulton College," he boomed

again, "to all my darling daughters." He stopped. I tossed the screws and file back in the bag, smacked the plate, and flung myself back in bed.

"Who was that?" Zibet whispered.

"Our founding father," I said, and then remembering the effect the word "father" seemed to be having on everyone in this edge place, I added hastily, "That's the last time you'll have to hear him. I'll put some plast in the works tomorrow and put the screws back in so the dorm mother won't figure it out. We will live in blessed silence for the rest of the semester."

She didn't answer. She was already asleep, gently snoring. Which meant so far I had misguessed every single thing today. Great start to the semester.

The admin knew all about the party. "You *do* know the meaning of the word restricks, I presume?" he said.

He was an old scut, probably forty-five. Dear Daddy's age. He was fairly good-looking, probably exercising like edge to keep the old belly in for the freshman girls. He was liable to get a hernia. He probably jig-jigged into a plastic bag, too, just like Daddy, to carry on the family name. Jiggin' Jesus, there oughta be a law.

"You're a trust student, Octavia?"

"That's right." You think I'd be stuck with a fucked name like Octavia if I wasn't?

"Neither parent?"

"No. Paid mother-surr. Trust name till twenty-one." I watched his face to see what effect that had on him. I'd seen a lot of scared faces that way.

"There's no one to write to, then, except your lawyers. No way to expel you. And restricks don't seem to have any appreciable effect on you. I don't quite know what would."

I'll bet you don't. I kept watching him, and he kept watching me, maybe wondering if I was his darling daughter, if that expensive jism in the plastic bag had turned out to be what he was boning after right now.

"What exactly was it you called your dorm mother?"

"Scut," I said.

"I've longed to call her that myself a time or two."

The sympathetic buildup. I waited, pretty sure of what was coming.

"About this party. I've heard the boys have something new going. What is it?"

The question wasn't what I expected. "I don't know," I said and then realized I'd let my guard down. "Do you think I'd tell you if I knew?"

"No, of course not. I admire that. You're quite a young woman, you know. Outspoken, loyal, very pretty, too, if I may say so."

Um-hmm. And you just happen to have a job for me, don't you?

"My secretary's quit. She likes younger men, she says, although if what I hear is true, maybe she's better off with me. It's a good job. Lots of extras. Unless, of course, you're like my secretary and prefer boys to men."

Well, and here was the way out. No more virgie freshman, no more restricks. Very tempting. Only he was at least forty-five, and somehow I couldn't quite stomach the idea of jig-jig with my own father. Sorry, sir.

"If it's the trust problem that's bothering you, I assure you there are ways to check."

Liar. Nobody knows who their kids are. That's why we've got these storybook trust names, so we can't show up on Daddy's doorstep: Hi, I'm your darling daughter. The trust protects them against scenes like that. Only sometimes with a scut like the admin here, you wonder just who's being protected from whom.

"Do you remember what I told my dorm mother?" I said.

"Yes."

"Double to you."

Restricks for the rest of the year and a godspit alert band welded onto my wrist.

"I know what they've got," Arabel whispered to me in class. It was the only time I ever saw her. The godspit alert band went off if I even mastied without permission.

"What?" I asked, pretty much without caring.

"Tell you after."

I met her outside, in a blizzard of flying leaves and cotton. The circulation system had gone edge again. "Animals," she said.

"Animals?"

"Little repulsive things about as long as your arm. Tessels, they're called. Repulsive little brown animals."

"I don't believe it," I said. "It's got to be more than beasties. That's elementary school stuff. Are they bio-enhanced?"

"You mean pheromones or something?" She frowned. "I don't know. I sure didn't see anything attractive about them, but the boys—Brown brought his to a party, carrying it around on his arm, calling it Daughter Ann. They all swarmed around it, petting it, saying things like 'Come to Daddy.' It was really edge."

I shrugged. "Well, if you're right, we don't have anything to worry about. Even if they're bio-enhanced, how long can beasties hold their attention? It'll all be over by midterms."

"Can't you come over? I never see you." She sounded like she was ready to go lezzy.

I held up the banded wrist. "Can't. Listen, Arabel, I'll be late to my next class," I said, and hurried off through the flailing yellow and white. I didn't have a next class. I went back to the dorm and took some float.

When I came out of it, Zibet was there, sitting on her bunk with her knees hunched up, writing busily in a notebook. She looked much better than the first time I saw her. Her hair had grown out some and showed enough curl at the ends to pick up on her features. She didn't look strained. In fact she looked almost happy.

"What are you doing?" I hoped I said. The first couple of sentences out of float it's anybody's guess what's going to come out.

"Recopying my notes," she said. Jiggin', the things that make some people happy. I wondered if she'd found a boyfriend and that was what had given her that pretty pink color. If she had, she was doing better than Arabel. Or me.

"For who?"

"What?" She looked blank.

"What boy are you copying your notes for?"

"Boy?" Now there was an edge to her voice. She looked frightened.

I said carefully, "I figure you've got to have a boyfriend." And watched her go edge again. Mary doing

Jesus, that must not have come out right at all. I wondered what I'd really said to send her off like that.

She backed up against the bunk wall like I was after her with something and held her notebook flat against her chest. "Why do you think that?"

Think what? Holy scut, I should have told her about float before I went off on it. I'd have to answer her now like it was still a real conversation instead of a caged rat being poked with a stick, and hope I could explain later. "I don't know why I think that. You just looked—"

"It's true, then," she said, and the strain was right back, blinking red and white.

"What is?" I said, still wondering what it was the float had garbled my innocent comment into.

"I had braids like you before I came here. You probably wondered about that." Holy scut, I'd said something mean about her choppy hair.

"My father . . ."—she clutched the notebook like she had clutched the wallplate that night, hanging on for dear life. "My father cut them off." She was admitting some awful thing to me and I had no idea what.

"Why did he do that?"

"'He said I tempted . . . men with it. He said I was a—that I made men think wicked thoughts about me. He said it was my fault that it happened. He cut off all my hair."

It was coming to me finally that I had asked her just what I thought I had: whether she had a boyfriend.

"Do you think I—do that?" she asked me pleadingly.

Are you kidding? She couldn't have tempted Brown in one of his bone-a-virgin moods. I couldn't say that to her, though, and on the other hand, I knew if I said yes it was going to be toss-up time in dormland again. I felt sorry for her, poor kid, her braids chopped off and her scut of a father scaring the hell out of her with a bunch of lies. No wonder she'd been so edge when she first got here.

"Do you?" she persisted.

"You want to know what I think," I said, standing up a little unsteadily. "I think fathers are a pile of scut." I thought of Arabel's story. Little brown animals as long as your arm and Brown saying, "Your father only wants to protect you." "Worse than a pile of scut," I said. "All of them."

She looked at me, backed up against the wall, as if she would like to believe me.

"You want to know what my father did to me?" I said. "He didn't cut my braids off. Oh, no, this is lots better. You know about trust kids?"

She shook her head.

"Okay. My father wants to carry on his precious name and his precious jig-juice, but he doesn't want any of the trouble. So he sets up a trust. He pays a lot of money, he goes jig-jig in a plastic bag, and presto, he's a father, and the lawyers are left with all the dirty work. Like taking care of me and sending me someplace for summer break and paying my tuition at this godspit school. Like putting one of these on me." I held up my wrist with the ugly alert band on it. "He never even saw me. He doesn't even know who I am. Trust me. I know about scutty fathers."

"I wish . . ." Zibet said. She opened her book and started copying her notes again. I eased down onto my bunk, starting to feel the post-float headache. When I looked at her again, she was dripping tears all over her precious notes. Jiggin' Jesus, everything I said was wrong. The most I could hope for in this edge place was that the boys would be done playing beasties by midterms and I could get my grades up.

By midterms the circulation system had broken down completely. The campus was knee-deep in leaves and cotton. You could hardly walk. I trudged through the leaves to class, head down. I didn't even see Brown until it was too late.

He had the animal on his arm. "This is Daughter Ann," Brown said. "Daughter Ann, meet Tavvy."

"Go jig yourself," I said, brushing by him.

He grabbed my wrist, holding on hard and pressing his fingers against the alert band until it hurt. "That's not polite, Tavvy. Daughter Ann wants to meet you. Don't you, sweetheart?" He held the animal out to me. Arabel had been right. Hideous little things. I had never gotten a close look at one before. It had a sharp little brown face, with dull eyes and a tiny pink mouth. Its fur was coarse and brown, and its body hung limply off Brown's arm. He had put a ribbon around its neck.

"Just your type," I said. "Ugly as mud and a hole big enough for even you to find."

His grip tightened. "You can't talk that way to my . . ."

"Hi," Zibet said behind me. I whirled around. This was all I needed.

"Hi," I said, and yanked my wrist free. "Brown, this is my roommate. My *freshman* roommate. Zibet, Brown."

"And this is Daughter Ann," he said, holding the animal up so that its tender pink mouth gaped stupidly at us. Its tail was up. I could see tender pink at the other end, too. And Arabel wonders what the attraction is?

"Nice to meet you, freshman roommate," Brown muttered and pulled the animal back close to him. "Come to Papa," he said, and stalked off through the leaves.

I rubbed my poor wrist. Please, please let her not ask me what a tessel's for? I have had about all I can take for one day. I'm not about to explain Brown's nasty habits to a virgie.

I had underestimated her. She shuddered a little and pulled her notebooks against her chest. "Poor little beast," she said.

"What do you know about sin?" she asked me suddenly that night. At least she had turned off the light. That was some improvement.

"A lot," I said. "How do you think I got this charming bracelet?"

"I mean really doing something wrong. To somebody else. To save yourself." She stopped. I didn't answer her, and she didn't say anything more for a long time. "I know about the admin," she said finally.

I couldn't have been more surprised if Old Scut Moulton had suddenly shouted, "Bless you, my daughter," over the intercom.

"You're a good person. I can tell that." There was a dreamy quality to her voice. If it had been anybody but her I'd have thought she was masting. "There are things you wouldn't do, not even to save yourself."

"And you're a hardened criminal, I suppose?"

"There are things you wouldn't do," she repeated sleepily, and then said quite clearly and irrelevantly, "My sister's coming for Christmas."

Jiggin', she was full of surprises tonight. "I thought you were going home for Christmas," I said.

"I'm never going home," she said.

"Tavvy!" Arabel shouted halfway across campus. "Hello!"

The boys are over it, I thought, and how in the scut am I going to get rid of this alert band? I felt so relieved I could have cried.

"Tavvy," she said again. "I haven't seen you in weeks!"

"What's going on?" I asked her, wondering why she didn't just blurt it out about the boys in her usual break-neck fashion.

"What do you mean?" she said, wide-eyed, and I knew it wasn't the boys. They still had the tessels, Brown and Sept and all the rest of them. They still had the tessels. It's only beasties, I told myself fiercely, it's only beasties and why are you so edge about it? Your father has your best interests at heart. Come to Daddy.

"The admin's secretary quit," Arabel said. "I got put on restricks for a samurai party in my room." She shrugged. "It was the best offer I'd had all fall."

Oh, but you're trust, Arabel. You're trust. He could be your father. Come to Papa.

"You look terrible," Arabel said. "Are you doing too much float?"

I shook my head. "Do you know what it is the boys do with them?"

"Tavvy, sweetheart, if you can't figure out what that big pink hole is for—"

"My roommate's father cut her hair off," I said. "She's a virgie. She's never done anything. He cut off all her hair."

"Hey," Arabel said, "you are really edging it. Listen, how long have you been without jig-jig? I can set you up, younger guys than the admin, nothing to worry about. Guaranteed no trusters. I could set you up."

I shook my head. "I don't want any."

"Listen, I'm worried about you. I don't want you to go edge on me. Let me ask the admin about your alert band at least."

"No," I said clearly. "I'm all right, Arabel. I've got to get to class."

"Don't let this tessel thing get to you, Tavvy. It's only beasties."

"Yeah." I walked steadily away from her across the spitting, leaf-littered campus. As soon as I was out of her line of sight, I slumped against one of the giant cotton-woods and hung on to it like Zibet had clung to that wallplate. For dear life.

Zibet didn't say another thing about her sister until right before Christmas break. Her hair, which I had thought was growing out, looked choppier than ever. The old look of strain was back and getting worse every day. She looked like a radiation victim.

I wasn't looking that good myself. I couldn't sleep, and float gave me headaches that lasted a week. The alert band started a rash that had worked its way halfway up my arm. And Arabel was right. I was going edge. I couldn't get the tessels off my mind. If you'd asked me last summer what I thought of beasties, I'd have said it was great fun for everyone, especially the animals. Now the thought of Brown with that hideous little brown and pink thing on his arm was enough to make me toss up. I keep thinking about your father. If it's the trust thing you're worried about, I can find out for you. He has your best interests at heart. Come to Papa.

My lawyers hadn't succeeded in convincing the admin to let me go to Aspen for Christmas, or anywhere else. They'd managed to wangle full privileges as soon as ev-erybody was gone, but not to get the alert band off. I figured if the dorm mother got a good look at what it was doing to my arm, though, she'd let me have it off for a few days and give it a chance to heal. The circulation system was working again, blowing winds of hurricane force all across Hell. Merry Christmas, everybody.

On the last day of class, I walked into our dark room, hit the wallplate, and froze. There sat Zibet in the dark. On my bed. With a tessel in her lap.

"Where did you get that?" I whispered.

"I stole it," she said.

I locked the door behind me and pushed one of the desk chairs against it. "How?"

"They were all at a party in somebody else's room."

"You went in the boys' dorm?"

She didn't answer.

"You're a freshman. They could send you home for that," I said, disbelieving. This was the girl who had gone quite literally up the wall over the sheets, who had said, "I'm never going home again."

"Nobody saw me," she said calmly. "They were all at a party."

"You're edge," I said. "Whose is it, do you know?"

"It's Daughter Ann."

I grabbed the top sheet off my bunk and started lining my shuttle bag with it. Holy scut, this would be the first place Brown would look. I rifled through my desk drawer for a pair of scissors to cut some air slits with. Zibet still sat petting the horrid thing.

"We've got to hide it," I said. "This time I'm not kidding. You really are in trouble."

She didn't hear me. "My sister Henra's pretty. She has long braids like you. She's good like you, too," and then in an almost pleading voice, "she's only fifteen."

Brown demanded and got a room check that started, you guessed it, with our room. The tessel wasn't there. I'd put it in the shuttle bag and hidden it in one of the spins down in the laundry room. I'd wadded the other slickspin sheet in front of it, which I felt was fitting irony for Brown, only he was too enraged to see it.

"I want another check," he said after the dorm mother had given him the grand tour. "I know it's here." He turned to me. "I know you've got it."

"The last shuttle's in ten minutes," the dorm mother said. "There isn't time for another check."

"She's got it. I can tell by the look on her face. She's hidden it somewhere. Somewhere in this dorm."

The dorm mother looked like she'd like to have him in her Skinner box for about an hour. She shook her head.

"You lose, Brown," I said. "You stay and you'll miss your shuttle and be stuck in Hell over Christmas. You leave and you lose your darling Daughter Ann. You lose either way, Brown."

He grabbed my wrist. The rash was almost unbearable under the band. My wrist had started to swell, puffing out purplish-red over the metal. I tried to free myself with my other hand, but his grip was as hard and vengeful as his face. "Octavia here was at a samurai party in the boys' dorm last week," he said to the dorm mother.

"That's not true," I said. I could hardly talk. The pain from his grip was making me so nauseated I felt faint.

"I find that difficult to believe," the dorm mother said, "since she is confined by an alert band."

"This?" Brown said, and yanked my arm up. I cried out. "This thing?" He twisted it around my wrist. "She can take it off any time she wants. Didn't you know that?" He dropped my wrist and looked at me contemptuously. "Tavvy's too smart to let a little thing like an alert band stop her, aren't you, Tavvy?"

I cradled my throbbing wrist against my body and tried not to black out. It isn't beasties, I thought frantically. He would never do this to me just for beasties. It's something worse. Worse. He must never, never get it back.

"There's the call for the shuttle," the dorm mother said. "Octavia, your break privileges are canceled."

Brown shot a triumphant glance at me and followed her out. It took every bit of strength I had to wait till the last shuttle was gone before I went to get the tessel. I carried it back to the room with my good hand. The restricks hardly mattered. There was no place to go anyway. And the tessel was safe. "Everything will be all right," I said to the tessel.

Only everything wasn't all right. Henra, the pretty sister, wasn't pretty. Her hair had been cut off, as short as scissors could make it. She was flushed bright red and crying. Zibet's face had gone stony white and stayed that way. I didn't think from the looks of her that she'd ever cry again. Isn't it wonderful what a semester of college can do for you?

Restricks or no, I had to get out of there. I took my books and camped down in the laundry room. I wrote two term papers, read three textbooks, and, like Zibet, recopied all my notes. He cut off my hair. He said I tempted men and that was why it happened. Your father was only trying to protect you. Come to Papa. I turned on all the spins at once so I couldn't hear myself think and typed the term papers.

I made it to the last day of break, gritting my teeth to keep from thinking about Brown, about tessels, about everything. Zibet and her sister came down to the laundry room to tell me Henra was going back on the first shuttle. I said goodbye. "I hope you can come back," I said, knowing I sounded stupid, knowing there was nothing in the world that could make me go back to Marylebone Weep if I were Henra.

"I am coming back. As soon as I graduate."

"It's only two years," Zibet said. Two years ago Zibet had the same sweet face as her sister. Two years from now, Henra too would look like death warmed over. What fun to grow up in Marylebone Weep, where you're a wreck at seventeen.

"Come back with me, Zibet," Henra said.

"I can't."

Toss-up time. I went back to the room, propped myself on my bunk with a stack of books, and started reading. The tessel had been asleep on the foot of the bunk, its gaping pink vaj sticking up. It crawled onto my lap and lay there. I picked it up. It didn't resist. Even with it living in the room, I'd never really looked at it closely. I saw now that it couldn't resist if it tried. It had tiny little paws with soft pink underpads and no claws. It had no teeth, either, just the soft little rosebud mouth, only a quarter of the size of the opening at the other end. If it had been enhanced with pheromones, I sure couldn't tell it. Maybe its attraction was simply that it had no defenses, that it couldn't fight even if it wanted to.

I laid it over my lap and stuck an exploratory finger a little way into the vaj. I'd done enough lezzing when I was a freshman to know what a good vaj should feel like. I eased the finger farther in.

It screamed.

I yanked the hand free, balled it into a fist, and crammed it against my mouth hard to keep from screaming myself. Horrible, awful, pitiful sound. Helpless. Hopeless. The sound a woman must make when she's being raped. No.

Worse. The sound a child must make. I thought, I have never heard a sound like that in my whole life, and at the same instant, this is the sound I have been hearing all semester. Pheromones. Oh, no, a far greater attraction than some chemical. Or is fear a chemical, too?

I put the poor little beast onto the bed, went into the bathroom, and washed my hands for about an hour. I thought Zibet hadn't known what the tessels were for, that she hadn't had more than the vaguest idea what the boys were doing to them. But she had known. Known and tried to keep it from me. Known and gone into the boys' dorm all by herself to steal one. We should have stolen them all, all of them, gotten them away from those scutting god-fucking . . . I had thought of a lot of names for my father over the years. None of them was bad enough for this. Scutting Jesus-jiggers. Fucking piles of scut.

Zibet was standing in the door of the bathroom.

"Oh, Zibet," I said, and stopped.

"My sister's going home this afternoon," she said.

"No," I said, "Oh, no," and ran past her out of the room.

I guess I had kind of a little breakdown. Anyway, I can't account very well for the time. Which is edge, because the thing I remember most vividly is the feeling that I needed to hurry, that something awful would happen if I didn't hurry.

I know I broke restricks because I remember sitting out under the cottonwoods and thinking what a wonderful sense of humor Old Man Moulton had. He sent up Christmas lights for the bare cottonwoods, and the cotton and the brittle yellow leaves blew against them and caught fire. The smell of burning was everywhere. I remember thinking clearly, smokes and fires, how appropriate for Christmas in Hell.

But when I tried to think about the tessels, about what to do, the thoughts got all muddy and confused, like I'd taken too much float. Sometimes it was Zibet Brown wanted and not Daughter Ann at all, and I would say, "You cut off her hair. I'll never give her back to you. Never." And she would struggle and struggle against him. But she had no claws, no teeth. Sometimes it was the admin, and he would say, "If it's the trust thing you're worried about, I can find out for you," and I would say, "You only want the tessels for yourself." And sometimes Zibet's father said, "I am only trying to protect you. Come to Papa." And I would climb up on the bunk to unscrew the intercom but I couldn't shut him up. "I don't need protecting," I would say to him. Zibet would struggle and struggle.

A dangling bit of cotton had stuck to one of the Christmas lights. It caught fire and dropped into the brown broken leaves. The smell of smoke was everywhere. Somebody should report that. Hell could burn down, or was it burn up, with nobody here over Christmas break. I should tell somebody. That was it, I had to tell somebody. But there was nobody to tell. I wanted my father. And he wasn't there. He had never been there. He had paid his money, spilled his juice, and thrown me to the wolves. But at least he wasn't one of them. He wasn't one of them.

There was nobody to tell. "What did you do to it?" Arabel said. "Did you give it something? Samurai? Float? Alcohol?"

"I didn't . . ."

"Consider yourself on restricks."

"It isn't beasties," I said. "They call them Baby Dear and Daughter Ann. And they're the fathers. They're the fathers. But the tessels don't have any claws. They don't have any teeth. They don't even know what jig-jig is."

"He has her best interests at heart," Arabel said.

"What are you talking about? He cut off all her hair. You should have seen her, hanging onto the wallplate for dear life! She struggled and struggled, but it didn't do any good. She doesn't have any claws. She doesn't have any teeth. She's only fifteen. We have to hurry."

"It'll all be over by midterms," Arabel said. "I can fix you up. Guaranteed no trusters."

I was standing in the dorm mother's Skinner box, pounding on her door. I did not know how I had gotten there. My face looked back at me from the dorm mother's mirrors. Arabel's face: strained and desperate. Flashing red and white and red again like an alert band: my roommate's face. She would not believe me. She would put me on restricks. She would have me expelled. It didn't matter.

When she answered the door, I could not run. I had to tell somebody before the whole place caught on fire.

"Oh, my dear," she said, and put her arms around me.

I knew before I opened the door that Zibet was sitting on my bunk in the dark. I pressed the wallplate and kept my bandaged hand on it, as if I might need it for support. "Zibet," I said. "Everything's going to be all right. The dorm mother's going to confiscate the tessels. They're going to outlaw animals on campus. Everything will be all right."

She looked up at me. "I sent it home with her," she said.

"What?" I said blankly.

"He won't . . . leave us alone. He—I sent Daughter Ann home with her."

No. Oh, no.

"Henra's good like you. She won't save herself. She'll never last the two years." She looked steadily at me. "I have two other sisters. The youngest is only ten."

"You sent the tessel home?" I said. "To your *father*?"

"Yes."

"It can't protect itself," I said. "It doesn't have any claws. It can't protect itself."

"I told you you didn't know anything about sin," she said, and turned away.

I never asked the dorm mother what they did with the tessels they took away from the boys. I hope, for their own sakes, that somebody put them out of their misery.

OF SPACE/TIME AND THE RIVER

Gregory Benford

It's hard to predict just which areas of human civilization might attract alien visitors to our planet. In this increasingly strange novelette, Gregory Benford shows us powerful aliens whose interests center on Egypt and the remains of its ancient civilization. Now why might that be?

Benford's most recent novels are Artifact *and* Heart of the Comet, *the latter written in collaboration with David Brin.*

DECEMBER 5

Monday.

We took a limo to Los Angeles for the 9 A.M. flight, LAX to Cairo.

On the boost up we went over 1.4 G, contra-reg, and a lot of passengers complained, especially the poor thins in their clank-shank rigs, the ones that keep you walking even after the hip replacements fail.

Joanna slept through it all, seasoned traveler, and I occupied myself with musing about finally seeing the ancient Egypt I'd dreamed about as a kid, back at the turn of the century.

> *If thou be'st born to strange sights,*
> *Things invisible go see,*
> *Ride ten thousand days and nights*
> *Till Age snow white hairs on thee.*

I've got the snow powdering at the temples and steadily expanding waistline, so I suppose John Donne applies. Good to see I can still summon up lines I first read as a teenager. There are some rewards to being a Prof. of Comp. Lit. at UC Irvine, even if you do have to scrimp to afford a trip like this.

The tour agency said the Quarthex hadn't interfered with tourism at all—in fact, you hardly noticed them, they deliberately blended in so well. How a seven-foot insectoid thing with gleaming russet skin can look like an Egyptian I don't know, but what the hell, Joanna said, let's go anyway.

I hope she's right. I mean, it's been fourteen years since the Quarthex landed, opened the first diplomatic interstellar relations, and then chose Egypt as the only place on Earth where they cared to carry out what they called their "cultural studies." I guess we'll get a look at that, too. The Quarthex keep to themselves, veiling their multi-layered deals behind diplomatic dodges.

As if 6 hours of travel weren't numbing enough, including the orbital delay because of an unannounced Chinese launch, we both watched a holoD about one of those new biotech guys, called *Straight from the Hearts.* An unending string of single-entendres. In our stupefied state it was just about right.

As we descended over Cairo it was clear and about 15°. We stumbled off the plane, sandy-eyed from riding ten thousand days and nights in a whistling aluminum box.

The airport was scruffy, instant third world hubbub, confusion, and filth. One departure lounge was filled exclusively with turbaned men. Heavy security everywhere. No Quarthex around. Maybe they do blend in.

Our bus across Cairo passed a decayed aqueduct, about which milled men in caftans, women in black, animals eating garbage. People, packed into the most unlikely living spots, carrying out peddler's business in dusty spots between buildings, traffic alternately frenetic or frozen.

We crawled across Cairo to Giza, the pyramids abruptly looming out of the twilight. The hotel, Mena House, was the hunting lodge-cum-palace of 19th century kings. Elegant.

Buffet supper was good. Sleep came like a weight.

DECEMBER 6

Joanna says this journal is good therapy for me, might even get me back into the habit of writing again. She says every Comp. Lit. type is a frustrated author and I should just spew my bile into this diary. So be it:

> Thou, when thou return'st, wilt tell me
> All strange wonders that befell thee.

World, you have been warned.

Set off south today—to Memphis, the ancient capital lost when its walls were breached in a war and subsequent floods claimed it.

The famous fallen Rameses statue. It looks powerful still, even lying down. Makes you feel like a pygmy tip-toeing around a giant, à la Gulliver.

Saqqara, principal necropolis of Memphis, survives 3 km away in the desert. First Dynasty tombs, including the first pyramid, made of steps, 5 levels high. New Kingdom graffiti inside are now history themselves, from our perspective.

On to the Great Pyramid!—by camel! The drivers proved to be even more harassing than legend warned. We entered the pyramid Khefren, slightly shorter than that of his father, Cheops. All the 80 known pyramids were found stripped. These passages have a constricted vacancy to them, empty now for longer than they were filled. Their silent mass is unnerving.

Professor Alvarez from UC Berkeley tried to find hidden rooms here by placing cosmic ray detectors in the lower known rooms, and looking for slight increases in flux at certain angles, but there seem to be none. There are seismic and even radio measurements of the dry sands in the Giza region, looking for echoes of buried tombs, but no big finds so far. Plenty of echoes from ruins of ordinary houses, etc., though.

No serious jet lag today, but we nod off when we can. Handy, having the hotel a few hundred yards from the pyramids.

I tried to get Joanna to leave her wrist comm at home.

Since her breakdown she can't take news of daily disasters very well. (Who can, really?) She's pretty steady now, but this trip should be as calm as possible, her doctor told me.

So of course she turns on the comm and it's full of hysterical stuff about another border clash between the Empire of Israel and the Arab Muhammad Soviet. Smart rockets vs. smart defenses. A draw. Some things never change.

I turned it off immediately. Her hands shook for hours afterward. I brushed it off.

Still, it's different when you're a few hundred miles from the lines. Hope we're safe here.

DECEMBER 7

Into Cairo itself, the Egyptian museum. The Tut Ankh Amen exhibit—huge treasuries, opulent jewels, a sheer wondrous plenitude. There are endless cases of beautiful alabaster bowls, gold-laminate boxes, testifying to thousands of years of productivity.

I wandered down a musty marble corridor and then, coming out of a gloomy side passage, there was the first Quarthex I'd ever seen. Big, clacking and clicking as it thrust forward in that six-legged gait. It ignored me, of course—they nearly always lurch by humans as though they can't see us. Or else that distant, distracted gaze means they're ruminating over strange, alien ideas. Who knows why they're intensely studying ancient Egyptian ways, and ignoring the rest of us? This one was cradling a stone urn, a meter high at least. It carried the black granite in three akimbo arms, hardly seeming to notice the weight. I caught a whiff of acrid pungency, the fluid that lubricates their joints. Then it was gone.

We left and visited the oldest Coptic church in Egypt, supposedly where Moses hid out when he was on the lam. Looks it. The old section of Cairo is crowded, decayed, people laboring in every nook with minimal tools, much standing around watching as others work. The only sign of really efficient labor was a gang of men and women hauling long, cigar-shaped yellow things on wagons. Something the Quarthex wanted placed outside the city, our guide said.

In the evening we went to the Sound & Light show at the Sphinx—excellent. There is even a version in the Quarthex language, those funny sputtering, barking sounds.

Arabs say, "Man fears time; time fears the pyramids." You get that feeling here.

Afterward, we ate in the hotel's Indian restaurant; quite fine.

DECEMBER 8

Cairo is a city being trampled to death.

It's grown by a factor of 14 in population since the revolution in 1952, and shows it. The old Victorian homes which once lined stately streets of willowy trees are now crowded by modern slab concrete apartment houses. The aged buildings are kept going, not from a sense of history, but because no matter how rundown they get, somebody needs them.

The desert's grit invades everywhere. Plants in the courtyards have a weary, resigned look. Civilization hasn't been very good for the old ways.

Maybe that's why the Quarthex seem to dislike anything built since the time of the Romans. I saw one running some kind of machine, a black contraption that floated two meters off the ground. It was laying some kind of cable in the ground, right along the bank of the Nile. Every time it met a building it just slammed through, smashing everything to frags. Guess the Quarthex have squared all this with the Egyptian gov't, because there were police all around, making sure nobody got in the way. Odd.

But not unpredictable, when you think about it. The Quarthex have those levitation devices which everybody would love to get the secret of. (Ending sentence with preposition! Horrors! But this is vacation, dammit.) They've been playing coy for years, letting out a trickle of technology, with the Egyptians holding the patents. That must be what's holding the Egyptian economy together, in the face of their unrelenting population crunch. The Quarthex started out as guests here, studying the ruins and so on, but now it's obvious that they have free run of the place. They *own* it.

Still, the Quarthex haven't given away the crucial devices which would enable us to find out how they do it—or so my colleagues in the physics department tell me. It vexes them that this alien race can master space/time so completely, manipulating gravity itself, and we can't get the knack of it.

We visited the famous alabaster mosque. It perches on a hill called The Citadel. Elegant, cool, aloofly dominating the city. The Old Bazaar nearby is a warren, so much like the movie sets one's seen that it has an unreal, Arabian Nights quality. We bought spices. The calls to worship from the mosques reach you everywhere, even in the most secluded back rooms where Joanna was haggling over jewelry.

It's impossible to get anything really ancient, the swarthy little merchants said. The Quarthex have bought them up, trading gold for anything that might be from the time of the Pharaohs. There have been a lot of fakes over the last few centuries, some really good ones, so the Quarthex have just bought anything that might be real. No wonder the Egyptians like them, let them chew up their houses if they want. Gold speaks louder than the past.

We boarded our cruise ship, the venerable *Nile Concorde*. Lunch was excellent, Italian. We explored Cairo in midafternoon, through markets of incredible dirt and disarray. Calf brains displayed without a hint of refrigeration or protection, flies swarming, etc. Fun, especially if you can keep from breathing for five minutes or more.

We stopped in the Shepheard's Hotel, the site of many Brit spy novels (Maugham especially). It has an excellent bar—Nubians, Saudis, etc., putting away decidedly non-Islamic gins and beers. A Quarthex was sitting in a special chair at the back, talking through a voicebox to a Saudi. I couldn't tell what they were saying, but the Saudi had a gleam in his eye. Driving a bargain, I'd say.

Great atmosphere in the bar, though. A cloth banner over the bar proclaims,

> *Unborn tomorrow and dead yesterday,*
> *why fret about them if today be sweet.*

Indeed, yes, ummm—bartender!

DECEMBER 9

Friday, Moslem holy day.

We left Cairo at 11 P.M. last night, the city gliding past our stateroom windows, lovelier in misty radiance than in dusty day. We cruised all day. Buffet breakfast & lunch, solid eastern and Mediterranean stuff, passable red wine.

A hundred meters away, the past presses at us, going about its business as if the pharaohs were still calling the tune. Primitive pumping irrigation, donkeys doing the work, women cleaning gray clothes in the Nile. Desert ramparts to the east, at spots sending sand fingers—no longer swept away by the annual flood—across the fields to the shore itself. Moslem tombs of stone and mud brick coast by as we lounge on the top deck, peering at the madly waving children through our binoculars, across a chasm of time.

There are about fifty aboard a ship with capacity of 100, so there is plenty of room and service as we sweep serenely on, music flooding the deck, cutting between slabs of antiquity; not quite decadent, just intelligently sybaritic. (Why so few tourists? Guide guessed people are afraid of the Quarthex. Joanna gets jittery around them, but I don't know if it's only her old fears surfacing again.)

The spindly, ethereal minarets are often the only grace note in the mud brick villages, like a lovely idea trying to rise out of brown, mottled chaos. Animal power is used wherever possible. Still, the villages are quiet at night.

The flip side of this peacefulness must be boredom. That explains a lot of history and its rabid faiths, unfortunately.

DECEMBER 10

Civilization thins steadily as we steam upriver. The mud brick villages typically have no electricity; there is ample power from Aswan, but the power lines and stations are too expensive. One would think that, with the Quarthex gold, they could do beter now.

Our guide says the Quarthex have been very hard-nosed—no pun intended—about such improvements. They will not let the earnings from their patents be used to modernize Egypt. Feeding the poor, cleaning the Nile, rebuilding monuments—all fine (in fact, they pay hand-somely for restoring projects). But better electricity—no. A flat no.

We landed at a scruffy town and took a bus into the western desert. Only a kilometer from the flat floodplain, the Sahara is utterly barren and forbidding. We visited a Ptolemaic city of the dead. One tomb has a mummy of a girl who drowned trying to cross the Nile and see her lover, the hieroglyphs say. Nearby are catacombs of mummified baboons and ibises, symbols of wisdom.

A tunnel begins here, pointing SE toward Akhenaton's capital city. The German discoverers in the last century followed it for 40 kilometers—all cut through limestone, a gigantic task—before turning back because of bad air.

What was it for? Nobody knows. Dry, spooky atmo-sphere. Urns of desiccated mummies, undisturbed. To duck down a side corridor is to step into mystery.

I left the tour group and ambled over a low hill—to take a pee, actually. To the west was sand, sand, sand. I was standing there, doing my bit to hold off the dryness, when I saw one of those big black contraptions come slipping over the far horizon. Chuffing, chugging, and laying what looked like pipe—a funny kind of pipe, all silvery, with blue facets running through it. The glittering shifted, chang-ing to yellows and reds while I watched.

A Quarthex riding atop it, of course. It ran due south, roughly parallel to the Nile. When I got back and told Joanna about it she looked at the map and we couldn't figure what would be out there of interest to anybody, even a Quarthex. No ruins around, nothing. Funny.

DECEMBER 11

Beni Hassan, a nearly deserted site near the Nile. A steep walk up the escarpment of the eastern desert, after crossing the rich flood by donkey. The rock tombs have fine drawings and some statues—still left because they were cut directly from the mountain, and have thick wedges securing them to it. Guess the ancients would steal any-thing not nailed down. One thing about the Quarthex, the guide says—they take nothing. They seem genuinely interested in restoring, not in carting artifacts back home to their neck of the galactic spiral arm.

Upriver, we landfall beside a vast dust plain, which we crossed in a cart pulled by a tractor. The mud brick palaces of Akhenaton have vanished, except for a bit of Nefertiti's palace, where the famous bust of her was found. The royal tombs in the mountain above are defaced—big chunks pulled out of the walls by the priests who undercut his monotheist revolution, after his death.

The wall carvings are very realistic and warm; the women even have nipples. The tunnel from yesterday probably runs under here, perhaps connecting with the passageways we see deep in the king's grave shafts. Again, nobody's explored them thoroughly. There are narrow sections, possibly warrens for snakes or scorpions, maybe even traps.

While Joanna and I are ambling around, taking a few snaps of the carvings, I hear a rustle. Joanna has the flashlight and we peer over a ledge, down a straight shaft. At the bottom something is moving, something big.

It takes a minute to see that the reddish shell isn't a sarcophagus at all, but the back of a Quarthex. It's planting suckerlike things to the walls, threading cables through them. I can see more of the stuff farther back in the shadows.

The Quarthex looks up, into our flashlight beam, and scuttles away. Exploring the tunnels? But why did it move away so fast? What's to hide?

DECEMBER 12

Cruise all day and watch the shore slide by.

Joanna is right; I needed this vacation a great deal. I can see that, rereading this journal—it gets looser as I go along.

As do I. When I consider how my life is spent, ere half my days, in this dark world and wide . . .

The pell-mell of university life dulls my sense of wonder, of simple pleasures simply taken. The Nile has a flowing, infinite quality, free of time. I can *feel* what it was like to live here, part of a great celestial clock that brought the perpetually turning sun and moon, the perennial rhythm of the flood. Aswan has interrupted the ebb and flow of the waters, but the steady force of the Nile rolls on.

> *Heaven smiles,*
> *and faiths and empires gleam,*
> *Like wrecks of a dissolving dream.*

The peacefulness permeates everything. Last night, making love to Joanna, was the best ever. Magnifique!

(And I know you're reading this, Joanna—I saw you sneak it out of the suitcase yesterday! Well, it *was* the best—quite a tribute, after all these years. And there's tomorrow and tomorrow . . .)

> *He who bends to himself a joy.*
> *Does the winged life destroy;*
> *But he who kisses the joy as it flies*
> *Lives in eternity's sunrise.*

Perhaps next term I shall request the Romantic Poets course. Or even write some of my own . . .

Three Quarthex flew overhead today, carrying what look like ancient rams-head statues. The guide says statues were moved around a lot by the Arabs, and of course the archaeologists. The Quarthex have negotiated permission to take many of them back to their rightful places, if known.

DECEMBER 13

Landfall at Abydos—a limestone temple miraculously preserved, its thick roof intact. Clusters of scruffy mud huts surround it, but do not diminish its obdurate rectangular severity.

The famous list of pharaohs, chiseled in a side corridor, is impressive in its sweep of time. Each little entry was a lordly pharaoh, and there is a whole wall jammed full of them. Egypt lasted longer than any comparable society, and the mass of names on that wall is even more impressive, since the temple builders did not even give it the importance of a central location.

The list omits Hatchepsut, a mere woman, and Akhenaton the scandalous monotheist. Rameses II had all carvings here cut deeply, particularly on the immense columns, to forestall defacement—a possibility he was much aware of, since he was busily doing it to his ancestor's temples. He chiseled away earlier work, adding his own cartouches, apparently thinking he could fool the gods themselves into believing he had built them all himself. Ah, immortality.

Had an earthquake today. Shades of California!

We were on the ship, Joanna dutifully padding back and forth on the main deck to work off the opulent lunch. We saw the palms waving ashore, and damned if there wasn't a small shock wave in the water, going east to west, and then a kind of low grumbling from the east. Guide says he's never seen anything like it.

And tonight, sheets of ruby light rising from both east and west. Looked like an aurora, only the wrong directions. The rippling aura changed colors as it rose, then met overhead, burst into gold, and died. I'd swear I heard a high, keening note sound as the burnt-gold line flared and faded, and flared and faded, spanning the sky.

Not many people on deck, though, so it didn't cause much comment. Joanna's theory is, it was a rocket exhaust.

An engineer says it looks like something to do with magnetic fields. I'm no scientist, but it seems to me whatever the Quarthex want to do, they can. Lords of space/time they called themselves in the diplomatic ceremonies. The United Nations representatives wrote that off as hyperbole, but the Quarthex may mean it.

DECEMBER 14

Dendera. A vast temple, much less well known than Karnak, but quite as impressive. Quarthex there, digging at the foundations. Guide says they're looking for some secret passageways, maybe. The Egyptian gov't is letting them do what they damn well please.

On the way back to the ship we pass a whole mass of people, hundreds, all dressed in costumes. I thought it was some sort of pageant or tourist foolery, but the guide frowned, saying he didn't know what to make of it.

The mob was chanting something even the guide couldn't make out. He said the rough-cut cloth was typical of the old ways, made on crude spinning wheels. The procession was ragged, but seemed headed for the temple. They looked drunk to me.

The guide tells me that the ancients had a theology based on the Nile. This country is essentially ten kilometers wide and seven hundred kilometers long, a narrow band of livable earth pressed between two deadly deserts. So they believed the gods must have intended it, and that the Nile was the center of the whole damned world.

The sun came from the east, meaning that's where things began. Ending—dying—happened in the west, where the sun went. Thus they buried their dead on the west side of the Nile, even 7,000 years ago. At night, the sun swung below and lit the underworld, where everybody went finally. Kind of comforting, thinking of the sun doing duty like that for the dead. Only the virtuous dead, though. If you didn't follow the rules . . .

> *Some are born to sweet delight,*
> *Some are born to endless night.*

Their world was neatly bisected by the great river, and they loved clean divisions. They invented the 24 hour day but, loving symmetry, split it in half. Each of the 12 daylight hours was longer in summer than in winter—and, for night, vice versa. They built an entire nation-state, an immortal hand or eye, framing such fearful symmetry.

On to Karnak itself, mooring at Luxor. The middle and late pharaohs couldn't afford the labor investment for pyramids, so they contented themselves with additions to the huge sprawl at Karnak.

I wonder how long it will be before someone rich notices that for a few million or so he could build a tomb bigger than the Great Pyramid. It would only take a million or so limestone blocks—or, much better, granite—and could be better isolated and protected. If you can't conquer a continent or scribble a symphony, pile up a great stack of stones.

> *L'eternité,*
> *ne fut jamais perdue.*

The light show this night at Karnak was spooky at

times, and beautiful, with booming voices coming right out of the stones. Saw a Quarthex in the crowd. It stared straight ahead, not noticing anybody but not bumping into any humans, either.

It looked enthralled. The beady eyes, all four, scanned the shifting blues and burnt-oranges that played along the rising columns, the tumbled great statues. Its lubricating fluids made shiny reflections as it articulated forward, clacking in the dry night air. Somehow it was almost reverential. Rearing above the crowd, unmoving for long moments, it seemed more like the giant frozen figures in stone than like the mere mortals who swarmed around it, keeping a respectful distance, muttering to themselves.

Unnerving, somehow, to see

> *. . . a subtler Sphinx renew*
> *Riddles of death Thebes never knew.*

DECEMBER 15

A big day. The Valleys of the Queens, the Nobles, and finally of the Kings. Whew! All are dry washes (wadis), obviously easy to guard and isolate. Nonetheless, all of the 62 known tombs except Tut's were rifled, probably within a few centuries of burial. It must've been an inside job.

There is speculation that the robbing became a needed part of the economy, recycling the wealth, and providing gaudy displays for the next pharaoh to show off at *his* funeral, all the better to keep impressing the peasants. Just another part of the socio-economic machine, folks.

Later priests collected the pharaoh mummies and hid them in a cave nearby, realizing they couldn't protect the tombs. Preservation of Tuthmosis III is excellent. His hook-nosed mummy has been returned to its tomb—a big, deep thing, larger than our apartment, several floors in all, connected by ramps, with side treasuries, galleries, etc. The inscription above reads,

> *You shall live again forever.*

All picked clean, of course, except for the sarcophagus, too heavy to carry away. The pyramids had portcullises, deadfalls, pitfalls, and rolling stones to crush the unwary robber, but there are few here. Still, it's a little creepy to think of all those ancient engineers, planning to commit murder in the future, long after they themselves are gone, all to protect the past. Death, be not proud.

An afternoon of shopping in the bazaar. The old Victorian hotel on the river is atmospheric, but has few guests. Food continues good. No dysentery, either. We both took the EZ-DI bacteria before we left, so it's living down in our tracts, festering away, lying in wait for an ugly foreign bug. Comforting.

DECEMBER 16

Cruise on. We stop at Kom Ombo, a temple to the crocodile god, Sebek, built to placate the crocs who swarmed in the river nearby. (The Nile is cleared of them now, unfortunately; they would've added some zest to the cruise . . .) A small room contains 98 mummified crocs, stacked like cordwood.

Cruised some more. A few km south, there were gangs of Egyptians working beside the river. Hauling blocks of granite down to the water, rolling them on logs. I stood on the deck, trying to figure out why they were using ropes and simple pulleys, and no powered machinery.

Then I saw a Quarthex near the top of the rise, where the blocks were being sawed out of the rock face. It reared up over the men, gesturing with those jerky arms, eyes glittering. It called out something in a halfway human voice, only in a language I didn't know. The guide came over, frowning, but he couldn't understand it, either.

The laborers were pulling ropes across ruts in the stone, feeding sand and water into the gap, cutting out blocks by sheer brute abrasion. It must take weeks to extract one at that rate! Farther along, others drove wooden planks down into the deep grooves, hammering them with crude wooden mallets. Then they poured water over the planks, and we could hear the stone pop open as the wood expanded, far down in the cut.

That's the way the ancients did it, the guide said kind of quietly. The Quarthex towered above the human teams, that jangling, harsh voice booming out over the water, each syllable lingering until the next joined it, blending in the dry air, hollow and ringing and remorseless.

NOTE ADDED LATER

Stopped at Edfu, a well preserved temple, buried 100 feet deep by Moslem garbage until the late 19th century. The best aspect of river cruising is pulling alongside a site, viewing it from the angles the river affords, and then stepping from your stateroom directly into antiquity, with nothing to intervene and break the mood.

Trouble is, this time a man in front of us goes off a way to photograph the ship, and suddenly something is rushing at him out of the weeds and the crew is yelling—it's a crocodile! The guy drops his camera and bolts.

The croc looks at all of us, snorts, and waddles back into the Nile. The guide is upset, maybe even more than the fellow who almost got turned into a free lunch. Who would introduce crocs back into the Nile?

DECEMBER 17

Aswan. A clean, delightful town. The big dam just south of town is impressive, with its monument to Soviet excellence, etc. A hollow joke, considering how poor the USSR is today. They could use a loan from Egypt!

The unforeseen side effects, though—rising water table bringing more insects, rotting away the carvings in the temples, rapid silting up inside the dam itself, etc.—are getting important. They plan to dig a canal and drain a lot of the incoming new silt into the desert, make a huge farming valley with it, but I don't see how they can drain enough water to carry the dirt, and still leave much behind in the original dam.

The guide says they're having trouble with it.

We then fly south, to Abu Simbel. Lake Nasser, which claimed the original site of the huge monuments, is hundreds of miles long. They enlarged it again in 2008.

In the times of the pharaohs, the land below these had villages, great quarries for the construction of monuments, trade routes south to the Nubian kingdoms. Now it's all underwater.

They did save the enormous temples to Rameses II—built to impress aggressive Nubians with his might and majesty—and to his queen, Nefertari. The colossal statues of Rameses II seem personifications of his egomania. Inside, carvings show him performing *all* the valiant tasks in the great battle with the Hittites—slaying, taking prisoners, then presenting them to himself, who is in turn advised by the gods—which include himself! All this, for a battle which was in fact an iffy draw. Both temples have been lifted about a hundred feet and set back inside a wholly artificial hill, supported inside by the largest concrete dome in the world. Amazing.

> *Look upon my works, ye Mighty,*
> *and despair!*

Except that when Shelley wrote *Ozymandias*, he'd never seen Rameses II's image so well preserved.

Leaving the site, eating the sand blown into our faces by a sudden gust of wind, I caught sight of a Quarthex. It was burrowing into the sand, using a silvery tool that spat ruby-colored light. Beside it, floating on a platform, were some of those funny pipelike things I'd seen days before. Only this time men and women were helping it, lugging stuff around to put into the holes the Quarthex dug.

The people looked dazed, like they were sleep-walking. I waved a greeting, but nobody even looked up. Except the Quarthex. They're expressionless, of course. Still, those glittering popeyes peered at me for a long moment, with the little feelers near its mouth twitching with a kind of anxious energy.

I looked away. I couldn't help but feel a little spooked by it. It wasn't looking at us in a friendly way. Maybe it didn't want me yelling at its work gang.

Then we flew back to Aswan, above the impossibly narrow ribbon of green that snakes through absolute bitter desolation.

DECEMBER 18

I'm writing this at twilight, before the light gives out. We got up this morning and were walking into town when the whole damn ground started to rock. Mud huts slamming down, waves on the Nile, everything.

Got back to the ship but nobody knew what was going on. Not much on the radio. Cairo came in clear, saying there'd been a quake all right, all along the Nile.

Funny thing was, the captain couldn't raise any other radio station. Just Cairo. Nothing else in the whole Middle East.

Some other passengers think there's a war on. Maybe so, but the Egyptian army doesn't know about it. They're standing around, all along the quay, fondling their AK 47s, looking just as puzzled as we are.

More rumblings and shakings in the afternoon. And now that the sun's about gone, I can see big sheets of light in the sky. Only it seems to me the constellations aren't right.

Joanna took some of her pills. She's trying to fend off the jitters and I do what I can. I hate the empty, hollow look that comes into her eyes.

We've got to get the hell out of here.

DECEMBER 19

I might as well write this down, there's nothing else to do.

When we got up this morning the sun was there all right, but the moon hadn't gone down. And it didn't, all day.

Sure, they can both be in the sky at the same time. But all day? Joanna is worried, not because of the moon, but because all the airline flights have been cancelled. We were supposed to go back to Cairo today.

More earthquakes. Really bad this time.

At noon, all of a sudden, there were Quarthex everywhere. In the air, swarming in from the east and west. Some splashed down in the Nile—and didn't come up. Others zoomed overhead, heading south toward the dam.

Nobody's been brave enough to leave the ship—including me. Hell, I just want to go home. Joanna's staying in the cabin.

About an hour later, a swarthy man in a ragged gray suit comes running along the quay and says the dam's gone. Just *gone*. The Quarthex formed little knots above it, and there was a lot of purple flashing light and big crackling noises, and then the dam just disappeared.

But the water hasn't come pouring down on us here. The man says it ran *back the other way*. South.

I looked over the rail. The Nile was flowing north.

Late this afternoon, five of the crew went into town. By this time there were fingers of orange and gold zapping across the sky all the time, making weird designs. The clouds would come rolling in from the north, and these radiant beams would hit them, and they'd *split* the clouds, just like that. With a spray of ivory light.

And Quarthex, buzzing everywhere. There's a kind of high sheen, up above the clouds, like a metal boundary or something, but you can see through it.

Quarthex keep zipping up to it, sometimes coming right up out of the Nile itself, just splashing out, then zooming up until they're little dwindling dots. They spin around up there, as if they're inspecting it, and then they drop like bricks, and splash down in the Nile again. Like frantic bees, Joanna said, and her voice trembled.

A technical type on board, an engineer from Rockwell, says *he* thinks the Quarthex are putting on one hell of a light show. Just a weird alien stunt, he thinks.

While I was writing this, the five crewmen returned from Aswan. They'd gone to the big hotels there, and then to police headquarters. They heard that TV from Cairo went out two days ago. All air flights have been grounded because of the Quarthex buzzing around and the odd lights and so on.

Or at least, that's the official line. The captain says his cousin told him that several flights *did* take off two days back, and they hit something up there. Maybe that blue metallic sheen?

One crashed. The others landed, although damaged.

The authorities are keeping it quiet. They're not just keeping us tourists in the dark—they're playing mum with everybody.

I hope the engineer is right. Joanna is fretting and we hardly ate anything for dinner, just picked at the cold lamb. Maybe tomorrow will settle things.

DECEMBER 20

It did. When we woke, the Earth was rising.

It was coming up from the western mountains, blue-white clouds and patches of green and brown, but mostly tawny desert. We're looking west, across the Sahara. I'm writing this while everybody else is running around like a chicken with his head chopped off. I'm sitting on deck, listening to shouts and wild traffic and even some gunshots coming from ashore.

I can see farther east now—either we're turning, or we're rising fast and can see with a better perspective.

Where central Egypt was, there's a big, raw, dark hole.

The black must be the limestone underlying the desert. They've scraped off a rim of sandy margin enclosing the Nile valley, including us—and left the rest. And somehow, they're lifting it free of Earth.

No Quarthex flying around now. Nothing visible except that metallic blue smear of light high up in the air.

And beyond it—Earth, rising.

DECEMBER 22

I skipped a day.

There was no time even to think yesterday. After I wrote the last entry, a crowd of Egyptians came down the quay, shuffling silently along, like the ones we saw back at Abu Simbel. Only there were thousands.

And leading them was a Quarthex. It carried a big disclike thing that made a humming sound. When the Quarthex lifted it, the pitch changed.

It made my eyes water, my skull ache. Like a hand squeezing my head, blurring the air.

Around me, everybody was writhing on the deck, moaning. Joanna, too.

By the time the Quarthex reached our ship I was the only one standing. Those yellow-shot, jittery eyes peered at me, giving nothing away. Then the angular head turned and went on. Pied piper, leading long trains of Egyptians.

Some of our friends from the ship joined at the end of the lines. Rigid, glassy-eyed faces. I shouted but nobody, not a single person in that procession, even looked up.

Joanna struggled to go with them. I threw her down and held her until the damned eerie parade was long past.

Now the ship's deserted. We've stayed aboard, out of pure fear.

Whatever the Quarthex did affects all but a few percent of those within range. A few crew stayed aboard, dazed but ok. Scared, hard to talk to.

Fewer at dinner.

The next morning, nobody.

We had to scavenge for food. The crew must've taken what was left aboard. I ventured into the market street nearby, but everything was closed up. Deserted. Only a few days ago we were buying caftans and alabaster sphinxes and beaten-bronze trinkets in the gaudy shops, and now it was stone cold dead. Not a sound, not a stray cat.

I went around to the back of what I remembered was a filthy corner cafe. I'd turned up my nose at it while we were shopping, certain there was a sure case of dysentery waiting inside . . . but now I was glad to find some days-old fruits and vegetables in a cabinet.

Coming back, I nearly ran into a bunch of Egyptian men who were marching through the streets. Spooks.

They had the look of police, but were dressed up like Mardi Gras—loincloths, big leather belts, bangles and beads, hair stiffened with wax. They carried sharp spears.

Good thing I was jumpy, or they'd have run right into me. I heard them coming and ducked into a grubby alley. They were systematically combing the area, searching the miserable apartments above the market. The honcho barked orders in a language I didn't understand—harsh, guttural, not like Egyptian.

I slipped away. Barely.

We kept out of sight after that. Stayed below deck and waited for nightfall.

Not that the darkness made us feel any better. There were fires ashore. Not in Aswan itself—the town was utterly black. Instead, orange dots sprinkled the distant hillsides. They were all over the scrub desert, just before the ramparts of the real desert that stretches—or did stretch—to east and west.

Now, I guess, there's only a few dozen miles of desert, before you reach—what?

I can't discuss this with Joanna. She has that haunted expression, from the time before her breakdown. She is drawn and silent. Stays in the room.

We ate our goddamn vegetables. Now we go to bed.

DECEMBER 23

There were more of those patrols of Mardi Gras spooks today. They came along the quay, looking at the tour ships moored there, but for some reason they didn't come aboard.

We're alone on the ship. All the crew, the other tourists— all gone.

Around noon, when we were getting really hungry and I was mustering my courage to go back to the market street, I heard a roaring.

Understand, I hadn't heard an airplane in days. And those were jets. This buzzing, I suddenly realized, is a rocket or something, and it's in trouble.

I go out on the deck, checking first to see if the patrols are lurking around, and the roaring is louder. It's a plane with stubby little wings, coming along low over the water, burping and hacking and finally going dead quiet.

It nosed over and came in for a big splash. I thought the pilot was a goner, but the thing rode steady in the water for a while and the cockpit folded back and out jumps a man.

I yelled at him and he waved and swam for the ship. The plane sank.

He caught a line below and climbed up. An American, no less. But what he had to say was even more surprising.

He wasn't just some sky jockey from Cairo. He was an astronaut.

He was part of a rescue mission, sent up to try to stop the Quarthex. The others he'd lost contact with, although it looked like they'd all been drawn down toward the floating island that Egypt has become.

We're suspended about two Earth radii out, in a slowly widening orbit. There's a shield over us, keeping the air in and everything—cosmic rays, communications, space-ships—out.

The Quarthex somehow ripped off a layer of Egypt and are lifting it free of Earth, escaping with it. Nobody had ever guessed they had such power. Nobody Earthside knows what to do about it. The Quarthex who were outside Egypt at the time just lifted off in their ships and rendezvoused with this floating platform.

Ralph Blanchard is his name, and his mission was to fly under the slab of Egypt, in a fast orbital craft. He was supposed to see how they'd ripped the land free. A lot of it had fallen away.

There is an array of silvery pods under the soil, he says, and they must be enormous anti-grav units. The same kind that make the Quarthex ships fly, that we've been trying to get the secret of.

The pods are about a mile apart, making a grid. But between them, there are lots of Quarthex. They're building stuff, tilling soil, and so on—upside down! The gravity works opposite on the underside. That must be the way the whole thing is kept together—compressing it with artificial gravity from both sides. God knows what makes the shield above.

But the really strange thing is the Nile. There's one on the underside, too.

It starts at the underside of Alexandria, where *our* Nile meets—met—the Mediterranean. It then flows back, all the way along the underside, running through a Nile valley of its own. Then it turns up and around the edge of the slab, and comes over the lip of it a few hundred miles upstream of here.

The Quarthex have drained the region beyond the Aswan dam. Now the Nile flows in its old course. The big temples of Rameses II are perched on a hill high above the river, and Ralph was sure he saw Quarthex working on the site, taking it apart.

He thinks they're going to put it back where it was, before the dam was built in the 1960s.

Ralph was supposed to return to Orbital City with his data. He came in close for a final pass and hit the shield they have, the one that keeps the air in. His ship was damaged.

He'd been issued a suborbital craft, able to do reentries, in case he should penetrate the airspace. That saved him.

There were other guys who hit the shield and cracked through, guys with conventional deepspace shuttle tugs and the like, and they fell like bricks.

We've talked all this over but no one has a good theory of what is going on. The best we can do is stay away from the patrols.

Meanwhile, Joanna scavenged through obscure bins of the ship, and turned up an entire case of Skivva, a cheap Egyptian beer. So after I finish this ritual entry—who knows, this might be in a history book someday, and as a good academic I should keep it up—I'll go share it out in one grand bust with Ralph and Joanna. It'll do her good. It'll do us both good. She's been rocky. As well,

> *Malt does more than Milton can*
> *To justify God's ways to man.*

DECEMBER 24

This little diary was all I managed to take with us when the spooks came. I had it in my pocket.

I keep going over what happened. There was nothing I could do, I'm sure of that, and yet . . .

We stayed below decks, getting damned hungry again but afraid to go out. There was chanting from the distance. Getting louder. Then footsteps aboard. We retreated to the small cabins aft, third class.

The sounds got nearer. Ralph thought we should stand and fight but I'd seen those spears and hell, I'm a middle-aged man, no match for those maniacs.

Joanna got scared. It was like her breakdown. No, worse. The jitters built until her whole body seemed to vibrate, fingers digging into her hair like claws, eyes squeezed tight, face compressed as if to shut out the world.

There was nothing I could do with her, she wouldn't keep quiet. She ran out of the cabin we were hiding in, just rushed down the corridor screaming at them.

Ralph said we should use her diversion to get away and I said I'd stay, help her, but then I saw them grab her and hold her, not rough. It didn't seem as if they were going to do anything, just take her away.

My fear got the better of me then. It's hard to write this. Part of me says I should've stayed, defended her—but it was hopeless. You can't live up to your ideal self. The world of literature shows people summoning up courage, but there's a thin line between that and stupidity. Or so I tell myself.

The spooks hadn't seen us yet, so we slipped overboard, keeping quiet.

We went off the loading ramp on the river side, away from shore. Ralph paddled around to see the quay and came back looking worried. There were spooks swarming all over.

We had to move. The only way to go was across the river.

This shaky handwriting is from sheer, flat-out fatigue. I swam what seemed like forever. The water wasn't bad, pretty warm, but the current kept pushing us off course. Lucky thing the Nile is pretty narrow there, and there are rocky little stubs sticking out. I grabbed onto those and rested.

Nobody saw us, or at least they didn't do anything about it.

We got ashore looking like drowned rats. There's a big hill there, covered with ancient rock-cut tombs. I thought of taking shelter in one of them and started up the hill, legs wobbly under me, and then we saw a mob up top.

And a Quarthex, a big one with a shiny shell. It wore something over its head. Supposedly Quarthex don't wear clothes, but this one had a funny rig on. A big bird head, with a long narrow beak and flinty black eyes.

There was madness all around us. Long lines of people carrying burdens, chanting. Quarthex riding on those lifter units of theirs. All beneath the piercing, biting sun.

We hid for a while. I found that this diary, in its zippered leather case, made it through the river without a leak. I started writing this entry. Joanna said once that I'd retreated into books as a defense, in adolescence—she was full of psychoanalytical explanations, it was a hobby. She kept thinking that if she could figure herself out, then things would be all right. Well, maybe I did use words and books and a quiet, orderly life as a place to hide. So what? It was better than this "real" world around me right now.

I thought of Joanna and what might be happening to her. The Quar can—

(New Entry)

I was writing when the Quarthex came closer. I thought we were finished, but they didn't see us. Those huge heads turned all the time, the glittering black eyes scanning. Then they moved away. The chanting was a relentless, singsong drone that gradually faded.

We got away from there, fast.

I'm writing this during a short break. Then we'll move on.

No place to go but the goddamn desert.

DECEMBER 25

Christmas.

I keep thinking about fat turkey stuffed with spicy dressing, crisp cranberries, a dry white wine, thick gravy—

No point in that. We found some food today in an abandoned construction site, bread at least a week old and some dried-up fruit. That was all.

Ralph kept pushing me on west. He wants to see over the edge, how they hold this thing together.

I'm not that damn interested, but I don't know where else to go. Just running on blind fear. My professorial instincts—like keeping this journal. It helps keep me sane. Assuming I still am.

Ralph says putting this down might have scientific value. If I can ever get it to anybody outside. So I keep on. Words, words, words. Much cleaner than this gritty, surreal world.

We saw people marching in the distance, dressed in loincloths again. It suddenly struck me that I'd seen that clothing before—in those marvelous wall paintings, in the tombs of the Valley of Kings. It's ancient dress.

Ralph thinks he understands what's happening. There was an all-frequencies broadcast from the Quarthex when they tore off this wedge we're on. Nobody understood much—it was in that odd semi-speech of theirs, all the words blurred and placed wrong, scrambled up. Something about their mission or destiny or whatever being to enhance the best in each world. About how they'd make a deal with the Egyptians to bring forth the unrealized promise of their majestic past and so on. And that meant isolation, so the fruit of ages could flower.

Ha. The world's great age begins anew, maybe—but Percy Bysshe Shelley never meant it like this.

Not that I care a lot about motivations right now. I spent the day thinking of Joanna, still feeling guilty. And hiking west in the heat and dust, hiding from gangs of glassy-eyed workers when we had to.

We reached the edge at sunset. It hadn't occurred to me, but it's obvious—for there to be days and nights at all means they're spinning the slab we're on.

Compressing it, holding in the air, adding just the right rotation. Masters—of space/time and the river, yes.

The ground started to slope away. Not like going downhill, because there was nothing pulling you down the face of it. I mean, we *felt* like we were walking on level ground. But overhead the sky moved as we walked.

We caught up with the sunset. The sun dropped for a while in late afternoon, then started rising again. Pretty soon it was right overhead, high noon.

And we could see Earth, too, farther away than yesterday. Looking cool and blue.

We came to a wall of glistening metal tubes, silvery and rippling with a frosty blue glow. I started to get woozy as we approached. Something happened to gravity—it pulled your stomach as if you were spinning around. Finally we couldn't get any closer. I stopped, nauseated. Ralph kept on. I watched him try to walk toward the metal barrier, which by then looked like luminous icebergs suspended above barren desert.

He tried to walk a straight line, he said later. I could see him veer, his legs rubbery, and it looked as though he rippled and distended, stretching horizontally while some force compressed him vertically, an egg man, a plastic body swaying in tides of gravity.

Then he starting stumbling, falling. He cried out—a horrible, warped sound, like paper tearing for a long, long time. He fled. The sand clawed at him as he ran, strands grasping at his feet, trailing long streamers of glittering, luminous sand—but it couldn't hold him. Ralph staggered away, gasping, his eyes huge and white and terrified.

We turned back.

But coming away, I saw a band of men and women marching woodenly along toward the wall. They were old, most of them, and diseased. Some had been hurt—you could see the wounds.

They were heading straight for the lip. Silent, inexorable.

Ralph and I followed them for a while. As they approached the wall, they started walking up off the sand—right into the air.

And over the tubes.

Just flying.

We decided to head south. Maybe the lip is different there. Ralph says the plan he'd heard, after the generals had studied the survey-mission results, was to try to open the shield at the ground, where the Nile spills over. Then they'd get people out by boating them along the river.

Could they be doing that, now? We hear roaring sounds in the sky sometimes. Explosions. Ralph is ironic about it all, says he wonders when the Quarthex will get tired of intruders and go back to the source—*all* the way back.

I don't know. I'm tired and worn down.

Could there be a way out? Sounds impossible, but it's all we've got.

Head south, to the Nile's edge.

We're hiding in a cave tonight. It's bitterly cold out here in the desert, and a sunburn is no help.

I'm hungry as hell. Some Christmas.

We were supposed to be back in Laguna Beach by now. God knows where Joanna is.

DECEMBER 26

I got away. Barely.

The Quarthex work in teams now. They've gridded off the desert and work across it systematically in those floating platforms. There are big tubes like cannon mounted on each end and a Quarthex scans it over the sands.

Ralph and I crept up to the mouth of the cave we were in and watched them comb the area. They worked out from the Nile. When a muzzle turned toward us I felt an impact like a warm, moist wave smacking into my face, like being in the ocean. It drove me to my knees. I reeled away. Threw myself farther back into the cramped cave.

It all dropped away then, as if the wave had pinned me to the ocean floor and filled my lungs with a sluggish liquid.

And in an instant was gone. I rolled over, gasping, and saw Ralph staggering into the sunlight, heading for the Quarthex platform. The projector was leveled at him so that it no longer struck the cave mouth. So I'd been released from its grip.

I watched them lower a rope ladder. Ralph dutifully climbed up. I wanted to shout to him, try to break the hold that thing had over him, but once again the better part of valor—I just watched. They carried him away.

I waited until twilight to move. Not having anybody to talk to makes it harder to control my fear.

God I'm hungry. Couldn't find a scrap to eat.

When I took out this diary I looked at the leather case and remembered stories of people getting so starved they'd eat their shoes. Suitably boiled and salted, of course, with a tangy sauce.

Another day or two and the idea might not seem so funny.

I've got to keep moving.

DECEMBER 27

Hard to write.

They got me this morning.

It grabs your mind. Like before. Squeezing in your head.

But after a while it is better. Feels good. But a buzzing all the time, you can't think.

Picked me up while I was crossing an arroyo. Didn't have any idea they were around. A platform.

Took me to some others. All Egyptians. Caught like me.

Marched us to the Nile.

Plenty to eat.

Rested at noon.

Brought Joanna to me. She is all right. Lovely in the long draping dress the Quarthex gave her.

All around are the bird-headed ones. Ibis, I remember, the bird of the Nile. And dog-headed ones. Lion-headed ones.

Gods of the old times. The Quarthex are the gods of the old time. Of the greater empire.

We are the people.

Sometimes I can think, like now. They sent me away from the work gang on an errand. I am old, not strong. They are kind—give me easy jobs.

So I came to here. Where I hid this diary. Before they took my old uncomfortable clothes I put this little book into a crevice in the rock. Pen too.

Now writing helps. Mind clears some.

I saw Ralph, then lost track of him. I worked hard after the noontime. Sun felt good. I lifted pots, carried them where the foreman said.

The Quarthex-god with ibis head is building a fresh temple. Made from the stones of Aswan. It will be cool and deep, many pillars.

They took my dirty clothes. Gave me fresh loincloth, headband, sandals. Good ones. Better than my old clothes.

It is hard to remember how things were before I came here. Before I knew the river. Its flow. How it divides the world.

I will rest before I try to read what I have written in here before. The words are hard.

Days Later

I come back but can read only a little.

Joanna says you should not. The ibis will not like it if I do.

I remember I liked these words on paper, in my days before. I earned my food with them. Now they are empty. Must not have been true.

Do not need them any more.

Ralph, science. All words too.

Later

Days since I find this again. I do the good work, I eat, Joanna is there in the night. Many things. I do not want to do this reading.

But today another thing howled overhead. It passed over the desert like a screaming black bird, the falcon, and then fell, flames, big roar.

I remembered Ralph.

This book I remembered, came for it.

The ibis-god speaks to us each sunset. Of how the glory of our lives is here again. We are one people once more again yes after a long long time of being lost.

What the red sunset means. The place where the dead are buried in the western desert. To be taken in death close to the edge, so the dead will walk their last steps in this world, to the lip and over, to the netherworld.

There the lion-god will preserve them. Make them live again.

The Quarthex-gods have discovered how to revive the dead of any beings. They spread this among the stars.

But only to those who understand. Who deserve. Who bow to the great symmetry of life.

One face light, one face dark.

The sun lights the netherworld when for us it is night. There the dead feast and mate and laugh and live forever.

Ralph saw that. The happy land below. It shares the sun.

I saw Ralph today. He came to the river to see the falcon thing cry from the clouds. We all did.

It fell into the river and was swallowed and will be taken to the netherworld where it flows over the edge of the world.

Ralph was sorry when the falcon fell. He said it was a mistake to send it to bother us. That someone from the old dead time had sent it.

Ralph works in the quarry. Carving the limestone. He looks good, the sun has lain on him and made him strong and brown.

I started to talk of the time we met but he frowned.

That was before we understood, he says. Shook his head. So I should not speak of it.

The gods know of time and the river. They know.
I tire now.

Again

Joanna sick. I try help but no way to stop the bleeding
from her.

In old time I would try to stop the stuff of life from
leaving her. I would feel sorrow.

I do not now. I am calm.

Ibis-god prepares her. Works hard and good over her.

She will journey tonight. Walk the last trek. Over the
edge of the sky and to the netherland.

It is what the temple carving says. She will live again
forever.

Forever waits.

I come here to find this book to enter this. I remember
sometimes how it was.

I did not know joy then. Joanna did not.

We lived but to no point. Just come-go-come-again.

Now I know what comes. The western death. The rising
life.

The Quarthex-gods are right. I should forget that life.
To hold on is to die. To flow forward is to live.

Today I saw the pharaoh. He came in radiant chariot,
black horses before, bronze sword in hand. The sun was
high above him. No shadow he cast.

Big and with red skin the pharaoh rode down the avenue
of the kings. We the one people cheered.

His great head was mighty in the sun and his many arms
waved in salute to his one people. He is so great the horses
groan and sweat to pull him. His hard gleaming body is all
armor for he will always be on guard against our enemies.

Like those who fall from the sky. Every day now more
come down, dying fireballs to smash in the desert. All
fools. Black rotting bodies. None will rise to walk west.
They are only burned prey of the pharaoh.

The pharaoh rode three times to the avenue. We threw
ourselves down to attract a glance. His huge glaring eyes
regarded us and we cried out, our faces wet with joy.

He will speak for us in the netherworld. Sing to the
undergods.

Make our westward walking path smooth.

I fall before him.

I bury this now. No more write in it.

This kind of writing is not for the world now. It comes from the old dead time when I knew nothing and thought everything.

I go to my eternity on the river.

A GIFT FROM THE GRAYLANDERS

Michael Bishop

True science fiction horror stories are rare, and despite the surfeit of monster movies they are seldom about attacks on Earth by alien beasties. Here is a quietly written sf story whose undercurrent of fear builds gradually, as in the best horror stories. But its ending isn't at all what you might expect.

Michael Bishop won a Nebula Award for his novelette "The Quickening." His many novels include No Enemy but Time *and* Ancient of Days.

In the house where Mommy took him several months after she and Daddy stopped living together, Cory had a cot downstairs. The house belonged to Mommy's sister and her sister's husband Martin, a pair of unhappy people who already had four kids of their own. Aunt Clara's kids had real bedrooms upstairs, but Mommy told Cory that he was lucky to have a place to sleep at all and that anyway a basement was certainly a lot better than a hot-air grate on a Denver street or a dirty stable like the one that the Baby Jesus had been born in.

Cory hated the way the basement looked and smelled. It had walls like the concrete slabs on the graves in cemeteries. Looking at them, you could almost see those kinds of slabs turned on their ends and pushed up against one another to make this small square prison underground. The slabs oozed wetness. You could make a handprint on the walls just by holding your palm to the concrete. When you took your hand away, it smelled gray. Cory knew that dead people smelled gray too, especially when they had been dead a long time—like the people who were only bones and whom he had seen grinning out of magazine photographs without any lips or eyeballs or hair. Cory sometimes lay down on his cot wondering if maybe an army of those gray-smelling skeletons clustered on the other side of the basement walls, working with oddly silent picks and shovels to break through the concrete and carry him away to the GrayLands where their deadness made them live.

Maybe, though, the gray-smelling creatures beyond the basement walls were not really skeletons. Maybe they were Clay People. On his cousins' black-and-white TV set, Cory had seen an old movie serial about a strange planet. Some of the planet's people lived underground, and they could step into or out of the walls of rock that tied together a maze of tunnels beneath the planet's surface. They moved through dirt and rock the way that a little boy like Cory could move through water in summer or loose snow in winter. The brave, blond hero of the serial called these creatures the Clay People, a name that fit them almost perfectly, because they looked like monsters slapped together out of wet mud and then put out into the sun to dry. Every time they came limping into view with that tinny movie-serial music rum-tum-tumping away in the background, they gave Cory a bad case of the shivers.

Later, lying on his cot, he would think about them trying to come through the oozy walls to take him away from Clara's house the way that Daddy had tried to kidnap him from that motel in Ratón, New Mexico. For a long time that day, Daddy had hidden in the room with the vending machines. Going in there for a Coke, Cory had at first thought that Daddy was a monster. His screams had brought Mommy running and also the motel manager and a security guard; and the "kidnap plot"—as Mommy had called it later—had ended in an embarrassing way for Daddy, Daddy hightailing it out of Ratón in his beat-up Impala like a drug dealer making a getaway in a TV cop show. But what if the Clay People were better kidnappers than Daddy? What if they came through the walls and grabbed him before he could awake and scream for help? They would surely take him back through the clammy grayness to a place where dirt would fill his mouth and stop his ears and press against his eyeballs, and he would be as good as dead with them forever and ever.

So Cory hated the basement. Because his cousins disliked the windowless damp of the place as much as he did, they seldom came downstairs to bother him. Although that was okay when he wanted to be by himself, he never really wanted to be by himself *in the basement*. Smelling its mustiness, touching its greasy walls, feeling like a bad guy in solitary, Cory could not help but imagine unnamable danger and deadness surrounding him. Skeletons. Clay People. Monsters from the earthen dark. It was okay to be alone on a mountain trail or even in a classroom at school, but to be alone in this basement was to be punished for not having a daddy who came home every evening the way that daddies were supposed to. Daddy himself, who had once tried to kidnap Cory, would have never made him spend his nights in this kind of prison. Or, if for some reason Daddy could not have prevented the arrangement, he would have stayed downstairs with Cory to protect him from the creatures burrowing toward him from the Gray-Lands.

"Cory, there's *nothing* down here to be afraid of," Mommy said. "And you don't want your mother to share your bedroom with you, do you? A big seven-year-old like you?"

"No," he admitted. "I want my daddy."

"Your daddy can't protect you. He can't or won't provide for you. That's why we had to leave him. He only tried to grab you back, Cory, to hurt me. Don't you understand?"

Daddy hurt Mommy? Cory shook his head.

"I'm sorry it's a basement," Mommy said. "I'm sorry it's not a chalet with a big picture window overlooking a mountain pass, but things just haven't been going that way for us lately."

Cory rolled over on his cot so that the tip of his nose brushed the slablike wall.

"Tell me what you're afraid of," Mommy said. "If you

tell me, maybe we can handle it together—whatever it is."

After some more coaxing, but without turning back to face her, Cory began to talk about the skeletons and the Clay People from the GrayLands beyond the sweating concrete.

"The GrayLands?" Mommy said. "There aren't any GrayLands, Cory. There may be skeletons, but they don't get up and walk. They certainly don't use picks and shovels to dig their way into basements. And the Clay People, well, they're just television monsters, make-believe, nothing at all for a big boy like you to worry about in real life."

"I want to sleep on the couch upstairs."

"You can't, Cory. You've got your own bathroom down here, and when you wake up and have to use it, well, you don't disturb Uncle Martin or Aunt Clara or any of the kids. We've been through all this before, haven't we? You know how important it is that Marty get his sleep. He has to get up at four in order to make his shift at the fire station."

"I won't use the bathroom upstairs. I won't even drink nothin' before I go to bed."

"Cory, hush."

The boy rolled over and pulled himself up onto his elbows so that he could look right into Mommy's eyes. "I'm scared of the GrayLands. I'm scared of the gray-smellin' monsters that're gonna come pushin' through the walls from over there."

Playfully, Mommy mussed his hair. "You're impossible, you know that? Really impossible."

It was as if she could not wholeheartedly believe in his fear. In fact, she seemed to think that he had mentioned the GrayLands and the monsters who would come forth from them only as a boy's cute way of prompting adult sympathy. He did not like the basement (Mommy was willing to concede that point), but this business of a nearby subterranean country of death and its weird gray-smelling inhabitants was only so much childish malarky. The boy missed his father, and Mommy could not assume Daddy's role as protector—as bad as Clinton himself had been at it—because in a young boy's eyes a woman was not a

man. And so she mussed his hair again and abandoned him
to his delusive demons.

Cory never again spoke to anyone of the GrayLands.
But each night, hating the wet clayey smell of the basement and its gummy linoleum floor and the foil-wrapped
heating ducts bracketed to the ceiling and the naked light
bulb hanging like a tiny dried gourd from a bracket near
the unfinished stairs, he would huddle under the blankets
on his cot and talk to the queer creatures tunneling stealth-
ily toward him from the GrayLands—the Clay People, or
Earth Zombies, or Bone Puppets, that only he of all the
members of this mixed-up household actually believed in.

"Stay where you are," Cory would whisper at the wall.
"Don't come over here. Stay where you are."

The monsters—whatever they were—obeyed. They did
not break through the concrete to grab him. Of course,
maybe the concrete was too thick and hard to let them
reach him without a lot more work. They could still be
going at it, picking away. The Clay People on that movie
planet had been able to walk through earth without even
using tools to clear a path for themselves, but maybe
Earth's earth was packed tighter. Maybe good old-fashioned
Colorado concrete could hold off such single-minded creatures for months. Cory hoped that it could. For safety's
sake, he would keep talking to them, begging them to stay
put, pleading with them not to undermine the foundations
of his uncle's house with their secret digging.

Summer came, and they still had not reached him. The
walls still stood against them, smooth to the touch here,
rough there. Some of the scratches in the ever-glistening
grayness were like unreadable foreign writing. These
scratches troubled Cory. He wondered if they had always
been there. Maybe the tunneling creatures had scribbled
them on the concrete from the other side, not quite getting
the tips of their strange writing instruments to push through
the walls but by great effort and persistence just managing
to press marks into the outer surface where a real human
being like him could see them. The boy traced these marks
with his finger. He tried to spell them out. But he had
gone through only his first year in school, and the task of
decipherment was not one he could accomplish without

help. Unfortunately, he could not apply for help without breaking the promise that he had made to himself never to speak of the GrayLanders to anyone in Aunt Clara's family. If Mommy could muster no belief in them, how could he hope to convince his hard-headed cousins, who liked him best when he was either running errands for them or hiding from them in the doubtful sanctuary of the basement?

Then Cory realized that maybe he was having so much trouble reading the GrayLanders' damp scratches not because he was slow or the scratches stood for characters in a foreign tongue, but because his tormentors' painstaking method of pressing them outward onto the visible portions of the walls made the characters arrive there *backwards*. Cory was proud of himself for figuring this out. He filched a pocket mirror from the handbag of the oldest girl and brought it down the creaking stairs to test his theory.

This girl, fifteen-year-old Gina Lynn, caught him holding the mirror against one of the rougher sections of wall, squinting back and forth between the concrete and the oval glass. Meanwhile, with the nub of a broken pencil, he was struggling to copy the reversed scratches onto a tatter of paper bag. Cory did not hear Gina Lynn come down the stairs because he was concentrating so hard on this work. He was also beginning to understand that his wonderful theory was not really proving out. The mysterious calligraphy of the GrayLanders continued to make no sense.

"You're just about the weirdest little twerp I've ever seen," Gina Lynn said matter-of-factly. "Give me back my mirror."

Startled and then shame-faced, Cory turned around. He yielded the mirror. Gina Lynn asked him no questions, knowing from past experience that he would respond with monosyllables if at all, but began to bruit it around the house that he could read the marks in concrete the way that some people could read cloud formations or chicken entrails. Uncle Martin, who was home for a long weekend, thought this discovery about his sister-in-law's son hilarious. He called Cory into the living room to rag him about taking the mirror but especially about holding it up to the shallow striations in the otherwise blank gray face of a basement wall.

"Out with it," he said. "What'd that stupid wall tell

you? No secrets, now. I want me a tip straight from the
cee-ment itself. What's a rock-solid investment for a fella
like Uncle Marty with only so much cash to spare?''

Cory could feel his face burning.

"Come on, cuz. This is a relative talkin', kid. Let me
in—let us *all* in—on what's goin' down, basement-wise.''

"Who's gonna take the World Series this year?'' twelve-
year-old David promptly asked.

"Is Hank Danforth gonna ask Gina Lynn to his pool
party?'' Faye, disturbingly precocious for nine, wondered
aloud.

("Shut up,'' Gina Lynn cautioned her.)

And thirteen-year-old Deborah said, "Is war gonna break
out? Ask your stupid wall if the Russians're gonna bomb
us.''

"Maybe the wall was askin' him for some cold cream,''
Uncle Martin said. "You know, to put on its wrinkles.''
All four of Uncle Martin's bratty kids laughed. "You were
just writin' down the brand, weren't you, Cory? Don't
wanna bring home the wrong brand of cold cream to smear
on your favorite wall. After all, you're the fella who's
gotta face the damn thing every morning, aren't you?''

"Silica Lotion,'' Gina Lynn said. "Oil of Grah-velle.''

Mommy had a job as a cash-register clerk somewhere.
She was not at home. Cory fixed his eyes on Uncle
Martin's belt buckle, a miniature brass racing car, and
waited for their silly game to end. When it did, without his
once having opened his mouth to reply to their jackass
taunts, he strode with wounded dignity back down to the
corner of the basement sheltering his cot. Alone again, he
peered for a time at the marks that Gina Lynn's mirror had
not enabled him to read. The scratches began to terrify
him. They coded a language that he had not yet learned.
They probably contained taunts—threats, in fact—crueler
and much more dangerous than any that his uncle and
cousins had just shied off him for sport.

Two days later, in Uncle Martin's detached garage,
Cory found a gallon of yellow paint that Aunt Clara had
bought nearly three summers ago to take care of the house's
peeling shutters. He also found a brush and an aerosol can
of black enamel that David had recently used to touch up

the frame of his ten-speed. These items the boy carried downstairs to his private sanctuary.

Stripped to his jockey briefs, he began to slap runny gouts of latex brilliance all over the disturbing hieroglyphs. At first, he hid a few of them behind the dripping image of a huge lopsided egg yolk. Then, swinging his arm in ever-widening arcs, he expanded this clownish shape into the brim of a festive straw sombrero. The sombrero rim grew to be gong-sized, and the gong ballooned to the dimensions of one of those giant yellow teacups whirling around and around in a local amusement park. Finally, though, Cory had his circle as big as a small sun, a ball of good cheer radiating into the basement as if the very paint itself had caught fire.

He outlined the sun with the black spray paint and added flares and fiery peninsulas that cried out for yet more yellow. Then he painted smaller lamps on other portions of this wall and on the other walls too, and squat tropical birds with combs and wattles, and pineapples as big as the lamps, and a long yellow beach under the glowering sun. His arms ran yellow, as did his pipe-cleaner thighs, as did his caved-in belly and chest, while his face seemed to reflect back the brightness of the obliterated gray that he strove to cover over permanently. If he had to live and sleep in this dank hole in the ground, let it be a happy hole in the ground. Let the light of artificial suns, two-dimensional lamps, and crudely drafted fruits and cockatoos spill into his basement through the pores of the very cement.

Let there be light.

Let there be light to hold the GrayLanders at bay. For Cory believed that the work he had done, the symbols he had splashed up around his cot like a fence of sunlight, would keep the creatures beyond the subterranean walls from bursting through them to steal him away from Mommy and the real world of automobiles and mountains and football stadiums—the real world in which she was trying to make a place for both of them. Maybe he was safer now.

But while Cory was admiring what he had done, David came down the steps to ask him to go to the store. His older cousin saw him three-quarters naked and striped like an aborigine in the midst of a yellow-gray jungle unlike any terrain that David had expected to find only a floor below the family's TV room.

"Holy shit," he said and backed away up the steps as if Cory might be planning to slit his throat on the spot.

A moment or two later, Uncle Martin came storming down the steps in a pair of rope-soled boots that made the whole unfinished structure tremble like a medieval assault tower in an old Tyrone Power movie. He could not believe what Cory had done. He bruised the boy's arm and upper chest shaking him this way and that to demonstrate his disbelief and his unhappiness. He threw Cory onto his cot with such force that it collapsed under the blow and dumped the boy sidelong so that his head struck a section of painted concrete. Yellow paint smudged the whorl pattern of hair on Cory's crown, and a trickle of red worked through the smudge to enrage Uncle Martin even further.

"This is *my* house!" he shouted, slapping Cory again. "No one gave you permission to do this!"

Aunt Clara's pant-suited legs appeared halfway up the trembling stairs. More of her came into view as she descended. When Uncle Martin drew back his forearm to administer another cracking wallop, she cried, "Marty, don't! Something's happenin' on the news. You like the news. Come see what's goin' on. Try to relax. I'll take care of this. Come watch the news."

Uncle Martin's forearm halted inches from Cory's eyes. "Ain't nobody gonna take care of this, Clara!" he shouted. "We'll jes' leave our little Piggaso down here to moon over his shitty goddamn yellow masterpieces! Forever, maybe!" He thrust Cory into the wall to punctuate this last threat, kicked the crumpled cot, and pounded back up the steps, pulling Aunt Clara along with him. Then the door slammed. Soon after, the naked light bulb near the staircase went out; and the boy knew that one of his cousins, at Uncle Martin's bidding, had flipped the circuit breaker controlling the power supply to the basement.

But for a narrow line of light beneath the door at the top of the steps, Cory crouched beside his cot in utter darkness. Then someone—maybe Uncle Martin himself—put something—probably a rolled-up towel—along the base of the door; and the not quite utter darkness of his prison took on a thoroughness that made the boy think that someone—

possibly a GrayLander—had stuck an altogether painless needle into his eyeballs and injected them with ink. He still had eyeballs, of course, but they had gone solid black on him, like licorice jawbreakers or moist ripe olives. With such eyes, he could "see" only darkness.

What about the fat yellow sun that he had painted? What about the beach, the pineapples, the sunlamps, and the cockatoos? He put his hands on the damp slabs of the basement walls and felt each invisible figure for reassurance. Was the dampness only the sweat of soil-backed concrete, or was it instead an indication of undried paint? Cory could not tell. When he sniffed his hands, they gave off the familiar odor of grayness—but even bright yellow pigment could acquire that smell when, like a glaze of fragile perfume, it was applied to an upright slab of earthen gray. The boy wiped his hands on his chest. Was he wiping off a smear of latex sunshine or the clammy perspiration of underground cement? Because he would never be able to tell, he gave up trying.

Then he heard a pounding overhead and knew that Mommy had come home from work. She and Uncle Martin were just beyond the door at the top of the stairs, arguing.

"For Chrissake, Marty, you can't keep him locked up in the basement—no matter what he's done!"

"Watch me, Claudia! Jes' you watch me!"

"I'm going down there to see him! I'm his mother, and I've got a right to see him! Or else he's gonna come up here to see us!"

"What he's gonna do, woman, is stew in the dumb-fuckin' Piggaso mess he's made!"

"He hasn't even had his dinner!"

"Who says he deserves any?"

"He's my son, and I'm going to let him out!"

Then Cory's darkness was riven by the kind of noise that a big dog makes when it slams its body into a fence slat, and Mommy was screaming, and Aunt Clara was cursing both Mommy and Uncle Martin, and the staircase scaffolding was doing the shimmy-shimmy in its jerrybuilt moorings. Crash followed crash, and curses curses, and soon all the upper portions of the house seemed to be waltzing to the time-keeping of slaps and the breakage of dinnerware or random pieces of bric-a-brac. Cory waited for the rumpus to end, fully expecting Mommy to triumph and the door to open and the darkness to give way to a liberating spill of wattage that would light up the big yellow sun and all the other happy symbols that he had painted. Instead, when the noise ceased and the house stopped quaking, the darkness kept going, and so did the silence, and the only reasons that Cory could think of were that Mommy and her brother-in-law had killed each other or that Mommy had finally agreed with Uncle Marty that Cory really did deserve to sit alone in the dark for trying to beautify the dumb-ass basement walls.

Whatever had happened upstairs, the door did not open, and the ink in his eyeballs got thicker and thicker, and he came to realize that he would have to endure both the dark and the steady approach of the GrayLanders—Clay People, Earth Zombies, Bone Puppets—as either a premeditated punishment or a spooky sort of accident. (Maybe a burglar had broken in during the argument and stabbed everybody to death before Mommy could tell him that her son was locked in the basement. Maybe Mommy had purposely said nothing to the bad guy about him, for fear that the bad guy would get worried and come downstairs to knife Cory too.) Anyway, he was trapped, with no lights and nothing to eat and streaks of yellow paint all over his invisible body and only a tiny bathroom and trickles of rusty tap water for any kind of comfort at all.

Cory crept up the rickety stairs, putting a splinter into one palm when he gripped the guard rail too hard. At the top, he beat on the door in rapid tatoos that echoed on his side like the clatter of a fight with bamboo staves at the bottom of an empty swimming pool. "Let me out!" he shouted. "Let me out of here!" Which was not dignified, he knew, but which was necessary, here at the beginning of his confinement, as a test of Uncle Martin's will to hold him. If noise would make his uncle nervous, if pleading would make the man relent, the boy knew that he had to try such tactics, for Mommy's sake as well as his. But it was no use, and finally he sat down and bit at the splinter in his palm until he had its tip between his baby teeth and managed to pull it free of the punctured flesh sheathing it.

* * *

Darkness swallows time. Cory decided that darkness swallows time when he had been alone in the black basement so long that he could not remember being anywhere else even a quarter of the time that he had spent hunched on his cot waiting for the darkness to end. He could not tell whether time was stretching out like a pull of salt-water taffy or drawing up like a spider when you hold a match over its body. Time was not something that happened in the dark at all. The dark had swallowed it. It was trying to digest time somewhere deep in its bowels, but when time emerged again, Cory felt sure that it would be a foul thing, physically altered and hence bad-smelling—gray-smelling, probably—and unwelcome. He almost hoped that the dark would swallow him, too, so that he would not have to confront the stench of time when, altered in this bad but inevitable way, it came oozing into the world again.

Once, he thought he heard sirens. Maybe Uncle Martin had gone to a fire somewhere.

Later, though, he was more concerned that the Gray-Landers were getting closer to breaking through the basement's outer wall than that some poor stranger's house had caught fire. He put his hands on the upright slab next to him. He did this to hold the slab in place, to prop it up against the gritty GrayLanders straining their molecules through the earth—straining them the way that Aunt Clara strained orange juice on Saturday mornings—to scratch backward messages into the cement in a language so alien that not even a mirror could translate it for Cory. No longer able to *see* these messages, then, he began to *feel* the striations embodying them. Maybe the Bone Puppets, the Earth Zombies, the Clay People, or whatever they were, preferred to contact living human beings with *feel*able rather than *see*able symbols.

Like Braille, sort of.

Didn't that make sense? It was smart to think that monsters living underground, in everlasting subterranean dark, would be blind, wasn't it? Cory's first-grade teacher had taught them about moles, which could only see a little, and had even shown them a film about cave animals that had no eyes at all because, in their always-dark environments, they had *revolved* that way. Well, the GrayLanders were probably like those cave animals, eyeless, blind, totally and permanently blind, because by choice and biological development they made their home in darkness. Which was why they would write backwards on the walls in symbols that you had to feel and then turn around in your head to get the meaning of.

Cory worked hard to let the alien Braille of the GrayLanders talk to him through his fingertips. Probably, their messages would let him know what sort of horrible things they planned to do to him when they at last got through the concrete. Probably, the symbols were warnings. Warnings meant to terrify. A really smart kid would leave them be, but because he had been locked into a place that he could not escape without the aid of the adults upstairs—grownups a kid would ordinarily expect to make some responsible decisions for him and maybe for themselves too—Cory had to struggle to parse the queer dents and knobbles on his own. Alone, in the dark, it was better to know than not to know, even if what you learned made your gut turn over and the hair in the small of your back prickle. So far, though, he was learning nothing. All their stupid tactile messages made no sense, either forwards at the tips of his fingers or backwards or sideways or upside-down in the ever-turning but ever-slipping vise of his mind.

"You're blind and you can't even write blind-writing!" Cory shouted. He pounded on the sweaty slab beside his cot as centuries ago he had pounded on the door at the top of the staircase. Thwap! thwap! thwap! and not even the satisfaction of an echo. Bruised fists and a bit lip, only.

Cory forced the bent legs on his cot back under the canvas contraption, but pinched the web between his thumb and forefinger. He lay down on his cot nursing the pinch and staring through ink-filled eyes at the heavy nothing pressing down on him like the bleak air pressure of a tomb. With a bleak black here and a bleak black there (he crooned to himself), here a black, there a black, everywhere a bleak black, Uncle Marty had a tomb, ee-ai, ee-ai-oh. The melody of this nursery song kept running in his head in almost exactly the way that the darkness kept restating itself all around him. They were both inescapable, and pretty soon they got mixed up in Cory's mind as if they were mirror-image phenomena that he could not quite see straight and hence could not distinguish between or make any useful sense of.

Upstairs, as faint as the buzzing of a single summer mosquito, sirens again.

And then, somehow, the sun that Cory had painted on the wall—the humongous yellow orb with hair-curler geysers and flares around its circumference—lit up like a flash bulb as big as a Mobile Oil sign. But unlike any kind of flash bulb, Cory's sun did not go out again. Instead, in the bargain-basement catacombs of his aunt and uncle's house, it continued incandescently to glow. Everything in the basement was radiated by its light. Cory had to lift one paint-smeared forearm to shield his eyes from the fierce intensity of its unbearable glowing. The images of sunlamps on this and other walls, and of birds of paradise, and of bananas, pineapples, and papayas—*all* these clumsy two-dimensional images began to burn. They did so with a ferociousness only a little less daunting than that of Cory's big latex sun. It seemed to the boy that God Himself had switched the power back on. For some private reason, though, He had chosen not to use the orthodox avenue of the wiring already in place.

No, instead He had moved to endow with blinding brightness the symbols of life and sunshine that *Cory* had splashed on the walls. If Mommy would not help him, God would. If his aunt, uncle, and four bratty cousins would not release him to daylight, well, God would bring a gift of greatly multiplied daylight right down into the basement to him. Although grateful for this divine favor, the boy helplessly turned aside from the gift. It was too grand, too searing, and that for a brief instant he had actually been able to see the bone inside the forearm shielding his eyes fretted Cory in a way that his gratitude was unable to wipe from his memory.

And then, almost as if he had dreamed the divine gift, darkness reasserted itself, like a television screen shrinking down to one flickering central spot and going black right in the middle of a program that he had waited all day to see.

Ei-ai, ei-ai-oh.

Cory sat still on his cot. *Something* had happened. For

an instant or two, the ink had been squeezed out of his eyeballs, and a liquid like lighter fluid had been poured into them. Then the liquid had ignited, and burned, and used itself up, whereupon the ink had come flooding back. Or something like that. Cory was still seeing fuzzy haloes of light on the congealed blackness of the ink. Fireflies. Glowing amoebas. Migrating match flames. Crimson minnows. They swam and they swam, and no one gave a damn but the boy in the basement.

And then it seemed to him that overhead a whirlwind had struck the neighborhood. The darkness roared, and the staircase began doing the shimmy-shimmy again. But this time the shaking got so violent that the steps and guard rails—a tiny din within the great bombast of the Rocky Mountain hurricane raging above him—broke loose of the scaffolding and like the bars of a big wooden xylophone tumbled into and percussed down upon one another with the discordant music of catastrophe, plink! plunk! crash! ka-BOOM-bah! clatter-clatter!

It would have been funny, sort of, except that the roaring and the quaking and the amplified sighing of whatever was going on upstairs—*what* stairs?—in the real world, the terrifying playground of wild beasts and grownups, would not stop. Cory feared that his head might soon explode with the noise. In fact, he began to think that the noise was *inside* his skull, a balloon of sound inflating toward a ka-BOOM! that would decorate the gray-smelling walls with glistening oysterlike bits of his brain. Gray on gray.

The endless roaring swallowed time. Cory began to forget that the world had not always entertained such noise. It seemed a kind of constant, like air. He wondered if maybe the GrayLanders were the culprits, howling from all the topless basements in his aunt and uncle's neighborhood that they had succeeded in breaking into from their earthen grottos. If so, they would soon be here too, and time would both begin again and stop forever when they opened the sky for him with their grating godforsaken howls.

Maybe air was not a constant. Cory was suddenly having trouble breathing. Also, the clammy walls had begun to hiss, as if the ooze invisibly streaking them had heated to a temperature enabling them to steam. Gasping, he got down off the cot and crawled along the floor to the niche where an old-timey water heater, unemployed since the final days of the Eisenhower administration, squatted like the sawed-off fuselage of a rocket. Cory could not see it now, of course, but he remembered what it looked like. The metal wrapping the cylinder scalded his naked shoulder as he crawled past the antique.

Still gasping, bewildered by the difficulty of refilling his lungs, the boy slumped behind the old heater and turned his face toward an aperture in the concrete wall—an accident of pouring—through which a faint breath of warm rather than desert-hot air blew. He twisted his itching, enflamed body around so that he could thrust his entire head into this anomalous vent. The lip of concrete at its bottom sliced into his neck, but he ignored the minor discomfort to gulp the air leaking through. A gift from the GrayLanders? Maybe. Cory refused to question it, he just gulped and gulped, meanwhile praying that the noise would die down and the heat ease off and his oxygen supply return to normal.

In this unlikely posture, the boy fell asleep. Or, at least, consciousness left him.

When Cory awoke, his ears were buzzing, but the whirlwind had ceased. He pulled his head out of the rough spout in the concrete and found that he could comfortably breathe. He crawled out from behind the old gas water heater. An eerie kind of darkness held the day, but he could see again, as if through blowing smoke or murky water. Parts of the basement ceiling had fallen in, but all the walls were standing, and on them, as dim as the markings on the bottom of a scummy swimming pool, wavered the childish symbols that he had brushed and spray-painted onto the cement. Soot and grime dusted his handiwork, giving a disheartening dinginess to the latex yellow that a while ago—an hour, a day, a millennium— had shouted God's glory at him. Soot and dust drifted around the dry sump of the basement like airborne chaff in the grainery of a farm in western Kansas.

He looked up. The staircase had collapsed, and the door that he had pounded on, well, that door no longer occupied the doorjamb framing an empty portal at the top of the fallen stairs. In fact, the doorjamb was gone. Where it should have stood, a refrigerator slouched, its hind rollers hanging off the edge of the oddly canted floor. How it had wound up in that place, in that position, Cory could not clearly say, but because the walls of the upper portions of the house had evaporated, along with the ceiling, the furniture, and its human occupants, he did not spend much time worrying about the recent adventures of the parboiled refrigerator. High above the ruins of the house, the sky looked like a crazy-quilt marbling of curdled mayonnaise and cold cocoa and dissolving cotton candy and burnt tomato paste. Yucky-weird, all of it.

Just as gut-flopping as the sky, everything stank and distant moans overlay the ticks of scaled metal or occasionally pierced the soft static of down-sifting black snow. Although summer, this snow was slanting out of the nightmare sky. Appropriately, it was nightmare snow, flakes like tarnished-silver cinders, as acrid as gunpowder, each cinder the size of a weightless nickel, quarter, or fifty-cent piece. Right now, the boy was sheltered from their fall by a swag-bellied warp of ceiling, but he had made up his mind to climb out of the basement and to go walking bareheaded through the evil ebony storm.

Bareheaded, barechested, and barefoot.

Before the GrayLanders came.

Which they surely would, now that the grownups, by flattening everything, had made their tunneling task so much the easier. One of the outer basement walls had already begun to crumble. It would be a relaxing breaststroke for the Clay People, Earth Zombies, or Bone Puppets to come weaving their cold molecules through that airy stuff. And they had to be on their way.

Cory got out of the basement. It took a while, but by mounting the staircase rubble and leaping for the edge of the floor near the teetering refrigerator and pulling himself up to chin height and painstakingly boosting one leg over, he was finally able to stand on the tilting floor. Then, propellering his arms to maintain his balance, he watched with astonished sidelong glances as his Aunt Clara's big Amana toppled from its perch and dropped like a bomb into the staircase ruins below it. A geyser of dust rose to meet the down-whirling cinders.

But he kept from falling, and looked around, and saw that no longer did the tall buildings of Denver, whose tops it had once been easy to see from his aunt and uncle's neighborhood, command the landscape, which had been horribly transfigured. Debris and charred dead people and blasted trees and melted automobiles lay about the boy in every direction, and the mountains to the west, although still there, were veiled by the photographic-negative snow-fall, polarized phosphor dots of lilting deadliness.

Cory pulled his vision back from the mountains. "Mommy!" he cried. "Mommy!" Because he had no reasonable hope of an answer in this unrecognizable place, he started walking. Some of the burnt lumps in the rubble were probably all that remained of certain people he had known, but he had no wish to kneel beside them to check out this nauseating hunch. Instead, he walked. And it was like walking through a dump the dimensions of . . . well, of Denver itself. Maybe it was even bigger than that. The ubiquitous black snow and the yucky-weird sky suggested as much.

And then he saw his first GrayLander. The sight made him halt, clench his fists, and let go of a harsh yelping scream that scalded his throat the way that the down-whirling cinders had begun to burn his skin. The GrayLander paid him no mind, and although he wanted to scream again, he could not force his blistered voicebox to do as he bid it. For which reason, frozen to the plane of crazed asphalt over which he had been picking his way, Cory simply gaped.

Well over six feet tall, the GrayLander was almost as naked as he. The boy could not tell if it were Clay Person, Earth Zombie, or Bone Puppet—it seemed to be a little of all three, if not actually a hybrid of other ugly gray-smelling ogres of which he had never even dreamed. The GrayLander's ungainly head looked like a great boiled cauliflower, or maybe a deflated basketball smeared with some kind of milky paste. If the creature had eyes, Cory could not see them, for its brow, an almost iridescent purple ridge in the surrounding milkiness, overlapped the sockets where most earth-born animals would have eyes.

The creature's heavy lips, each of which reminded Cory of albino versions of the leeches that sometimes attacked people in television horror movies, were moving, ever moving, like greasy toy-tank treads that have slipped off their grooves. Maybe it had heard the boy approach—the huge, stunned creature—for it turned toward him and pushed an alien noise from between its alien lips.

"Haowah meh," it said. "Haowah meh."

When it turned, the purple-gray skin on its breasts, belly, and thighs slumped like hotel draperies accidentally tilted off their rods. Cory took a careful step back. One of the monster's arms showed more bone below the elbow than flesh, as did its leg below the knee on the same side. Pale lips still moving, the GrayLander extended its other arm toward the boy, the arm that might almost have been mistaken for a man's, and opened its blackened paw to reveal a tiny glistening spheroid. The monster shoved this object at Cory, as if urging him either to contemplate it at length or to take it as a memento of their meeting.

Squinting at the object in the unceasing rain of cinders, Cory understood that it was an eyeball. The GrayLander, blind, wanted him to have its eyeball. Just as he had suspected, the GrayLanders whom he had been waiting to come after him were sightless. They had eyes, apparently, but years of living in the dark, ignoring the realms of light just above their heads, had robbed their optical equipment of the ability to see. What, then, could be more useless than the gift of a GrayLander's eyeball? Cory was outraged. The whirlwind had finally freed this stupid creature—and all its equally ugly relatives wandering like benumbed zombies across the blasted landscape—from its subterranean darkness, and it was trying to give him something that had never been of the least value to itself or to any of its kind.

"Haoweh meh," it said again.

The boy's anger overcame his fear. He jumped forward, snatched the eye from the monster's paw, and flung it off the hideous body of the GrayLander so that it bounced back at him like the tiny red ball connected to a bolo paddle by a rubber tether.

Then, knowing nothing at all about where he was going or what he would do when he got there, Cory began to run. The dump that Denver and its suburbs had become seemed too big to escape easily, but he had to try, and he had to try in spite of the fact that as he ran many of the yucky GrayLanders loitering bewilderedly in the rubble called to him to stop—to stop and help them, to stop and share both their pain and their bewilderment. Cory would not stop. He was angry with the blind monsters. They were people in disguise, people just like his dead mommy, his dead aunt and uncle, and his dead cousins. He was angry with them because they had fooled him. All along, he had been living among the GrayLanders and they had never once—until now—stepped forward to let him know that, under their skins, they and their human counterparts were absolutely identical.

PRAXIS

Karen Joy Fowler

This story, set on a future world where political intrigue goes on against a backdrop of "cybers" used as slaves and "simulations" that enact Shakespeare's plays, is a . . . murder mystery? Well, there's a killing and much is mysterious, but it's more the mystery of what-is-reality as in the works of writers such as Shirley Jackson and Philip K. Dick.

Karen Joy Fowler studied writing in a class taught by Kim Stanley Robinson; "Praxis" was her first sale, but she's already published several more fine stories and we can look forward to her byline for years to come.

The price of a single ticket to the suicides would probably have funded my work for a month or more, but I do not let myself think about this. After all, I didn't pay for the ticket. Tonight I am the guest of the Baron Claude Himmlich and determined to enjoy myself.

I saw *Romeo and Juliet* five years ago, but only for one evening in the middle of the run. It wasn't much. Juliet had a cold and went to bed early. Her nurse kept wrapping her in hot rags and muttering under her breath. Romeo and Benvolio got drunk and made up several limericks. I thought some of them were quite good, but I'd been drinking a little myself.

Technically it was impressive. The responses of the stimulants were wonderfully lifelike and the amphitheater had just been remodeled to allow the audience to walk among the sets, viewing the action from any angle. But the story itself was hardly dramatic. It wouldn't be, of course, in the middle of the run.

Tonight is different. Tonight is the final night. The audience glitters in jewels, colorful capes, extravagant hairstyles. Only the wealthy are here tonight, the wealthy and their guests. There are four in our own theater party: our host, the Baron; his beautiful daughter, Svanneshal; a wonderfully eccentric old woman dressed all in white who calls herself the Grand Duchess de Vie; and me. I work at the university in records and I tutor Svanneshal Himmlich in history.

The Grand Duchess stands beside me now as we watch Juliet carried in to the tombs. "Isn't she lovely?" the Duchess says. "And very sweet, I hear. Garriss wrote her program. He's a friend of the Baron's."

"An absolute genius." The Baron leans towards us, speaking softly. There is an iciness to Juliet, a sheen her false death has cast over her. She is like something carved from marble. Yet even from here I can see the slightest rise and fall of her breasts. How could anyone believe she was really dead? But Romeo will. He always does.

It will be a long time before Romeo arrives and the Baron suggests we walk over to the Capulets' to watch Juliet's nurse weeping and carrying on. He offers his arm to the Duchess though I can see his security cyber dislikes this.

It is one of the Baron's own models, identical in principle to the simulants on stage—human body, software brain. Before the Baron's work the cybers were slow to respond and notoriously easy to outwit. The Baron made his fortune streamlining the communications link-up and introducing an element of deliberate irrationality into the program. There are those who argue this was an ill-considered, even dangerous addition. But the Baron has never lacked for customers. People would rather take a chance on a cyber than on a human and the less we need to depend on the poor, the safer we become.

The Duchess is looking at the cyber's uniform, the sober blues of the House of Himmlich. "Watch this," she says to me, smiling. She reaches into her bodice. I can see how the cyber is alert to the movement, how it relaxes when her hand reappears with a handkerchief. She reverses the action; we watch cyber tense again, relaxing when the hand reemerges.

The Baron shakes his head, but his eyes are amused. "Darling," he says, "you must not play with it."

"Then I shall walk with Hannah instead." The Duchess slips her hand around my arm. Her right hand is bare and feels warm pressed into my side. Her left hand is covered by a long white glove; its silky fingers rest lightly on the outside of my arm.

The Baron precedes us, walking with Svanneshal, the cyber close behind them. The Duchess leans against me and takes such small steps we cannot keep up. She looks at the Baron's back. "You've heard him called a 'self-made man'?" she asks me. "Did it ever occur to you that people might mean it literally?"

She startles me. My eyes go at once to the Baron, recognizing suddenly his undeniable perfection—his dark, smooth skin, his even teeth, the soft timbre of his voice. But the Duchess is teasing me. I see this when I look back at her.

"I like him very much," I answer. "I imagine him to be exactly like the ancient aristocracy at their best—educated, generous, courteous . . ."

"I wouldn't know about that. I have never studied history; I have only lived it. How old would you guess I am?"

It is a question I hate. One never knows what the most polite answer would be. The Duchess' hair, twisted about her head and held into place with ivory combs, is as black as Svanneshal's, but this can be achieved with dyes. Her face, while not entirely smooth, is not overly wrinkled. Again I suspect cosmetic enhancements. Her steps are undeniably feeble. "You look quite young," I say. "I couldn't guess."

"Then look at this." The Duchess stops walking and removes the glove from her left hand. She holds her palm flat before me so that I see the series of ciphers burnt into her skin. IPS3552. It is the brand of a labor duplicate. I look up at her face in astonishment and this amuses her. "You've never seen anything like that before, have you, historian? But you've heard perhaps how, in the last revolution, some of the aristocracy branded themselves and hid in the factories? *That's* how old I am.''

In fact, I have heard the story, a two-hundred-year-old story, but the version I know ends without survivors. Most of those who tried to pass were detected immediately; a human cannot affect the dead stare of the duplicates for very long. Those few who went in to the factories gave themselves up eventually, preferring, after all, to face the mob rather than endure the filth, the monotony, and the endless labor. ''I would be most interested in interviewing you,'' I say. ''Your adventures should be part of the record.'' *If true*, but of course that is something I do not say.

''Yes.'' The Duchess preens herself, readjusting an ivory comb, replacing her glove. We notice the Baron, still some distance away, returning to us. He is alone and I imagine he has left the cyber with Svanneshal. The Duchess sweeps her bare hand in the direction of the hurrying figure. ''I am a true member of the aristocracy,'' she tells me. ''Perhaps the only surviving member. I am not just some wealthy man who chooses to call himself *Baron*.''

This I discredit immediately as vanity. Revolution after revolution—no one can verify a blood claim. Nor can I see why anyone would want to. I am amazed at the willingness of people to make targets of themselves, as if every time were the last time and now the poor are permanently contained.

''I must apologize.'' The Baron arrives, breathless. ''I had no idea you had fallen so far behind.''

''Why should you apologize,'' the Duchess chides him, ''if your guest is too old for such entertainments and too proud to use a chair as she should?'' She shifts herself from my arm to his. ''Verona is so lovely,'' she says. ''Isn't it?''

We proceed slowly down the street. I am still thinking of the Duchess' hand. When we rejoin Svanneshal it is as though I have come out of a trance. She is so beautiful tonight I would rather not be near her. The closer I stand, the less I can look. Her eyes are very large inside the dark hood of her gown which covers her hair and shoulders in a fine net of tiny jewels. In the darkened amphitheater the audience shines like a sky full of stars, but Svanneshal is an entire constellation—Svanneshal, the Swan's throat, and next to her, her father, the Dragon. I look around the amphitheater. Everyone is beautiful tonight.

Juliet's nurse is seated in a chair, rocking slowly back and forth in her agony. She is identical to the nurse I saw before and I tell the Baron so.

"Oh, I'm sure she *is* the one you saw before. I saw her once as Amanda in *The Glass Menagerie*. You didn't imagine they started from scratch every time, did you? My dear Hannah, anyone who can be recycled after the run certainly will be. The simulations are expensive enough as it is." The Baron smiles at me, the smile of the older, the wiser, to the young and naive. "What's amazing is the variation you get each time, even with identical parts. Of course, that's where the drama comes in."

Before, when I saw *Romeo and Juliet*, Friar Lawrence was killed on the second night, falling down a flight of stairs. That's mainly why I went. I was excited by the possibilities opened by the absence of the Friar. Yet the plot was surprisingly unchanged.

It makes me think of Hwang-li and I say to the Baron, "Did you know it was a historian who created the simulations?"

"I don't have your knowledge of history," he answers. "Svanneshal tells me you are quite gifted. And you have a specialty . . . forgive me. I know Svanneshal has told me."

"Mass movements. They don't lend themselves to simulation." The Duchess has not heard of Hwang-li either, but then only a historian would have. It was so many revolutions ago. I could argue that the historians are the true revolutionary heroes, retaining these threads of our past, bringing them through the upheaval. Many historians have died to protect the record. And *their* names are lost to us forever. I am glad for a chance to talk about Hwang-li.

"Hwang-li was not thinking of entertainment, of course. He was pondering the inevitability of history. Is the course of history directed by personalities or by circumstances?" I ask the Baron. "What do you think?"

The Baron regards me politely. "In the real world," he says, "personalities and circumstances are inseparable.

The one creates the other and vice versa. Only in simulation can they be disjoined.''

"It follows then," I tell him, "that if you could intervene to change one, you would simultaneously change both and, therefore, the course of history. Could you make a meaningful change? How much can depend upon a single individual taking a single action at a single moment? Or not taking it?"

"Depending on the individual, the action, and the moment," the Duchess says firmly, "everything could change."

I nod to her. "That is what Hwang-li believed. He wished to test it by choosing an isolated case, a critical moment in which a series of seeming accidents resulted in a devastating war. He selected the Mancini murder, which was manageable and well-documented. There were seven personality profiles done on Philip Mancini at the time and Hwang-li had them all."

The Baron has forgotten Juliet's nurse entirely and turns to me with gratifying attention. "But this is fascinating," he says. "Svanneshal, you must hear this." Svanneshal moves in closer to him; the cyber seems relieved to have both standing together.

"Go on," says the Baron.

"I was telling your father about Hwang-li."

"Oh, I know this story already." Svanneshal smiles at the Baron coquettishly. "It's the murder that interests him," she says to me. "Aberrant personalities are sort of a hobby of his."

The Baron tells me what he already knows of the murder, that Frank Mancini was killed by his brother Philip.

"Yes, that's right," I say encouragingly. This information survives in a saying we have—enmity is sometimes described as "the love of the Mancinis."

It is the Duchess who remembers the saying. But beyond that, she says she knows nothing of the case. I direct my statements to her. "Frank Mancini was a security guard, back in the days when humans functioned in that capacity. He was responsible for security in the Irish sector. He had just learned of the terrorist plot against Pope Peter. The Pope was scheduled to speak in an open courtyard at noon; he was to be shot from the window of a nearby library. Frank was literally reaching for the phone at the moment

Philip Mancini burst into his study and shot him four times for personal reasons.''

Svanneshal is bored with the discussion. Although she is extremely intelligent, it is not yet something she values. But she will. I look at her with the sudden realization that it is the only bit of inherited wealth she can be certain of holding on to. She is playing with her father's hair, but he catches her hand. "Go on," he says to me.

"Philip had always hated his brother. The murder was finally triggered by a letter Philip received from their mother—a letter we know he wrongly interpreted. What if he had read the letter more carefully? What if it had arrived ten minutes later? Hwang-li planned to replay the scene, running it through a number of such minute variations. Of course he had no simulants, nor did he need them. It was all to be done by computer.''

"The whole project seems to me to raise more questions than it answers." Svanneshal is frowning. "What if the Pope had survived? How do you assess the impact of that? You cannot say there would have been no revolution. The Pope's death was a catalyst, but not a cause.''

I am pleased to see that she not only knows the outlines of the incident, but has obviously been giving it some thought. I begin to gesture emphatically with my hands as though we were in class, but I force myself to stop. This is, after all, a social occasion. "So, war is not averted, but merely delayed?" I ask her. "Another variation. Who would have gained from such a delay? What else might have been different if the same war was fought at a later time? Naturally nothing can be proved absolutely—that is the nature of the field. But it is suggestive. When we can answer these questions we will be that much closer to the day when we direct history along the course we choose.''

"We already do that," the Duchess informs me quietly. "We do that every day of our lives." Her right hand smooths the glove over her left hand. She interlaces the fingers of the two.

"What happened in the experiment?" the Baron asks.

"Hwang-li never finished it. He spent his life perfecting the Mancini programs and died in a fire before he had finished. Another accident. Then there were the university purges. There's never been that kind of money for history again.'' I look into Svanneshal's eyes, deep within her hood. ''It's too bad, because I've an experiment of my own I've wanted to do. I wanted to simulate Antony and Cleopatra, but make her nose an inch longer.''

This is an old joke, but they do not respond to it. The Baron says politely that it would provide an interesting twist the next time *Antony and Cleopatra* is done. He'll bring it up with the Arts Committee.

Svanneshal says, ''You see, Daddy, you owe Hwang-li everything. He did the first work in synthetic personalities.''

It occurs to me that the Baron may think Svanneshal and I are trying to persuade him to fund me and I am embarrassed. I search for something to say to correct this impression, but we are interrupted by a commotion onstage.

Lady Capulet has torn her dress at the collar, her hair is wild and uncombed. Under her tears, her face is ancient, like a tragic mask. She screams at her husband that it is his fault their baby is dead. If he hadn't been so cold, so unyielding . . .

He stands before her, stooped and silent. When at last she collapses, he holds her, stroking the hair into place about her sobbing face. There is soft applause for this gentleness. It was unexpected.

''Isn't it wonderful?'' Svanneshal's face glows with appreciation. ''Garriss again,'' she informs me although I know Garriss did the programming for the entire Capulet family. It is customary to have one writer for each family so that the similarities in the programming can mirror the similarities of real families created by genetics and upbringing.

The simulants are oblivious to this approval. Jaques tells us, every time, that the world is a stage, but here the stage is a world, complete in itself, with history and family, with even those random stagehands, death and disease. This is what the stimulants live. If they were told that Juliet is no one's daughter, that everything they think and say is software, could they believe it? Would it be any less tragic?

Next to me I hear the beginning of a scream. It is choked off as suddenly as it started. Turning, I see the white figure of the Duchess slumping to the ground, a red stain spreading over her bodice. The gloved hand is pressed against her breast; red touches her fingers and moves down her arm. Her open eyes see nothing. Beside her, the cyber is returning a bloody blade to the case on its belt.

It was all so fast. "It killed her," I say, barely able to comprehend the words. "She's dead!" I kneel next to the Duchess, not merely out of compassion, but because my legs have given way. I look up at the Baron, expecting to see my own horror reflected in his face, but it is not.

He is calmly quiet. "She came at me," he says. "She moved against me. She meant to kill me."

"No!" I am astounded. Nothing is making sense to me. "Why would she do that?"

He reaches down and strips the wet glove from the warm hand. There is her lifeline—IPS3552. "Look at this," he says to me, to the small group of theater-goers who have gathered around us. "She was not even human."

I look at Svanneshal for help. "You knew her. She was no cyber. There is another explanation for the brand. She told me. . . ." I do not finish my sentence, suddenly aware of the implausibility of the Duchess' story. But what other explanation is there? Svanneshal will not meet my eyes. I find something else to say. "Anyway, the cybers have never been a threat to us. They are not programmed for assassination." It is another thought I do not finish, my eyes distracted by the uniform of the House of Himmlich. I get to my feet slowly, keeping my hands always visible and every move I make is watched by the Baron's irrational cyber. "The autopsy will confirm she is human," I say finally. "Was human."

Svanneshal reaches for my arm below the shoulder, just where the Duchess held me. She speaks into my ear, so low that I am the only one who hears her. Her tone is ice. "The cybers are all that stand between us and the mob. You remember that!"

Unless I act quickly, there will be no autopsy. Already maintenance duplicates are scooping up the body in the manner reserved for the disposal of cybers. Three of them are pulling the combs from her hair, the jewels from her ears and neck and depositing them in small, plastic bags. The Baron is regarding me, one hand wiping his upper lip. Sweat? No, the Baron feels nothing, shows no sign of unease.

Svanneshal speaks to me again. This time her voice is clearly audible. "It tried to kill my father," she says. "You weren't watching. I was."

It would be simpler to believe her. I try. I imagine that the whole time we were talking about the Mancinis, the Duchess was planning to murder her host. For political reasons? For personal reasons? I remember the conversation, trying to refocus my attention to her, looking for the significant gesture, the words which, listened to later, will mean so much more. But, no. If she had wanted to kill the Baron, surely she would have done it earlier, when the Baron returned to us without his cyber.

I return Svanneshal's gaze. "Did anyone else see that?" I ask, raising my voice. I look from person to person. "Did anyone see anything?"

No one responds. Everyone is waiting to see what I will do. I am acutely conscious of the many different actions I can take; they radiate out from me as if I stood at the center of a star, different paths, all ultimately uncontrollable. Along one path I have publicly accused the Baron of murder through misjudgment. His programs are opened for examination; his cybers are recalled. He is ruined. And, since he has produced the bulk of the city's security units, Svanneshal is quite right. We are left unprotected before the mob. Could I cause that?

I imagine another, more likely path. I am pitted alone against the money and power of the Himmlichs. In this vision the Baron has become a warlord with a large and loyal army. He is untouchable. Wherever I try to go, his cybers are hunting me.

The body has been removed, a large, awkward bundle in the arms of the maintenance duplicates. The blood is lifting from the tile, like a tape played backwards, like a thing which never happened. The paths radiating out from me begin to dim and disappear. The moment is past. I can do nothing now.

In the silence that has fallen around us, we suddenly hear that Romeo is coming. Too early, too early. What will it mean? The knot of spectators around us melts away; everyone is hurrying to the tombs. Svanneshal takes my arm and I allow myself to be pulled along. Her color is high and excited, perhaps from exertion, perhaps in antici-

pation of death. When we reach the tombs we press in
amongst the rest.

On one side of me, Svanneshal continues to grip my
arm. On the other is a magnificent woman imposingly tall,
dressed in Grecian white. Around her bare arm is a coiled
snake, fashioned of gold, its scales in the many muted
colors gold can wear. A fold of her dress falls for a
moment on my own leg, white, like the gown of the Grand
Duchess de Vie and I find myself crying. "Don't do it," I
call to Romeo. "It's a trick! It's a trap. For God's sake,
look at her." The words come without volition, part of me
standing aside, marveling, pointing out that I must be
mad. He can't hear me. He is incapable of hearing me.
Only the audience turns to look, then turns away politely,
hushed to hear Romeo's weeping. He is so young, his
heart and hands so strong, and he says his lines as though
he believed them, as though he made them up.

The Baron leans into Svanneshal. "Your friend has
been very upset by the incidents of the evening." His
voice is kind. "As have we all. And she is cold. Give her
my cape."

I am not cold, though I realize with surprise that I am
shaking. Svanneshal wraps the red cape about me. "You
must come home with us tonight," she says. "You need
company and care." She puts an arm about me and whispers, "Don't let it upset you so. The simulants don't feel
anything."

Then her breath catches in her throat. Romeo is drinking
his poison. I won't watch the rest. I turn my head aside
and in the blurred lens of my tears, one image wavers,
then comes clear. It is the snake's face, quite close to me,
complacency in its heavy-lidded eyes. "Don't look at me
like that," I say to a species which vanished centuries ago.
"Who are you to laugh?"

I think that I will never know the truth. The Duchess
might have been playing with the cyber again. Her death
might have been a miscalculation. Or the Baron might
have planned it, have arranged the whole evening around
it. I would like to know. I think of something Hwang-li is
supposed to have said. "Never confuse the record with the
truth. It will always last longer." I am ashamed that I did
nothing for the Duchess, accuse myself of cowardice, tears

dropping from my cheeks onto the smooth flesh of my palms. In the historical record, I tell myself, I will list her death as a political assassination. And it will be remembered that way.

Next to me Svanneshal stiffens and I know Juliet has lifted the knife. This is truly the end of her; the stab wounds will prevent her re-use and her voice is painfully sweet, like a song.

One moment of hesitation, but that moment is itself a complete world. It lives onstage with the simulants, it lives with the mob in their brief and bitter lives, it lives where the wealthy drape themselves in jewels. If I wished to find any of them, I could look in that moment. "But how," I ask the snake, "would I know which was which?"

THE PEOPLE ON THE PRECIPICE

Ian Watson

Sometimes sf writers can present very imaginative worlds just by changing our perspective a bit. Here, for instance, is a world where people live on an endless vertical wall, a kind of Flatland set on edge. And when changes invade this world . . .

Ian Watson's most recent novels are the "Book of the River" trilogy.

One evening Smear climbed down to our ledge and told us a story about people who lived in a two-dimensional world.

He had made the story up, of course. To amuse and enlighten. (This could have been Smear's motto.)

"Just suppose," he said, as the daylight dimmed, "that a whole world is as flat as a leaf! And suppose that creatures live within that leaf, who themselves are perfectly flat. Imagine that this narrow ledge here simply carries on"—he chopped his hand out into empty space—"in that direction forever! Imagine that it is a simple, infinite surface with nothing above it and nothing below it. And with no precipice to jut out from."

Bounce giggled at this idea so much that she almost fell out of her bower of vine-rope.

Tumbler, our chief—who had no sense of humour—said, "Preposterous! What would hold your ledge up? How would we ever get over the lip, to harvest sweet fungi below?"

293

"I'm asking you to imagine a different kind of world. A plane—with no 'below' or 'above.' With no 'up' or 'down.' The inhabitants are flat, too."

"But how can they grip anything? They'll all slide away, and slide forever."

"No they won't. You see, they don't live *upon* the flat surface. They're *part* of the surface."

"You'll do me an injury!" squealed Bounce.

"So how do they make love?" enquired Fallen. "How can they squeeze on to one another?"

"Aha," and Smear winked at her, "now you're asking."

"Tell us!" cried Bounce.

But Tumbler interrupted. "I hear that young Clingfast from three ledges down fell off yesterday. That was his mother's fault for giving him such an unlucky name. 'Bounce' is a risky name, too, in my opinion."

This remark annoyed Bounce. "Just you try to invade my bower, Tumbler, and *you'll* get bounced—right off the cliff. That'll teach you what my name's all about."

"Can I please tell my story?" asked Smear.

And so he did.

He regaled us with the hilarious adventures of Ma and Pa Flat in their flatworld; and what preposterous antics those were, to be sure! Still, his story seemed to have a couple of sly morals buried in it. Compared with the imaginary flat-people we were fortunate indeed—being gifted with all sorts of mobility denied to Ma and Pa Flat. In other words, things might be a lot worse. But also, Ma and Pa at least tried to make the very best of a bad job—did we always do likewise?

By the time Smear finished it was black dark, and we had long since tightened our tethers for the night. Obviously Smear would be spending the time of darkness on our ledge.

Soon after, I heard suspicious scraping sounds, suggesting that Smear was recklessly edging his way along to reach Bounce's bower. (He had positioned himself close to her.) Subsequent smothered giggles and gasps indicated that he had succeeded: a surmise proven true in the morning when light brightened and we saw Bounce and Smear clinging together asleep in her harness of vines.

Smear quickly roused himself and departed upward, his

horny toes in all the proper cracks, his left hand holding a guidevine, his right hand reaching up in approved style for well-remembered, reliable holds. You could never wholly trust guidevines with your total weight. They might snap or rip their roots free. Then you would be taking the long trip down through empty air.

We breakfasted on the leftovers from yesterday's harvest of berries and lichen, rockworms and beetles.

The pearly void was bright; the day was warm. Below, the precipice descended forever. Above, it rose forever. To left and right, it stretched out unendingly. Occasionally, thin silver water-licks oozed from the rock, dribbling down till the droplets bounced into space. Here and there were still some surviving pastures of moss and fungus and fleshier plants; though by now our appetites had stripped most decent rock-fields bare, adding to the area of naturally occurring barrens. Soon we would all have to migrate—just as we had already migrated at least a hundred times since I was born. A planning conference was slated for today high up on Badbelay's ledge. Tumbler as our chief would attend.

As our tribe clung to the rockface considering which way to forage, a scream from above made us tighten our holds. We tried to flatten ourselves completely—just like Smear's mythical beings. A young lad plunged past, an arm's length away. I could have reached out to touch him, if I was foolish enough.

"Butterfingers!" shrieked Fallen in sympathy. The lad probably never heard her.

The falling body diminished until it was a mere speck deep below.

Bounce surprised us by saying, "Next time we migrate we ought to head upwards and *keep on* migrating upwards for a whole lifetime, to see what happens."

"That'll be one of friend Smear's fancy ideas, I suppose?" Tumbler spat contemptuously into space. "What a strain *that* would be, and what peril, compared with migrating sideways. My dear Bounce, it's all very well to climb up a few ledges, and down a few ledges. Indeed this keeps all our muscles in trim. But to climb one way only? Faugh! Do you imagine our grandchildren would reach a *top*? Or a *bottom*, suppose we migrated downwards? And what would be at this imaginary bottom? Bones and rubbish and shit, floating in foul water, I shouldn't be surprised!''

"I didn't mention any bottom."

"And what would be at this top of yours? Not that it exists! I'll tell you: a place where our muscles would weaken through disuse so that we could no longer harvest the precipice. We'd starve within a generation. Our present way of life is perfect."

"Clinging on by your fingertips all life long is perfect?" she retorted. "There might be a huge flat space up at the top—with oodles of really big plants all over, because they wouldn't have to worry about their weight ripping them away."

"What's wrong with hanging on by one's fingertips, pray?"

"A certain tendency to *fall*," she said. "Especially when you get old and sick and mad and exhausted."

I spoke up, since something had been worrying me for a while. "When we migrated here, it seemed to me that this particular patch of precipice hereabouts was . . . well, strangely familiar. When we arrived I felt as if I'd been here before—when I was only a child. All the cracks and finger-grips were somehow known to me."

"That," said Tumbler, "is purely because of the expertise you develop at clinging on after twenty or thirty years."

"So why do experienced adults ever fall off?"

"They get tired and ill and crazy," said Bounce. "Everyone does, in the end, after a lifetime of clinging on."

"We always migrate leftward," I pointed out.

"Obviously! Who on earth would migrate back to a patch which had been stripped the time before?"

"What if," I asked, "the sum total of our migrations has brought us back to the very same place where we were years ago? What if our precipice isn't a straight wall but a vast . . . um . . .''

"A vast cylinder," said Bounce.

Tumbler pointed impatiently to the right where the view was more barren. "Look: if that isn't straight—!"

"Maybe it only seems straight," said Splatty unexpectedly, "because it's so enormous. Maybe it bends ever so slightly? We can't actually see the bend, but after tens of years of travel . . . if so, what's the sense in migrating?"

"To find food, slippy-thumb! To survive! Suppose we do come back to the same patch eventually—so what? The pastures have fleshed out again."

"It's hardly *progress*," said Bounce.

"Progress? Cylinders? Bends? Have you people gone nuts? Are you planning to let go and dive into the abyss? This is all Smear's fault. Listen: we hang on by the skin of our teeth. We make daily forays up and down for food. When we've scalped a patch we migrate sideways. That's life."

Even Topple joined in. "It's life. That's true. But is it *living*?"

"Damn it, it's as good a life as any! In fact I can't imagine any other. How about you?"

Topple shook his head. "I've been clinging on for a lifetime. What else do I know?"

"And you'll die clinging on. Or rather, you'll die pretty soon after you *stop* clinging on. Now, today I'm climbing up to the Chief-of-Chiefs for the conference. Bounce will guard our ledge and keep the kids tied up. Loosepiton"
—that's me—"will escort me upwards."

"Why me, Boss?"

"Perhaps you would like to plead your notion that we're climbing round in a circle. That ought to raise some laughs." (Aye, and likely damage Smear's advocacy of migrating upwards. . . .)

"The rest of you will forage. Splatty and Fallen and Plunge can head far to the left, and chart the distant cracks while they're about it. Slip and Flop can forage to the right for what's left of the familiar pickings. Gather well, my tribe! We need to store some supplies in case we have to cross wide barrens." To me he said, "Come on, Loosepiton. Best foot upward!"

And he began to ascend the sheer precipice, toehold by toehold.

"On what wide surface shall we store our huge harvest, oh Chief?" Bounce called after him. He ignored her.

When Tumbler and I paused on Smear's Ledge for a

quick rest we learned that Chief Smear had already pre-
ceded us upwards. Apparently Smear had done a lot of
shinning about, visiting other ledges and telling merry
stories, recently.

"He's campaigning to change our lives," I remarked to
Tumbler.

However, our chief seemed more annoyed with Bounce.
"That woman's a fool," he groused. "A vertical cliff puts
constraints on the amount we can store. Of course it does.
That stands to reason. So this limits the amount we can
sensibly harvest. Consider the alternative! If we could tear
up everything and pile it all on some vast ledge we'd
exhaust our resources much more rapidly. What's more,
we'd over-eat. We'd grow fat and clumsy and far too
heavy to haul ourselves up and down."

We climbed onward together.

Another body fell past us; a woman's. She held her
arms wide out on either side of her, as down she flew.

"Diver," puffed Tumbler. "Deliberate dive."

"Dive of despair."

"What's there to be desperate about, eh Loosepiton?
Beautiful weather today. Soft breezes. No slippery stone."
He plucked a crimson rock-worm loose with a 'plop' and
popped it into his mouth.

Not long after, some excrement hit him on the shoulder.
Excrement usually falls well clear of the wall but some
freak contour must have directed otherwise. Without comment Tumbler wiped himself clean on a nearby danglevine.

We passed six more ledges, rested and ate a meal
courtesy of the tribe clinging to the seventh, then climbed
past fifteen more. We reached Chief-of-Chief Badbelay's
ledge in the early afternoon.

The ledge was already crowded with a line of chiefs—
and in the middle Smear was chanting out another of his
stories about bizarre worlds. In this case: about people
with suckers like a gripworm's on their feet who lived on a
huge ball afloat in a void. Smear was leaning quite far
back to call his words past the intervening bodies.

"Shit in your eye," Tumbler greeted him grumpily as
we two forced a space for ourselves on the ledge.

"Aha," responded Smear, "but up here, where would
that crap fall from? Either another tribe of tribes clings

immeasurably high above us—or else not. If not, why not? Why do no strangers ever fall from above? Because no strangers live higher up! Yet if our precipice extends upwards infinitely, surely other people must dwell somewhere higher up. *Ergo*—''

''Unless those other people have migrated further along than us!'' broke in Tumbler. ''Unless they're further to the left—or to the right, for that matter.''

''The reason,'' Smear continued suavely, ''is that our precipice isn't infinitely high. It has a top.''

''The real reason,'' growled Badbelay, ''may simply be that we are the *only* people. All that exists is the precipice, and us.''

''Maybe we're the only people on the precipice itself. But maybe hundreds of tribes live on top—and every now and then they gaze down and have a good laugh at us.''

''Why should anyone laugh at us? Are we not courageous and ingenious, persevering and efficient, compassionate and clever?''

''Undoubtedly,'' Smear replied, ''but perhaps if we were fools, liars, cheats, thieves, and slovens we would have slid down to the bottom years ago instead of trying to cling on here; and we would have been living in rich pastures.''

''So now it's the *bottom* that's our goal, is it?'' challenged Tumbler. ''Kindly make your mind up!''

''I spoke by way of illustration. Obviously, with all our fine qualities, it is ever upward that we ought to aspire. We may reach the top within a single lifetime.''

''Then what do we do?'' asked another chief. ''Sprawl and sleep?''

The argument went on all afternoon.

Eventually Badbelay gave his judgment. We would all migrate in ten days' time—diagonally. Leftwards, as was traditional; but also upwards, as Smear had urged.

''If we do find lush pastures leftward and upward,'' explained Badbelay, ''we can always steepen our angle of ascent. But if we run into difficulties we can angle back down again on to the time-approved route.''

Some chiefs applauded the wisdom of this compromise. Others—particularly Tumbler—voiced discontent. Smear looked disappointed at first but then perked up.

That night we slept in vine-harnesses on Badbelay's ledge; and in the morning we all climbed back down again.

A couple of days later Smear paid another visit to our ledge—with apprehension written on his face.

The rest of our tribe had already fanned out across the precipice, a-gathering. I myself was about to depart.

"Tumbler! Loosepiton! Have you looked out across the void lately?"

"Why should we waste our time looking at nothing?" demanded Tumbler with a scowl.

Smear pointed. "Because there's *something*."

To be sure, far away in the pearly emptiness there did seem to me to be some sort of enormous shadow.

Tumbler rubbed his eyes then shrugged. "I can't see anything."

I cleared my throat. "There *is* something, Chief. It's very vague and far away."

"Rubbish! Nonsense! There's never been anything there. How can there be something?"

Tumbler, I realized, must be short-sighted.

Smear must have arrived at a similar diagnosis. However, he didn't try to score any points off Tumbler. He just said diplomatically to me, "Just in case, let's keep watch, Loosepiton—you and I, hmm?"

I nodded agreement.

Whatever it was seemed to thicken day by day. At first the phenomenon was thin, then it grew firmer, denser. No one else glanced in the empty direction—until the very morning when we were due to migrate.

Then at last some fellow's voice cried out, "Look into the void! Look, everyone!"

Presently other voices were confirming what the man had noticed. For a while minor pandemonium reigned, though Tumbler still insisted: "Fantasy! Smear has been spreading rumours. Smear has stirred this up!" Which was the very opposite of the truth.

Bounce clung to me. "What is it?" Now that her attention had been directed, she could see the thing clearly; though as yet none of us could make out any details. All I

could be sure of, was that something enormous existed out
in the void beyond the empty air; and that something was
changing day by day in a way which made it more
noticeable.

"I've no idea, dear Bounce."

"Migrate!" ordered Tumbler. "Commence the migration!"

And so we began to migrate, leftward and upward; as
did the tribes above us, and the tribes above them.

Over the course of the next ten days the business of
finding novel fingerholds and toeholds occupied a huge
amount of our attention. Besides, we had our kids to shep-
herd, or to carry if they were still babies. Consequently
there wasn't much opportunity for staring out into the void.
Splatty made the mistake of doing so while we were traversing
unfamiliar rock. He forgot himself, lost his poise, and fell.

On the tenth evening Smear climbed down to our camp-
ing ledge.

"Don't you recognize what it is by now, Loosepiton?"
he asked.

"There *might* be some kind of dark cloud out there,"
allowed Tumbler, peeved that Smear was addressing me.

"It isn't any cloud, old chief—nor any sort of weird
weather. Look keenly, Loosepiton. That's another precipice."

I perceived . . . a faintly wrinkled vertical plane. Like a
great sheet of grey skin.

"It's another precipice just like ours; and it's moving
slowly towards our precipice day by day. It's closing in on
us. As though it ain't bad enough clinging on by our
fingertips all life long . . . !" Smear crooked a knee around
a vine for stability and held his hands apart then brought
them slowly together and ground them, palm to palm,
crushingly.

The wrinkles in that sheet of skin out there were ledges.
Without any doubt. The hairs on the skin were vines. My
heart sank.

"We oughtn't to have migrated in this direction," declared Tumbler. He was simply being obtuse.

Smear gently corrected him. "We aren't migrating into
an angle between two walls. Oh no. That other precipice

faces us flat on. And it began to move towards us before we ever started our migration. Or perhaps *our* precipice began to move towards it. The result is the same.''

''We'll be squashed between the two.'' I groaned.

To have survived bravely for so many years of hanging on by our fingernails! We had never railed excessively against our circumstances. Sometimes certain individuals took the dive of despair. But children were born and raised. Life asserted itself. We had hung on.

All so that we could meet a second precipice head on—a mobile precipice—and be crushed!

This seemed a little unfair. A little—yes—hateful and soul-twisting.

Days passed by. We had settled on our new cliff pastures. We explored the cracks and ledges. We wove vines. We foraged. We ate worms and beetles.

All the while the approaching precipice became more clearly discernible as just that: another infinite precipice, limitlessly high and deep, limitlessly wide.

As the gap narrowed pearly daylight began to dim dangerously.

Smear had conceived a close affinity for me. ''Maybe it's just a reflection,'' I said to him one day.

''If that's the case, then we should see ourselves clinging on over there. I see no one. If I could bend my arm back far enough to throw a chunk of stone, my missile would hit solid rock and bounce off.''

Several people from upper ledges took the dive of despair. A few parents even cast their children down; and that is real despair.

Yet consider the difference between taking the dive—and being slowly crushed to death between two walls of stone. Which would you prefer? Maybe those individuals who dived died peacefully from suffocation on the way down. Or maybe they did reach a bottom and were instantly destroyed, before they knew it, by impact.

The remaining daylight was appallingly dim by now. The other precipice with its cracks and ledges and vines was only a few bodies' lengths away. In another day or two it might be possible to leap over and cling on—though that hardly spelled any avenue of escape.

I paid a visit to Smear.

"Friend," I said, "some of those ledges over there are going to fit into space where we don't have ledges. But others won't. Others will touch our own ledges."

"So?"

"So maybe there'll be a little gap left between the two precipices. A gap as big as a human body."

"Leaving us uncrushed—but locked inside rock?"

"We'll have to wait and see."

"See?" he cried. "With no light to see by? Yet I suppose," he added bitterly, "it *will* be a different sort of world. For a while."

Different. Yes.

Yesterday—though 'days' are now irrelevant—the two precipices met.

All light had disappeared but with my hand I could feel the inexorable pressure of the other rocky wall pushing forward—until from above, from below, from left and right there came a grating, groaning, crackling noise; then silence for a while.

Nobody had screamed. Everybody had waited quietly for the end. And as I had begun to suspect some days earlier, the end—the absolute end—did not come.

I was still alive on a ledge in utter darkness, sandwiched between one wall and the other.

Voices began to call out: voices which echoed strangely and hollowly down the gap of space that remained.

Yes, we survive.

There's even a little light now. Fungi and lichen have begun to glow. Maybe they always did glow faintly; and only now have our deprived eyes grown sensitive enough to detect their output.

We can still travel about—along a ledge to the end, then by way of cracks up or down to the end of another ledge. We scarcely see where we're going, and have to guess our way through the routes of this vertical stone maze. Also, it's still possible to fall down a gap, which would cause terrible injuries.

Yet in a sense travel is also easier nowadays. We can brace ourselves between both walls and shuffle upward or downward or left or right by "chimneying."

Perhaps I should mention a disadvantage which has actually stimulated travel. Excrement can't tumble away now into the void. Stools strike one wall or the other.

What's more, the collision of the two walls destroyed a lot of vines; nor can lush foliage thrive in the ensuing darkness.

Consequently we are ascending steadily, just as Smear once recommended.

Instead of living one above the other, our tribes are now strung out in a long line; and all of us climb slowly upward, foraging as we go, eating all the available lichen and fungi, worms and beetles. Now we're permanently migrating.

Are we moving towards somewhere? Towards Smear's mythical top? Maybe.

And maybe that place is infinitely far away.

The new kids who are born to us on the move will enter a world utterly different from the world of my own childhood. A vertical world confined between two irregular walls. A world of near-total gloom.

They will live in a narrow gap which extends sideways forever, drops downward forever, and rises forever.

How will Bounce's child (who is also either mine or Smear's) ever conceive of the old world which we will describe: that world where one precipice alone opened forever upon the vastness of empty, bright space? Will he (or she) think of it as a paradise which might yet exist again some time in the future if the two walls ever move apart? Or will the child be unable even to understand such a concept?

Sometimes I dream of the old world of open air and light, and of clinging to the cliff. Then I awaken to darkness, to the faint glow of a few fungi, to the confinement of the walls.

The other day Smear said to me, "We didn't know how well off we were, did we, Loosepiton? But at least we survive, and climb. And maybe, just maybe, right *now* we're well off—compared with some future state of the world which will limit us even more severely!"

"How could we be more limited?" I asked in surprise. "What new disaster could occur?"

"Maybe this gap will shrink to become a single upright chimney! Maybe *that'll* happen next."

"Life forbid! It hasn't happened yet."

"Not yet."

Meanwhile we climb upward. And upward.

Amazingly Smear still tells his peculiar tales about imaginary worlds; and tells them with gusto.

THE ONLY NEAT THING TO DO

James Tiptree, Jr.

We journey now to the far future and the far reaches of space, past the boundaries of exploration to the Great North Rift that lies between arms of the galaxy. The protagonist is sixteen-year-old Coati Cass, who wants to become an explorer and who ventures into that unknown space. She finds more than her share of adventure.

James Tiptree, Jr.'s most recent novel is Brightness Falls From the Air.

Heroes of space! Explorers of the starfields!

Reader, here is your problem:

Given one kid, yellow-head, snub-nose-freckles, green-eyes-that-stare-at-you-level, rich-brat, girl-type, fifteen-year-old. And all she's dreamed of, since she was old enough to push a hologram button, are heroes of the First Contacts, explorers of far stars, the great names of Humanity's budding Star Age. She can name you the crew of every Discovery Mission; she can sketch you a pretty accurate map of Federation Space and number the Frontier Bases; she can tell you who first contacted every one of .the fifty-odd races known; and she knows by heart the last words of Han Lu Han when, himself no more than sixteen, he ran through alien flame-weapons to drag his captain and pilot to safety on Lyrae 91-Beta. She does a little math, too; it's easy for her. And she haunts the spaceport and makes friends with everybody who'll talk to her, and begs rides, and knows the controls of fourteen models of craft. She's a late bloomer, which means the nubbins on her little chest could almost pass for a boy's; and love, great Love, to her is just something pointless that adults do, despite her physical instruction. But she can get into her junior space suit in seventy seconds flat, including safety hooks.

So you take this girl, this Coati Cass—her full name is Coatillia Canada Cass, but everyone calls her Coati—

And you give her a sturdy little space-coupe for her sixteenth birthday.

Now, here is your problem:

Does she use it to jaunt around the star-crowded home sector, visiting her classmates and her family's friends, as her mother expects, and sometimes showing off by running a vortex beacon or two, as her father fears?

Does she? Really?

Or—does she head straight for the nearest ship-fitters and blow most of her credit balance loading extra fuel tanks and long-range sensors onto the coupe, fuel it to the nozzles, and then—before the family's accountant can raise questions—hightail for the nearest Federation frontier, which is the Great North Rift beyond FedBase 900, where you can look right out at unknown space and stars?

That wasn't much of a problem, was it?

The exec of FedBase 900 watches the yellow head bobbing down his main view corridor.

"We ought to signal her folks c-skip collect," he mutters. "I gather they're rich enough to stand it."

"On what basis?" his deputy inquires.

They both watch the little straight-backed figure marching away. A tall patrol captain passes in the throng; they see the girl spin to stare at him, not with womanly appreciation but with the open-eyed unselfconscious adoration of a kid. Then she turns back to the dazzling splendor of the view beyond the port. The end of the Rift is just visible from this side of the asteroid Base 900 is dug into.

"On the basis that I have a hunch that that infant is trouble looking for a place to happen," Exec says mournfully. "On the basis that I don't believe her story, I guess. Oh, her ident's all in order—I've no doubt she owns that ship and knows how to run it, and knows the regs; and it's her right to get cleared for where she wants to go—by a couple of days. But I cannot believe her parents consented to her tooting out here just to take a look at unknown stars. . . . On the basis that if they did, they're certifiable imbeciles. If she were my daughter—"

His voice trails off. He knows he's overreacting emotionally; he has no adequate excuse for signaling her folks.

"They must have agreed," his deputy says soothingly. "Look at those extra fuel tanks and long-range mechs they gave her."

(Coati hadn't actually lied. She'd told him that her parents raised no objection to her coming out here—true, since they'd never dreamed of it—and added artlessly, "See the extra fuel tanks they put on my ship so I'll be sure to get home for long trips? Oh, sir, I'm calling her the *CC-One*; will that sound too much like something official?")

Exec closes the subject with a pessimistic grunt, and they turn back into his office, where the patrol captain is waiting. FedBase 900's best depot supply team is long overdue, and it is time to declare them officially missing, and initiate and organize a search.

Coati Cass continues on through the surface sections of the base to the fueling port. She had to stop here to get clearance and the holocharts of the frontier area, and she can top off her tanks. If it weren't for those charts, she might have risked going straight on out, for fear they'd stop her. But now that she's cleared, she's enjoying her first glimpse of a glamorous Far FedBase—so long as it doesn't delay her start for her goal, her true goal, so long dreamed of: free, unexplored space and unknown, unnamed stars.

Far Bases *are* glamorous; the Federation had learned the hard way that they must be pleasant, sanity-promoting duty. So, the farther out a base is, and the longer the tours, the more lavishly it is set up and maintained. Base 900 is built mostly inside a big, long-orbit, airless rock, yet it has gardens and pools that would be the envy of a world's richest citizen. Coati sees displays for the tiny theater advertising first-run shows and music, all free to station personnel; and she passes half a dozen different exotic little places to eat. Inside the rock the maps show sports and dance shells, spacious private quarters, and winding corridors, all nicely planted and decorated, because it has been found that stress is greatly reduced if there are plenty of alternate, private routes for people to travel to their daily duties.

Building a Far Base is a full-scale Federation job. But it conserves the Federation's one irreplaceable resource—her people. Here at FedBase 900 the people are largely Human, since the other four spacefaring races are concentrated to the Federation's south and east. This far north, Coati has glimpsed only one alien couple, both Swain; their greenish armor is familiar to her from the spaceport back home. She won't find really exotic aliens here.

But what, and who, lives out there on the fringes of the Rift?—not to speak of its unknown farther shores? Coati pauses to take a last look before she turns in to Fuels and Supply. From this port she can really see the Rift, like a strange irregular black cloud lying along the northern zenith.

The Rift isn't completely lightless, of course. It is merely an area that holds comparatively few stars. The scientists regard it as no great mystery; a standing wave or turbulence in the density-texture, a stray chunk of the same gradients that create the galactic arms with their intervening gaps. Many other such rifts are seen in uninhabited reaches of the starfield. This one just happens to form a useful northern border for the irregular globe of Federation Space.

Explorers have penetrated it here and there, enough to know that the usual distribution of star systems appears to begin again on the farther side. A few probable planetary systems have been spotted out there; and once or twice what might be alien transmissions have been picked up at extreme range. But nothing and no one has come at them from the far side, and meanwhile the Federation of Fifty Races, expanding slowly to the south and east, has enough on its platter without hunting out new contacts. Thus, the Rift has been left almost undisturbed. It is the near presence of the Rift that made it possible for Coati to get to a real frontier so fast, from her centrally located home star and her planet of Cayman's Port.

Coati gives it all one last ardent look, and ducks into the suiting-up corridor, where her small suit hangs among the real spacers'. From here she issues onto a deck over the

asteroid surface, and finds *CC-One* dwarfed by a new
neighbor; a big Patrol cruiser has come in. She makes her
routine shell inspection with disciplined care despite her
excitement, and presently signals for the tug to slide her
over to the fueling stations. Here she will also get oxy,
water, and food—standard rations only. She's saved enough
credit for a good supply if she avoids all luxuries.

At Fuels she's outside again, personally checking every
tank. The Fuels chief, a big rosy woman whose high color
glows through her faceplate, grins at the kid's eagerness.
A junior fuelsman is doing the actual work, kidding Coati
about her array of spares.

"You going to cross the Rift?"

"Maybe next trip. : . . Someday for sure," she grins
back.

A news announcement breaks in. It's a pleasant voice
telling them that DRS Number 914 B-K is officially declared missing, and a Phase One search will start. All
space personnel are to keep watch for a standard supply
tug, easily identifiable by its train of tanks, last seen in the
vicinity of Ace's Landing.

"No, correction, negative on Ace's Landing. Last depot
established was on a planet at seventeen-fifty north, fifteen-
thirty west, RD Eighteen." The voice repeats. "That's far
out in Quadrant Nine B-Z, out of commo range. They
were proceeding to a new system at thirty-twenty north,
forty-two-twenty-eight west, RD Thirty.

"All ships within possible range of this course will
maintain a listening watch for one minim on the hour.
Anything heard warrants return to Base range. Meanwhile
a recon ship will be dispatched to follow their route from
Ace's Landing."

The announcer repeats all coordinates; Coati, finding
no tablet handy, inscribes the system they're headed to on
the inside of her bare arm with her stylus.

"If they were beyond commo range, how did they
report?" she asks the Fuels chief.

"By message pipe. Like a teeny-weeny spaceship. They
can make up to three *c*-skip jumps. When you work beyond
range, you send back a pipe after every stop. There'll soon
be a commo relay set up for that quadrant, is my guess."

"Depot Resupply 914 B-K," says the fuelsman. "That's

Boney and Ko. The two boys who—who're—who aren't—I mean, they don't have all their rivets, right?''

"There's nothing wrong with Boney and Ko!" The Fuels chief's flush heightens. "They may not have the smarts of some people, but the things they do, they do 100 percent perfect. And one of them—or both, maybe—has uncanny ability with holocharting. If you go through the charts of quadrants they've worked, you'll see how many B-K corrections there are. That work will save lives! And they haven't a gram of meanness or pride between them; they do it all on supply pay, for loyalty to the Fed." She's running down, glancing at Coati to see if her message carried. "That's why Exec took them off the purely routine runs and let them go set up new depots up north. . . . The Rand twins have the nearby refill runs now; they can take the boredom because of their music.''

"Sorry," the fuelsman says. "I didn't know. They never say a word.''

"Yeah, they don't talk," the chief grins. "There, kid, I guess you're about topped up, unless you want to carry some in your ditty bag. Now, how about the food?''

When Coati gets back inside Base and goes to Charts for her final briefing, she sees what the Fuels chief meant. On all the holocharts that cover the fringes of 900's sector, feature after feature shows corrections marked with a tiny glowing "B-K." She can almost follow the long, looping journeys of the pair—what was it? Boney and Ko—by the areas of richer detail in the charts. Dust clouds, g-anomalies, asteroid swarms, extra primaries in multiple systems—all modestly B-K's. The basic charts are composites of the work of early explorers—somebody called Ponz has scrawled in twenty or thirty star systems with his big signature (B-K have corrected six of them), and there's an "L," and a lot of "YBCs," and more that Coati can't decipher. She'd love to know their names and adventures.

"Who's 'SS'?" she asks Charts.

"Oh, he was a rich old boy, a Last War vet, who tried to take a shortcut he remembered and jumped himself out of fuel way out there. He was stuck about forty-five standard days before anybody could get to him, and after he calmed down, he and his pals kept themselves busy with a little charting. Not bad, too, for a static VP. See how the SS's all center around this point? That's where he sat. If you go near there, remember the error is probably on the radius. But you aren't thinking of heading out *that* far, are you, kid?''

"Oh, well," Coati temporizes. She's wondering if Charts would report her to Exec. "Someday, maybe. I just like to have the charts to, you know, dream over."

Charts chuckles sympathetically, and starts adding up her charges. "Lots of daydreaming you got here, girl."

"Yeah." To distract him she asks, "Who's 'Ponz'?"

"Before my time. He disappeared somewhere after messaging that he'd found a real terraform planet way out that way." Charts points to the northwest edge, where there's a string of GO-type stars. "Could be a number of good planets there. The farthest one out is where the Lost Colony was. And that you stay strictly away from, by the way, if you ever get that far. Thirty-five-twelve N—that's thirty-five minutes twelve seconds north—thirty-forty west, radial distance—we omit the degrees; out here they're constants—eighty-nine degrees north by seventy west—that's from Base 900, they all are—thirty-two Bkm. Some sort of contagion wiped them out just after I came. We've posted warning satellites. . . . All right, now you have to declare your destination. You're entitled to free charts there; the rest you pay for."

"Where do you recommend? For my first trip?"

"For your first trip . . . I recommend you take the one beacon route we have, up to Ace's Landing. That's two beacons, three jumps. It's a neat place: hut, freshwater lake, the works. Nobody lives there, but we have a rock hound who takes all his long leaves there, with a couple of pals. You can take out your scopes and have a spree; everything you're looking at is unexplored. And it's just about in commo range if you hit it lucky."

"How can places be out of commo range? I keep hearing that."

"It's the Rift. Relativistic effects out here where the density changes. Oh, you can pick up the frequency, but the noise, the garble factor is hopeless. Some people claim even electronic gear acts up as you really get into the Rift itself."

"How much do they charge to stay at the hut?"

"Nothing, if you bring your own chow and bag. Air and water're perfect."

"I might want to make an excursion farther on to look at something I've spotted in the scope."

"Green. We'll adjust the chart fee when you get back. But if you run around, watch out for this vortex situation here." Charts pokes his stylus into the holo, north of Ace's Landing. "Nobody's sure yet whether it's a bunch of little ones or a great big whopper of a g-pit. And remember, the holos don't fit together too well—" He edges a second chart into the first display; several stars are badly doubled.

"Right. And I'll keep my eyes open and run a listening watch for that lost ship, B-K's."

"You do that. . . ." He tallies up an amount that has her credit balance scraping bottom. "I sure hope they turn up soon. It's not like them to go jazzing off somewhere. . . . Green, here you are."

She tenders her voucher-chip. "It's go," she grins. "Barely."

Still suited, lugging her pouch of chart cassettes, Coati takes a last look through the great view-wall of the main corridor. She has a decision to make. Two decisions, really, but this one isn't fun—she has to do something about her parents, and without giving herself away to anybody who checks commo. Her parents must be signaling all over home sector by now. She winces mentally, then has an idea: Her sister on a planet near Cayman's has married enough credits to accept any number of collect 'skips, and it would be logical— Yes.

Commo is two doors down.

"You don't need to worry," she tells a lady named Paula. "My brother-in-law is the planet banker. You can check him in that great big ephemeris there. Javelo, Hunter Javelo."

Cautiously, Paula does so. What she finds on Port-of-Princes reassures her enough to accept this odd girl's message. Intermittently sucking her stylus, Coati writes:

"Dearest Sis, Surprise! I'm out at FedBase 900. It's wonderful. Will look around a bit and head home stopping by you. Tell folks all O.K., ship goes like dream and million thanks. Love, Coati."

There! That ought to do it without alerting anybody. By the time her father messages FedBase 900, if he does, she'll be long gone.

And now, she tells herself, heading out to the port, now for the big one. Where exactly should she go?

Well, she can always take Charts' advice and have a good time on Ace's Landing, scanning the skies and planning her next trip. She's become just a little impressed by the hugeness of space and the chill of the unknown. Suppose she gets caught in an uncharted gravity vortex? She's been in only one, and it was small, and a good pilot was flying. (That was one of the flights she didn't tell her folks about.) And there's always next time.

On the other hand, she's *here* now, and all set. And her folks could raise trouble next time she sets out. Isn't it better to do all she can while she can do it?

Well, like what, for instance?

Her ears had pricked up at Charts' remark about those GO-type suns. And one of them was where the poor lost team was headed for; she has the coordinates on her wrist. What if she found them! Or—what if she found a fine terraform planet, and got to name it?

The balance of decision, which had never really leveled, tilts decisively toward a vision of yellow suns—as Coati all but runs into the ramp edge leading out.

A last flicker of caution reminds her that, whatever her goal, her first outward leg must be the beacon route to Ace's. At the first beacon turn, she'll have time to think it over and really make up her mind.

She finds that *CC-One* has been skidded out of Fuels and onto the edge of the standard-thrust takeoff area. She hikes out and climbs in, unaware that she's broadcasting a happy hum. This is IT! She's really, really, at last, on her way!

Strapping in, preparing to lift, she takes out a ration snack and bites it open. She was too broke to eat at Base. Setting course and getting into drive will give her time to digest it; she has a superstitious dislike of going into cold-sleep with a full tummy. Absolutely nothing is supposed to go on during cold-sleep, and she's been used to it since she was a baby, but the thought of that foreign lump of food in there always bothers her. What puts it in stasis before it's part of her? What if it decided to throw itself up?

So she munches as she sets the holochart data in her computer, leaving FedBase 900 far below. She's delightedly aware that the most real part of her life is about to begin. Amid the radiance of unfamiliar stars, the dark Rift in her front view-ports, she completes the course to Beacon 900-One AL, and listens to the big c-skip converters, the heart of her ship, start the cooling-down process. The c-skip drive unit must be supercooled to near absolute zero to work the half-understood miracle by which reciprocal gravity fields will be perturbed, and *CC-One* and herself translated to the target at relativistic speed.

As the first clicks and clanks of cooling resound through the shell, she hangs up her suit, opens her small-size sleep chest, gets in, and injects herself. Her feelings as she pulls the lid down are those of a child of antique earth as it falls asleep to awake on Christmas morning. Thank the All for cold-sleep, she thinks drowsily. It gave us the stars. Imagine those first brave explorers who had to live and age, to stay awake through all the days, the months, the years. . . .

She wakens in what at first glance appears to be about the same starfield, but when she's closed the chest, rubbing her behind where the antisleep injections hit she sees that the Rift looks different.

It's larger, and—why, it's all around the ship! Tendrils of dark almost close behind her. She's in one of the fringy star-clumps that stick out into the Rift. And the starfield looks dull, apart from a few blazing suns—of course, there aren't any nearby stars! Or rather, there are a few very near, and then an emptiness where all the middle-distance suns should be. Only the far, faint star-tapestry lies beyond.

The ship is full of noise; as she comes fully awake she understands that the beacon signal and her mass-proximity indicator are both tweeting and blasting away. She tunes them down, locates the beacon, and puts the ship into a slow orbit around it. This beacon, like FedBase, is set on a big asteroid that gives her just enough g's to stabilize.

Very well. If she's going to Ace's Landing, she'll just set in the coordinates for Beacon 900-Two AL, and go back to sleep. But if she's going to look at those yellow

suns, she must get out her charts and work up a safe two-
or three-leg course to one of them.

She can't simply set in their coordinates and fly straight
there, even if there were no bodies actually in the way,
because the 'skip drive is built to turn off and wake her up
if she threatens to get too deep in a strong gravity field, or
encounters an asteroid swarm or some other space hazard.
So she has to work out corridors that pass really far away
from any strong bodies or known problems.

Decide. . . . But, face it, hasn't she already decided,
when she stabilized here? She doesn't need that much time
to punch in Beacon Two! . . . Yes. She *has* to go somewhere really wild. A hut on Ace's Landing is just not what
she came out here for. Those unknown yellow suns *are*
. . . and maybe she could do something useful, like finding the missing men; there's an off chance. The neat thing
to do might be to go by small steps, Ace's Landing
first—but the *really* neat course is to take advantage of all
she's learned and not to risk being forbidden to come
back. Green, go!

She's been busy all this while, threading cassettes and
getting them lined up for those GO suns. As Charts had
warned her, edges don't fit well. She's working at forcing
two holos into a cheap frame made for one, when her
mass-proximity tweeter goes off.

She glances up, ready to duck or deflect a sky-rock.
Amazed, she sees something unmistakably artificial ahead.
A ship? It grows larger—but not large enough, not at the
rate it's coming. It'll pass her clean. Whatever can it be?
Visions of the mythical tiny ship full of tiny aliens jump to
her mind.

It's so small—why, she could pick it up! Without really
thinking, she spins *CC-One*'s attitude and comes parallel,
alongside the object. She's good at tricky little accelera-
tions. The thing seems to put on speed as she idles up.
Touched by chase fever, she mutters, "Oh, no, you don't!"
and extrudes the rather inadequate manipulator arm.

As she does so, she realizes what it is. But she's too
excited to think, she plucks it neatly out of space, and after
a bit of trying, twists it into her cargo lock, shuts the port
behind it, and refills with air.

She's caught herself a message pipe! Bound from the

gods know where to FedBase. It was changing course at Beacon One, like herself, hence moving slowly. Has she committed an official wrong? Is there some penalty for interfering with official commo?

Well, she's put her spoon in the soup, she might as well drink it. It'll take a while for the pipe to warm to touchability. So she goes on working her charts, intending merely to take a peek at the message and then send the little thing on its way. Surely such a small pause won't harm anything—pipes are used because the sender's out of range, not because they're fast.

She hasn't a doubt she can start it going, again. She's seen that it's covered with instructions. Like all Federation space gear, it's fixed to be usable by amateurs in an emergency.

Impatiently she completes a chart and goes to fish the thing out of the port while it's still so cold she has to put on gloves. When she undogs its little hatch, a cloud of golden motes drifts out, distracting her so that she brushes her bare wrist against the metal when she reaches for the cassette inside. Ouch!

She glances at her arm, hoping she hasn't given herself a nasty cold-burn. Nothing to be seen but an odd dusty scratch. No redness. But she can feel the nerve twitch deep in her forearm. Funny! She brushes at it, and takes out the cassette with more care. It's standard record; she soon has it threaded in her voder.

The voice that speaks is so thick and blurry that she backs up and restarts, to hear better.

"Supply and Recon Team Number 914 B-K reporting," she makes out. Excitedly she recognizes the designation. Why, that's the missing ship! That *is* important. She should relay it to Base at once. But surely it won't hurt to listen to the rest?

The voice is saying that a new depot has been established at thirty-twenty north, forty-two-twenty-eight west, RD Thirty. That's one of the yellow suns' planets, and the coordinates Coati has on her wrist. "Ninety-five percent terraform." The voice has cleared a little.

It goes on to say that they will work back to FedBase, stopping to check a highly terraform planet they've spotted at eighteen-ten north, twenty-eight-thirty west, RD Thirty, in the same group of suns. "But—uh—" The voice stops, then resumes.

"Some things happened at thirty-twenty. There're people there. I guess we have to report a, uh, First Contact. They—"

A second voice interrupts abruptly.

"We did just like the manual! The manual for First Contacts."

"Yeah," resumes the first voice. "It worked fine. They were really friendly. They even had a few words from Galactic, and the signals. But they—"

"The wreck. The wreck! Tell them," says the other voice.

"Oh. Well, yeah. There's a wreck there, an old RB. Real old. You can't see the rescue flag; it has big stuff growing on it. We think it's Ponz. So maybe it's his First Contact." The voice sound unmistakably downcast. "Boss can decide. . . . Anyway, they have some kind of treatment they give you, like a pill to make you smart. It takes two days; you sleep a lot. Then they let you out and you can understand everything. I mean—everything! It was—we never had anything like that before. Everybody talking and understanding everybody! See how we can talk now? But it's funny. . . . Anyway, they helped us find a place with a level site, and we fixed up a fuel dump really nice. We—"

"What they looked like!" the other voice bursts in. "Never mind us. Tell about them, what they looked like and how they did."

"Oh, sure. Well. Big white bodies with fur all over. And six legs—they mostly walk on the back four; the top two are like arms. They have like long bodies, long white cats, big; when they rear up to look, they're over our heads. And they have. . . ." Here the voice stammers, as if finding it hard to speak. "They have like two, uh, private parts. Two sets, I mean. Some of them. And their faces"—the voice runs on, relieved—"their faces are *fierce*. Some teeth! When they came and looked in first, we were pretty nervous. And big eyes, sort of like mixed-up people and animals. Cats. But they acted friendly, they gave back the signals, so we came out. That was when they grabbed us and pushed their heads onto ours. Then they let go, and acted like something was wrong. I heard one say 'Ponz,' and like 'Lashley' or 'Leslie.' "

"Leslie was with Ponz, I told you," says the second.

"Yeah. So then they grabbed us again, and held on, and that was when they gave the treatment. I think something went into me, I can still hear like a voice. Ko says, him, too. . . . Oh, and there were young ones and some others running around on an island; they said they're not like them until they get the treatment. 'Drons,' they called the young ones. And afterward they're 'Ee-ah-drons.' The ones we talked to. It's sort of confusing. Like the Ee-ah are people, too. But you don't see them." His voice—it must be Boney—runs down. "Is that all?" Coati hears him ask aside.

"Yeah, I guess so," the other voice—Ko—replies. "We better get started, we got one more stop . . . and I don't feel so good anymore. I wish we was home."

"Me, too. Funny, we felt so great. Well, DRS 914 B-K signing off. . . . I guess this is the longest record we ever sent, huh? Oh, we have some corrections to send. Stand by."

After a long drone of coordinate corrections, the record ends.

Coati sits pensive, trying to sort out the account. It's clear that a new race has been contacted, and they seem friendly. Yet something about it affects her negatively— she has no desire to rush off and meet the big white six-legs and be given the "smart treatment." Boney and Ko were supposed to be a little—innocent. Maybe they were fooled in some way, taken advantage of? But she can't think why, or what. It's beyond her. . . .

The other thing that's clear is that this should go to Base, fastest. Wasn't there a ship going to follow Boney and Ko's route? That would take them to the cat planet, which is at—she consults her wrist—thirty-twenty north, et cetera. Oh, dear, must she go back? Turn back, abort her trip to deliver this? Why had she been so smart, pulling in other people's business?

But wait. If it's urgent, she could speed it by calling base and reading the message, thus bypassing the last leg. Then surely they wouldn't crack her for interfering! Maybe she's still in commo range.

She powers up the transponder and starts calling FedBase 900. Finally a voice responds, barely discernible through the noise. She fiddles with the suppressors and gets it a bit clearer.

"FedBase 900, this is *CC-One* at AL. Beacon One. Do you read me? I have intercepted a message pipe from Supply Ship DRS 914 B-K, the missing ship, Boney and Ko." She repeats. "Do you read that?"

"Affirmative, *CC-One*. Message from ship 914 B-K intercepted. What is the message?"

"It's too long to read. But listen—important. They are on their way to a planet at—wait a minim—" She rolls the record back and gets the coordinates. "And before that they stayed at that planet thirty-twenty north—you have the specs. There are people there! It's a First Contact, I think. But listen, they say something's funny. I don't think you should go there until you get the whole message. I'm sending it right on."

"*CC-One*, I lost part of that. Is planet at thirty-twenty north a First Contact?"

Garble is breaking up Commo's voice. Coati shouts as clearly as she can, "Yes! Affirmative! But don't, repeat, do—not—go—there—until you get B-K's original message. I—will—send—pipe—at once. Did you get that?"

"Repeating. . . . Do not proceed to planet thirty-twenty north, forty-two-twenty-eight west until B-K message received. Pipe coming soonest. Green, *CC-One*?"

"Go. If I can't make the pipe work, I'll bring it. *CC-One* signing off." She finishes in a swirl of loud static, and turns her attention to getting the pipe back on its way.

But before she takes the cassette out of the voder, she rechecks the designation of the planet B-K are headed for. Eighteen-ten north. Twenty-eight-thirty west. RD Thirty. That's closer than the First Contact planet; that's right, they said they'd stop there on their way home. She copies the first coordinates off on her workpad, and replaces them on her wrist with the new ones. If she wants to help look for Boney and Ko, she could go straight there—but of course she hasn't really made up her mind. As she rolls back her sleeve, she notices that her arm still feels odd, but she can't see any trace of a cold-burn. She rubs the arm a couple of times, and it goes away.

"Getting goosey from excitement," she mutters. She has a childish habit of talking aloud to herself when she's alone. She figures it's because she was alone so much as a child, happily playing with her space toys and holos.

Putting the message pipe back on course proves to be absurdly simple. She blows it clean of the yellow powdery stuff, reinserts the cassette, and ejects it beside the viewports. Fascinated, she watches the little ship spin slowly, orienting to its homing frequency broadcast from Base 900. Then, as if satisfied, it begins to glide away, faster and faster. Sure enough, as well as she can judge, it's headed down the last leg from Beacon One to FedBase. Neat! She's never heard of pipes before; there must be all kinds of marvelous frontier gadgets that'll be new to her.

She has a guilty twinge as she sees it go. Isn't it her duty to go nearer back to Base and read the whole thing? Could the men be in some kind of trouble where every minim counts? But they sounded green, only maybe a little tired. And she understands it's their routine to send a pipe after every stop. If some of those corrections are important, she could never read them straight; her voice would give out. Better they have Boney's own report.

She turns back to figuring out her course, and finds she was fibbing: she has indeed made up her mind. She'll just go to the planet B-K were headed for and see if she can find them there. Maybe they got too sick to move on, maybe they found another alien race they got involved with. Maybe their ship's in trouble. . . . Any number of reasons they could be late, and she *might* be helpful. And now she knows enough about the pipes to know that they can't be sent from a planet's surface. Only from above atmosphere. So if Boney and Ko can't lift, they can't message for help—by pipe, at least.

She's half-talking this line of reasoning out to herself as she works on the holocharts. Defining and marking in a brand-new course for the computer is far more work than she'd realized; the school problems she had done must have been chosen for easy natural corridors. "Oh, gods . . . I've got to erase again; there's an asteroid path there.

Help! I'll never get off this beacon at this rate—explorers must have spent half their time mapping!''

As she mutters, she becomes aware of something like an odd little echo in the ship. She looks around; the cabin is tightly packed with shiny cases of supplies. ''Got my acoustics all buggered up,'' she mutters. That must be it. But there seems to be a peculiar delay; for example, she hears the word ''Help!'' so tiny-clear that she actually spends a few minim searching the nearby racks. Could a talking animal pet or something have got in at Far Base? Oh, the poor creature. Unless she can somehow get it in cold-sleep, it'll die.

But nothing more happens, and she decides it's just the new acoustical reflections. And at last she achieves a good, safe three-leg course to that system at eighteen-ten north. She's pretty sure an expert could pick out a shorter, elegant, two-leg line, but she doesn't want to risk being waked up by some unforeseen obstacle. So she picks routes lined by well-corrected red dwarfs and other barely visible sky features. These charts are living history, she thinks. Not like the anonymous holos back home, where everything is checked a hundred times a year, and they give you only tripstrips. In these charts she can read the actual hands of the old explorers. The man Ponz, for instance—he must have spent a lot of time working around the route to the yellow suns, before he landed on thirty-twenty and crashed and died. . . . But she's dawdling now. She stacks the marked cassettes in order in her computer take-up, and clicks the first one in. To the unknown, at last!

She readies her cold-sleep chest and hops in. As she relaxes, she notices she still has a strange sensation of being accompanied by something or someone. ''Maybe because I'm sort of one of the company of space now,'' she tells herself romantically, and visualizes a future chart with a small ''CC'' correction. Hah! She laughs aloud, drowsily, in the darkness, feeling great. An almost physical rosy glow envelops her as she sinks to dreamless stasis.

She can take off thus unconscious amid pathless space with no real fear of getting lost and being unable to return, because of a marvelously simple little gadget carried by all jumpships—a time-lapse recorder in the vessel's tail, which clicks on unceasingly, recording the star scene behind. It's accelerated by motion in the field, and slows to resting state when the field is static. So, whenever the pilot wishes to retrace his route, he has only to take out the appropriate cassette and put it up front in his guidance computer. The computer will hunt until it duplicates the starfield sequences of the outward path, thus bringing the ship infallibly, if somewhat slowly, back along the course it came.

She wakes and jumps out to see a really new star scene—a great sprawl of radiant golden suns against a very dark arm of Rift. The closest star of the group, she finds, is eighteen-ten north, just as she's calculated! The drive has cut off at the margin of its near gravity field; it will be a long thrust drive in.

Excitement like a sunrise is flooding her. She's made it! Her first solo jump!

And with the mental joy is still that physical glow, so strong it puzzles her for a minim. Physical, definitely; it's kind of like the buzz of self-stimulation, but without the sticky-sickly feeling that self-stimulation usually gives her. Their phys ed teacher, who'd showed them how to relieve sex tension, said that the negative quality would go away, but Coati hasn't bothered with it all that very much. Now she thinks that this shows that sheer excitement can activate sex, as the teacher said. "Ah, go away," she mutters impatiently. She's got to start thrust drive and run on in to where the planets could be.

As soon as she's started, she turns to the scope to check. Planets—yes! One—two—four—and there it is! Blue-green and white even at this distance! Boney and Ko had said it tested highly terraform. It looks it, all right, thinks Coati, who has seen only holos of antique Earth. She wonders briefly what the missing nonterraform part could be: irregularities of climate, absence of some major life-forms? It doesn't matter—anything over 75 percent means livable without protective gear, air and water present and good. She'll be able to get out and explore in the greatest comfort—on a *new* world! But are Boney and Ko already there?

When she gets into orbital distance from the planet, she must run a standard search pattern around it. All Federation ships have radar-responsive gear to help locate them.

But her little ship doesn't have a real Federation search-scope. She'll have to use her eyes, and fly much too narrow a course. This could be tedious; she sighs.

She finds herself crossing her legs and wriggling and scratching herself idly. Really, this sex overflow is too much! The mental part is fairly calm, though, almost like real happiness. Nice. Only distracting. . . . And, as she leans back to start waiting out the run in, she feels again that sense of *presence* in the ship. Company, companionship. Is she going a little nutters? "Calm down," she tells herself firmly.

A minim of dead silence . . . into which a tiny, tiny voice says distinctly, "Hello . . . hello? Please don't be frightened. Hello?"

It's coming from somewhere behind and above her.

Coati whirls, peers up and around everywhere, seeing nothing new.

"Wh-where are you?" she demands. "Who are you, in here?"

"I am a very small being. You saved my life. Please don't be frightened of me. Hello?"

"Hello," Coati replies slowly, peering around hard. Still she sees nothing. And the voice is still behind her when she turns. She doesn't feel frightened at all, just intensely excited and curious.

"What do you mean, I saved your life?"

"I was clinging to the outside of that artifact you call a message. I would have died soon."

"Well, good." But now Coati *is* a bit frightened. When the voice spoke, she definitely detected movement in her own larynx and tongue—as if she were speaking the words herself. Gods—she *is* going nutters, she's hallucinating! "I'm talking to myself!"

"No, no," the voice—her voice—reassures her. "You are correct—I am using your speech apparatus. Please forgive me; I have none of my own that you could hear."

Coati digests this dubiously. If this is a hallucination, it's really complex. She's never done anything like this before. Could it be real, some kind of alien telekinesis?

"But where are you? Why don't you come out and show yourself?"

"I can't. I will explain. Please promise me you won't

be frightened. I have damaged nothing, and I will leave anytime you desire.''

Coati suddenly gets an idea, and eyes the computer sharply. In fantasy shows she's seen holos about alien minds taking over computers. So far as she knows, it's never happened in reality. But maybe—

''Are you in my computer?''

''Your computer?'' Incredibly, the voice gives what might almost be a giggle. ''In a way, yes. I told you I am very, very small. I am in empty places, in your head.'' Quickly it adds, ''You aren't frightened, please? I can go out anytime, but then we can't speak.''

''In my head!'' Coati exclaims. For some reason she, too, feels like laughing. She knows she should be making some serious response, but all she can think of is, this is why her sinuses feel stuffy. ''How did you get in my head?''

''When you rescued me I was incapable of thought. We have a primitive tropism to enter a body and make our way to the head. When I came to myself, I was here. You see, on my home we live in the brains of our host animals. In fact, we are their brains.''

''You went through my body? Oh—from that place on my arm?''

''Yes, I must have done. I have only vague, primitive memories. You see, we are really so small. We live in what I think you call intermolecular, maybe interatomic spaces. Our passage doesn't injure anything. To me, your body is as open and porous as your landscape is to you. I didn't realize there was so much large-scale solidity around until I saw it through your eyes! Then, when you went cold, I came to myself and learned my way around, and deciphered the speech centers. I had a long, long time. It was . . . lonely. I didn't know if you would ever awaken. . . .''

''Yeah. . . .'' Coati thinks this over. She's pretty sure she couldn't imagine all this. It must be *real*! But all she can think of to say is, ''You're using my eyes, too?''

''I've tapped into the optic nerve, at the second juncture. *Very* delicately, I assure you. And to your auditory channels. It's one of the first things we do, a primitive

program. And we make the host feel happy, to keep from
frightening it. You do feel happy, don't you?''

"Happy?—Hey, are *you* doing that? Listen, if that's
you, you're overdoing it! I don't want to feel quite so
'happy,' as you call it. Can you turn it down?''

"You don't? Oh, I *am* sorry. Please wait—my movements are slow.''

Coati waits, thinking so furiously about everything at
once that her mind is a chaos. Presently there comes a
marked decrease in the distracting physical glow. More
than all the rest, this serves to convince her of the reality
of her new inhabitant.

"Can you read my mind?'' she asks slowly.

"Only when you form words,'' her own voice replies.
"Subvocalizing, I think you call it. I used all that long
cold time tracing out your vocabulary and language. We
have a primitive drive to communication; perhaps all life-
forms have.''

"Acquiring a whole language from a static, sleeping
brain is quite a feat,'' says Coati thoughtfully. She is
beginning to feel a distinct difference in her voice when
the alien is using it; it seems higher, tighter—and she
hears herself using words that she knows only from reading, not habitual use.

"Yes. Luckily I had so much time. But I was so dis-
mayed and depressed when it seemed you'd never awaken.
All that work would be for nothing. I am so happy to find
you alive! Not just for the work, but for—for life. . . .
Oh, and I have had one chance to practice with your
species before. But your brain is quite different.''

However flustered and overwhelmed by the novelty of
all this, Coati isn't stupid. The words about "home'' and
"hosts'' are making a connection with Boney and Ko's
report.

"Did the two men who sent that message you were
riding on visit your home planet? They were two Humans—
that's what I am—in a ship bigger than this.''

"Oh, yes! I was one of those who took turns being with
them! And I was visiting one of them when they left.''
. . . The voice seems to check itself. "Your brain is really
very different.''

"Thanks,'' says Coati inanely. "I've heard that those

two men—those two Humans—weren't regarded as exactly bright.''

'' 'Bright?' Ah, yes. . . . We performed some repairs, but we couldn't do much.''

Coati's chaotic thoughts coalesce. What she's sitting here chatting with is an alien—an *alien* who is possibly deadly, very likely dangerous, who has invaded her head.

"You're a *brain parasite!*" she cries loudly. "You're an intelligent brain parasite, using my eyes to see with and my ears to hear with, and talking through my mouth as if I were a zombie—and, and for all I know, you're taking over my whole brain!"

"Oh, please! P-please!" She hears her own voice tremble. "I can leave at any moment—is that what you wish? And I damage nothing—nothing at all. I use very little energy. In fact, I have cleared away some debris in your main blood-supply tube, so there is more than ample for us both. I need only a few components from time to time. But I can withdraw right now. It would be a slow process, because I've become more deeply enmeshed and my mentor isn't here to direct me. But if that's what you want, I shall start at once, leaving just as I came. . . . Maybe—n-now that I'm refreshed, I could survive longer, clinging to your ship.''

The pathos affects Coati; the timbre of the voice calls up the image of a tiny, sad, frightened creature shivering in the cold prison of space.

"We'll decide about that later," she says somewhat gruffly. "Meanwhile I have your word of honor you aren't messing up my brain?''

"Indeed not," her own voice whispers back indignantly. "It is a beautiful brain.''

"But what do you want? Where are you trying to go?''

"Now I want only to go home. I thought, if I could reach some central Human place, we could find someone who would carry me back to my home planet and my proper host.''

"But why did you leave Boney and Ko and go with that message pipe in the first place?''

"Oh—I had no idea then how *big* the empty spaces are; I thought it would be like a long trip out-of-body at home. Brrr-rr! There's so much I don't know. Can you tell that I am quite a young being? I have not at all finished my instructions. My mentors tell me I am foolish, or fool-hardy. I—I wanted adventure?" The little voice sounds suddenly quite strong and positive. "I still do, but I see I must be better prepared."

"Hmm. Hey, can you tell I'm young, too? I guess that makes two of us. I guess I'm out here looking for adventure, too."

"You do understand."

"Yeah." Coati grins, sighs. "Well, I can carry you back to FedBase, and I'm sure they'll be sending parties to your planet soon. It's a First Contact for us, you know; that's what we call meeting a new non-Human race. We know about fifty so far, but no one just like you. So I'm certain people will be going."

"Oh, thank you! Thank you so much."

Coati feels a surge of physical pleasure, an urge—

"Hey, you're doing *that* again! Stop it."

"Oh, I am sorry." The glow fades. "It's a primitive response to gratitude. To give pleasure. You see, our normal hosts are quite mindless; they can be thanked only by physical sensation."

"I see." Pondering this, Coati sees something else, too.

"I suppose you could make them feel pain, too, to punish them, if they did something you didn't like?"

"I suppose so. But we don't like pain; it churns up the delicate brain. Those are some of the lessons I haven't had yet. I had to only once, when my host was playing too near a dangerous cliff. And then I soothed it with pleasure right after it moved back. We use it only in emergencies, if the host threatens to harm itself, rare things like that. . . . Or, wait, I remember, if the host gets into what you call a *fight*. . . . You can see it's complicated."

"I see," Coati repeats. Uneasily she realizes that this young alien passenger might have more control over her than was exactly neat. But it seems to be so well-meaning, to have no intent at all to harm her. She relaxes—unable to suppress a twinge of wonder whether her easy emotional acceptance of its presence in—whew!—her brain might not be a feeling partly engineered by the alien. Maybe the *really* neat thing to do would be to ask her passenger to withdraw, right now. Could she fix some comfortable place for it to stay outside her? Maybe she'll do that, when they get a bit closer to FedBase.

Meanwhile, what about her plan for visiting the planet Boney and Ko were headed for? If she could pick up a trace of them, it would be a real help to FedBase. And wouldn't it be a shame to come all this way without taking a look?

That argument with herself is soon over. And her young appetite is making itself felt. She picks out a ration snack and starts to set the drive course for the planets, explaining between munches what she plans to do before returning to FedBase. Her passenger raises no objection to this delay.

"I am so grateful, so grateful you would think to deliver me," her voice says with some difficulty around the cheese bites.

As Coati opens the cold-keeper, a flash of gold attracts her attention. It's more of that gold dust, clinging to the chilly surface. She bats it away, and some floats to her face.

"By the way, what is this stuff? It came in the message pipe, with you. Can you see it? Hey, it's on my legs, too." She extends one.

"Yes," her "different" voice replies. "They are seeds."

She's getting used to this weird dialogue with herself. It reminds her of a show she saw, where a ventriloquist animated a dummy. "I'm a ventriloquist's dummy," she chuckles to herself. "Only I'm the ventriloquist, too.

"What kind of seeds, of what?" she asks aloud.

"Ours." There's a sound, or feeling, like a sigh, as if a troubling thought had passed. Then the voice says more briskly, "Wait, I forgot. I should release a chemical to keep them off you. They are attracted to—to the phero-mones of life."

"I didn't know I knew those words," Coati tells her invisible companion. "I guess you were really into my vocabulary while I slept."

"Oh, yes. I labored."

A moment later Coati feels a slight flush prickling her skin. Is this the "chemical"? Before she can feel alarmed, it passes. And she sees that the floating dust—or seeds—has fallen away from her as if repelled by a charge.

"Good-o." She eats a bit more, finishing the course-set. "That reminds me, what do you call your race? And you, you must have a name. We should get better acquainted!" She laughs for two; all sense of trouble has gone.

"I am of the Eea, or Eeadron. Personally I'm called Syllobene."

"Hello, Syllobene! I'm Coati Cass. Coati."

"Hello, Coati Cass Coati."

"No, I meant, just Coati. Cass is my family name."

"Ah, 'family.' We wondered about that, with the other Humans."

"Sure, I'll be glad to explain. But later—" Coati cuts herself off. "I mean, there'll be plenty of time to explain everything while we slowly approach the planet orbiting that star. And I think I'm entitled to your story first, Syllobene, since I'm providing the body. Don't you agree that's fair?"

"Oh, yes. I must take care not to be selfish, when you do so much."

Somehow this speech for the first time conveys to Coati that her passenger really is a young, almost childish being. The big words it had found in her mind had kept misleading her. But now Syllobene sounds so much like herself reminding herself of her manners. She chuckles again, benignly. Could it be that they are two kids—even two females—together, out looking for adventure in the starfields? And it's nice to have this unexpected companion; much as Coati loves to read and view, she's beginning to get the idea that a lot of space voyaging consists of lonely sitting and waiting, when you aren't in cold-sleep. Of course, she guiltily reminds herself, she could be checking the charts to see if all the coordinates of the relatively few stars out here are straight. But Boney and Ko have undoubtedly done all that—after all, this was their second trip to this sun; on the first one they merely spotted planets. And learning about an alien race is surely important.

She leans back comfortably and asks, "Now, what about your planet? What does it look like? And your hosts—how does that work? How did such a system ever evolve in the first place? Hey, I know—can you make me see an image, a vision of your home?"

"Alas, no. Such a feat is beyond my powers. Making speech is the utmost I can do."

"Well, tell me about it all."

"I will. But first I must say, we have no such—no such material equipment, no such *technology* as you have. What techniques we have are of the mind. I am filled with amazement at all you do. Your race has achieved marvels! I saw a distant world when I looked through your device—a world! And you speak of visiting it as casually as we would go to a lake or a tree farm. A wonder!"

"Yes, we have a lot of technology. So do some other races, like the Swain and the Moom. But I want *yours*, Syllobene! To start with, what's this business of Eea and Eeadron?"

"Ah. Yes, of course. Well, I personally, just myself, am an Eea. But when I am in my proper host, which is a Dron, I am an Eeadron. An Eea by itself is almost nothing. It can do nothing but wait, depending on its primitive tropisms, until a host comes by. It is very rare for Eea to become detached as you found me—except when we are visiting another Eeadron for news or instruction. And then we leave much of ourselves in place, in our personal Dron, to which we return. I, being young, was able to detach myself almost completely to go with the Humans as one of their visitors."

"Oh—were there other Eea inside Boney and Ko when they took off?"

"Yes—one each, at least."

"What would you call that—Eeahumans?" Coati laughs.

But her companion does not seem to join in. "They were very old," she hears herself mutter softly. And then something that sounds like, "no idea of the length of the trip. . . ."

"So you came away when they messaged. Whew—wild act! Oh, Syllobene, I'm so glad I intercepted it and saved you."

"I too, dear Coati Cass."

"But now we've got to get serious about this crazy system of yours. Are you the only people on your planet that have their brains in separate bodies?—Oh, wait. I just realized we should record all this; we'll never be able to go over it twice. Hold while I put in a new cassette."

She gets set up, and bethinks herself to make it sound professional with an introduction.

"This is Coati Cass recording, on board the *CC-One*, approaching unnamed planet at—" She gives all the coordinates, the standard date and time, and the fact that Boney and Ko were last reported to be headed toward this planet.

"Before that they landed on a planet at thirty-twenty north and reported a First Contact with life-forms there. Their report is in a message forwarded to Base before I came here. Now it seems that when they left the planet, some of the life-forms came with them; specifically, two at least of the almost invisible Eea, in their heads. And some seeds, and another Eea, a very young one, who came along, she says, for the adventure. This young Eea moved to the message pipe, not realizing how long the trip would be, and was almost dead when I opened the pipe. She—I call it 'she' because we haven't got sexes, if any, straightened out yet—she moved over to me when I opened the pipe, and is right now residing in my head, where she can see and hear through my senses, and speak with my voice. I am interviewing her about her planet, Nolian. Now remember, all the voice you hear will be mine—but I myself am the one asking the questions. I think you will soon be able to tell when Syllobene—that's her name—is speaking with my voice; it's higher and sort of constricted, and she uses words I didn't know I knew. She learned all that while I was in cold-sleep coming here. Now, Syllobene, would you please repeat what you've told me so far, about the Eea and the Eeadron?"

Coati has learned to relax a little while her own voice goes on, and she hears Syllobene start with a nice little preface: "Greetings to my Human hearers!" and go on to recite the Eea-Eeadron system.

"Now," says Coati, "I was just asking her whether the Eea are the only life-forms on their planet to have their brains in separate animals, so to speak?"

"Oh, no," says her Syllobene voice, "it is general in our, ah, animal world. In fact, we are still amazed that there is another way. But always in other animals, the two are very closely attached. For instance, in the Enquaalons the En is born with the Quaalon, mates when it mates, gives birth when it does, and dies when it dies. The same for all the En—that is what we call the brain animal—except for ourselves, the Eea. Only the Eea are so separate from the Dron, and do not die when their Dron dies. . . . But we have seen aged Endalamines—that is the nearest animal to the Eeadron—holding their heads against new-born Dalamines, as though the En were striving to pass to a new body, while the seed-Ens proper to that newborn hovered about in frustration. We think in some cases they succeed.''

''So you Eea can pass to a new body when yours is old! Does that make you immortal?''

''Ah, no; Eea, too, age and die. But very slowly. They may use many Dron in a lifetime.''

''I see. But tell about your society, your government, and how you get whatever you eat, and so on. Are there rich or poor, or servants and master Eeadron?''

''No, if I understand those words. But we have farms—''

And so, by random stages and probings, Coati pieces together a picture of the green and golden planet Syllobene calls Nolian, with its sun Anella. All ruled over by the big white Eeadron, who have no wars, and only the most rudimentary monetary system. The climate is so benign that housing is largely decorative, except for shelter from the nightly mists and drizzles. It seems a paradise. Their ferocious teeth, which had so alarmed Boney and Ko, derive from a forgotten, presumably carnivorous past; they now eat plant products and fruits. (Here Coati recollects that certain herbivorous primates of antique Earth also had fierce-looking canines.)

As to material technology, the Eeadron have the wheel, which they use for transporting farm crops and what few building materials they employ. And long ago they learned to control fire, which they regard almost as a toy except for some use in cooking. Their big interest now appears to be the development of a written code for their language; they picked up the idea from Ponz and Leslic. It's a source of great pleasure and excitement, although some of the older Eea, who serve as the racial memory, grumble a bit at this innovation.

Midway through this account, Coati has an idea, and when Syllobene runs down, she bursts out, ''Listen! Oh—

this is Coati speaking—you said you cleaned out my arteries, my blood tubes. And you cure other hosts. Would you—I mean, your race—be interested in being healers to other races like mine, who can't heal themselves? We call such healers *doctors*. But our doctors can't get inside and really fix what's wrong, without cutting the sick person up. Why, you could travel all over the Federation, visiting sick people and curing them—or, wait, you could set up a big clinic, and people, Humans and others, would come from everywhere to have the Eea go into them and fix their blood vessels, or their kidneys, or whatever was wrong. Oh, hey, they'd *pay* you—you're going to need Federation credits—and everybody would love you! You'd be the most famous, valuable race in the Federation!''

"Oh, oh—" replies the Syllobene voice, sounding breathless, "I don't know your exclamations! We would say—" She gives an untranslatable trill of excitement. "How amazing, if I understand you—"

"Well, we can talk about that later. Now, you learned about Humans from what you call visiting, in the brains of Boney or Ko, is that right?"

"Yes. But if I had not had the experience of visiting my mentor and a few other Eeadron, I would not have known how to enter and live there without causing damage. You see, the brains of the Dron are just unformed matter; one can go anywhere and eat anything without ill effect on the host's brain. In fact, it is up to the Eea to form them. . . . And, I almost forgot, my mentor was old; and was one of those who had known the living Humans Ponz and Leslie. The two who landed violently and died. They were beyond our powers to cure then, but we could abolish their pain. I believe they mated before they died, but no seeds came. My mentor told me how your brains are developed and functioning. We are still amazed.''

"Why do you visit other Eeadron?"

"To learn many facts about some subject in a short time. We send out tendrils—I think you have a word, for your fungus plants—mycelia. Very frail threads and knots, permeating the other brain—I believe that is what I look like in your brain now—and by making a shadow pattern in a certain way, we acquire all sorts of information, like history, or the form of landscapes, and keep it intact when we withdraw.''

"Look, couldn't you learn all about Humans and the Federation by doing that in my head?''

"Oh, I would not dare. Your speech centers alone frightened me with their complexity. I proceeded with infinite care. It was lucky I had so much time while you slept. I wouldn't dare try anything more delicate and extensive and emotion-connected.''

"Well, thanks for your consideration . . .'' Coati doesn't want to stall the interview there, so she asks at random, "Do you have any social problems? Troubles or dilemmas that concern your whole race?''

This seems to puzzle the Eea. "Well. If I understand you, I don't think so. Oh, there is a heated disagreement among two groups of Eeadron as to how much interest we should take in aliens, but that has been going on ever since Ponz. A panel of senior councillors—is that the word for old wise ones?—is judging it.''

"And will the factions abide by the panel's judgment?''

"Oh, naturally. It will be wiped from memory.''

"Whew!''

"And . . . and there is the problem of a shortage of *faleth* fruit trees. But that is being solved. Oh—I believe I know one social problem, as you put it. Since the Eea are becoming personally so long-lived, there is arising a reluctance to mate and start young. Mating is very, ah, disruptive, especially to the Dron body. So people like to go along as they are. The elders have learned how to suppress the mating urge. For example, I and my siblings were the only young born during one whole season. There are still plenty of seeds about—you saw them—but they are becoming just wasted. Wasted . . . I think I perceive something applicable in your verbal sayings, about nature.''

"Huh? Oh—'Nature's notorious wastefulness,' right?''

"Yes. But our seeds are very long-lived. Very. And that golden coat, which is what you see, is impervious to most everything. So maybe all will be well.''

Her informant seems to want to say no more on this topic, so Coati seizes the pause to say, "Look, our throat—*my* throat—is about to close up or break into flames. Water!'' She seizes the flask and drinks. "I always thought that business of getting a sore throat from talking too much was a joke. It isn't. Can't you *do* something, Dr. Syllobene?''

"I can only block off some of the inflamed channels, and help time do its work. I could abolish the pain, but if we use the throat, it would quickly grow much worse."

"You sound like a doctor already," Coati grumbles hoarsely. "Well, we'll just cut this off here— Oh, I wish I had one of those message pipes! Ouch. . . . Then we'll have some refreshments—I got some honey, thank the gods—and take a nap. Cold-sleep doesn't rest us, you know. Could you take a sleep, too, Syllobene?"

"Excellent idea." That hurts.

"Look, couldn't you learn just to nod my head like this for 'yes' or like this for 'no'?"

Nothing happens for a moment, then Coati feels her head nod gently as if elfin fingers were brushing her chin and brow, yes.

"Fantastic," she rasps. "Ouch."

She clicks off the recorder, takes a last look through the scope at the blue-green-white planet—still far, far ahead—sets an alarm, and curls up comfortably in the pilot couch.

"Sleep well, Syllobene," she whispers painfully. The answer is breathed back, "You, too, dear Coati Cass."

Excitement wakes her before the alarm. The planet is just coming into good bare-eye view. But when she starts to speak to Syllobene, she finds she has no voice at all. She hunts up the med-kit and takes out some throat lozenges.

"Syllobene," she whispers. "Hello?"

"Wha—er, what? Hello?" Syllobene discovers whispering.

"We've lost our voice. That happens sometimes. It'll wear off. But if it's still like this when we get on the planet, you'll *have* to do something so we can record. You can, can't you?"

"Yes, I believe so. But you must understand it will make it worse later."

"Green."

"What?"

"Green . . . means 'I understand, too.' Listen, I'm

sorry about your turn to ask questions. That'll be later. For now we'll just shut up.''

"I wait.''

"Go.''

"What?''

"Oh, green, go—that means 'Understood, and we will proceed on that course.' '' Coati can scarcely force out the words.

"Ah, informal speech . . . most difficult. . . .''

"Syl, this is killing me. We shut up *now*, green?''

A painful giggle. "Go.''

Some hot tea from the snack pack proves soothing. Meanwhile the enforced silence for the first time gives Coati a chance to think things over. She is, of course, entranced by the novelty of it all, and seriously stirred by the idea that Syllobene's race could provide the most astounding, hitherto inconceivable type of medical help to the others. If they want to. And if a terrible crowd-jam doesn't ensue. But that's for the big minds to wrestle out.

And, like the kid she is, Coati relishes the sensation she fancies her return will provoke—with a real live new alien carried in her head! But, gods, they won't be able to *see* Syllobene—suppose they jump to the obvious conclusion that Coati's gone nutters, and hustle her off to the hospital? She and Syl better talk that over before they get home; Syllobene has to be able to think of some way to prove she exists.

Funny how firmly she's thinking of Syllobene as "she," Coati muses. Is that just sheer projection? Or—after all, they're in pretty intimate contact—is this some deep instinctive perception, like one of Syl's "primitive tropisms"? Whatever, when they get it unscrambled, it'll be a bit of a shock if Syl's a young "he" . . . or gods forbid, an "it" or a "them." What was it that Boney had said about the Dron, that some of them had two sets of "private parts"? That'd be his modest term for sex organs; he must have meant they were like hermaphrodites. Whew. Well, that still doesn't necessarily mean anything about the Eea.

When they can talk, she must get things straightened out. And until then not get too romantically fixated on the idea that they're two girls together.

All this brings her to a sobering sense of how little she

really knows about the entity she's letting stay in her
head—in her very brain. If indeed Syl was serious about
being able to leave. . . . With this sobriety comes—or
rather, surfaces—a slight, undefined sense of *trouble*. She's
had it all along, Coati realizes. A peculiar feeling that
there's more. That all isn't quite being told her. Funny,
she doesn't suspect Syl herself of some bad intent, of
being secretly evil. No. Syllobene is *good*, as good as she
can be; all Coati's radar and perceptions seem to assure her
of that. But nevertheless this feeling persists—it's becoming clearer as she concentrates—that something was making the alien a little sad and wary now and then—that
something troubling to Syl had been touched on but not
explored.

The lords know, she and Syl had literally talked all they
could; Syl had answered every question until their voice
gave out. But Coati's sense of incompleteness lingers.
Let's see, when had it been strongest? . . . Around that
business of the seeds in the message pipe, for one. Maybe
every time they touched on seeds. Well, seeds were being
wasted. That meant dying. And a seed is a living thing; an
encysted, complete beginning of a new life. Not just a
gamete, like pollen, say. Maybe they're like embryos, or
even living babies, to Syllobene. The thought of hundreds
of doomed babies surely wouldn't be a very cheerful one
for Coati herself.

Could that be it? That Syl didn't want to go into the
sadness? Seems plausible. Or, wait—what about Syl herself? By any chance did she want to mate, and now she
can't—or *had* she, and that's the mystery of where those
seeds in the message pipe had come from? Whew! Is Syl
old enough, is she sexually mature? Somehow Coati doesn't
think so, but again, she knows so little—not even that
Syl's a she.

As Coati ruminates, her eyes have been on the front
view-ports, where the planet is rapidly growing bigger and
bigger. She must put her wonderment aside, with the
mental note to question Syl at the first opportunity. In a
few minim it'll be time to kill the torches and go on
antigrav for the maneuvers that will bring her into a close-
orbit search pattern. She will have to fly a lot of extra
orbits, doing the best she can by eye and with her narrow

little civilian radarscope. It'll be tedious; not for the first time, she deplores the unsuitability of a little space-coupe for serious exploration work.

The planet still looks remarkably like holos of Terra. It has two big ice caps, but only three large landmasses set in blue ocean. It looks cold, too. Cloud cover is thin, wispy cirrus. And for many degrees south of the northern ice, the land is a flat gray-green, featureless except for an intricate, shallow lake system, which changes from silver to black as the angle of reflection changes. Like some exotic silken fabric, Coati thinks. The technical name for such a plain is tundra, or maybe muskeg.

No straight lines or curves, no dams, no signs of artificial works appear. The place seems devoid of intelligent life.

Hello, what's this ahead? A twinkling light is rounding the shadowed curve of the planet, far enough out to catch the sun. That's reflected light; the thing is tumbling slowly. Coati slows and turns to the scope. Big sausage tanks! Such tanks must belong to a DRS, a depot resupply ship. Boney and Ko must have left them in orbit before they landed. And they wouldn't fail to pick them up when they left; that means the men are here. Oh, good. That'll give her the enthusiasm to sit out a long, boring search.

She tunes up every sensor on *CC-One* and starts the pattern while she's still, really, too far out. This is going to be a long chore, unless some really wild luck strikes.

And luck does strike! On her second figure eight orbit, she sees an immense blackened swath just south of the northern ice cap. A burn. Can it have been caused by lightning, or volcanism? Or even a natural meterorite?

No . . . on the next pass she can see a central line of scorch, growing as it leads north, with a perceptible zigzag such as no incoming natural object could make. She clicks on the recorder and whispering reports the burn and the tanks in orbit.

On the third pass she's sure. There's a gleam at the north end of the burn scar.

"Oh, the poor men! They must have been sick; they had to correct course with rockets. . . . Syl! Syllobene! Are you awake?"

"Uh—hello?" her voice mumbles. Funny to hear herself sounding sleepy.

"Look, you have to do something about our throat so I can report. I think I've found the men."

"Oh. Yes. Wait . . . I fear I need nourishment. . . ."

"Go right ahead. Be my guest."

For an instant Coati pictures Syl sipping blood, like a vampire; but no, Syl is too small. It'll be more like the little being snagging a red blood corpuscle or two as they rush by. Weird. Coati doesn't feel the least bit nervous about this. Syl had said she's increased the blood flow overall. And in fact Coati herself feels great, very alert and well. They *would* make wonderful healers, she thinks.

The gleam at the end of the burn is definitely a ship; the scope shows her a big Federation supply tug. Her calls on Fed frequencies bring no response. She kills the search pattern and prepares to land on antigrav. The plain beside the strange ship looks good. But maybe there was another reason for their use of torches, she thinks; those two men were super-experienced planetary pilots. Maybe this place has weird mascons or something that had to be corrected for? She'd better keep alert, and be ready to torch if she finds her course going unsteady.

When she calls the supply ship again, her voice is back and her throat suddenly feels great.

"Hey, thanks Syl."

"Coati, why are we landing?"

"The Humans you left are down somewhere on the planet. They were never heard of after you left them; they're officially missing. That means, everybody search. Now I've found their ship, but they don't answer. I have to land and find out what's happening to them. So you'll get to see a strange planet."

The news doesn't seem to cheer her little passenger, who only repeats, "We must land?"

"Oh, yes. Among other things, they may need help."

"Help. . . ." Syllobene's voice repeats, with an odd, almost bitter inflection.

But Coati is too busy to brood over this. "What condition were they in when you left them, Syl?"

"Oh. . . ." her throat sighs. "I do not know your race well enough to tell what is normal. They were speaking of going to cold-sleep when I withdrew and left them. I was trying to hurry because I understood that the message device would soon be sent out. As I said, it's a slow process. As soon as I was dependent on my Eea senses, the men were too large to perceive—for example, I could no longer discern the sound waves of their voices.''

Coati thinks this over as she gentles the ship down through thick atmosphere. Her ablation shielding isn't all that good.

''Syl, you have just as much technology in your way as we do. Imagine going back and forth from the molecular to the molar scales!''

''Yes. It *is* a big learning. Very frightening the first time, when we're taught to visit.''

''You said there were other Eea in Boney and Ko?''

''Yes . . . but I couldn't establish good contact, and they controlled everything. That's why I slipped away, when I understood about the message device.''

Coati grins. ''I can understand that, Syl. But you took an awful chance.''

She feels the elfin hands nod her head emphatically. ''You are my savior.''

''Oh, well. I didn't know it. But if I had known it, I would have got you off there, Syllobene. I *couldn't* have let you die in space.''

A feeling of indefinable warmth and real happiness glows within her. Coati understands. There is genuine friendship between her and her tiny alien passenger.

The recorder has been clicking away as they talked. But of course it won't show her feelings. Pity.

''Just for the record,'' she says formally, ''I have, uh, subjective reasons to believe that this alien has sincere feelings of friendship of me. I mean for me, not just as a convenience. I think that's important. I feel the same toward Syl.''

It's time to set *CC-One* down. With all care, Coati jockeys her little ship in above the big supply tug and comes down neatly beside it. Nothing untoward shows up. That must mean that Boney and/or Ko were really in wobbly condition when they came in.

The atmosphere tests out green, but still she suits up for

her first trip out. As her ports open, she gets her first good look at the DRS.

"Their ramp's down," she tells the 'corder. "And, hey, the port's ajar! Not good. I'm going in. . . . Hello! Hello in there! . . . Oh!''

Her voice breaks off. Sounds of footsteps, squeaks of ports being pulled.

"Oh, my. What a mess. There were gloves on the ramp—and the inside looks like they didn't clean anything up for a long time. I see food dishes and cassettes and a suit—wait, two suits—in a heap on the deck, as if they'd just jumped out of them. Oh, dear, this looks like trouble . . . I think somebody threw up here. . . . There're a lot of those goldy seeds around everywhere, too.''

She prowls the cabin, reporting as she checks the sleep chests and anyplace a man-sized body could be. Nothing. And the big cargo hold is empty, too, except for a carton of supplies bound somewhere.

She comes outside, saying, "I think I should try to find them. The ground here is soft, like peat, with low vegetation or whatever, and I can see trampled places. There's one big place that looks like a trail leading"—she checks her bearings—"leading north, of all things. The atmosphere is highly Human-compatible, lots of oxy. I have my helmet off. So I'm going to try to follow their trail. But just in case I get into trouble, I think I better send this record off first. It has all about Syl's planet on it. Lords, I wish I could send it from the surface. I guess I'll have to lift above atmosphere. I'm taking some of their message pipes over to my ship. So here goes. It's the only neat thing to do.''

She sighs, clicks off, and gets back into her ship.

Preparing to lift off, she says, "You're very quiet, Syllobene. Are you all right?''

"Oh, yes. But I am—I am afraid.''

"Afraid of what? Walking around on a strange planet? Listen, I do have a hand weapon in case we run into big, wild, vicious beasts. But I don't think there's anything like that around here. Nothing for a carnivore to eat.''

"No . . . I am not afraid of the planet. I fear . . . what you will find.''

Coati is maneuvering her ship up for a fast single orbit

and return. "What do you mean, Syl?" she asks a trifle absently.

"Coati, my friend"—it sounds weird to hear her name in her own voice—"I wish to wait until you search. Perhaps I am wrong. I hope so."

"Well-ll, green, if you must," Coati is preoccupied with opening a message pipe. "Oh, bother, there're some of those little yellow dust seeds in here. How do I clear them out? I don't want to kill them—you say they can live in space, like you—but I don't think they should get loose in FedBase, do you?"

"No! No!"

"Look, I'm sorry about your seeds. I just want to make them get out of this pipe. How do I do that?"

"Heat. High heat."

"Huh . . . oh, I know." She clicks the recorder on and tells it what she's doing. "I'm going to put the pipe in my food heater and run the heater up to 120 degrees C. That won't hurt the cassette. . . . All right, I'm taking it out with tongs. By the gods, there're a couple of those seeds coming out of the 'corder as it gets near heat. All out, you. I will now end this record as I remove the cassette to send. *CC-One* signing off, before returning to planet to search for B and K."

"Good thing we did that," she tells Syl as she closes the pipe and puts it in the lock to be blown out. "Here goes the air. —And there goes the pipe! I hope the Base frequency reaches this far. . . . Yes, it does. Neat, how the little thing knows where to go. Bye-bye, you. . . . Funny, I'm getting a feeling like we're a long, long ways from anywhere. Being a space adventurer can be a trifle spooky." She noses the ship over into landing mode, thinking, "I'm going down to hike over a strange planet looking for two people who, face it, may be dead. . . .

"Syllobene?"

"Yes?"

"I'm really glad I have you for a friend here. Hey, maybe there's another thing your people could do . . . I mean, for credits: Going with lonely space people on long trips!"

"Ah. . . ."

"I was just joking. . . . Or was I?"

Soon they are back on the planet, beside the abandoned DRS. Coati puts on planetary weather gear and tramping shoes. It's sunny but bleak outside. She packs a week's rations and some water, although the ground is spongy-wet. Then she clips the recorder to her shoulder and carefully loads it with a fresh cassette.

A long time later, after Coati has been officially declared missing, that same fresh cassette, its shine somewhat dimmed, is in the hands of the deputy to the exec of FedBase 900. It is about to be listened to by a group of people in the exec's conference room.

Weeks before, the message that Coati had lifted off-planet to send had arrived at FedBase. The staff has heard all about Syllobene and the Eea, and the Eeadron, and the Dron, and all the other features of Syllobene's planet Nolian, and her short trip with Boney and Ko; they have left Coati and her brain passenger about to go back down to the unnamed planet on which sits Boney and Ko's empty ship.

One of the group of listeners now is not of FedBase.

When that first message had come in, the exec had signaled the Cass family, and Coati's father is now in the room. He looks haggard; he has worn out his vocabulary of anger—particularly when he found that no rescue mission was being planned.

"Very convenient for you, Commander," he had sneered. "Letting a teenage girl do your dirty work. I say it's your responsibility to look for your own missing men, and to go get my daughter out of there and free her from that damn brain parasite. You should never have let her go way out there in the first place! If you think I'm not going to report this—"

"How do you suggest I could have stopped her, Myr Cass? She injected herself of her free will into an ongoing search, without consulting anyone. If anyone is to blame for her being out here, it's you. It was your responsibility to have some control over your daughter's travels in that ship you gave her. Meanwhile my responsibility is to my people, and I'm not justified in risking another ship pursuing a Federation citizen on her voluntary travels."

"But that cursed alien in her—"

"Yes. To be blunt about it, Myr Cass, your daughter is already infected, if that's the word, and she has given us evidence of the great mobility and potential for contagion of these small beings. We have probably already lost the men who first visited them. Now I suggest we quiet down and listen to what your daughter has to say. It may be that your concerns are baseless."

Grumblingly, Cass senior subsides.

"This message pipe has been heated, too," says the deputy. "The plastic shows it. From which we can infer that she was compos mentis and possibly in her own ship when she sent it."

The recording starts with a few miscellaneous bangs and squeaks.

"I've decided to take another look at B-K's ship before I start," Coati's voice says. "Maybe they left a message or something."

The 'corder clicks off and on again.

"I've been hunting around in here," says Coati. "No message I can see. There's a holocam focused on the cabin, but it's been turned off. Hey, I bet the Feds like to keep an eye on things, for cases like this. I'll root around by the shell."

Clicks—off, on.

"I've spotted what I think is another holocam up in the bow; I heard it click. . . . How can I get at it? Oh, wait, maybe from outside." Off, on. "Yoho! I got it. It's in time-lapse mode; I think it caught the terrain around the ship. We'll just take it over to my ship and run it."

Click—off.

Exec shifts uneasily. "I believe she's discovered the planetary recorder. I'm not sure the two men knew it was there."

"That must be the additional small cassette in this pipe," the deputy says.

The recorder has come on. "It's really small," Coati is saying. "Hey, it's full of your seeds, Syllobene. Those things must like cassettes. I'm threading it—here we go. Oh, my, oh, my—Syllobene!"

"That is my home," says Coati in what they have come to recognize as the voice of the alien speaking through

Coati's throat. "Oh, my beautiful home! . . . But what a marvel, how do you—"

"Later," Coati cuts herself off. "Later we'll look at it all you want. Right now we have to run it ahead to where it shows this planet and maybe the two men we're looking for."

"Yes— Oh, that was my mentor—"

"Oh, gods, I'd love to look. But I'm speeding up now." Sounds of fast clicking, incoherent small sounds from Coati's Syllobene voice.

"See, now they've taken off. It'll be stars for a long time, nothing but the starfield." Furious clicks. "Gods, I hope it doesn't run out."

"No fear," says the deputy. "These things are activated by rapid action in the field. When the action is as slow as a passing starfield, it reverts to its resting rate of about a frame an hour—maybe a frame a day; I forget. Only a passing rock or whatnot will speed them up briefly."

"Here we are," says Coati's voice, "I can see that great string of GO suns. . . . Yes, they seem to be heading in to the planet now; I'd need a scope to tell—ah! It's getting bigger. That's it, all right. . . . Closer, closer . . . they're going into orbit. But Syl, look at that frame wobble. I tell you, whoever's flying is not all right. . . . Oo-oops—that could be changing pilots, or maybe switching over to the rockets. Oh, dear . . . yes, they're coming in like a load of gravel; I'm glad I know they made it. . . . Smoke now, nothing but smoke. Their torches have hit. Down—I see flames. This must be action-activated; there'll be a pause now, but we can't tell how long. I know this doesn't mean much to you, Syl, but wait till the smoke clears—ah! Look, there's the landscape we saw around the ship, right?"

The alien voice makes a small murmur.

"Action again—that's the edge of the ramp. Here comes one of the men—now the other—which is which? I'll call the tall, thin one Boney. Oh, dear gods, they're staggering. See, they dropped those gloves. And look, the vegetation around the ship outside the burn is all untrampled. This is their first exit, of course—oh, the Boney one fell down! Could the cold-sleep have done that, have they come out too soon? I don't think so; I think they're sick.

Look, there's a funny place on Ko's face, over the nose; he keeps scratching. They're not stopping to look around or anything. This isn't good, Syl. . . . Now they're both down on their hands and knees, in the burn. Oh, I wish I could help them. Look, do you see the goldy cloud, like your spores, by the ramp?''

A pause, with small "ohs" and murmurs.

"They're up now; I hope they're not burned—why, they're running or trying to run! Away from the ship. Toward the trampled place we saw, only it isn't trampled now. Oh. Boney is—and Ko—they're *stripping*! What are they trying to do, take a bath? But there's no— Oh! Oh, wait, *what*? Oh, no! Oh! Oh, dear gods, I don't like this much. I thought all spacers operated under the Code. I didn't know recon teams did sex!''

"They don't," growls Exec, startling everybody.

General stirrings in the room as Coati's voice goes on haltingly, "Well, this is weird . . . I don't much want to look at it; it's not happy-looking like our demo teams back at school. Huh . . . I don't think they know what to do, exactly. . . . Their faces look crazy; why, one of them has his mouth open like he was yelling or screaming. They look terrible. . . . Whoever's listening to this, I'm sorry. I hope I'm not saying anything bad. But this is weird, it's like *ugly*. . . . They have to stop soon, I hope. Oh, *no*—'' Her voice is shaking on the verge of some kind of outcry.

"Oh, oh, oh—'' But it's the other voice that begins sobbing frankly now. The recorder blurs in a confusion of, "Syl! What's the matter? What's wrong?'' and "Oh, I was afraid, oh, I'm afraid, oh, Coati, it's terrible—''

"Yeah, it's ugly. That's not the way Humans really mate, Syl.''

"No,'' says Syl's tones, "I don't mean that. I mean we—oh, oh—'' And she's sobbing again.

"Listen, Syl!'' Coati gulps back alien tears, cuts her off. "I think you know something you aren't telling me! You tell me what's frightening you this instant, or I'll— I'll bash my own brains so hard it'll shake you loose. See?''

There's the sound of a hard slap on flesh, and then a sudden sharp outcry.

"Hey—what—*you hurt me*, Syl. I th-thought you never—''

"Oh, I'm sorry," the alien voice moans. "I p-panicked when you said you would harm yourself—"

"Or harm *you*, huh? Look, I can stand a lot of pain if I have to. You tell me right now what's got into those men. Look, they've collapsed again. *Tell* me!"

"It—it's the young ones."

"The young what?"

"The young Eea—from s-seeds in th-the ship."

"But you said there were grown-up Eea in each of the men. Didn't they keep the seeds off, like you did for me?"

"They— Oh, Coati, I told you, they were very old. They must have died, and the seeds went into the men. I saw them getting feeble. That's when I got frightened and l-left. Before the Humans went in cold-sleep. . . . Oh, Coati, it's so horrible—I feel so bad—"

"Hush up now, Syl, and let me understand. What could seeds do?"

"Seeds hatch, when they're in—they hatched into young ones. With no mentors, no one to train them, they're like wild animals. They grow. They eat—they eat anything. And then in the cold-sleep, some of them must have matured. No teachers, no one to teach them discipline. Oh, the others should have known the seeds and spores would seek hosts, they should have seen that those visitors who went with them were too old. B-but nobody knew how long, how far. . . . When I began to understand how long a time it was going to be, I knew something bad would happen. And I c-couldn't *do* anything; they wouldn't listen to me. So I-I ran away." The alien is convulsing Coati with sobs.

"Well-ll. . . ." Long sigh from Coati. "Oh, dear gods, the poor men. You mean the young ones just ate their brains out?"

"Y-yes, I fear so. As if they were Dron. Worse, because no teachers."

"And that sex stuff—that was the mature ones making them do it?"

"Yes! Oh, yes! Like wild animals. We're taught strictly to control it; we're shown. It takes much training to be fully Eea. Even I am not fully trained. . . . Oh, I wish I'd died there in space instead of seeing this—"

"Oh, no. Brace up, Syl. It's not your fault. Nobody

who isn't used to space could grasp how long the distances are. They probably thought it would be like a long trip in your country. . . . Oh, look—the men have gotten up. God, they're holding each other up; their legs keep going out of control. Motor centers gone, maybe. They're going— they went up the path north; only it wasn't a path then. They're making the path, trampling. . . . That's where we go, Syl, unless this shows them coming back. It'll have to be soon; we're almost at where the camera stopped. I wish I knew how long ago this was. The sun looks kind of different, and the colors of the vegetation, but that could be the camera. I'm going to speed up. Syl, stop crying, honey; it's *not your fault*.''

Rapid clicking from the recorder.

"Nothing, nothing," Coati's voice says. "Still nothing. I doubt they came back. Nothing—wait, what's that? Oh, my goodness, it's the wake—it's our ship landing. Well! I don't think I want to see us, do you? Let's take out this cassette and go.''

Click.

In the executive office the deputy stops the recorder for a moment.

"Is that clear to everyone?''

Grunts of assent answer him.

"I think this casts a new light on the potentials of Coati's little friend's race," the medical officer says. "I suggest that we all keep a sharp eye open for anything that looks like grains of yellow powder, in case the young woman's heat treatment did not completely clean out this pipe. Or the preceding one. Her initial precautions were very wise.''

Before he's finished speaking, Exec has turned on stronger lights. There is a subdued shuffling as people look themselves over, brushing at imaginary golden spots.

"Gods, if a pipeful of that stuff had got loose in here, and nobody warned!'' Zenology mutters. "H'mm . . . Boney and Ko.''

"Yes,'' Exec understands Xenology's shorthand. "If we get any indication that their ship lifted off, we have some hard decisions to make. I gather the seeds can affix themselves to the *outside* of space vessels, too. Well, we'd best continue and see what our problem is.''

"Right." The deputy douses the top light, restarts the 'corder.

"We are now proceeding north on the trail left by Boney and Ko," says Coati's voice. "We've come about five kiloms. The trail is very plain because the vegetation, or whatever this is, is very delicate and frail. I don't think it's built to have animals walk over it to graze. But the trail isn't all that fresh, because there're little tips of new growth. We haven't seen any animals or birds, only plant-like things and an occasional insect going by fast, like a bullet. It's a pretty cold, quiet, weird place. The ground is almost level, but I think we're headed roughly for one of those lakes we saw from above.

"Syllobene is so shook up by what happened to the men that she won't talk much. I keep trying to tell her it's not her fault. One thing she said shows you—she said the grown-up Eea must have assumed that we could make ourselves immune to the seeds, just as they can, since we're so *complete*. They can't get used to the idea of whole, single animals born that way. And the ship . . . we had so many wild, powerful things. It never occurred to them that the men would be as vulnerable as the Dron. . . . Syl, do you hear what I'm telling my people? Nobody's going to think for a minim that you're at fault. Please brace up, honey, it's awfully lonesome here on this primordial tundra or whatever it is."

". . . After you saved my life," murmurs the Syllobene voice sadly.

"Oh-h-h! Listen, hey—Syl, you saved my life, too, for the lords' sake. Don't you realize?"

"I? How?"

"By being on that message pipe, dopus. It was full of seeds, remember? If you hadn't been there, at the risk of your life, if you hadn't been there to keep them off me, I'd have gone just like Boney and Ko. They'd have eaten my brains out. *Now* will you cheer up? You've personally saved my life, too. Hey, Syl, how about that? Hello!"

"Hello . . . oh, dear Coati Cass—"

"That's my Syl. Listen, I've about had the hiking for today; these boots aren't the greatest. I see a little hummock ahead; maybe it's drier. I'll tramp down a flat place and lay out my bag and screen—I don't want one of those bullet-bugs to hit me. I don't think this sun is going to set, either: it must be summer up here, with a big axial tilt." She chuckles. "I've heard of the lands of the midnight sun! Now I've seen one. This is Coati Cass, en route to I don't know where, signing off."

"Your daughter is a remarkable young woman, Myr Cass," Exec says thoughtfully. Cass grunts. Looking more carefully at him, Exec sees that Cass's eyes are wet.

The record continues with a few words by Coati on awakening. Apparently she—they—have slept undisturbed.

"Green, on we go. Now, Syl, I hope you feel better. Think of me, having to lug a Weeping Willie—that means a sad lump of a person—all over the face of this godlost planet. Hey, don't you know any songs? I'd really like that!"

"Songs?"

"Oh, for the gods' sake. Well, explaining and demonstrating will give me something to do. But I don't think our audience needs it."

Click.

In an instant her voice is back again, sounding tired.

"We've been walking eighteen hours total," she says. "My pedometer says we're sixty-one kiloms from the ships. The trail is still clearly visible. We're nearing an arm of one of the glaciers that extend south from the ice cap. I can see a line of low clouds—yes, with rainbows in them!—like a miniature weather front. The men seem to have been making straight toward it. Syl says the seeds have a primitive tropism to cold. That they can live a very, very long time if it's cold enough. I don't think anybody should come near this planet for a very, *very* long time. All right, onward."

Click—off. Click—on.

"The glacier edge and a snowbank are right ahead. I think I see them—I mean, their bodies. . . . There's a cold wind from under the glacier; it smells bad."

Click . . . click.

"We found them. It's pretty bad." The voice sounds drained. "I did what I could. They're like frozen. They crawled under the edge of the ice; it stands off the ground and makes a cave there, with deep green lightcracks. Nothing had been at them that I could tell, but they both have big, nasty-looking holes above their noses, where the sinuses are.

"I don't know their last names, so I just scratched 'Boney and Ko, brave Spacers for the Federation, Fed Base 900' on a slaty piece.

"Oh—they left a message, on the same sort of rock. It says: 'Danger. WE are Infekted. Fatel.' All misspelled, like a kid. I guess the . . . things . . . kept eating their brains out.

"And there are seeds all over around here, like gold dust on the snow. They rise up in a cloud when a shadow falls on them. Syllobene says these are new seeds and spores that the young Eea formed; they mated when the men did, and the seeds grew while the men walked here. Anyway, those holes in their faces are where the new seeds sprouted out in a big clump or stream.

"I got out my glass and looked at a group of seeds. That gold color is their coat or sheath. Syl says it is just about impermeable from outside. There's a big difference in the seeds, too—some are much, much larger and solid-looking; others are more like empty husks. Syl says the big ones beat out the others when competing for a host, and the earliest big one takes all." . . . A sigh.

"Let's see, have I said everything? Oh, maybe I should add that I don't think those holes were bad enough to cause the men's deaths. It must have been what went on inside. I didn't see any other wounds, except scratches and bruises from falling down, I think. They . . . they were holding each other by the hand. I fixed them up, but I didn't change that.

"Now I guess that's all. I don't want to sleep here; I'm going to get as far back toward the ships as I can tonight. It may not be night; I told you the sun doesn't set, but it makes some pretty reddish glow colors. Syl is so sad she'll hardly talk at all. . . . Signing off now, unless something drastic happens."

The deputy clicked the 'corder off.

"Is that all?" someone asked.

"Oh, no. I merely wanted to know if everyone is satisfied that they're hearing clearly so far. Did everyone get enough on the men's conditions, or would Doc like me to run back over that?"

"Not at present, thanks," says Medical. "I would assume that the action of forming a large number of embryos requires extra energy, and consequently, during the men's last walk, their parasites were consuming nutrients—brain tissue and blood—at an ever-increasing rate. As to the exact cause of death, it could be a combination of trauma, hypothermia, malnutrition, and loss of blood; or perhaps the parasites attacked brain structures essential to life. We won't know until we can—I guess we won't know, period."

"Anyone else?" says the deputy in his "briefing session" manner.

Coati's father makes an ambiguous throat-clearing noise but says nothing. No one else speaks, despite the sense of large, unuttered questions growing in the room.

"Oh, get on with it, Fred," Exec says.

"Right."

"We're back at the ship, resting up," says Coati's voice. "Syl, you've been very quiet for a long time. Are you all right? Are you still shook from seeing what the young ones did?"

"Oh, yes."

"Well, push it aside, honey. If I can, you can. Try."

"Yes. . . ."

"You don't sound like you're trying. Listen, I can't carry a melancholy, dismal person *in my head* all the way back to FedBase. I'll go nutters, even in cold-sleep. Don't you think you could cheer up a little? Wasn't it fun when we tried singing? After all, the men all happened a long time back; it's all over. There's nothing you can do."

In the room at Fed Base, Coati's father recognizes a piece of his own advice to his daughter in long-ago days, and blinks back a tear.

"And we've done something useful—actually invaluable, because only you and I are safe on this planet. Right? So maybe we've saved the lives of whoever might have come to look."

"Um'm. . . ."

"She's right," says Exec.

"Of course, it's only Human lives, but it was the Human men made you sad, wasn't it, Syl. So really, it's all even. And those two had a really nice time on your planet first. Hey, think how good you'll feel when you get home.

Would it make you feel better if I showed you the scenes from Nolian when we get going?''

"Yes . . . oh, I don't know.''

"Syl, you're hopeless. Or is something else bothering you? I'm getting hunches. . . . Anyway, we've done everything we can here, I'm taking *CC-One* up. I collected Boney and Ko's last charting cassettes; I'll put them in a pipe with this, and with the little cassette from the bow camera. I don't think they have left anything else of value. I closed the door and wrote a sign on the port to stay out. If you at the Fed want to salvage that ship, you're going to have to go in with flamers. Or get an Eea to go in with you. Personally I think it isn't worth the danger: some seeds could be on the outside, and get left wherever you went with the ship. Hey, something I've been thinking—I wonder if possibly this could be the plague that wiped out the Lost Colony. Seeds drifting in from space. This whole great group of suns could be dangerous. Oh, lords. What a blow. . . . Hey, that's something that Syl and I could check someday! Syl, after you get home and have a nice rest-up, how would you like to come with me on another trip? If they'd let me—I'm sure they would, because we'd be their only seedproof scouts! Only, my poor folks. That reminds me: my father may have messaged Far Base; it'd be great if somebody could message him and mother, collect, that all's well and I'm coming back. Thanks a million. My address is Cayman's Port, and all is on record there. Syl, there's another thing we could do—how'd you like to meet my folks? You could learn all about families, and go back and be a big mentor on Nolian. They'd love to meet you, I know . . . I guess. Green. I'm taking the ship up now.''

Click. Click.

"We're up, and I'm setting in course for the first leg back to Far Base. Whew, these yellow suns are really beautiful. But Syl is still in a funk. It *can't* be because of what we saw on the planet. I keep feeling sure there's something you aren't telling me, Syl. What is it?''

"Oh, no, I—''

"Syl! Listen, you're thinking with *my* brain, and I can *sense* something! Like every time I suggested something we could do, I got drenched in some kind of sadness. And there's a feeling like a big thing tickling when you won't talk. You've got to tell me, Syl. What *is* it?''

"I . . . oh, I am so ashamed!"

"See, there *is* something you're hiding! Ashamed of what? Go on, Syl, tell me or I'll—I'll bash us both. *Tell me!*"

"Ashamed," repeats the small voice. "I'm afraid, I'm afraid. My training. . . . Maybe I'm not so completely developed as I thought. I don't know how to stop— Ohhh," Coati's voice wails. "I wish my mentor were here!"

"Huh?"

"I have this feeling. Oh, dear Coati Cass, it is increasing; I can't suppress it!"

"What? . . . Don't tell me you're about to have some kind of primitive fit? Did that mating business—?"

"No. Well, maybe, yes. Oh, I *can't*—"

"Syl, you must."

"No. All will be well. I will recollect all my training and recover myself."

"Syl, this sounds terrible. . . . But, face it, you're all alone—*we're* all alone. You can't mate, if that's what's coming over you."

"I know. But—"

"Then that's it. The sooner we get going, the sooner we'll be at FedBase and you can start home. I was going to take a nice nap first, but if you've got troubles, maybe I better just go right into the chest. Couldn't you try to sleep, too? You might wake up feeling better.''

"Oh, no! Oh, no! Not the cold! It stimulates us."

"Yes, I forgot. But look, I can't live through all those light-years awake!"

"No—not the cold-sleep!"

"Syl. Myr Syllobene. Maybe you better confess the whole thing *right now*. Just what are you afraid of?"

"But I'm not sure—"

"You're sure enough to be glooming for days. Now you tell Coati exactly what you're afraid of. Take a deep breath—here, I'll do it for you—and start. Now!"

"Perhaps I must," the alien voice says, small but newly resolute. "I don't remember if I told you: If the mating cycle overtakes us when an Eea is alone, we can still . . . reproduce. By—I know your word—spores. Just like seeds, only they are all identical with the parent. And the Eea grows them and gives birth like seeds, as you saw. Then the Eea comes back to itself.'' Syl's words are coming in a rush now, as from relief at speaking out. ''It's very rare, because of course we are taught to stop it when the feeling begins. I—I never had it before. I'm supposed to seek out my mentor at once, to be instructed how to stop it, or the mentor will visit the young one and make it stop. But my mentor is far away! I keep hoping this is not really the feeling that begins all that, but it won't go away; it's getting stronger. Oh, Coati, my friend, I am so afraid—so fearful—'' The voice trails off in great sobs.

The Coati voice says, slowly, ''Oh, whew. You mean, you're afraid you're going to be grabbed by this mating thing and make spores in my head? And they'll bore a hole?''

''Y-yes.'' The alien is in obvious misery.

''Wait a minute. Will it make you go crazy and stop being you, like a Human who gets intoxicated? Oh, you couldn't know about that. But you'll act like those untrained young ones? I mean, what will you do?''

''I may—eat blindly. Oh-h-h . . . don't leave me alone in your cold-sleep!''

''Well. Well. I have to think.''

Click—the deputy has halted the machine.

''I thought we should take a minim to appreciate this young woman's dilemma, and the dilemma of the alien.''

The xenobiologist sighs. ''This urge, or cycle is evidently not so very rare, since instructions are given to the young to combat it. Instructions that unfortunately depend on the mentor being available. But it doesn't appear to be a normal part or stage of maturing—more like an accidental episode. I suggest that here it was precipitated by the experience with the two Humans infected by untrained young. That awakened what the Eea seem to regard as part of their primitive system.''

''How fast can they get back to that Eea planet, ah, Nolian?'' someone asks.

''Not fast enough, I gather,'' Exec says. ''Even if she took the heroic measure of traveling without cold-sleep.''

''She's got to get rid of that thing!'' Coati's father

bursts out. "Cut into her own head and pull it out if she has to! Can't somebody get to her and operate?"

He is met by the silence of negation. The moments they are hearing passed, for good or ill, long back.

"The alien said it could leave," the deputy observes. "We will see if that solution occurs to them." He clicks on.

As if echoing him, Coati's voice comes in. "I asked Syl if she could pull out and park somewhere comfortable until the fit passed. But she says—tell them, Syl."

"I have been trying to withdraw for some time. Early on, I could have done so easily. But now the strands of my physical being have been penetrating so very deeply into Coati's brain, into the molecular and—is atomic the word? —atomic structure. So I have attempted to cut loose from portions of myself, but whenever I succeed in freeing one part, I find that the part I freed before has rejoined. I-I have not had much instruction in this technique, not since I was much smaller. I seem to have grown greatly while with Coati. Nothing I try works. Oh, oh, if only another Eea were here to help! I would do anything, I'd cut myself in half—"

"It's a god-cursed cancer," Coati's father growls. He perceives no empathetic young alien, but only the threat to his child.

"But dear Coati Cass, I cannot. And there is no mistake now; the primitive part of myself that contains this dreadful urge is growing, growing, although I am fighting it as well as I can. I fear it will soon overwhelm me. Is there not something you can do?"

"Not for you, Syl. How could I? But tell me—after it's all passed, and you've, well, eaten my brains out, will you come back to yourself and be all right?"

"Oh—I could never be all right, knowing I had murdered you! Killed my friend! My life would be a horrible thing. Even if my people accepted me, I could not. I mean this, Coati Cass."

"H'mm. Well. Let me think." The recorder clicks off—on. Coati's voice comes back. "Well, the position is: If we carry out our plan to go back to FedBase, I'll be a zombie, or dead, when I get there, and you'll be miserable. And the ship'll be full of spores. I wouldn't be able to land it, but somebody'd probably manage to intercept us. And the people who opened it would get infected with your spores, and by the time things got cleared up, a lot of Humans would have died, and maybe nobody would feel like taking you back to your planet. Ugh.''

The alien voice echoes her.

''On the other hand, if we cut straight for Nolian, even at the best, you'd have made spores and they'd have chewed up my brains and it'd be impossible for me to bring the ship down and let you out. So you'd be locked up with a dead Human and a lot of spores, flying on to gods know where, forever. Unless somebody intercepted us, in which case the other scenario would take over. . . . Syl, I don't see any out. What I do see is that this ship will soon be a flying time bomb, just waiting for some non-Eea life to get near it.''

''Yes. That is well put, Coati-my-friend,'' the small voice says sadly. ''Oh!''

''What?''

''I felt a strong urge to—to hurt you. I barely stopped it. Oh, Coati! Help! I don't want to become a wild beast!''

''Syl, honey . . . it's not your fault. I wonder, shouldn't we sort of say our good-byes while we can?''

''I see . . . I see.''

''Syllobene, my dear, whatever happens, remember we were great friends, and had adventures together, and saved each other's lives. And if you do something bad to me, remember I know it isn't really you; it's just an accident because we're so different. I . . . I've never had a friend I loved more, Syl. So good-bye, and remember it all with joy if you can.''

A sound of sobbing. ''G-good-bye, dear Coati Cass. I am so sad with all my being that it is through me that badness has come. Being friends with you has lifted my life to lightness I never dreamed of. If I survive, I will tell my people how good and true Humans are. But I don't think I will have that chance. One way or another, I will end my life with yours, Coati Cass. Above all, I do not wish to bring more trouble on Humans.''

''Syl. . . .'' Coati says thoughtfully. ''If you mean that about going together, there's a way. Do you mean it?''

''Y-yes. Yes.''

"The thing is, in addition to what happens to us, our ship will be a menace to anybody, Human or whatever, who gets at it. It's sort of our duty not to do a thing like that, you know? And I really don't want to go on as a zombie. And I see that beautiful yellow sun out there, the sun we saw all those days and nights down on the planet . . . like it's waiting for us . . . Syl?"

"Coati, I understand you."

"Of course, there're a lot of things I wanted to do; you d-did, too—maybe this is the b-big one—"

The recorder lapses to a fuzzy sound.

"Something has been erased," the deputy says.

It comes back in a minim or two with Coati's voice saying, "—didn't need to hear all that. The point is, we've decided. So—ow! Oh-h-h—*ow!* What?"

"Coati!" The small voice seems to be screaming. "Coati, I'm losing—I'm losing myself! Something wants to hurt you, to stop you—to make you go into cold-sleep—I'm fighting it— Oh, forgive me, forgive me—"

"OW! Hey, I forgive you, but— Oh, *ouch!* Wait, hold it, baby, I just have to set our course, and then I'll hop right into the chest. I *have* to set the computer; try to understand."

Undecipherable noise from the alien. Then, to everyone's surprise, the unmistakable sound of a young Human voice humming fills the room.

"I know that tune," the computer chief says suddenly. "It's old—wait—yes. It's 'Into the Heart of the Sun.' . . . She's trying to tell us what she's doing without alerting that maniacal parasite."

"We'd better listen closely," the deputy observes superfluously.

A moment later the humming gives place to a softly sung bar of words—yes, it's "Into the Heart of the Sun." It ends in a sharp yelp. "Hey, Syl, try not to, *please*—"

"I try! I try!"

"We get into cold-sleep just as soon as I possibly can. Don't hurt me, you doppelgänger, or I'll make a mistake and you'll end up as fried spores— Owwwww! For an amateur, you're a little d-devil, Syl." The voice seems to be trying to conceal the wail of real agony. Exec is reminded of the wounded patrolmen he tended as a young med-aid long ago during the Last War.

"I just have to regoogolate the fribilizer that keeps us from penetrating high g-fields," says Coati. "You wouldn't want *that* to happen, would you?"

Her own throat growls at her. "Hurry."

"That's an old nonsense phrase," Computers speaks up. " 'Googolating the fribilizer'—she's trying to tell us she's killing the automatic-drive override. Oh, good girl."

"And now I *must* send this message pipe off. It's in your interests, Syl; it shows you doing all those useful things. And I have to heat it first— Oh, ow—please let me, Syl, please try to let m-me—"

Sounds that might be a heat oven, roughly handled, punctuated by yelps from Coati. Her father is gripping his chair arms so hard they creak.

"Yes, I know that big yellow sun is getting pretty hot and bright. Don't let it worry you. If we go close by it, we'll save a whole leg of our trip. It's the only neat thing to do. Han Lu Han, anybody there? Here, I'll pull the bow blinds.

"And now the cassettes from Boney and Ko go in the pipe—*ow!*—and where's that little one from their bow camera? Syl, try to tell your primitive self you're just slowing me down with these jabs. Please, please— Ah, here it is. And out come the spores—I mean, the seeds that were in there. . . . That pipe is *hot!*

"And now it's time to say good-bye, put this in the pipe, and climb into the chest. I really hope the pipe's frequency can pull it through these g's. On second thought, maybe I'd like to see where we're going while it lasts. As long as I can stand the pain, I think I'll stay out and watch."

Loud sounds of the cassette being handled.

"Good-bye, all. To my folks, oh, I do love you, Dad and Mum. Maybe somebody at FedBase can explain—*OW!!* Oh . . . Oh . . . I can't . . . Hey, Syl, is there anybody you want to say good-bye to? Your mentor?"

A confused vocalization, then, faintly: "Yes. . . ."

"Remember Syl. She's the real stuff, she's doing this for Humans. For an alien race. She could have stopped me, believe it. . . . Bye, all."

A crash, and the recorder goes to silence.

"Han Lu Han," says the xenobiologist quietly into the silence. "He was that boy in the Lyrae mission. 'It's the only really neat thing to do.' He said that before he took the rescue run that killed him."

Exec clears his throat. "Myr Cass, we will send a reconnaissance mission to check the area. But I fear there is no reason to believe, or hope, that Myr Coati failed in her plan to eliminate the contagious menace of herself, her passenger, and the ship by flying into a sun. By the end of the message, she was close enough to feel its heat, and it was doubtless the effect of the gravity that delayed this message pipe so much longer than the preceding one, which was sent only a few days earlier. She had, moreover, carefully undone the precautions that prevent a ship on automatic drive from colliding with a star. Myr Cass, when confronted by a terrifying and painful dilemma capable of causing great harm to others, your daughter took the brave and honorable course, and we must be grateful to her."

Silence, as all contemplate the sudden ending of a bright young life. Two bright young lives.

"But you said she was alive and well when the message was sent." Coati's father makes a last, confused protest.

"Sir, I said she was compos mentis and probably in her ship," the deputy reminds him.

"Thank the gods her mother didn't come here. . . ."

"You can pinpoint the star she was headed for?" Exec asks Charts.

"Oh, yes. The B-K coordinates are good."

"Then, if nobody has a different idea, I suggest that it be appropriately named in the new ephemeris."

"Coati's Star," says Commo. People are rising to leave.

"And Syllobene," a quiet voice says. "Have we forgotten already?"

"Myr Cass, I think you may perhaps prefer to be alone for a moment," Exec tells him. "Anytime you wish to see me, I'll be at your service in my office."

"Thank you."

Exec leads his deputy out, and opts for a quiet lunch in their small private dining room. Added to the list of things that were on his mind before he entered the conference chamber to hear Coati's message are now the problem of when and how to contact the Eea; how to determine the degree of danger from their seeds or spores, in space near the promising GO suns; the Lost Colony question; whether to quarantine the area; and whether there is any chance of any seeds in FedBase itself from the earlier messages. Also, a sample of the chemical that Syllobene had immunized Coati with would seem to be a rather high priority.

But behind all these practical thoughts, an image floats in his mind's eye, accompanied by the sound of a light young voice humming. It's the image in silhouette of two children—one Human, the other not—advancing steadfastly, hand in hand, toward an inferno of alien solar fire.

1985, THE SF YEAR IN REVIEW

Charles N. Brown

First the good news: Science fiction had its best year ever in commercial terms. More books were published, more books were sold, authors' advances were up, sf books routinely made the general bestseller lists, and sf was treated with respect by the general media.

The bad news: Theodore Sturgeon died, Judy Lynn del Rey did not recover from a stroke, and, early in 1986, we lost Frank Herbert. More on this in the obituary section.

Publishing

There were 1,332 sf or fantasy books published in 1985—up 13% from 1984 and higher than the previous 1979 record of 1,288. They sold well, too. Nearly all publishers of sf agreed it was the best year yet. Science fiction did much better than general publishing last year for at least two reasons. There were more hardcovers than usual which were packaged, advertised, and sold along with the paperbacks. The hardcover mass market book is coming into its own in general publishing, but the sf field was there first. The chain stores dramatically increased their sf sales. Waldenbooks' sf club had a year-end membership of 300,000 compared to 150,000 for romance and 60,000 for mystery.

As any science fiction reader should know, any advance brings more problems and the seeds of its own destruction. Because sf was selling so well, publishers overproduced both hardcovers and paperbacks, and upped advances. Now there are too many books, returns are way up, and prices are going higher. The average paperback has gone from $2.95 to $3.50. The chains were also forced into a price war with many top sf novels as loss leaders. Unlike other areas where prices can vary tremendously and wholesale cost is much lower, books carry a retail price tag and cost about 60% of that price wholesale. Bookstore overhead averages 20%, so any book sold for 20% or more under list price is probably a money loser.

The sf field is dominated by seven publishers, although 122 companies did sf and fantasy books last year. The Berkley/Ace combine did the most, had the most originals, and was second only to Del Rey in the bestseller department. Science fiction editor-in-chief Susan Allison was promoted to Vice President and given more say in running the company. Del Rey was very strong in fantasy and in general bestsellers. Executive editor Owen Lock took over control in October. Tor expanded tremendously and more than doubled their output; they actually passed Del Rey in total number of books and were third in bestsellers. Beth Meacham was promoted to science fiction editor-in-chief. The revitalized program at Bantam, under publishing director Lou Aronica, did an excellent job on all fronts. They hired Shawna McCarthy as senior editor. DAW increased production slightly. Betsy Wollheim took over the company when her father, Donald Wollheim, was felled by serious illness. She hired Sheila Gilbert as her second in command. New companies Baen and Bluejay had excellent expansion years. Warner/Popular Library launched a new line, Questar Books, and Arbor House under editor David Hartwell expanded into original publishing.

All was not completely well with publishers. Pinnacle Books went bankrupt, tying up authors' properties for possibly years to come. Pocket Books finished dismantling their Timescape program in an orgy of self-destruction.

Books of the Year

The most popular novels of 1985 included *Robots and Empire* by Isaac Asimov (Doubleday), the latest item cementing together his future history; *The Cat Who Walks*

Through Walls by Robert A. Heinlein (Putnam), which reprises characters from a number of past Heinlein books; *Chapterhouse: Dune* by the late Frank Herbert (Putnam), which brings the old saga to an end—with room for new beginnings which, alas, will now never be written; *The Invaders Plan* by L. Ron Hubbard (Bridge), the first part of a ten-volume satire which the author finished before he died; *Footfall* by Larry Niven and Jerry Pournelle (Del Rey), where sf writers help save the world; *Contact* by Carl Sagan (Simon & Schuster), a first novel by the famed science writer; *The Wishsong of Shannara* by Terry Brooks (Del Rey), the conclusion of a simplified Tolkien-like trilogy; *The Vampire Lestat* by Anne Rice (Knopf), sequel to her *Interview With the Vampire*; *With a Tangled Skein* by Piers Anthony (Del Rey), book three of the "fates personified" series; and *Killashandra* by Anne McCaffrey (Del Rey), a blend of sf and romance.

The book that created the most controversy was *Always Coming Home* by Ursula K. Le Guin (Harper & Row), a utopian future history told in poetry, prose, music (it comes with a cassette), sayings, etc.

My personal favorites of the year were *Eon* by Greg Bear (Bluejay) and *Between the Strokes of Night* by Charles Sheffield (Baen), two books with mind-boggling concepts; *Artifact* by Gregory Benford (Tor), a fine blend of thriller and sf; *Dinner at Deviant's Palace* by Tim Powers (Ace), for its rich imagery; *Helliconia Winter* by Brian Aldiss (Atheneum), a stunning conclusion to the trilogy; *Lovecraft's Book* by Richard A. Lupoff (Arkham House), an almost believable alternate history; *Cuckoo's Egg* by C. J. Cherryh (DAW), for the best aliens of the year; and *Five-Twelfths of Heaven* by Melissa Scott (Baen), a unique brand of space opera and quasi-magic.

Other excellent 1985 novels were *Brightness Falls From the Air* by James Tiptree, Jr. (Tor), *Blood Music* by Greg Bear (Arbor House), *The Summer Tree* by Guy Gavriel Kay (Arbor House), *Human Error* by Paul Preuss (Tor), *Trumps of Doom* by Roger Zelazny (Arbor House), *The Enchantress* by Han Suyin (Bantam), and *Lyonesse II: The Green Pearl* by Jack Vance (Underwood-Miller).

There were more good first novels in 1985 than we can possibly list. Pay special attention to *Saraband of Lost*

Time by Richard Grant (Avon), *Emprise* by Michael P. Kube-McDowell (Berkley), *Terrarium* by Scott Russell Sanders (Tor), *The Torch of Honor* by Roger MacBride Allen (Baen), *Walk the Moons Road* by Jim Aikin (Del Rey), *Skirmish* by Melisa C. Michaels (Tor), and *Tailchaser's Song* by Tad Williams (DAW).

There are also exciting stories by new authors in *Writers of the Future* edited by Algis Budrys (Bridge) and a whole course in sf writing in *Medea: Harlan's World* edited by Harlan Ellison (Bantam).

Small Press

The small press publishers, most of whom have specialized in high-priced limited signed editions in the past decade, are doing more original fiction and hardcover library editions of books only available in paperback.

The high-priced limited edition is still there—especially for Stephen King collectors. Special signed editions of *The Talisman* (Donald Grant) and *Skeleton Crew* (Scream/Press) were selling for hundreds of dollars just days after their publication. *The Eyes of the Dragon* (Philtrum Press), a King original and the most lavishly produced book of the year, is worth at least six times its published price of $125.00 already.

Small press books should usually be ordered directly from the publisher—especially for limited signed editions. Write them for availability of past books and for advance notice of future works. Phantasia Press (5536 Crispin Way, West Bloomfield MI 48033) was outstanding for straight science fiction in 1985, with special editions of *Cuckoo's Egg* and *The Kif Strike Back* by C. J. Cherryh, *Medea* edited by Harlan Ellison, a revised hardcover of the Hugo and Nebula winner David Brin's *Startide Rising*, as well as others. Donald M. Grant (West Kingston RI 02892) did a lavishly illustrated version of *The Talisman* by King and Straub which is still available, as well as *The Book of Kane* by Karl Edward Wagner and a new special edition of *Kull* by Robert E. Howard. And don't miss the wonderfully macabre illustrated poem *A Monster at Christmas* by Thomas Canty. Underwood-Miller (651 Chestnut St., Columbia PA 17512) specializes in Jack Vance. They did the first editions of *Lyonesse II: The Green Pearl* as well as some fantasy work. They also did limited editions of Zelazny's *Trumps of Doom*, Silverberg's *Sailing to Byzantium*, etc. Scream/Press (Box 8531, Santa Cruz CA 95061) specializes in horror books chillingly illustrated by J. K. Potter and Harry O. Morris. Their 1985 offerings included the lavish *Skeleton Crew* by King, *Cold Print* by Ramsey Campbell, the *Books of Blood* by Clive Barker, and *Toplin* by Michael McDowell. Mark V. Ziesing (Box 806, Willimantic CT 06226) does excellent sf collections such as *Beastmarks* by A. A. Attanasio and *The Book of Ian Watson*. Corroboree Press (2729 Bloomington Ave. S., Minneapolis MN 55407) publishes editions of R. A. Lafferty's works. They also did Philip K. Dick's screenplay for his novel *Ubik*. NESFA Press (Box G, MIT Branch, Cambridge MA 02139) produces short story collections honoring guests of honor at conventions. *Late Knight Edition* by Damon Knight and *Light from a Lone Star* by Jack Vance were their 1985 books. Dark Harvest (Box 48134, Niles IL 60648) did a collection of original horror stories, *Night Visions 2*, edited by Charles L. Grant, for the World Fantasy Convention. Dragon Press (Box 78, Pleasantville NY 10570) produced a non-sf original by Philip K. Dick, *In Milton Lumky Territory*. There were many others, some of which I'll try to cover if they still exist next year.

Obituaries

Theodore Sturgeon, 67, died May 8, 1985 of fibrosis complicated by pneumonia. Sturgeon was unquestionably one of the greats of science fiction. He started writing in the thirties and produced a handful of good to excellent stories in 1939 and 1940 including "It," "Microcosmic God," "Shottle Bop," and "Bianca's Hands"—which was rejected many times before appearing as a prize-winning story in England half a decade later. It was his most important early work and explored his main themes of love and empathy for strange characters. In the late forties and fifties he developed these themes brilliantly in "The World Well Lost," "The Wages of Synergy," "Saucer of Loneliness," "To Here and the Easel," and the classic *More Than Human* (1953), arguably one of the ten best novels ever written. It won the 1954 International Fantasy Award. Sturgeon never attained that height again at novel length, but continued to turn out excellent shorter work. There are successful and unsuccessful stories, but few bad ones. Sturgeon's stories always had something to say but were rarely didactic, and his command of imagery and language was awesome. His first novel *The Dreaming Jewels* (1950) is still a reading experience, as are *The Cosmic Rape* (1958) and *Venus Plus X* (1960). Sturgeon's best work is in the short story collections *A Way Home* (1955), *Caviar* (1955), *E Pluribus Unicorn* (1953), and *A Touch of Strange* (1958). His 1970 story "Slow Sculpture" won both Hugo and Nebula Awards. Sturgeon wrote few stories after 1962, turning more to reviewing, teaching, and lecturing. Both his writing and teaching left a lasting impression on most who came in contact with them.

Frank Herbert, 65, author of *Dune*, died February 11, 1986 of complications following cancer surgery. Although he wrote over two dozen books and numerous short stories, his reputation rests on *Dune* (1965), probably the best selling sf novel of all time. The series has an estimated twenty-five million copies in print. Herbert's first novel, *The Dragon in the Sea* (1956) aka *Under Pressure*, was a fully mature work exploring his lifelong preoccupations with man and his environment. *Dune* was rejected by over a dozen publishers because of its length and complexity. It was finally printed in a small edition by Chilton, a non-fiction publisher, to satisfy their editor, sf writer Sterling Lanier. It won both Hugo and Nebula, achieved cult status over the next decade, and earned author and publisher millions of dollars. It usually heads lists of the top sf novels of all time. The third book of the series, *Children of Dune* (1976), was the first genuine science fiction bestseller—75,000 copies in hardcover. Herbert became one of the earliest sf authors able to command a million-dollar advance. He was an excellent didactic writer whose books are filled with ideas and concepts frequently tinged with mysticism. In many ways, he was the opposite of Sturgeon, whose stories are about humanism and understanding. Herbert's best work is at novel length. Outside the

"Dune" series, I would particularly recommend *Whipping Star* (1964), *The Dosadi Experiment* (1977), and the non-sf novel *Soul Catcher* (1972).

Judy-Lynn del Rey, 43, publisher of Del Rey Books, suffered a massive brain hemorrhage on October 16, 1985. She died four months later, on February 20, 1986, without ever regaining consciousness. Judy-Lynn Benjamin began her editorial career in 1965 at *Galaxy* magazine, where she became managing editor in 1969, replacing Lester del Rey, whom she married in 1971. She was hired by Betty Ballantine in 1973 and became Ballantine sf editor in 1974 when the Ballantines suddenly left the company. She had an unerring eye for commercial fiction and was a genius at promotion and at conveying her enthusiasms to the sales force. She hired her husband in 1975 as fantasy editor and, between them, they produced the most successful sf and fantasy publishing list of all time. In 1977 she was given her own imprint, Del Rey Books. Her first two efforts were *Star Wars*, which she bought a year before the movie appeared (it sold nearly four million copies), and *The Sword of Shannara* by Terry Brooks, the first fantasy trade paperback to make the *New York Times* bestseller list. It wasn't a fluke. Del Rey Books did the same with Anne McCaffrey, Stephen Donaldson, Piers Anthony, David Eddings, Larry Niven, Marion Zimmer Bradley, and many others. She was particularly proud of being the publisher of Heinlein, Asimov, and Clarke. One industry insider described her as "the E. F. Hutton of publishing. When she talks, everybody listens."

L. Ron Hubbard, 74, Golden Age science fiction author, founder of Dianetics and Scientology, and, most recently, a bestselling science fiction writer, died of a stroke on January 24, 1986. Hubbard was a prodigious pulp writer in the thirties and forties, famed for being able to write salable first draft fiction very quickly. He wrote for *Astounding* and *Unknown* from 1939 to 1950, when he announced Dianetics, the Science of Mental Health, in some *Astounding* articles and in the bestselling book *Dianetics* (1950). Many sf writers were early converts, but dropped out when Dianetics blossomed into Scientology and the Church of Scientology. In 1982, he returned to science fiction with the bestselling *Battlefield Earth*. He also finished a ten-part novel, *Mission Earth*; the first two volumes have appeared, and the rest are scheduled. He also sponsored the "Writers of the Future" contest, awards, and publications. His early magazine fiction was republished in book form. The best ones are *Final Blackout* (1948), *Slaves of Sleep* (1948), *Fear and Typewriter in the Sky* (1951), and *Old Doc Methuselah* (1970).

Jack Gaughan, 54, died July 21, 1985 of cancer. He was a four-time Hugo winner and the field's most popular artist in the late sixties.

Larry T. Shaw, 60, a well-known editor, died April 1, 1985 of cancer. He edited *Infinity* magazine in the fifties, and was a book editor at Regency, Lancer, and Dell in the sixties. Harlan Ellison described him as "the single most important editor in my life." Shaw also developed the "Conan" properties for Lancer. He was given a moving tribute in his last public appearance at the 1984 world convention.

Robert P. Mills, 65, two-time Hugo-winning editor of *The Magazine of Fantasy & Science Fiction* (1958–1962) and well-known literary agent, was found dead of a heart attack on February 8, 1986.

Other deaths included Italo Calvino, 62, famed Italian writer and winner of the World Fantasy Award; Leo R. Summers, 59, a major artist for *Astounding/Analog*; Robert Nathan, 91, author of *Portrait of Jennie* (1940); T. L. Sherred, 69, author of "E for Effort" (1947); Douglass Wallop, 65, who wrote *The Year the Yankees Lost the Pennant* (1954); Bernard Wolfe, 70, author of *Limbo* (1952); Walter B. Gibson, 88, author of "The Shadow" series; Rene Barjavel, 74, well-known French sf author; and Robert Graves, 90, whose heretical views on mythology and history affected several generations of fantasy writers.

Magazines

The specialty magazines published some excellent fiction this year. *Asimov's* and *Analog* did especially well, but it didn't help circulation: *Asimov's* dropped 20% while *Analog's* was flat. *Fantasy & Science Fiction* and *Twilight Zone* lost circulation, while *Amazing* went up slightly. Only *Omni* did well.

Three new magazines appeared. *Far Frontiers*, a hybrid anthology/magazine in paperback form, edited by Jerry Pournelle and Jim Baen, published four issues. *Night Cry*, a *Twilight Zone* spinoff edited by Alan Rodgers and specializing in pure horror, also published four issues. *Stardate*, a former games/media magazine now edited by David Bischoff, added one-third fiction; it published two issues. The long-awaited *L. Ron Hubbard's To the Stars* did not appear. *Weird Tales* and *The Last Wave* disappeared. *If* and *Aboriginal SF* have been announced for 1986.

Michael Blaine replaced T.E.D. Klein as editor of *The Twilight Zone* and plans to move the fiction away from pure horror to "more human-centered fantasy." Gardner Dozois replaced Shawna McCarthy at *Asimov's*. Patrick L. Price replaced George Scithers at *Amazing* early in 1986.

There were 58 issues of specialty magazines plus 26 original anthologies plus lots of stories in *Omni* and other general magazines—about 840 stories all told—up more than 20% from last year.

Movies

1985 wasn't a good year for sf movies. *Back to the Future* and *Cocoon* did well enough. *Mad Max: Beyond Thunderdome* did okay. *The Black Cauldron*, *D.A.R.Y.L.*, *My Science Project*, *Silver Bullet*, *Ladyhawke*, and *Return to Oz* were all failures. *Enemy Mine* failed commercially but got good reviews within the sf field.

The three new television anthology shows, *Amazing Stories*, *Twilight Zone*, and *Alfred Hitchcock*, all had middle ratings and might or might not last. *Twilight Zone* got the best critical reception.

Science fiction and fantasy do very well on videotape and video disk. The release of *Star Trek* episodes helped sales tremendously. 1985 also saw the expansion of the sf audio market. You can now listen to dramatized tape versions of Clarke's *Childhood's End*, Heinlein's *Green Hills of Earth*, Asimov's *The Gods Themselves*, Le Guin's *Left Hand of Darkness*, Farmer's *To Your Scattered Bodies Go*, etc.

1986, with *Aliens* and *Star Trek IV*, should be a much better year for movies.

Headliners

Stephen King continued to be a whole industry unto himself. When it was revealed he was also Richard Bachman, the latest Bachman novel, *Thinner*, zoomed to the top of the bestseller list, as did an omnibus reissue of the four earlier Bachman novels. *Skeleton Crew* and *The Talisman* also were up there on the lists, as was *Pet Sematary*. King set a new advance record with $5 million per book on a two-book contract with NAL. His *Talisman* co-author, Peter Straub, got a mere $1 million per book on a three-book contract. Between September 1986 and November 1987, a new King novel is set to appear every 3½ months. Perhaps a separate Stephen King bestseller list?

Robert A. Heinlein sold *The Cat Who Walks Through Walls* for a multi-million-dollar advance, celebrated his 78th birthday, and started a new novel.

Arthur C. Clarke turned in *The Songs of Distant Earth* for Spring 1986 publication.

Isaac Asimov turned in *Foundation and Earth* for Fall 1986 publication.

Harlan Ellison did not turn in *The Last Dangerous Visions*.

Martin H. Greenberg edited eight of the thirty-eight reprint anthologies and became the consulting editor of *Amazing Stories*.

Awards

Robin McKinley won the Newbery Award, presented annually for the outstanding juvenile book of the year, with her fantasy *The Hero and the Crown*.

William Gibson won the Philip K. Dick Memorial Award for best original paperback of 1984 with *Neuromancer*.

The John W. Campbell Memorial Award for best novel of 1984 went to Frederik Pohl for *The Years of the City*.

The 1984 Nebula Awards were presented at an over-crowded banquet at the Warwick Hotel in New York City on May 4th, 1985. Winners were: Best Novel, *Neuromancer* by William Gibson; Best Novella, "PRESS ENTER ■" by John Varley; Best Novelette, "Bloodchild" by Octavia E. Butler; Best Short Story, "Morning Child" by Gardner

Dozois. A special award was given to Ian and Betty Ballantine for their pioneering contributions in publishing science fiction and fantasy. The Nebula Awards are nominated and voted on by members of the Science Fiction Writers of America.

The 1985 *Locus* Awards were announced on May 23rd, 1985, in Oakland, California. Winners were: Best SF Novel, *The Integral Trees* by Larry Niven; Best Fantasy Novel, *Job: A Comedy of Justice* by Robert A. Heinlein; Best First Novel, *The Wild Shore* by Kim Stanley Robinson; Best Novella, "PRESS ENTER ■" by John Varley; Best Novelette, "Bloodchild" by Octavia E. Butler; Best Short Story, "Salvador" by Lucius Shepard; Best Anthology, *Light Years and Dark* edited by Michael Bishop; Best Single Author Collection, *The Ghost Light* by Fritz Leiber; Best Related Non-Fiction Book, *Sleepless Nights in the Procrustean Bed* by Harlan Ellison; Best Artist, Michael Whelan; Best Magazine, *Locus*; Best Publisher, Ballantine/ Del Rey. The *Locus* Awards are chosen by subscribers to *Locus* magazine.

The 1985 Hugo Awards were presented in Melbourne, Australia on August 25th. Winners were: Best Novel, *Neuromancer* by William Gibson; Best Novella, "PRESS ENTER ■" by John Varley; Best Novelette, "Bloodchild" by Octavia E. Butler; Best Short Story, "The Crystal Spheres" by David Brin; Best Non-Fiction Book, *Wonder's Child: My Life in Science Fiction* by Jack Williamson; Best Dramatic Presentation, *2010*; Best Professional Editor, Terry Carr; Best Professional Artist, Michael Whelan; Best Semi-Prozine, *Locus*, edited by Charles N. Brown; Best Fanzine, *File 770*, edited by Mike Glyer; Best Fan Writer, Dave Langford; Best Fan Artist, Alexis Gilliland. The John W. Campbell Award for best new writer went to Lucius Shepard. Nominations and voting for the Hugo Awards and the Campbell Award are open to any member of the World Science Fiction Convention in the year of presentation.

The 1985 World Fantasy Awards were presented at the World Fantasy convention in Tucson, Arizona on November 3rd. Winners were: Life Achievement, Theodore Sturgeon; Best Novel (tie) *Mythago Wood* by Robert Holdstock, *Bridge of Birds* by Barry Hughart; Best Novella, "The

Unconquered Country" by Geoff Ryman; Best Short Fiction (tie), "Still Life with Scorpion" by Scott Baker, "The Bones Wizard" by Alan Ryan; Best Anthology/Collection, *Clive Barker's Books of Blood, Vols. 1–3* by Clive Barker; Best Artist, Edward Gorey; Special Award (Professional), Chris Van Allsburg for *The Mysteries of Harris Burdick*; Special Award (Non-Professional), Stuart David Schiff for *Whispers* and Whispers Press; Special Convention Award, Evangeline Walton. The awards are chosen by a panel of judges.

Conventions

The 43rd World Science Fiction Convention, Aussiecon Two, was held in Melbourne, Australia August 22 to 26, 1985, with Gene Wolfe and Ted White as guests of honor and Bob Shaw as toastmaster. The total attendance was 1,600, making it the smallest worldcon since Aussiecon One ten years ago. There were between 300 and 400 Americans and about 100 other foreigners present, and we had a ball despite a somewhat poorly organized committee. The flavor of the yearly party was somewhat different—and that was all to the good. The point driven home time after time was that Australia is *big*, bigger than the United States but with a population smaller than California. Many Australian fans could not make the convention because the distance was too much and internal air costs are high. Those who did showed us a different, friendly culture which was not quasi-American despite a similar language. What held us together was science fiction—a truly international language. At the end of the convention, while others were continuing their tours or sightseeing, a hundred of the hardiest (or craziest) souls, including this reporter, packed their bags and headed for the American national convention in Texas.

The North American Science Fiction Convention, held whenever the world convention is outside the United States, took place in Austin, Texas August 29 to September 2, 1985. It was appropriately called The First Occasional Lone Star Science Fiction Convention and Chili Cookoff, and was certainly different from the world convention. The shock of going from an Australian winter to a hot Texas summer was—different. The chili cookoff was spicier, the attendance of 2,700 was higher, but the convention was spread out on both sides of a river, and it seemed smaller and less crowded. The guests of honor, Jack Vance, Richard Powers, Joanne Berger, and Chad Oliver, were friendly and approachable, and Orson Scott Card's Secular Humanism Revival was most popular. A good time was had by most—even those who complained the loudest.

The 44th World Science Fiction Convention will be held in Atlanta, Georgia August 28–September 1, 1986. Guests of Honor include Ray Bradbury, Terry Carr, and Bob Shaw. For information on membership, write Confederation/Worldcon 44, Suite 1986, 3277 Roswell Rd, Atlanta GA 30305.

The 45th World Science Fiction Convention, Conspiracy '87, will be held in Brighton, England, August 27–September 2, 1987. Guests of Honour will be Doris Lessing, Alfred Bester, Jim Burns, Joyce and Ken Slater, David Langford, and Brian W. Aldiss. For information, write to Conspiracy '87, P.O. Box 43, Cambridge, England CBI 3JJ; American agents: Bill and Mary Burns, 23 Kensington Court, Hempstead NY 11550.

The 1987 North American SF Convention, Cactuscon, will be held in Phoenix, Arizona, September 3–6, 1987, with Guests of Honor including Hal Clement and Marjii Ellers. For information, write to Cactuscon, Box 27201, Tempe AZ 85282.

—*Charles N. Brown*

Charles N. Brown is the editor of *Locus, the newspaper of the science fiction field*. Sample copies are $2.50 each anywhere in the world. Subscriptions in the United States are $24.00 for twelve issues, $45.00 for twenty-four issues, via second-class mail. First-class subscriptions in the U.S. or Canada are $32.00 for twelve issues, $61.00 for twenty-four issues. Overseas subscriptions are $27.00 for twelve issues, $51.00 for twenty-four issues, via sea mail. Airmail overseas subscriptions to Europe and South America are $45.00 for twelve issues, $85.00 for twenty-four issues; airmail to Australia, Asia, and Africa is $50.00 for twelve issues, $95.00 for twenty-four issues. All subscriptions are payable in U.S. funds to *Locus Publications*, P.O. Box 13305, Oakland CA 94661.

Locus also publishes *Science Fiction in Print: An Annotated Bibliography of All Science Fiction Books, Magazines, and Other Works Published During the Past Year.* For information, write to the above address.

RECOMMENDED READING

Terry Carr

MICHAEL ARMSTRONG: "Going After Arviq." *After-war*, edited by Janet Morris.

DAMIEN BRODERICK: "A Tooth for Every Child." *Urban Fantasies*, edited by David King and Russell Blackford, and *Omega Science Digest*, September 1985.

PAT CADIGAN: "After the Days of Dead-Eye 'Dee." *Isaac Asimov's Science Fiction Magazine*, May 1985.

ORSON SCOTT CARD: "The Fringe." *Fantasy and Science Fiction*, October 1985.

C. J. CHERRYH: "The Scapegoat." *Alien Stars*, edited by Elizabeth Mitchell.

MIKE CONNER: "Fergussen's Wraith." *Fantasy and Science Fiction*, August 1985.

AVRAM DAVIDSON: "The Slovo Stove." *Universe 15*, edited by Terry Carr.

THOMAS M. DISCH: "Eternity." *Shenandoah*, Vol. XXXV, No. 4.

TERRY DOWLING: "Shatterwrack at Breaklight." *Omega Science Digest*, July 1985.

GARDNER DOZOIS, JACK DANN, and MICHAEL SWANWICK: "The Gods of Mars." *Omni*, March 1985.

PHYLLIS EISENSTEIN: "Fair Exchange." *Analog*, Mid-December 1985.

GREGORY FROST: "In Media Vita." *Isaac Asimov's Science Fiction Magazine*, January 1985.

WILLIAM GIBSON: "Winter Market." *Vancouver Magazine*, November 1985.

ANDREW M. GREELEY: "Gaby." *Amazing Science Fiction Stories*, January 1985.

KARL HANSEN: "Dreams Unwind." *Omni*, May 1985.

CHARLES L. HARNESS: "George Washington Slept Here." *Analog*, July 1985.

DEAN ING: "Lost in Translation." *Far Frontiers #1*.

ALEXANDER JABLOKOV: "Beneath the Shadow of Her Smile." *Isaac Asimov's Science Fiction Magazine*, April 1985.

WOLFGANG JESCHKE: "The Land of Osiris." *Isaac Asimov's Science Fiction Magazine*, March 1985.

BILL JOHNSON: "Respect," *Analog*, June 1985.

GARRISON KEILLOR: "What Did We Do Wrong?" *The New Yorker*, Sept. 16, 1985.

JAMES PATRICK KELLY: "Solstice." *Isaac Asimov's Science Fiction Magazine*, June 1985.

NANCY KRESS: "Out of All Them Bright Stars." *Fantasy and Science Fiction*, March 1985.

GEORGE R. R. MARTIN: "Loaves and Fishes." *Analog*, October 1985. "Under Siege." *Omni*, October 1985.

FREDERIK POHL: "The Things that Happen." *Isaac Asimov's Science Fiction Magazine*, October 1985.

KEITH ROBERTS: "Kitemistress." *Interzone*, Spring 1985.

KIM STANLEY ROBINSON: "Green Mars." *Isaac Asimov's Science Fiction Magazine*, September 1985.

SCOTT RUSSELL SANDERS: "Travels in the Interior." *Omni*, December 1985.

JOHN SHIRLEY: "The Incorporated." *Isaac Asimov's Science Fiction Magazine*, July 1985.

ROBERT SILVERBERG: "Sunrise on Pluto." *The Planets*, edited by Byron Preiss.

JAMES TIPTREE, JR.: "All This and Heaven Too." *Isaac Asimov's Science Fiction Magazine*, Mid-December 1985.

GEORGE TURNER: "The Fittest." *Urban Fantasies*, edited by David King and Russell Blackford. "On the Nursery Floor." *Strange Attractors*, edited by Damien Broderick.

HARRY TURTLEDOVE/"ERIC G. IVERSON": "Archetypes." *Amazing Science Fiction Stories*, November 1985. "Hatching Season." *Analog*, December 1985. "Les Mortes d'Arthur." *Analog*, August 1985. "The

Road Not Taken." *Analog*, November 1985. "Vilest Beast." *Analog*, September 1985.

KATE WILHELM: "The Gorgon Field." *Isaac Asimov's Science Fiction Magazine*, August 1985.

WALTER JON WILLIAMS: "Side Effects." *Fantasy and Science Fiction*, June 1985.

CONNIE WILLIS: "The Curse of Kings." *Isaac Asimov's Science Fiction Magazine*, March 1985.

ROGER ZELAZNY: "24 Views of Mt. Fuji, by Hokusai." *Isaac Asimov's Science Fiction Magazine*, July 1985.

THE BEST IN SCIENCE FICTION

GORDON R. DICKSON

THE BEST IN FANTASY

POUL ANDERSON
Winner of 7 Hugos and 3 Nebulas